# Brotherhood in Grease and Dust

# also by P. Hartwell

Cailleach's Embrace
The Last Inhale
The Sacred Island
Beneath West Seneca
Time in Kilkenny

# BROTHERHOOD IN GREASE AND DUST

## P. HARTWELL

# Brotherhood in Grease and Dust


Copyright © 2025 by P. Hartwell

All rights reserved. This book or any portion thereof may not be reproduced, distributed or transmitted in any form or by any means without the express written consent of the copyright holder, except in the case of brief quotations for the purpose of reviews and certain other noncommercial uses permitted by copyright law.

This is a work of fiction. Names, characters, places, and incidents are a product of the author's imagination or are used fictitiously. Any resemblance to actual people, living or dead, or to businesses, companies, events, institutions, or locales is completely coincidental.


Cover art and design by Designer P. Hartwell


ISBN: 978-1-969929-08-3

# Dedication

To my brother, who has always been the spark, the troublemaker, and the irreplaceable cornerstone of my life. This story is a testament to the unbreakable, sometimes tested, bond that holds us together, even when the world tries to pull us apart. It's for the shared laughter in the grease-stained garage, the whispered dreams under a sky thick with city smog, and the silent understanding that passes between us—a language only we truly speak. For every setback, every near miss, and every moment of pure, unadulterated brotherhood, this is for you. May we always find our way back to each other, no matter how deep the dust or how thick the grease. And to all those who have navigated the labyrinth of addiction, loss, and the relentless pursuit of family, your strength is our inspiration. This is also for you.

# Chapter One
# The Weight of Legacy

### Echoes in the Garage

The air in the garage was thick, a familiar, comforting shroud woven from a thousand greasy memories. It was the scent of his childhood, the perfume of his parents' tireless dedication. Here, amidst the hulking carcasses of dormant automobiles, Joe felt their presence most acutely. The faint, metallic tang of spent oil mingled with the earthy musk of ancient rubber, a complex bouquet that was as much a part of him as his own blood. Sunlight, fractured and diffused by decades of grime on the high windows, cast hazy, golden shafts across the concrete floor, illuminating motes of dust that danced like spectral patrons. Each worn tool, from the hefty wrenches hanging in precise order on the pegboard to the delicate feeler gauges nestled in their velvet-lined case, was a silent testament to their lives, their labor, their love.

He ran a calloused hand over a workbench scarred with a thousand cuts and gouges, each mark a story whispered from the past. His father's steady hand, his mother's quick, decisive movements – he could almost see them, hear the clink of metal on metal, the low murmur of their shared language of mechanics. This wasn't just a business; it was an altar, a sanctuary built on sweat and sacrifice. Their sudden absence had left a void, a cavernous silence that the usual symphony of the shop had always filled. Now, only the occasional creak of the old building settling, the distant hum of traffic outside, or the frantic thumping of his own heart echoed in the vast emptiness.

Joe's gaze swept across the bays, each one a repository of memories. Bay 1, where his father had meticulously rebuilt the engine of a vintage Ford, the air thick with the smell of carb cleaner and victory. Bay 2, where his mother, her face smudged with grease but her eyes alight with fierce concentration, had wrestled with a stubborn transmission, coaxing it into submission with a blend of brute force and delicate persuasion. Bay 3, their shared workspace, where he and Mike had spent countless hours, their youthful exuberance often clashing with the methodical demands of the trade.

The worn countertops, smoothed by years of leaning elbows and the friction of rags, were etched with a roadmap of his life. The grease-stained floor, a mosaic of spilled fluids and tracked-in dirt, was a familiar landscape he'd navigated since he was tall enough to peer over the hood of a car. These weren't just imperfections; they were artifacts, tangible links to a past he was desperately trying to anchor himself to, a past that felt increasingly fragile, threatened by an encroaching future he couldn't yet fully comprehend. The weight of it all settled on his shoulders, a heavy, invisible mantle that had replaced the easy camaraderie of shared labor. He was the custodian now, the sole guardian of a legacy that was both a comfort and a crushing burden.

He found himself drawn to the office, a small, cluttered space that still held the faint scent of his mother's floral perfume, a ghost of her presence. The ledgers lay open on the desk, a testament to the meticulous records she'd kept. His father's favorite armchair, worn smooth and comfortable, sat by the window, a silent witness to countless hours of planning and problem-solving. He picked up a tarnished photograph from the desk – his parents, younger, vibrant, their smiles as bright as the chrome on a freshly polished fender. Beside them stood a young Joe and an even younger Mike, their arms slung around each other, a picture of brotherly affection and shared ambition. That image, so full of promise, now felt like a cruel taunt.

The silence in the garage was a palpable thing, more than just the absence of noise. It was the absence of his parents' laughter, their arguments, their easy banter. It was the absence of a shared future they had so diligently built. Each tool he touched, each familiar surface he ran his hand over, felt like a conversation with the ghosts of his past. He was adrift in a sea of memories, the scent of oil and metal a constant reminder of what he had lost and what he was now solely responsible for protecting. The weight of this legacy was immense, a physical pressure that seemed to emanate from the very foundations of the building, settling deep within his bones. He walked through the familiar bays, each step an echo in the vast, silent space, a solemn pilgrimage through the hallowed grounds of his family's history. The encroaching future, a vast unknown, loomed like a storm cloud on the horizon, and he stood alone, the sole sentinel of a fading light.

He remembered the boundless energy that had once pulsed through this place, the vibrant hum of machinery at work, the sharp, clean smell of new parts replacing the lingering aroma of old exhaust. Now, a quietude had settled, a heavy stillness that spoke of neglect and fading purpose. It was a stillness that mirrored the growing quietude within his brother. Mike, younger, once a whirlwind of youthful ambition, had been his shadow, eager to absorb every bit of knowledge, every nuance of the trade. They had shared dreams here, whispered secrets over greasy pizza boxes after long days, their brotherhood forged in the crucible of shared labor and common aspirations. Mike had spoken of expansion, of modernizing the shop, of making their parents proud, his eyes alight with a future Joe had readily embraced.

Now, standing amidst the dormant machinery, those dreams felt like distant, faded photographs. The easy camaraderie that had once defined their bond was fraying, strained by the pressures of their new reality. Joe clung to those memories, to the echo of Mike's enthusiastic voice, hoping that the shared history, the very blood that ran between them, could reignite the spark that had begun to dim in his brother's eyes. He needed Mike, needed that shared ambition, that youthful drive to face the daunting task ahead. But looking at the vacant space where his brother's tools should be, where his brother's energy should be fueling the revival of their legacy, Joe felt a chilling premonition creep into his gut. The silence wasn't just in the garage; it was in Mike's too-frequent absence, in his evasive answers, in the growing distance between them.

He remembered the way Mike used to approach a complex engine, his brow furrowed in concentration, a spark of challenge in his gaze. There was a joy in that struggle, a satisfaction in overcoming mechanical adversity that Mike had always seemed to relish. Now, that same focused intensity seemed to have shifted, its target unclear, its energy misdirected. The fire that had once burned so brightly in Mike's eyes seemed to be flickering, replaced by a restless, unsettled gleam that Joe couldn't decipher. It was as if an invisible force was steadily siphoning away his brother's essence, leaving behind a hollowed-out version of the man Joe knew and loved. He tried to reach him, to pull him back from whatever precipice he was teetering on, but his words seemed to bounce off an invisible barrier, lost in the echoing silence of the garage and the deepening silence within his brother. The weight of their parents' legacy, once a shared inheritance, now felt like a solitary burden, amplified by the growing chasm between the two brothers.

## A Brothers Promise

The scent of oil and worn leather had always been a comforting constant in Joe's life, a familiar anchor in the tempest of his existence. It was the aroma of his childhood, the sweet, acrid perfume of his parents' tireless dedication, a scent so deeply ingrained in his very being that he often forgot it was a product of the external world. The garage, his inheritance, his burden, was more than just a place of business; it was a sanctuary, a cathedral of steel and grease where the echoes of his parents' lives resonated with an almost palpable force. He could still see his father, a silhouette against the blinding glare of a welding torch, his mother, her hands sure and steady as she guided a recalcitrant bolt into place. Their presence was a spectral orchestra, playing a symphony of clanking metal, the hiss of pneumatic tools, and the low murmur of shared expertise. Now, the silence was deafening, a vast, empty cavern that amplified the frantic thrumming of his own heart.

He moved through the bays like a somnambulist, his calloused fingers tracing the familiar contours of worn tools, each one a tangible link to the past. Bay 1, where his father had breathed life back into a vintage Mustang, the air thick with the tang of gasoline and triumph. Bay 2, his mother's domain, where she'd wrestled with a particularly stubborn transmission, her usual quiet determination amplified by a fierce glint in her eyes. Bay 3, their shared kingdom, the crucible where he and Mike had forged their brotherhood amidst the demanding rhythm of the trade. The countertops, smoothed by the friction of countless rags and leaning elbows, bore the intricate calligraphy of years of labor, a roadmap of his own growth. The floor, a Jackson Pollock of spilled fluids and ingrained dirt, was a landscape he'd navigated since he was small enough to sit on his father's shoulders and peer over the hood of a gleaming Cadillac. These were not flaws; they were artifacts, solid proof of a life lived with purpose, a life he was now tasked with preserving. The weight of that responsibility settled on his shoulders, an invisible mantle woven from the threads of memory and obligation, a burden that grew heavier with each passing moment.

His steps inevitably led him to the small, cluttered office, a space that still held the faint, lingering trace of his mother's lavender perfume. It was a scent that could bring him to his knees, a poignant reminder of her nurturing presence. The ledgers, meticulously organized, spoke of her orderliness, her unwavering commitment to the business. His father's worn armchair, a testament to countless hours of contemplation and strategizing, sat sentinel by the window, its faded upholstery holding the ghosts of plans hatched and problems solved. He picked up a tarnished photograph from the desk, his parents frozen in time, their smiles radiating a youthful optimism that now seemed almost cruelly ironic. Beside them, two boys, Joe and Mike, stood with arms slung around each other, a tableau of sibling affection and shared dreams. That image, once a symbol of their unity, now felt like a sharp shard of glass, piercing the fragile armor of his resolve.

The silence in the garage was more than just the absence of sound; it was the void left by his parents' laughter, their occasional sharp disagreements, their easy camaraderie. It was the hollow echo of a shared future that had been so meticulously, so lovingly constructed. Every tool he touched, every familiar surface he brushed against, was a conversation with the phantoms of his past, a somber communion with the spirits of those he had lost. He was adrift on a sea of memories, the scent of oil and metal a constant, agonizing reminder of what was gone and what he was now solely responsible for protecting. The legacy, once a shared inheritance, now felt like a solitary burden, a physical weight that seemed to emanate from the very foundations of the building, settling deep within his bones. He walked through the familiar bays, each step an echo in the vast, silent space, a solemn pilgrimage through the hallowed grounds of his family's history. The encroaching future, a vast, untamed unknown, loomed like a storm cloud on the horizon, and he stood alone, the sole sentinel of a fading light.

He remembered the boundless energy that had once pulsed through this place, the vibrant hum of machinery at work, the sharp, clean smell of new parts replacing the lingering aroma of old exhaust. Now, a quietude had settled, a heavy stillness that spoke of neglect and fading purpose. It was a stillness that mirrored the growing quietude within his brother. Mike, younger, once a whirlwind of youthful ambition, had been his shadow, eager to absorb every bit of knowledge, every nuance of the trade. They had shared dreams here, whispered secrets over greasy pizza boxes after long days, their brotherhood forged in the crucible of shared labor and common aspirations. Mike had spoken of expansion, of modernizing the shop, of making their parents proud, his eyes alight with a future Joe had readily embraced.

Now, standing amidst the dormant machinery, those dreams felt like distant, faded photographs. The easy camaraderie that had once defined their bond was fraying, strained by the pressures of their new reality. Joe clung to those memories, to the echo of Mike's enthusiastic voice, hoping that the shared history, the very blood that ran between them, could reignite the spark that had begun to dim in his brother's eyes. He needed Mike, needed that shared ambition, that youthful drive to face the daunting task ahead. But looking at the vacant space where his brother's tools should be, where his brother's energy should be fueling the revival of their legacy, Joe felt a chilling premonition creep into his gut. The silence wasn't just in the garage; it was in Mike's too-frequent absence, in his evasive answers, in the growing distance between them.

He remembered the way Mike used to approach a complex engine, his brow furrowed in concentration, a spark of challenge in his gaze. There was a joy in that struggle, a satisfaction in overcoming mechanical adversity that Mike had always seemed to relish. Now, that same focused intensity seemed to have shifted, its target unclear, its energy misdirected. The fire that had once burned so brightly in Mike's eyes seemed to be flickering, replaced by a restless, unsettled gleam that Joe couldn't decipher. It was as if an invisible force was steadily siphoning away his brother's essence, leaving behind a hollowed-out version of the man Joe knew and loved. He tried to reach him, to pull him back from whatever precipice he was teetering on, but his words seemed to bounce off an invisible barrier, lost in the echoing silence of the garage and the deepening silence within his brother. The weight of their parents' legacy, once a shared inheritance, now felt like a solitary burden, amplified by the growing chasm between the two brothers.

"He used to practically vibrate with excitement when we'd get a challenging engine in," Joe murmured to the empty space, his voice rough with unshed emotion. He ran a hand over the smooth, worn surface of the workbench, a familiar ritual that usually brought a measure of solace. Today, it offered little comfort. "He'd sketch out diagrams on napkins, theorize about torque ratios and combustion cycles for hours. He *loved* this stuff, Mike loved proving he could figure it out, that he was as good as Dad, better, even." Joe's gaze drifted to the corner where Mike's workbench used to be, a space now unnervingly bare. It was a void that spoke volumes, a silence that screamed louder than any argument. "Remember that '67 Camaro? The one with the seized crankshaft? He spent three days straight on that, fueled by nothing but coffee and stubbornness. When he finally got it free, the look on his face... it was like he'd conquered Everest." A ghost of a smile touched Joe's lips, a fleeting memory of shared triumph, quickly overshadowed by the stark reality of the present.

He could vividly recall the late nights, the air thick with the metallic tang of exhaust fumes and the faint, sweet aroma of stale coffee. They would be hunched over the greasy innards of an engine, their faces illuminated by the harsh glare of portable work lamps, their conversation a rapid-fire exchange of technical jargon and boyish boasts. Mike, younger and leaner then, his youthful enthusiasm a palpable force, would often be the one to bounce new ideas off him, his mind a fertile ground for innovation. He'd sketch out proposals for modernizing the shop, his voice brimming with an almost evangelistic zeal. "We could put in a state-of-the-art diagnostic system, Joe," he'd enthuse, his eyes shining with a vision of the future. "And a proper customer waiting area, not just these dusty chairs. We could really make this place shine, make Mom and Dad proud." Joe had always been the anchor, the pragmatist, tempering Mike's wilder ambitions with a healthy dose of realism, but he'd also recognized the brilliance, the unshakeable belief that fueled his younger brother. They were a team, their differing strengths a perfect complement, their shared heritage a powerful unifying force.

"He was so damn proud of this place," Joe continued, the words catching in his throat. "He'd talk about it like it was our own private kingdom, built on our own sweat and smarts. He wanted to be the guy who took it to the next level, who showed everyone that the next generation could do it even bigger and better." He sighed, the sound heavy with a profound sense of loss. "And we were going to do it together. That was the plan, wasn't it? That was the promise we made, not out loud, maybe, but it was there. In every shared beer after a long day, every late-night strategy session." He picked up a greasy rag, turning it over and over in his hands, the rough fibers a familiar texture against his skin. "He used to say we were going to have three bays humming all the time, that we'd be the best damn auto shop in the tri-state area. He'd already picked out the colors for the new signage, remember? A deep blue, to signify… trust, or something like that."

The memory of Mike's unwavering optimism, his almost infectious belief in their shared future, was a bittersweet pang. It was a reminder of a time when their path seemed clear, when the weight of their parents' legacy felt like a shared inheritance, a beacon guiding them forward. Now, standing amidst the quiet hum of dormant machinery, those vibrant dreams felt like faded photographs, their colors leached away by the harsh light of reality. The easy camaraderie that had once bound them together, forged in the crucible of shared labor and whispered ambitions, had frayed, stretched thin by the unspoken pressures of their new lives. Joe clung to those memories, to the echo of Mike's enthusiastic voice, desperately hoping that the shared history, the very blood that ran between them, could somehow reignite the spark that had begun to dim in his brother's eyes. He needed Mike, needed that shared ambition, that youthful drive to face the daunting task ahead. He needed his brother to be the man he knew, the man who had once stood shoulder-to-shoulder with him, ready to conquer the world.

But the vacant space where Mike's tools should have been, the unsettling quiet that now permeated his brother's usual workspace, sent a chilling premonition creeping into Joe's gut. The silence wasn't confined to the garage; it had infiltrated Mike's life, manifesting in his too-frequent absences, his evasive answers, the growing chasm that separated them. It was a silence that gnawed at Joe, a hollow echo of a shared past that was rapidly becoming a distant, fading memory. He searched his mind for the turning point, the moment when the vibrant tapestry of their brotherhood had begun to unravel, but found only a blur of unspoken anxieties and diverging paths.

He remembered the fierce concentration that would settle on Mike's face when he encountered a particularly stubborn engine problem. His brow would furrow, his eyes would narrow with a determined gleam, and he would dive into the mechanical labyrinth with an almost primal intensity. There was a raw, visceral joy in that struggle, a profound satisfaction in dissecting a complex problem and coaxing it into submission that Mike had always seemed to relish. Now, that same focused intensity appeared to have shifted, its target obscure, its energy misdirected. The fire that had once burned so brightly in Mike's eyes seemed to be flickering, replaced by a restless, unsettled gleam that Joe couldn't decipher. It was as if an invisible force, insidious and relentless, was steadily siphoning away his brother's essence, leaving behind a hollowed-out version of the man Joe knew and loved. He'd tried to reach him, to pull him back from whatever precipice he was teetering on, but his words seemed to dissipate into the air, lost in the echoing silence of the garage and the deepening silence within his brother. The weight of their parents' legacy, once a shared inheritance, a guiding star, now felt like a solitary burden, its immense gravity amplified by the growing chasm between the two brothers, a chasm that threatened to swallow them both whole.

## Cracks in the Foundation

The spectral glow of the desk lamp cast long, dancing shadows across the worn linoleum floor, transforming the familiar office into a landscape of disquiet. Joe hunched over the ledger, his knuckles white where he gripped the edge of the scarred oak desk. The scent of stale coffee, a bitter counterpoint to the phantom lavender of his mother's perfume, filled his nostrils. It was late, the quiet of the garage now a profound, almost suffocating presence. Outside, the city hummed with a life that felt distant and alien, a world that continued to spin while his own had ground to a jarring halt. The figures on the page swam before his eyes, a relentless tide of red ink that threatened to drown him. Each entry was a fresh wound, a testament to the erosion of their once-thriving business. The invoices, stacked precariously high, were not mere pieces of paper; they were monuments to their declining fortunes, each one a silent accusation.

He traced a line with his finger, his breath catching in his throat. Another late payment, another service call pushed back. The clientele, once loyal and steady, had dwindled like melting snow. The regulars, the ones who had trusted his father's hands and his mother's sharp mind, were becoming fewer and farther between. New customers, attracted by the slick advertising of larger, more modern garages in town, rarely ventured down their quiet side street. Joe understood the allure of newness, of shiny chrome and state-of-the-art equipment. But this place, this sanctuary of oil and steel, wasn't just about the latest technology; it was about legacy, about the intricate dance of skilled hands and a deep understanding of the machines they serviced. It was about the trust built over decades, a trust that was now proving alarmingly fragile.

The weight of the bills pressed down on him, an invisible vise tightening around his chest. There were suppliers to pay, overdue notices from utility companies, the ever-present specter of property taxes. He felt a sickening lurch with each entry, a growing dread that gnawed at his resolve. He tried to remain stoic, to channel the unwavering pragmatism his father had always possessed, but the sheer volume of the financial challenges was overwhelming. He was a mechanic, a craftsman, not a financier. His hands were made for the grease and grime of the trade, for coaxing stubborn engines back to life, not for wrestling with spreadsheets and balance sheets. Yet, here he was, adrift in a sea of numbers, the captain of a sinking ship.

He closed his eyes for a moment, picturing his parents' faces, their proud smiles when the shop was bustling, their easy laughter as they discussed the day's work. He could almost hear his father's booming voice, "We'll get it done, Joey, we always do." But his father wasn't here, and the inherent optimism that had defined his outlook felt like a distant, unattainable dream. His mother, with her quiet strength and meticulous attention to detail, had always been the steady hand that balanced his father's more boisterous energy. She was the one who kept the books meticulously, who knew every customer by name, who could find a way to stretch every dollar. Her absence was a gaping wound, a void that no amount of effort could fill.

He ran a weary hand through his hair, the strands already slick with the day's accumulated grime. He had to keep this place afloat. It was more than just a business; it was his inheritance, the tangible manifestation of his parents' life's work, the very bedrock of his identity. He couldn't let it crumble into dust. But the sheer effort required to keep it from doing so was exhausting him, body and soul. He was working sixteen-hour days, meticulously tending to the few remaining customers, trying to stretch their budgets, offering payment plans where before there had been only straightforward transactions. He was trying to be his father and his mother rolled into one, a feat that felt increasingly impossible.

The strain was starting to show. He saw it in the reflection of the office window – the tired lines etched around his eyes, the slump of his shoulders, the ever-present shadow of exhaustion. He knew he was failing to hide it from Mike, though he tried. He would put on a brave face, offer reassurances, and try to keep the conversation light, focusing on the mechanics of the work rather than the precariousness of their financial situation. But he saw the worry in Mike's eyes too, a subtle mirroring of his own anxieties, even if Mike tried to mask it with a forced casualness or a restless energy that seemed to propel him away from the core problems.

He picked up a discarded invoice, the paper flimsy and creased. A simple oil change and tire rotation for Mrs. Henderson, a customer since the early days. Her check had been post-dated by two weeks. He understood the need, the hard times that could fall on anyone, but when these instances multiplied, they became a crushing burden. Each late payment, each deferred invoice, was a stone added to the ever-growing pile he was forced to carry. He felt a sense of responsibility so profound it threatened to suffocate him. He was the older brother, the one who was supposed to be strong, to have all the answers, to protect Mike from the harsh realities of the world. But the world, in the form of overdue bills and dwindling income, was encroaching, and he felt increasingly ill-equipped to defend their shared inheritance.

The silence of the office, punctuated only by the scratching of his pen and the distant wail of a siren, amplified the gnawing fear in his gut. He remembered Mike's boundless enthusiasm, his dreams of modernizing the shop, of putting in a new diagnostic system, of creating a customer lounge that wouldn't smell faintly of motor oil. Those dreams, once so vivid and shared, now seemed almost naive, a product of a time when the future felt assured and their parents' guiding presence was a constant, unwavering force. Now, that future was a question mark, shrouded in uncertainty, and the weight of their parents' legacy had shifted, settling entirely onto Joe's weary shoulders. He felt the edifice of the garage, once so solid and reliable, beginning to show hairline cracks, fissures spreading through the very foundation of their shared past and uncertain future. He was holding it together, but for how much longer, he didn't know. The relentless tide of numbers in the ledger was a stark, undeniable testament to that fact.

He closed the ledger, the snap of the cover echoing in the quiet room. The day's work was done, as much as it could be. But the worries, the financial anxieties, were far from over. They were a constant companion, a shadow that followed him from the garage to his meager apartment, clinging to him even in his sleep. He knew he had to find a way to stem the tide, to shore up the crumbling foundations of the business. But the path forward was obscured, shrouded in the same financial fog that seemed to have settled over their lives. He looked at his hands, calloused and stained with grease, the tools of his trade. They were strong hands, capable hands, but they felt inadequate against the intangible, yet formidable, force of economic hardship. He was a mechanic, not a miracle worker, and the miracle he needed felt increasingly out of reach. The weight of it all threatened to buckle his knees, to finally break him. He pushed himself up from the desk, the chair scraping loudly against the floor, a jarring intrusion into the stillness. He needed to get some air, to try and clear his head. But he knew, with a certainty that chilled him to the bone, that no amount of fresh air would truly dissipate the suffocating weight of their dwindling fortunes. He was trapped, it seemed, in the very legacy he was so desperate to preserve.

## The First Signs

The first few weeks after the funeral had been a blur of inherited responsibilities and unspoken grief. Joe had thrown himself into keeping the garage running, the familiar rhythms of engine repair a welcome distraction from the gnawing emptiness left by his parents. He'd stepped into the breach, shouldering the weight of management, customer relations, and the increasingly daunting financial ledgers with a grim determination. Mike, meanwhile, had retreated into himself, his presence a quiet, almost spectral thing in the garage. Joe had attributed it to shock, to the raw, unprocessed pain of losing both parents in quick succession. He'd tried to give him space, to let him grieve in his own way, while shouldering the lion's share of the burden. He'd found himself working longer hours, his own exhaustion a constant companion, but he'd told himself it was necessary. He was the older brother, the responsible one. He had to be.

But lately, a new kind of unease had begun to creep in, a subtle shift in the familiar dynamics that felt more significant than just grief. It started with the small things, the almost imperceptible deviations from Mike's usual routine. He'd begun showing up late, not by much, but enough to notice. Ten, fifteen minutes here and there, usually with a mumbled apology about traffic or a misplaced alarm. Joe, ever the pragmatist, initially chalked it up to Mike still adjusting to a life without their parents' structured routines. He remembered how their father had always been punctual to a fault, and their mother, though more forgiving of minor tardiness, had always emphasized the importance of a consistent start to the day. Mike had inherited a good deal of their father's easygoing nature, but also, Joe had thought, his reliability.

Then came the fatigue. It wasn't just the general weariness that came with long hours in the garage. Mike's eyes, usually bright and alert, often held a distant, unfocused look. There were dark circles etched beneath them, a testament to nights that Joe suspected were less about restful sleep and more about restless worry, or perhaps something else entirely. He'd try to engage Mike in conversation about a tricky repair, or ask his opinion on a new diagnostic tool they might need, but Mike's responses would be slow, hesitant, as if he were struggling to surface from a deep well of thought. His once-sharp focus, honed by years of working alongside their father, seemed to have dulled, replaced by a persistent distractedness that gnawed at Joe's patience. It was like talking to a radio station that kept fading in and out, the signal never quite strong enough to hold.

These lapses in concentration manifested in other ways, too. A crucial bolt left untightened on a brake job, a diagnostic code that Mike, usually so adept at deciphering them, seemed to overlook. Joe found himself double-checking Mike's work more often than he liked to admit, a silent accusation hanging in the air between them. It was a subtle erosion of the trust that had always underpinned their partnership, a trust built on shared experience and mutual reliance. He didn't want to confront Mike, not directly. He understood that Mike was hurting, that grief could manifest in myriad ways. But these weren't just random mistakes; they felt like symptoms of something deeper, something Joe couldn't quite pinpoint.

The arguments, when they did occur, were another troubling indicator. They were rare before, usually brief disagreements about the best approach to a particular engine problem, quickly resolved with a shared understanding of their common goal: getting the job done right. But now, their exchanges were tinged with an unfamiliar defensiveness from Mike, a bristling that suggested he felt attacked even when Joe was simply trying to guide him back to the task at hand. One afternoon, Joe had gently pointed out a missed step in a routine oil change. Mike's reaction was disproportionate, his voice sharp as he retorted, "I know what I'm doing, Joe. Don't treat me like I'm some green kid just starting out." The edge in his tone was like a physical blow. Joe had simply nodded, the words catching in his throat, unwilling to escalate the confrontation. But the exchange left a bitter residue, a growing chasm between them that Joe found himself increasingly reluctant to cross.

He noticed a new nervousness in Mike, a fidgeting that went beyond the usual restless energy of a mechanic at work. Mike would tap his fingers incessantly on the workbench, jiggle his leg under the counter, or chew on the inside of his cheek with a peculiar intensity. It was a palpable anxiety, a coiled tension that seemed to emanate from him. He'd also started to seem detached, as if he were physically present in the garage but his mind was miles away. Conversations would drift, his gaze would wander to the window, and his participation in their shared life – the casual banter, the shared lunches of lukewarm coffee and hastily made sandwiches – seemed to dwindle. It was as if a pane of invisible glass had settled between them, muffling their connection, distorting the shared reality they had inhabited for so long.

Joe tried to rationalize it all. Mike was younger, still finding his footing in the world, and the loss of their parents had undoubtedly hit him hard. Perhaps he was struggling with the transition from being the younger brother, the apprentice, to being an equal partner in the business. Maybe he felt the weight of responsibility differently, and his way of coping was to withdraw, to let Joe take the lead. Joe clung to these explanations, desperate to believe that it was all temporary, a phase that Mike would eventually outgrow. He reminded himself of their shared childhood, of the countless times they'd played in the dust of this very garage, dreaming of the day they'd take it over from their father. That shared history, that ingrained bond, had to count for something.

Yet, the signs continued to accumulate, each one a tiny crack in the foundation of their shared world. He'd overheard Mike on the phone a few times, his voice low and hushed, a stark contrast to his usual open demeanor. He couldn't make out the words, but the furtive nature of the conversations, the way Mike would abruptly end them or turn away to shield the receiver, raised a red flag. It felt… secretive. And secrecy, in their line of work, in their lives, had always been a breeding ground for trouble. Their father had always preached transparency, about keeping everything out in the open. "No matter how ugly the truth," he used to say, his voice gruff but kind, "it's always better than a well-kept lie."

One evening, Joe arrived at the garage after a late supply run. The place was locked up, the lights off, but he could hear faint music emanating from inside. He'd expected to find Mike still at his workbench, finishing up some odds and ends. Instead, he found him sitting in the small, cluttered office, bathed in the dim glow of the desk lamp, not with ledgers or repair manuals, but with a deck of cards spread out before him. He was playing solitaire, his movements slow and deliberate, his expression unreadable. When he looked up and saw Joe, a flicker of something – surprise? annoyance? shame? – crossed his face before he quickly masked it.

"Working late, Mike?" Joe asked, trying to keep his tone casual, friendly.

Mike shuffled the cards with a soft rustle. "Just… clearing my head," he said, his voice flat. He avoided Joe's gaze, his eyes fixed on the patterns on the playing cards.

Joe walked over, leaning against the doorframe. He could smell a faint, unfamiliar scent on the air, something vaguely sweet and cloying, not the usual honest smell of oil and metal. "Everything alright?"

Mike finally met his eyes, and for a fleeting moment, Joe saw a desperate plea in their depths. But it was gone as quickly as it appeared, replaced by a practiced nonchalance. "Yeah, Joe. Just… thinking about things." He picked up a card, his hand trembling slightly. "You know. The future."

The future. It was a word that loomed large, a nebulous concept that had once been a shared ambition, a canvas upon which they painted their dreams. Now, it felt like a threat, a dark unknown that was slowly, inexorably, consuming the present. Joe felt a knot tighten in his stomach. He couldn't shake the feeling that Mike wasn't just thinking about the future of the garage, or their inheritance. He was thinking about something else entirely, something that was pulling him further and further away from the life they'd always known, from him. The cards, the late nights, the secretive calls – they were all pieces of a puzzle Joe was struggling to assemble, a puzzle that promised to reveal a truth he wasn't sure he was ready to face. He could feel the legacy, the weight of it, pressing down not just on him, but on Mike too, and he feared that Mike was buckling under a pressure he couldn't, or wouldn't, share.

## A Looming Shadow

The hum of the fluorescent lights in the garage had always been a familiar, almost comforting sound to Joe. It was the soundtrack to his life, the steady thrum of the place where he and Mike had learned to wield wrenches, where their father's gruff laughter and their mother's gentle reprimands had echoed. Now, that hum felt strained, a discordant note in the symphony of his unease. He stood by the open bay door, watching as a battered sedan, its engine sputtering a mournful lament, was towed in. It was the kind of job they used to relish, a challenge that would have ignited a spark of competition between him and Mike, a silent push to see who could diagnose and fix it faster, more efficiently. But the fire seemed to have gone out of Mike, replaced by a dull, apathetic glow.

Joe felt the familiar gnaw of responsibility, amplified tenfold. It wasn't just about keeping the doors of "Miller & Sons Auto Repair" open; it was about salvaging the remnants of a life, a legacy, that felt like it was slipping through his fingers like fine sand. He'd always been the grounded one, the pragmatist who kept their feet planted firmly on the earth while Mike's head often drifted among the clouds. But now, it was as if Mike had fallen from the sky, landing hard and unable to get back up. The dreams they'd meticulously sketched out in faded notebooks – expanding the service, opening a second location, even just affording a decent vacation without worrying about the cash flow – felt like relics from a forgotten past. The vibrant hues of their shared future had leached away, leaving behind a monochrome canvas of worry and resignation.

The garage, once a sanctuary, had become a source of constant anxiety. Every squeaky hinge, every unanswered phone call, every delayed invoice seemed to echo the growing chasm between him and his brother. Joe found himself replaying conversations, scrutinizing Mike's fleeting expressions, searching for clues he might have missed. He'd always prided himself on his ability to read people, a skill honed by years of dealing with demanding customers and finicky engines. But Mike was an enigma, his usual openness replaced by a guarded silence that was more unnerving than any outright argument. It was as if a shadow had fallen over his brother, a darkness that seemed to emanate from within, distorting his familiar features, muffling his voice, and extinguishing the light in his eyes.

He tried to hold onto hope, clinging to the belief that this was merely a manifestation of grief, a temporary deviation from the norm. He remembered their father's stoic resilience in the face of setbacks, their mother's unwavering optimism even in the darkest of times. Surely, Mike would find his way back, would shake off this lethargy and reclaim the spirited young man he knew. But a more insidious thought, a chilling premonition, began to worm its way into Joe's consciousness. It whispered of something more profound than sadness, of a vulnerability that was being exploited, of a path Mike was treading that Joe couldn't see, but that he instinctively knew led to a precipice.

The subtle changes in Mike's behavior had escalated from mere curiosities to genuine causes for concern. The late arrivals were now the norm, punctuated by increasingly elaborate excuses that strained credulity. Joe had once caught Mike in the stockroom, ostensibly searching for a specific part, but instead finding him hunched over his phone, his face pale in the dim light, his thumbs flying across the screen with an urgency that belied the mundane task. When Joe had entered, Mike had flinched, his hand snapping the phone shut as if caught in the act of some illicit transgression. He'd mumbled something about checking a vendor's availability, but his averted gaze and the tremor in his voice had spoken volumes.

Then there were the financial irregularities. Joe, who meticulously managed their accounts, had begun noticing discrepancies that he couldn't reconcile. Small amounts, initially, that he'd attributed to his own oversight or an administrative error. But the pattern persisted, growing more pronounced with each passing week. Transactions that didn't add up, payments that seemed to have vanished into thin air. He'd confronted Mike about it, his voice tight with a carefully controlled frustration. "Mike, I don't understand these numbers. It's like money's just… disappearing."

Mike's reaction had been a defensive surge, his jaw tightening, his eyes narrowing. "Maybe you're not looking hard enough, Joe. Maybe you're too close to it." The accusation, sharp and unexpected, had landed like a blow. Joe had retreated, the unspoken implication hanging heavy in the air: that Joe, the elder brother, the one who had always been so meticulous, was now somehow incapable. He'd spent hours poring over the ledgers himself, his own fatigue a dull ache behind his eyes, searching for any logical explanation, any slip of his own. But the numbers remained stubbornly elusive, their story refusing to be told.

He remembered one particularly jarring incident. A customer, Mrs. Gable, a sweet elderly woman who always brought them homemade cookies, had called to inquire about a diagnostic report Joe had promised to have ready by noon. It was already three in the afternoon, and Mike had assured Joe that he'd handled it. When Joe checked the system, the report was nowhere to be found. He found Mike in the breakroom, staring blankly at a half-eaten sandwich, the diagnostic equipment sitting idle on a nearby counter. Mike's explanation was a mumbled apology about a sudden headache and a forgotten appointment. The lie, so blatant, so poorly constructed, was more disturbing than the oversight itself. It was a betrayal of their father's teachings, of the trust that had always been the bedrock of their business.

The weight of it all was crushing Joe. He felt like he was drowning, the familiar currents of their shared life now pulling him under. He'd always been the anchor, the steady hand that kept them from drifting. But now, he was flailing, trying to keep his head above water while the person who should have been swimming beside him was sinking. He found himself withdrawing too, not out of malice, but out of a desperate need for self-preservation. He couldn't bear to witness any more of Mike's subtle unraveling, couldn't face the constant barrage of his brother's evasiveness. He started working later, staying in the garage long after Mike had left, seeking solace in the quiet hum of machines that no longer held the same comfort.

He'd look at old photographs, sepia-toned images of them as children, their faces bright with innocence, their hands sticky with engine grease as they posed proudly beside their father. They'd been a unit, an inseparable force. Now, they were two strangers occupying the same space, bound by a shared past that felt increasingly alien. Joe longed for the easy camaraderie they once shared, the unspoken understanding that had flowed between them like a well-oiled machine. He missed the late-night conversations over lukewarm coffee, the shared jokes, the simple comfort of knowing that they were in it together.

The premonition, the gnawing sense of dread, was no longer a whisper; it was a roaring in his ears. He knew, with a certainty that chilled him to the bone, that this wasn't just grief. This was something darker, something that had sunk its claws deep into his brother's soul. He saw it in the way Mike's shoulders had begun to slump, in the increasing frequency of his vacant stares, in the way his hands, once so sure and steady, now seemed to tremble with an invisible force. It was a gradual decay, a slow poisoning of the spirit, and Joe felt utterly powerless to stop it. The legacy that had once seemed like a beacon of opportunity now felt like a looming shadow, casting a pall over their lives, and threatening to consume them both. He had to do something, but the thought of confronting Mike directly, of forcing him to reveal the truth he so desperately concealed, filled him with a dread that was almost as potent as the fear for his brother. He was caught in a vise, squeezed between his love for Mike and his growing certainty that something was terribly, terribly wrong.

# Chapter Two
# The Slow Erosion

## Missed Shifts and Evasive Answers

The silence in the garage was no longer a comforting hum; it had become a gnawing emptiness, punctuated only by the clatter of Joe's own tools and the whine of the hydraulic lift. Mike's absence was a gaping hole, a stark absence that Joe was forced to fill, not just with his own labor, but with the burden of explaining his brother's disappearing act to increasingly impatient customers. Each late arrival or outright no-show was a physical manifestation of Mike's desertion, a tangible weight added to Joe's already overloaded shoulders. He'd find himself muttering apologies under his breath, smoothing over the rough edges of Mike's unreliability with a practiced smile that felt increasingly like a grimace. Mrs. Henderson, whose '88 Buick was overdue for a transmission flush, had tapped her manicured fingernails on the service counter with thinly veiled impatience. "Is Mike alright, Joe? He promised he'd call me yesterday with an update." Joe's throat tightened. "He, uh… he had a family emergency, Mrs. Henderson. Really sorry about that. I'll get right on it." The lie tasted like ash in his mouth.

The excuses themselves were becoming a macabre, predictable liturgy. A sudden migraine, a flat tire on his own car (which Joe knew had been running smoothly for months after their last joint effort), a forgotten doctor's appointment that couldn't be rescheduled. Each explanation was delivered with a forced casualness that only highlighted its hollowness. Joe would watch Mike's eyes, desperately trying to find a flicker of truth, a shard of the brother he knew buried beneath the layers of evasion. But all he found were darting glances, a studied avoidance of eye contact, a nervous shift of weight from one foot to the other. It was the look of a man caught in a web of his own making, desperately trying to untangle himself without revealing the sticky threads that bound him. The transparent nature of the lies was almost more insulting than the lies themselves. It was as if Mike no longer even *tried* to make them believable, as if he'd resigned himself to being seen through, but still couldn't bring himself to face the consequences.

One sweltering Tuesday, a day where the heat inside the garage seemed to amplify the tension, Joe found himself wrestling with a stubborn exhaust manifold on a pickup truck. The bolts were seized, fused by years of road salt and neglect. He'd been at it for nearly an hour, his knuckles scraped raw, sweat stinging his eyes, when he realized Mike was supposed to be there an hour ago. He'd checked his phone. Nothing. No text, no call. Joe wiped his brow with the back of his grease-stained hand and trudged to the small office. Mike's toolbox, usually tucked neatly under his workbench, was gone. His faded blue work jacket, which he practically lived in, wasn't hanging on its usual hook. A knot of dread tightened in Joe's stomach, a familiar sensation these days. He picked up the phone and dialed Mike's cell. It went straight to voicemail. Again.

He spent the rest of the day fielding questions, running diagnostics, and performing repairs that should have been shared. By closing time, Joe was bone-weary, his muscles aching, his mind a fog of fatigue and simmering resentment. He knew Mike was usually at the diner down the street by now, drowning his sorrows or whatever else he was doing. He drove over, the truck's engine a familiar rumble that offered no solace. He found Mike at a corner booth, hunched over, nursing a beer, his face buried in his phone. Joe slid into the opposite seat, the worn vinyl squeaking a protest. Mike looked up, startled, his eyes a little too bright, a little too unfocused.

"Hey, Joe," he mumbled, his voice thick.

"Hey yourself," Joe replied, his tone carefully neutral, though the words felt brittle. "Long day?"

Mike shrugged, taking a long pull from his beer. "Yeah, you know. Stuff." He gestured vaguely with his phone. "Just trying to sort some things out."

"Mike, you didn't show up. Again. Customers were asking. I had to cover for you all day." Joe's voice was low, but the frustration was a palpable vibration between them. "What's going on?"

Mike's gaze flickered to the window, then back to his phone, his thumbs hovering over the screen. "I told you, man, family stuff. It's… complicated."

"Complicated how?" Joe pressed, leaning forward. "Because 'family stuff' usually involves telling your brother, not just vanishing. I'm worried about you, Mike. And frankly, I'm getting pretty fed up with covering your shifts."

Mike finally looked at him, his expression a mixture of defensiveness and something Joe couldn't quite decipher – guilt, maybe, or a profound weariness. "Look, I'm dealing with some… personal issues, okay? It's nothing you need to worry about. I'll be back tomorrow. I promise." The word 'promise' hung in the air, devoid of its usual weight. Joe had heard it before, or variations of it, too many times to count.

"Promises don't pay the bills, Mike. And they don't keep our customers happy. This place, our dad's legacy, it's falling apart while you're off 'sorting things out'." The words tumbled out, sharper than Joe intended, fueled by the exhaustion and the growing fear. Each missed shift felt like another brick being chipped away from the foundation of their business, another nail driven into the coffin of the dreams they'd once shared. The resentment, a slow-burning ember, began to curdle into something more bitter, a sour taste that coated Joe's tongue.

Mike's jaw tightened. "Don't you go talking about Dad's legacy like that, Joe. You think I don't care about this place?" His voice rose slightly, attracting the attention of a couple at a nearby table.

"Then act like it!" Joe countered, keeping his own voice down but the intensity undiminished. "Show up. Do the work. Be here. That's all I'm asking." He held Mike's gaze, searching for that spark of recognition, that flicker of the brother he remembered. But the spark was absent, replaced by a dull, smoky haze.

Mike pushed his phone away, the clatter against the oak tabletop sharp. He ran a hand through his already disheveled hair. "It's not that simple, Joe. You wouldn't understand."

"Try me," Joe said, the plea beneath the demand evident. "Because right now, I understand that you're not here, you're not talking to me, and I'm left picking up the pieces. That's the only thing I understand."

Mike leaned back, a impression of defeat washing over his features. "I… I can't right now, Joe. I just… I can't." He picked up his beer again, his knuckles white around the glass. The conversation, if it could even be called that, was over. He had retreated behind his wall of evasiveness, leaving Joe once again on the outside, staring in at a brother he no longer seemed to recognize.

As Joe drove home that night, the streetlights blurring into streaks of light, he replayed the encounter. The flimsy excuses, the averted eyes, the utter lack of accountability. Each missed shift was a wound, not just to their business, but to their bond. He felt a profound sense of loss, not just for the missing income or the extra work, but for the erosion of trust, for the quiet disintegration of his brother. The steady hum of the garage, once the soundtrack to their shared lives, now seemed to mock him with its emptiness. It was a hollow sound, echoing the hollowness he felt inside, the growing realization that Mike wasn't just struggling; he was pulling away, dragging their shared past, their shared future, down into some dark, uncharted territory. Joe knew he couldn't keep covering for him indefinitely. The pressure was building, and soon, something would have to break. He just prayed it wouldn't be him, or their father's legacy. But as he looked out at the dark, quiet streets, a chilling premonition settled in his gut: he was already breaking. He was watching his brother break, and he didn't know how to stop it. The missed shifts were just the symptom; the disease was something far more insidious, and Joe was starting to realize he might not have the tools, or the answers, to fix it. The frustration was a raw, open wound, and the resentment was a venom slowly spreading through his veins, tainting everything he felt for his brother.

## Arguments in the Dust

The air in the garage, usually thick with the comforting scent of oil and exhaust, now felt heavy with unspoken accusations. Joe watched Mike, his brother, his business partner, the man who was supposed to be his anchor, move with a restless energy that spoke volumes. Each clink of a dropped tool, each sharp exhaled breath, seemed to underscore the chasm that had opened between them. The last few weeks had been a slow, agonizing erosion of their shared foundation, and Joe could feel the ground crumbling beneath his feet. He'd tried to approach it with patience, with understanding, but patience was a finite resource, and understanding was becoming a luxury he could no longer afford.

"Another one, Mike," Joe said, his voice low and rough, barely cutting through the metallic echo of the cavernous space. He held up a crumpled piece of paper, a work order for Mrs. Gable's minivan. "She's been calling all morning. Said you promised her a call back yesterday with an update on the brakes." Joe let the paper fall back onto the greasy workbench, the sound a soft, defeated sigh. He didn't need to look at Mike to know his brother's posture would be defensive, his gaze fixed on some point beyond Joe's shoulder.

Mike didn't turn. He was bent over the engine block of a beat-up Ford pickup, his back a rigid wall. "Yeah, I'll get to it," he mumbled, the words muffled by the sheer indifference in his tone.

"You'll get to it?" Joe's voice cracked, the carefully constructed dam of his composure finally breached. He walked closer, the worn concrete floor feeling like a minefield under his boots. "That's what you said about Mr. Henderson's Buick, and Mrs. Gable's minivan, and God knows how many others this past month. I'm the one who's been fielding the calls, Mike. I'm the one making excuses, sounding like a damned fool, telling people you're dealing with 'family emergencies' when I don't even know what the hell you're doing." The words spilled out, a torrent of frustration and hurt that had been building for weeks, each missed shift, each flimsy excuse, a drop that had finally overflowed the cup.

Mike finally straightened, slowly, deliberately. He wiped his hands on a stained rag, his movements measured, as if trying to buy himself time, or perhaps to gather his own defenses. His eyes, when they met Joe's, held a familiar, yet newly sharpened, defensiveness. It wasn't the look of a man facing a problem he could solve, but the defiant glare of someone trapped. "You don't have to cover for me, Joe," he said, his voice flat, devoid of any hint of apology or remorse. "Just tell them I'm busy. Or tell them whatever you want. It's your circus, man."

"My circus?" Joe felt a cold dread creep into his gut. "This is *our* circus, Mike. Dad built this place with his bare hands, and you're acting like it's some kind of joke. I'm busting my ass here, day in and day out, trying to keep this place afloat, and you're… what? Off playing somewhere? Because that's what it looks like. That's what it *feels* like." He took a step closer, his voice dropping to a dangerous growl. "I'm worried about you, Mike. And I'm tired. I'm damn tired of the lies, of the dodging, of the not knowing."

Mike's jaw tightened. He turned back to the Ford, his attention seemingly riveted to a bolt that didn't need riveting. "You want to know what's going on? Fine. I'm dealing with some things. Personal things. Things you wouldn't understand."

"Try me!" Joe's voice rose, echoing off the metal walls. "Try explaining it to me, your brother, your partner. Because right now, all I understand is that I'm doing the work of two men, and you're nowhere to be found. And frankly, Mike, it feels like a betrayal." The word, once spoken, hung heavy in the air between them, a tangible accusation. Betrayal. It was a word Joe had never thought he'd associate with his brother.

Mike slammed his wrench down on the workbench, the clang reverberating through the garage. He spun around, his eyes blazing, but not with the fire of conviction. It was the desperate, cornered glare of a wild animal. "Betrayal? You think this is about betraying you? You think I
*like* this? You think I *want* to be out here, pretending everything's fine, when it's not?" His voice was ragged, laced with a raw, undisguised pain.

"Then tell me, damn it!" Joe pleaded, his anger momentarily overshadowed by a surge of genuine concern. He reached out, wanting to grab Mike's arm, to shake him, to make him see the damage he was doing. But he stopped himself, his hand falling uselessly to his side. "Tell me what's going on. Let me help. Whatever it is, we can face it together, like we always have."

Mike let out a harsh, humorless laugh. He ran a hand through his already messy hair, his gaze darting around the garage as if searching for an escape route. "Together? You really think it's that simple, Joe? You think I can just… unload all of this onto you, and everything magically gets better?" He scoffed. "You've got your own shit to deal with. You don't need my problems piled on top."

"Your problems *are* my problems, Mike! This business, our family, it's all connected. When you're hurting, I'm hurting. When you're not here, I'm drowning. Don't you get that?" Joe's voice was raw with emotion. He saw the flicker of something in Mike's eyes, a momentary softening, a hint of the brother he knew, but it vanished as quickly as it appeared, replaced by that hard, unyielding shell.

"What I get," Mike said, his voice dropping to a low, dangerous tone, "is that you're judging me. You're standing there, all high and mighty, thinking you've got it all figured out, while I'm the screw-up. You always have, haven't you, Joe? Always the responsible one, the golden boy. And me? I'm just the screw-up brother who can't even keep his shit together."

The accusation stung, sharp and unexpected. Joe felt a surge of heat rise up his neck. "That's not fair, Mike. I'm not judging you. I'm trying to help you. But you're making it impossible. You're shutting me out. You're shutting *everyone* out." He gestured around the garage, the silence amplifying his words. "This place, it needs both of us. Dad's legacy, it needs both of us. But you're not here. You're not showing up. And I can't keep carrying this alone."

"So what do you want me to do, Joe? Huh? You want me to crawl back here, all apologetic, and beg for your forgiveness? You want me to tell you all my dirty laundry so you can have something to hold over me later?" Mike's voice was rising again, the veneer of control cracking completely.

"I want you to be my brother!" Joe roared, the sound echoing off the concrete and steel. "I want you to be my partner! I want you to stop acting like this is some kind of game! This is our life, Mike!" He took a step back, the sheer exhaustion of the argument, of the situation, washing over him. He looked at Mike, really looked at him, and saw not the capable, if sometimes reckless, brother he'd always known, but a stranger, hollowed out and consumed by something Joe couldn't comprehend.

Mike stared back, his chest heaving, his eyes wild and unfocused. The fire that Joe had seen earlier was still there, but it was the fire of desperation, of someone who had finally reached the end of their rope. He looked like he wanted to say something, anything, but the words wouldn't come. He opened his mouth, then closed it again, the sound of his own ragged breathing filling the void.

"I can't," Mike finally whispered, the words barely audible. He turned away, his shoulders slumping, the fight draining out of him, replaced by a profound, weary resignation. "I just… I can't do this right now, Joe. I can't." He picked up the stained rag again, folding it meticulously, as if it were the most important task in the world.

Joe watched him, his heart sinking with a heavy, crushing finality. He knew, with a chilling certainty, that this wasn't a fight that could be won with words, not anymore. The damage had gone too deep. The trust had eroded too completely. He saw Mike's back, the rigid line of his shoulders, and felt the familiar, gnawing emptiness return, a hollow echo in the silence that had fallen between them, thicker and more suffocating than any argument. The dust motes danced in the shafts of sunlight slanting through the grimy windows, oblivious to the quiet devastation unfolding in their father's garage. And Joe knew, with a certainty that chilled him to the bone, that he was watching not just his business, but his brother, slowly but surely, disintegrate. He was losing Mike, not to another town, or another woman, but to something within himself, something dark and consuming that Joe, despite all his efforts, couldn't reach.

## The Whispers of Addiction

The silence that descended after Mike's near-confession was a different beast than the tense quiet of their arguments. This was a heavy, suffocating blanket, woven with the threads of unspoken truths and Joe's burgeoning dread. He watched Mike, or what remained of him in that moment, retreat further into himself, his gaze fixed on the grease-stained rag, his posture one of utter defeat. The words "I just… I can't do this right now, Joe. I can't" hung in the air, each syllable a hammer blow against the foundation of Joe's hope. It wasn't just about missed work orders or late nights anymore. It was about a void, a chasm that had opened up in his brother, a void that was swallowing him whole.

Joe's mind, already reeling from the emotional onslaught, began to churn, replaying the past few weeks, months even, through a new, horrifying lens. The late nights weren't just long hours at the shop; they were nights spent… elsewhere. The erratic behavior, the sudden mood swings, the almost manic bursts of energy followed by prolonged periods of lethargy – it wasn't just stress. The evasiveness, the constant deflections, the way Mike would abruptly change the subject or simply shut down – it wasn't just personal problems, as he'd claimed. Joe had heard the stories, the whispered warnings from friends, the hushed accounts from acquaintances who had navigated similar treacherous waters with their own loved ones. He'd always filed them away, abstract warnings that applied to other people, other families. Now, the abstract had crashed into his reality with the force of a wrecking ball.

He tried to fight it, to push the terrifying possibility away. Addiction. The word itself felt alien, a contaminant that didn't belong in their lives, in their family, in their father's legacy. Mike was strong, capable, a bit reckless, sure, but never weak. Not like this. This was a different kind of weakness, a surrender that Joe couldn't reconcile with the brother he knew. He latched onto any other explanation, grasping at straws in the suffocating darkness. Maybe it was a bad debt. Maybe he was being blackmailed. Maybe he was in trouble with someone dangerous. But even as these thoughts formed, they felt like flimsy paper shields against an oncoming tidal wave. The signs, once he allowed himself to see them, were too stark, too consistent.

He remembered the tremor in Mike's hands when he'd dropped the wrench, a tremor that wasn't from exertion. He recalled the almost feverish intensity in Mike's eyes when he'd talked about a job, only to have him disappear for days afterward, offering no coherent explanation. There were the times Mike would show up to work looking gaunt, his eyes bloodshot, his normally vibrant energy replaced by a jittery restlessness. Joe had attributed it to a bad flu, to staying up all night wrestling with a difficult engine. But now, the pieces clicked into place with sickening clarity. It wasn't a flu; it was withdrawal. It wasn't late nights with engines; it was binges and the subsequent attempts to function.

The hushed warnings from friends, once dismissed as gossip or overblown concerns, now echoed with chilling accuracy. Sarah, whose brother had battled heroin addiction for years, had once told Joe, "It starts subtly, Joe. Little changes. They become experts at hiding it, at lying. You'll doubt yourself, think you're overreacting. But when you see that emptiness in their eyes, that desperation to get whatever it is they need... there's no mistaking it." Joe remembered Sarah's haunted eyes, the weariness etched into her face, and he felt a cold dread seep into his bones. Was he seeing that emptiness in Mike now? Was he witnessing the same desperate need in the vacant stare that Mike kept fixed on the floor?

He'd always prided himself on being able to read people, especially Mike. They were brothers, after all, bound by years of shared experiences, triumphs, and failures. But the Mike in front of him now was a stranger. The familiar crinkles around his eyes, the easy grin that used to light up his face, the very essence of his brother – it was all obscured, hidden behind a veil of something dark and consuming. Joe felt a profound sense of disorientation, as if the ground beneath him had shifted, revealing an abyss where solid earth had been.

He thought about the money. The shop accounts were tighter than they should be, despite the steady stream of customers. There had been a few unexplainable withdrawals, small amounts at first, that Joe had chalked up to Mike covering some personal expenses. But then there were the larger sums, the money that seemed to vanish without a trace. Joe had confronted Mike about it once, weeks ago, suggesting they tighten up their budgeting, but Mike had become instantly defensive, accusing Joe of treating him like a child. At the time, Joe had felt unfairly accused, hurt by the implication that he didn't trust his own brother. Now, the missing money felt like another crucial piece of the puzzle, another damning piece of evidence.

The memory of Mike's defiant glare, the words "You don't have to cover for me, Joe," and "It's your circus, man," now carried a bitter, almost cynical undertone. Mike wasn't being dismissive; he was being protective, trying to shield Joe from the ugly truth of his own unraveling. He was trying to keep the chaos contained, to compartmentalize his addiction, and in doing so, he was isolating himself, pushing away the very person who could have helped him.

Joe's frustration, which had been simmering for weeks, now threatened to boil over into a raw, primal fear. It wasn't just about the business anymore. It wasn't just about his father's legacy. It was about Mike, his blood, his brother, disappearing before his very eyes, swallowed by an invisible enemy. He remembered their childhood, the scraped knees healed with band-aids and a reassuring hug, the fights settled with a shared understanding. They had always faced things together. What had happened to that? When had the unbreakable bond of brotherhood been replaced by this suffocating distance, this wall of secrets and lies?

He looked at Mike again, who was now sitting on an overturned bucket, his head bowed, his shoulders slumped in a posture of utter exhaustion. The fight had gone out of him, replaced by a chilling resignation. Joe felt a wave of pity wash over him, quickly followed by a surge of desperate resolve. He couldn't just stand there and watch his brother drown. He wouldn't.

He took a deep breath, the scent of oil and metal a stark contrast to the acrid scent of his own fear. He needed to be clear-headed, to approach this not with anger or accusation, but with the same quiet determination he used to diagnose a complex engine problem. This was a different kind of problem, infinitely more complex and heartbreaking, but perhaps, just perhaps, there was a way to fix it.

He walked over to Mike, his footsteps deliberately soft on the concrete floor. He didn't touch him, not yet. He just stood there, a silent presence in the cavernous space, a witness to his brother's quiet despair. The silence stretched, punctuated only by the distant hum of traffic outside and the ragged sound of Mike's breathing.

"Mike," Joe began, his voice quiet, almost hesitant. He cleared his throat, the sound unnaturally loud. "I'm not judging you. I never have, and I never will." He paused, choosing his words carefully. "But I can't ignore this anymore. I can't pretend I don't see it. I don't know what it is, exactly, what you're struggling with, but I know it's serious. And I know you're hurting."

He knelt down beside Mike, facing him directly. He saw the flicker of surprise, then a renewed wariness in Mike's eyes. "I've been thinking a lot," Joe continued, his voice gaining a steady, reassuring rhythm. "About the late nights, the excuses, the way you've been acting. And I've heard things, Mike. Things people have said about... about falling into bad habits." He hesitated, the word 'addiction' still too raw to utter aloud. "I don't want to believe it, but I can't deny the signs anymore. They're there."

Mike flinched, his gaze dropping to his lap. He hugged his knees to his chest, a protective, almost childlike gesture that twisted Joe's gut. "You're imagining things, Joe," Mike mumbled, the words muffled by his arms.

"Am I?" Joe asked softly. "Am I imagining the tremor in your hands? Am I imagining the way you get so agitated when you haven't had enough sleep, or when you're not… yourself? Am I imagining the money disappearing, Mike? The missed calls, the promises you can't keep? Because if I am, then I need you to tell me, and tell me clearly, what's really going on."

Joe reached out, his hand hovering over Mike's shoulder, then slowly, gently, he placed it there. Mike's body tensed under his touch, but he didn't pull away. Joe's thumb began to stroke a slow, steady rhythm on his brother's denim-clad shoulder. "I'm not going to let you go through this alone, Mike," Joe said, his voice thick with emotion. "Whatever this is, we'll face it together. Just like we've always faced everything. Dad taught us that. He taught us to be there for each other, no matter what."

Mike's breath hitched. Joe could feel the tension radiating from him, the internal struggle playing out in his rigid posture. He wanted to grab him, to pull him into a hug that would somehow convey all the love and worry and desperation that was churning inside him. But he knew that wouldn't be enough. Mike needed more than a hug; he needed a lifeline, and Joe was determined to be that lifeline.

"I'm scared, Mike," Joe admitted, the confession raw and honest. "I'm scared of losing you. And I can't stand to see you like this, hurting like this. Whatever you're dealing with, whatever you're using to cope, it's destroying you. And it's destroying us." He squeezed Mike's shoulder, trying to convey a message of unwavering support. "But there's help out there, Mike. There are people who understand, who can guide you through this. And I'll be right there with you, every step of the way. We can find help, Mike. We can get through this. Together."

Mike remained silent, his head still bowed. Joe could feel the tremors running through his brother's body, a silent testament to his internal turmoil. He didn't push, didn't demand an immediate confession. He just stayed there, his hand a steady anchor on Mike's shoulder, a silent promise of unwavering support. He knew this was just the beginning. The whispers of addiction had become a deafening roar in his mind, and the slow erosion of their shared life had finally brought them to this precipice. He could only hope that Mike would reach for his hand, that they could pull back from the edge, and begin the long, arduous journey of rebuilding what had been so carelessly, so tragically, broken. The garage, once a symbol of their shared past and future, now felt like a battleground, and Joe braced himself for the fight that lay ahead, a fight not against an external enemy, but against the darkness that had taken root within his own brother. He felt the immense weight of responsibility settle upon him, the lonely burden of being the one who had to see, the one who had to acknowledge, and the one who had to try and save them both.

## Financial Strain Mounts

The air in the garage, usually alive with the symphony of clanging metal and the roar of engines, had taken on a different, more somber tone. It was the sound of stagnation, of potential unfulfilled. The workbench, once a testament to Mike's meticulous organization, was now a chaotic testament to his absence. Tools lay scattered, half-disassembled engines sat gathering dust, and the familiar scent of fresh oil was often masked by the stale odor of neglect. Joe moved through this disarray with a heavy heart, each glance at the unfinished projects a fresh jab of anxiety. Customers who had once relied on their prompt service were now met with delays, polite excuses that wore thinner with each passing week.

"Can't you just… juggle it?" a customer, Mr. Henderson, had asked yesterday, his voice laced with a familiar mix of impatience and concern. His classic Mustang, a labor of love and a significant source of income for them, had been sitting in the bay for three weeks, awaiting a specific transmission part that Mike had promised to source. Joe had to admit, with a growing sense of dread, that the part hadn't even been ordered yet. Mike's evasiveness on the matter, his vague assurances that he was "handling it," were no longer credible. Joe had to tell Mr. Henderson, his stomach churning, that they needed to push the delivery date back

*again.* The look of disappointment on the older man's face was a mirror of Joe's own internal despair. Losing a customer like Mr. Henderson wasn't just a financial blow; it was a betrayal of the trust they had built over years of honest work.

Then there were the calls. They had started subtly, polite reminders from suppliers about outstanding invoices. But as the weeks bled into months, the tone had shifted. The voices on the other end of the line grew firmer, less patient. "Joe, we need that payment for the engine parts, or we'll have to suspend your account," one call had ended, the threat hanging in the air like a storm cloud. Joe found himself dreading the ringing of the shop phone, each incoming call a potential harbinger of bad news. He'd taken to answering it with a carefully constructed calm, a practiced veneer of control that masked the gnawing panic within. He'd explain that a payment was "in the mail," or that they were "just waiting on a big job to clear," all while his mind raced, calculating how much longer they could stretch their dwindling resources.

The shop's ledger, once a source of pride for Joe, now felt like a damning indictment. He'd spent hours poring over it in the quiet of his small office, the harsh fluorescent light illuminating the stark reality. Revenue was down, significantly. Expenses, however, remained stubbornly high. The cost of parts, the electricity for the lifts and the welders, the rent for the building – these were all non-negotiable, a constant drain on their already precarious finances. Mike's unreliability wasn't just a personal failing; it was a direct assault on the financial stability of their livelihood. Every missed appointment, every delayed repair, translated directly into lost income, a slow but steady erosion of their capital.

The mounting debt felt like a physical weight, pressing down on Joe's chest, making it difficult to breathe. He'd tried to have a frank conversation with Mike about it, sitting him down one evening amidst the organized chaos of the shop, the scent of old grease and metal thick in the air. "Mike, we've got to talk about the numbers," Joe had begun, his voice carefully neutral. "We're behind on a few key accounts, and I'm getting some… pointed calls."

Mike had, predictably, deflected. "Relax, Joe," he'd said, not meeting Joe's gaze, his fingers idly tracing the condensation on a cold soda can. "It's just a tight patch. Happens to every business. We'll catch up."

"But *how* will we catch up, Mike?" Joe had pressed, his patience wearing thin. "We're turning away work because we don't have the bodies, or because critical parts aren't being ordered. That's not just a tight patch; that's digging ourselves into a deeper hole." He'd gestured towards a half-finished engine on the hoist, its gleaming chrome now dulled by a film of dust. "This Jaguar, for instance. Mrs. Albright is going to be furious if we don't get it done by next week. You said you had the carburetor parts sorted."

Mike had finally looked up, a flicker of defensiveness in his eyes. "I'm working on it, Joe. Stop breathing down my neck. You're not the only one who knows how to run this place."

The retort had stung. Joe remembered their father, always fair, always trusting. He and Mike had built this shop together, a dream forged in the fires of their shared passion for mechanics. But lately, it felt like Joe was the only one tending the flames, while Mike was letting the embers die. The suggestion that Joe was somehow questioning his ability to run the business felt like a personal insult, but Joe couldn't afford to let pride get in the way of survival.

He'd tried to be strategic, to find ways to cut costs. He'd cancelled their subscriptions to trade magazines they no longer had time to read, switched to a cheaper brand of shop rags, even started brewing their own coffee instead of buying it from the diner next door. Small measures, insignificant in the grand scheme of things, but they were all he could think of. He knew, however, that these were merely band-aids on a gaping wound. The real problem, the one he was afraid to name, was Mike's unreliability, his increasingly erratic behavior that was directly impacting their ability to operate.

The pressure was relentless. It seeped into Joe's personal life, turning his evenings into a time of anxious contemplation rather than rest. He'd lie awake at night, the glow of his phone a constant reminder of overdue bills, his mind replaying conversations, replaying Mike's evasions, searching for a solution that seemed to elude him. He started to dread going to the bank, the automated deposit that usually brought a sense of relief now felt like a temporary reprieve, a mere postponement of the inevitable.

He found himself staring at the specialized tools in the shop, the expensive diagnostic equipment, the gleaming set of Snap-on wrenches that had been their father's pride and joy. The thought, at first, had been a fleeting, almost unthinkable notion. But as the financial strain mounted, as the creditor calls became more frequent and more demanding, the idea began to solidify, taking root in his desperate mind. Selling off some of their valuable assets. It was a betrayal, in a way, a dismantling of the legacy they were supposed to be building. But what was the alternative? Letting the business collapse entirely? Letting the bank foreclose on the shop, on their father's dream?

He pictured the specialized engine balancer, a piece of equipment they rarely used but had cost a small fortune. Or the heavy-duty lift, essential for working on larger trucks and buses, a job they'd recently had to turn down because Mike hadn't been around to assist. Each piece of equipment represented a significant investment, a chunk of their father's hard-earned money. To part with them felt like admitting defeat, a public declaration of their failure.

The thought of selling the Snap-on set was particularly agonizing. Their father had bought them piece by piece over decades, each wrench a symbol of his dedication and skill. Joe remembered watching him polish them, his calloused hands moving with a reverence that spoke volumes about his passion. "These are more than just tools, Joe," his father had told him once, his eyes twinkling. "They're an extension of yourself. Treat them right, and they'll serve you well." Now, the idea of pawning them off to cover Mike's... whatever it was... felt like a profound disrespect to his memory.

He knew he couldn't keep juggling the overdue invoices and the threatening calls indefinitely. He was starting to feel the strain in his own health. Sleep offered little respite, his nights plagued by anxiety dreams where the shop's doors were chained shut, and creditors formed an angry mob outside. He was making mistakes, small ones, like misplacing an order or forgetting to confirm a customer's appointment, mistakes he would never have made before. The constant stress was a corrosive agent, eating away at his focus and his resolve.

One afternoon, staring at a stack of bills that seemed to multiply overnight, Joe felt a wave of despair wash over him. He picked up a particularly stern letter from the parts supplier, his hand trembling slightly. They were threatening to send his account to collections. He tossed it onto the desk, the paper fluttering onto the floor. He looked around the garage, at the tools, the half-finished projects, the ghosts of his father's and brother's presence. He felt trapped, suffocated by the weight of responsibility and the growing certainty that Mike was no longer a partner, but a liability. The financial strain was no longer a distant threat; it was a tangible, crushing reality, and Joe knew he had to do something, anything, to stop the bleeding, even if it meant sacrificing pieces of their shared past to salvage a future, however uncertain it might be. The question of *what* to sell, and *when*, was becoming a desperate, daily calculation.

## A Growing Chasm

The silence in the shop, once a comfortable companion to Joe's focused work, had morphed into something oppressive. It was the silence of division, of two people occupying the same space but inhabiting entirely different worlds. Joe found himself working with a solitary intensity, the familiar clink of his wrench against an engine block the only sound to punctuate the heavy quiet. He'd learned to rely on himself, to anticipate problems, to shoulder the burdens that Mike had once shared, and in his absence, seemed to have abandoned altogether. The camaraderie, the easy banter that had fueled their early years, had evaporated, replaced by a growing, unbridgeable gulf. He felt the loneliness keenly, a phantom limb ache where his brother's presence used to be. Every decision, every crisis, every late-night inventory check now fell solely on his shoulders. The weight of it was immense, a constant pressure that made his shoulders ache and his sleep restless. He was the keeper of the ledger, the negotiator with suppliers, the apologizer to increasingly impatient customers, and the sole proprietor of a thousand unspoken anxieties.

Mike's withdrawal was a slow, insidious process, like a tide gradually receding, leaving behind a barren, unfamiliar shore. He'd become a spectral presence in the garage, his appearances sporadic and his contributions minimal. He'd drift in and out, offering vague pronouncements about needing to "handle some personal stuff," or disappearing for days at a time with no explanation, only to reappear as if no time had passed, no damage had been done. Joe no longer asked for details. The few times he'd dared to probe, to try and penetrate the fog that seemed to surround his brother, he'd been met with a wall of passive resistance, a subtle deflection that made him feel like an unwelcome intruder in Mike's increasingly private world. "Everything's fine, Joe. Just dealing with some things," was the usual refrain, delivered with a practiced, almost serene detachment that belied the turmoil Joe sensed simmering beneath the surface.

This detachment was perhaps the most unnerving aspect of Mike's transformation. It was as if he was observing their shared life from a distance, a spectator to the slow unraveling of their business, their partnership, their very brotherhood. Joe watched him, a helpless observer of a tragedy unfolding in slow motion. He saw the subtle changes in Mike's demeanor, the way his eyes seemed to hold a distant, unfocused gaze, the way he'd often retreat into his phone, scrolling through an endless stream of digital ephemera, shutting out the world around him, and most importantly, shutting out Joe. Their conversations, when they happened, were superficial, stilted affairs, like two strangers exchanging pleasantries. The deep, honest discussions they once had, about cars, about life, about their dreams for the shop, were gone, replaced by polite inquiries about the weather or the latest sports scores.

Joe felt a profound sense of loneliness that went beyond the business pressures. It was the loneliness of shared history, of a bond forged in childhood, in shared secrets and scraped knees, in the heady scent of engine oil and the shared ambition of building something of their own, something that would honor their father's legacy. He yearned for the brother he knew, the one who could anticipate his thoughts, who could finish his sentences, who shared his passion with an equal fervor. Instead, he was faced with a stranger, a phantom who haunted the edges of his life, leaving behind only a trail of unanswered questions and a growing sense of unease.

He remembered a particular incident a few weeks prior. Mrs. Albright, the owner of the classic Jaguar that was still languishing in the bay, had called again. This time, her voice, usually so warm and patient, had a sharp edge. "Joe," she'd said, her tone leaving no room for argument, "I understand you're busy. But this is becoming unacceptable. I need my car back by Friday. Is that clear?" Joe had been forced to offer yet another apology, another promise that he'd personally oversee the completion of her repair. As he hung up the phone, his stomach churning, he'd seen Mike leaning against the frame of the garage door, his arms crossed, a faint, almost imperceptible smirk playing on his lips. He hadn't offered to help, hadn't expressed any concern for Mrs. Albright's frustration, hadn't even acknowledged Joe's predicament. He'd simply stood there, an impassive observer, as Joe absorbed the brunt of the customer's displeasure. That look, that subtle smirk, had felt like a deliberate jab, a confirmation of Joe's growing suspicion that Mike no longer saw them as partners, but as individuals with separate, and perhaps even conflicting, interests.

The chasm between them widened with each passing day, an invisible rift that made any attempt at genuine connection feel futile. Joe tried to bridge it, to reach out, to pull Mike back from the precipice he seemed to be teetering on. He'd suggest they grab a beer after work, as they used to, hoping to recapture some semblance of their old dynamic. But Mike would invariably decline, citing an early morning or a prior engagement, always with that same vague, unconvincing air. The invitations, once a source of comfort and anticipation, now felt like desperate pleas, embarrassing in their persistence. Joe began to understand that he couldn't force Mike to engage, couldn't drag him back to the life they had once shared. The choice, it seemed, was entirely Mike's, and he was making it, deliberately or not, to drift further and further away.

The unspoken questions hung between them, heavy and suffocating. What was Mike doing with his time? Where was the money from the few jobs they

*were* completing actually going? Was he gambling again? Was there someone else? Joe didn't know, and the not knowing was a torment. He'd catch himself staring at Mike, searching his face for answers, for a flicker of the brother he'd known, for some sign that he wasn't alone in this struggle. But Mike's expression was often unreadable, his eyes a guarded secret. This lack of transparency was more damaging than any confession could have been. It fostered suspicion, bred resentment, and made it impossible for Joe to offer anything but a weary, resigned concern.

The loneliness was a gnawing ache in Joe's gut. He felt like he was carrying the weight of their entire lives, their business, their father's memory, all by himself. He longed for a confidante, someone to share the burden with, someone who understood the sheer exhaustion of it all. But Mike was no longer that person. He was a ghost in the machine, a silent partner in a business that was slowly grinding to a halt. Joe found himself talking to his father's photograph, a faded image of a man whose strong, kind face seemed to offer silent encouragement. "Dad," he'd whisper, his voice rough with emotion, "I don't know what to do. I'm losing him. I'm losing everything." The silence that followed was a familiar, painful answer.

He saw the disappointment in the eyes of their loyal customers, the subtle shift in their trust as delays mounted and excuses became thinner. He saw the weariness in his own reflection, the lines etched deeper around his eyes, the gray hairs that seemed to multiply with alarming speed. He was a man drowning, flailing for a lifeline, while the person who should have been there, the person who had once been his strongest support, had already let go. The bond that had once been their greatest strength, the bedrock of their shared enterprise, had begun to fracture, its once-unbreakable strands fraying and snapping one by one. Joe was left standing on the shifting sands of their fractured partnership, the familiar landscape of his life disintegrating around him, with only the hollow echo of his brother's absence for company. He was adrift, and the shore was nowhere in sight. The quiet in the shop was no longer just the absence of noise; it was the deafening roar of their broken connection.

# Chapter Three
# Vanishing Act

## The Empty Bay

The usual morning cacophony of the garage – the clatter of tools, the roar of an engine being coaxed into life, the back-and-forth banter between brothers – was absent. It was a void so profound, so utterly alien, that Joe initially mistook it for an early start. He'd been up since four, as always, the familiar ritual of brewing coffee and mentally ticking off the day's priorities a comforting anchor in the sea of his anxieties. But as the minutes stretched into ten, then twenty, a prickle of unease began to spread across his skin. Mike wasn't just late; he wasn't here at all.

Joe moved through the shop with a growing sense of dread, his eyes scanning the familiar bays. Mike's toolbox, usually a chaotic monument to his hurried efficiency, was still nestled in its usual spot by the workbench. The array of gleaming wrenches, the battered screwdrivers, the specialized tools that bore the nicks and scars of countless repairs – all were in place, undisturbed. It was the undisturbed nature of it all that felt wrong. Mike was never meticulous about his tools. He'd leave them scattered, testament to the urgency of the work, or the sheer passion that drove him to dive into an engine with an almost primal focus. Seeing them so neatly arranged, almost as if they hadn't been touched, sent a shiver down Joe's spine.

He walked over to Mike's locker, a battered metal cabinet that had seen better days, just like most things in their inherited garage. He'd often caught Mike rummaging through it, pulling out spare shirts, greasy rags, or the occasional half-eaten sandwich he'd forgotten about. Joe hesitated, his hand hovering over the cool metal. He didn't want to invade, not really, but the gnawing in his gut was becoming unbearable. He pulled the handle. The door swung open with a soft *squeak*, a sound that seemed amplified in the unnatural quiet.

It was empty.

Not just empty of clothes or personal effects. It was *scoured*. The single, dusty shelf was bare. The small hooks that usually held a belt or a worn-out baseball cap were naked. It was as if Mike had meticulously packed up his entire existence from this one small space, leaving behind only the faint, metallic tang of stale air. Joe's breath hitched. This wasn't the hurried departure of someone going on a spontaneous fishing trip. This was a deliberate, calculated absence.

His hands trembled as he reached for his phone, the rough texture of the screen a welcome familiarity. He scrolled to Mike's contact, his thumb hovering over the familiar name. He'd called him countless times in the past weeks, each call met with the same dead air or the abrupt click of voicemail. He still called, though. Hope, however foolish, was a persistent weed. He pressed the call button. The familiar, tinny ringtone echoed in the cavernous space, each pulse a hammer blow against Joe's mounting fear. Straight to voicemail. "Hey, it's Mike," the automated voice chirped, a cruel mockery of the brother he was desperately trying to reach. "Leave a message." Joe couldn't. The words wouldn't form. He ended the call, the silence rushing back in, heavier than before.

The decision to go to Mike's apartment was made with a desperate urgency that bypassed any semblance of rational thought. Mike's apartment was on the other side of town, a small, grimy walk-up above a struggling bodega. Joe hadn't been there in months, not since Mike had started to retreat into his shell. He drove with the windows down, the cool morning air doing little to dispel the heat that was building within him – a mixture of fear, anger, and a profound, suffocating confusion.

He pulled up to the curb, the familiar peeling paint and the overflowing dumpster a grim welcome. The landlord, a perpetually weary man named Mr. Henderson, was rarely around, and Joe knew the spare key was supposed to be kept in a magnetic box hidden beneath a loose brick by the back steps. He found it, his fingers fumbling with the cold metal. The key slid into the lock with a grating sound, and Joe pushed the door open, his heart hammering against his ribs.

The apartment was small, cramped, and usually a testament to Mike's bachelor chaos. But this was different. It wasn't messy; it was *vacant*. The air was cold, stale, as if no one had been there for days, yet there was a strange, hurried stillness to the place. A single suitcase lay open on the floor of the bedroom, its contents gone. A few books were missing from the small bookshelf, and a framed photo of him and Mike as kids, the one where they were both grinning, gap-toothed, had been removed from the bedside table. It wasn't a complete emptying, but a selective scavenging, as if someone had carefully picked through the remnants of a life, taking only what was deemed essential.

Joe walked through the small living area, his eyes darting from object to object, searching for any clue, any sign of where Mike might have gone, or why. The cheap coffee table was bare, no scattered mail, no half-empty beer cans, no remotes. The television, usually a constant hum of noise when Mike was home, was dark and silent. Even the worn armchair, where Mike would often slump after a long day, seemed to have a vacant air about it, as if waiting for a presence that would never return.

He moved into the kitchen. The sink was empty, no dirty dishes. The refrigerator hummed, but its contents seemed minimal – a carton of milk, a jar of pickles, a half-eaten tub of yogurt. It was the quiet, the utter lack of personal detritus, that was the most unsettling. Mike was a creature of habit, of little messes that accumulated over time, the silent markers of a life being lived. This absence of those markers felt deliberate, almost surgical.

A cold dread began to creep into Joe's gut, a fear far more potent than the anger and frustration he'd been nursing for weeks. This wasn't just Mike being irresponsible or disappearing for a while. This felt like an erasure. He imagined Mike, moving through his apartment with a quiet, determined efficiency, packing only what he needed, leaving behind the echoes of their shared life, the remnants of their brotherhood, without a word. It was a betrayal that cut deeper than any argument, any perceived slight.

He sank onto the edge of the bed, the springs groaning beneath his weight. His gaze fell on the empty suitcase, then drifted to the bare shelf where the photograph used to be. He remembered the last time he'd seen that photo, Mike had been holding it, tracing the outline of their younger faces with a rough finger, a flicker of something akin to nostalgia in his eyes. Had that been a moment of realization? A goodbye?

Joe ran a hand over his face, the rough stubble a mirror of his own disheveled state. He thought of all the unspoken words, the opportunities to connect that he had let slip by, the moments he'd been too consumed by his own worries to truly see the distress in his brother's eyes. Had he missed the signs? Had he been so caught up in keeping the business afloat, in dealing with the day-to-day grind, that he'd allowed Mike to drift away, to make plans, to disappear without a trace?

The gnawing fear intensified, morphing into a primal terror. Where was Mike? What was he running from? Or was he not running, but moving towards something, something Joe was entirely excluded from? The thought was a cold, sharp shard of ice in his chest. He stood up, his legs feeling unsteady. He had to find him. He couldn't let this be the end of it, not like this. Not with the silence screaming louder than any explanation. The empty bay of the garage had been a chilling prelude; this empty apartment was the terrifying crescendo. He turned and walked out, locking the door behind him, leaving the sterile silence of Mike's former life to settle back into its eerie emptiness. The questions, however, were far from settled. They were only just beginning to echo in the hollow spaces Mike had left behind.

## A Forced Closure

The silence was the first thing that truly registered. Not the absence of Mike's boisterous laughter or the rhythmic clank of his hammer, but a deeper, more pervasive quietude that had settled over the garage like a shroud. Joe had spent the better part of the morning in a haze of disbelief, oscillating between a desperate hope that Mike would walk through the door and a crushing certainty that he wouldn't. Now, as the afternoon sun began its slow descent, painting streaks of amber and rose across the grimy windows, the reality began to sink its teeth in. The garage, the heart and soul of their operation, the place where their father had first taught them the smell of oil and the satisfaction of a job well done, was to be shuttered.

He walked towards the main entrance, his boots echoing unnervingly on the concrete floor. The 'Open' sign, usually a beacon of their livelihood, felt like a cruel joke now. He reached for the large, red-painted metal lever that secured the heavy bay door. It was a mechanism worn smooth by years of use, familiar to his touch, yet today it felt alien, burdened with a finality that made his stomach clench. With a grunt, he pushed it down. The heavy metal groaned in protest, a mournful sound that seemed to reverberate through the very bones of the building. The thick steel door began its descent, slowly, inexorably, obscuring the last vestiges of daylight that dared to penetrate the space. Each inch of its closure felt like a nail being hammered into a coffin.

When the door finally settled into its housing with a heavy thud, plunging the interior into a semi-darkness broken only by the weak spill from the office light, Joe stood for a long moment, his hand still resting on the cold metal. The air inside the garage, once thick with the invigorating scent of gasoline and exhaust, now held a stale, almost musty odor, the smell of disuse. The hulking forms of cars, half-finished projects, and diagnostic equipment were reduced to shadowy monoliths, their potential silenced. The tools, still neatly arranged in

Mike's locker but now feeling like relics of a forgotten era, seemed to mock him with their inertness. The very air felt heavy, thick with the weight of unspoken goodbyes and the ghost of a future that would never materialize.

He turned and walked towards the smaller side door, the one that led to the cramped office where their father had once charted their course. On the inside of the glass, he knew, hung the 'Open' sign. He hesitated, his reflection staring back at him – a gaunt, hollow-eyed stranger. This wasn't just about closing shop; it was about the dissolution of a dream, a legacy fractured beyond repair. He'd watched their father pour his life into this place, seen the pride in his eyes as he taught Joe and Mike the intricacies of engine repair, the value of hard work, the bond of family forged through grease and sweat. Now, that legacy was being locked away, gathering dust alongside the silent machinery.

With a sigh that felt ripped from the depths of his soul, Joe reached for the small, worn wooden sign that usually hung by the office door, the one bearing the bold, hopeful declaration of their business hours. He didn't need to look; he knew the words by heart. "We're open," it proclaimed, a cheerful lie that had sustained them for years. Now, it was an anthem of their failure. He unhooked it, his fingers brushing against the smooth, lacquered surface. He walked to the front window, the one that faced the street, the one that proclaimed their presence to the world. The 'Open' sign felt like a betrayal of the truth. He took a deep breath, the stale air filling his lungs, and hung the 'Closed' sign in its place.

The sign itself was nothing remarkable – a simple, rectangular piece of painted wood, with stark, block letters spelling out the word. Yet, as it swung gently in the almost imperceptible breeze that found its way through a crack in the window frame, it felt monumental. It was a surrender. It was an admission of defeat. It was the tangible manifestation of his deepest fears, now staring back at him from the street. He stepped back, his gaze fixed on the sign. The familiar street outside, usually bustling with the comings and goings of customers and the general hum of city life, seemed to blur, the world outside receding as the stark reality of his present closed in.

He retreated into the dimness of the office, the silence amplifying the frantic beat of his own heart. The small space was a testament to their shared past. A faded photograph of him and Mike, younger, full of an unearned confidence, sat on the cluttered desk. Their father's worn leather armchair still held the imprint of his presence, the faint scent of pipe tobacco clinging to the worn upholstery. Joe sank into the chair, the familiar give of the springs a stark contrast to the rigid finality of the garage door. He ran a hand over the smooth wood of the desk, the same desk where Mike had sketched out his wildest dreams, where they'd hashed out deals, where they'd argued, and where, for a fleeting moment, they had been truly happy.

The financial ledger lay open, a stark white testament to their unraveling. The numbers swam before Joe's eyes, a sea of red ink that represented dwindling supplies, unpaid invoices, and the gnawing pressure of overdue rent. Without Mike's steady hand, his knack for finding workarounds, his ability to charm clients even when the going was tough, the business was simply unsustainable. Joe was a meticulous mechanic, a steady worker, but he lacked Mike's intangible spark, that certain something that had always pulled them through the lean times. Now, that spark had been extinguished, leaving Joe in the suffocating darkness of their shared failure.

He looked around the office, his gaze catching on every object, imbuing each with a painful significance. Mike's favorite coffee mug, chipped and stained with countless brews, sat by the stapler. He remembered Mike slamming it down in frustration during a particularly difficult repair, or cradling it in his hands during moments of quiet contemplation. Now, it was just another piece of debris in the wreckage of their lives. The tools of their trade – the wrenches, the sockets, the diagnostic computers – all sat in their designated places, awaiting a hand that would no longer guide them. The specialized equipment, the pride of their workshop, now seemed like expensive paperweights, their purpose rendered obsolete by Mike's vanishing act.

The realization of what this closure meant for him, beyond the financial ruin, was the hardest to bear. It wasn't just a business being shut down; it was the severing of a lifeline. Mike had been his anchor, his confidant, his partner in every sense of the word. They had grown up in this garage, their childhood inextricably linked to the smell of oil and the roar of engines. Their father's dying wish had been for them to keep the business, to build upon his legacy, to remain a united front. And Joe had failed him. He had failed Mike. He had failed himself.

He picked up the framed photograph of him and Mike, their younger selves frozen in time, their smiles wide and unburdened. He traced the outline of Mike's face with his thumb, a wave of raw grief washing over him. Where was he now? What had driven him to walk away from everything, from their shared history, from him? The questions circled in his mind, each one a tiny shard of glass, cutting deeper with every revolution. He had tried to reach him, bombarded his phone with calls and texts, but only silence had answered. The silence that had now permeated the entire garage, a deafening testament to their fractured bond.

Joe stood up, his legs stiff and unwilling. He walked over to the bay door, the massive steel barrier that now separated him from the outside world, from the life that continued without them. He placed his hand against it, the cold metal radiating a chilling indifference. This was it. The end of an era. The final chapter of a story that had started with their father's dreams and ended with his son's disappearance. He imagined the days and weeks to come: the creditors calling, the accounts being settled, the slow, painful process of liquidating assets. Each step would be a fresh reminder of what had been lost.

He walked back to the desk, the ledger still open, a stark reminder of the insurmountable debt. He knew, with a certainty that chilled him to the bone, that he couldn't keep this place afloat on his own. Not without Mike. Not without the shared vision, the complementary skills, the sheer force of their combined will. The garage, once a symbol of their shared ambition, was now a monument to their shared failure. He closed the ledger, the snap of the cover echoing in the cavernous space. It was a sound of finality, of a chapter definitively closed.

He looked around the office one last time, his gaze lingering on the worn armchair, the photograph, the tools that now seemed so utterly useless. He saw not just a garage, but a lifetime. He saw the endless hours of hard work, the sacrifices made, the dreams nurtured, the brotherhood that had been the bedrock of his existence. And he saw it all slipping away, dissolving into the silence, leaving him alone with the ghosts of what might have been. He walked out of the office, leaving the door ajar, the dim light spilling out onto the concrete floor, a tiny beacon of defiance in the encroaching darkness. He paused at the bay door, his hand instinctively reaching for the lever that would seal their fate, his heart a heavy, leaden weight in his chest. The 'Closed' sign in the window felt like a physical blow, a public declaration that their story, their family's legacy, was over. The silence that followed was not peaceful; it was the deafening roar of a dream that had died.

## The First Threads of a Search

The silence in the garage was no longer just an absence of noise; it was a suffocating blanket that pressed down on Joe's chest, each breath a struggle. The 'Closed' sign, stark against the grimy window, was a constant, mocking reminder of his brother's vanishing act. The finality of locking the heavy bay door, the mournful groan of the metal, still echoed in the hollow chambers of his memory. Joe had spent the last few days in a state of stunned paralysis, the ledger's damning numbers a constant phantom presence, but the sheer shock of Mike's disappearance had numbed him. Now, however, a different kind of ache had begun to surface – a gnawing, desperate urgency. Mike wouldn't just leave. Not like this. There had to be an explanation, a reason, however twisted, that had propelled his brother into the ether.

Fueled by a potent cocktail of desperation and a refusal to accept the unthinkable, Joe decided to move. He couldn't just sit there, drowning in the silence and the scent of stale oil. He needed to *do* something, anything, to pull back the curtain on this impossible charade. His first instinct, raw and unrefined, was to retrace Mike's steps, to find the physical manifestations of his brother's life outside the confines of their shared workshop. Mike had his routines, his places. Places Joe had always been too busy, too focused on the mechanics of their lives, to truly understand. Now, he had no choice but to immerse himself in them.

He started with the obvious: the watering holes. Mike wasn't a regular drinker, not in the way some of their older customers were, but he had his preferred haunts. Dive bars, the kind where the neon signs flickered with a weary defiance and the air was thick with stale beer and regret. Places where anonymity was a currency and conversation was often conducted in hushed tones. Joe pulled on a worn leather jacket, the familiar weight a small comfort, and stepped out into the late afternoon chill. The city, indifferent to the seismic shift in his own world, pulsed with its usual frenetic energy. Cars honked, sirens wailed in the distance, and the cacophony felt both alien and strangely comforting, a stark contrast to the void Mike had left behind.

His first stop was 'The Rusty Mug,' a place Mike occasionally mentioned when he'd had a particularly rough day, usually accompanied by a wry, self-deprecating smile. The entrance was a narrow, unassuming doorway sandwiched between a pawn shop and a tattoo parlor. As Joe pushed open the heavy, scarred wooden door, a wave of noise and stale smoke hit him. The interior was dim, lit by the lurid glow of ancient beer advertisements and the harsh glare of a few bare bulbs. A motley collection of patrons huddled around the sticky tables, their faces etched with the stories of hard living. The air vibrated with the tinny, distorted sound of a jukebox playing a forgotten country ballad.

Joe scanned the room, his gaze lingering on every face, searching for a flicker of recognition, a familiar slouch, a hint of Mike's restless energy. He approached the bar, a long, dark expanse of polished wood that had seen better decades. The bartender, a burly man with a faded tattoo snaking up his arm and eyes that seemed to have witnessed every kind of human folly, wiped down a glass with a practiced, almost bored, rhythm.

"Can I get you something?" the bartender's voice was a low rumble, devoid of any warmth.

Joe leaned closer, his voice barely audible above the din. "I'm looking for my brother. Mike. Mike Donovan." He held up a slightly crumpled photo of him and Mike, taken a few years back, their younger faces full of a careless optimism that felt a million miles away.

The bartender took the photo, his thick fingers dwarf on the glossy surface. He squinted at it, his expression unreadable. "Donovan, huh? Lots of guys named Mike come through here." He handed the photo back without missing a beat in his polishing. "Haven't seen him around lately. Not that I pay much attention to faces."

Joe's hope, which had flickered to life at the prospect of an answer, sputtered and died. "He sometimes comes in here, right? After work?"

The bartender shrugged, his gaze shifting to a group of boisterous men in the corner. "Maybe. Can't say I remember him. This place is a revolving door, pal."

Joe felt a familiar frustration begin to coil in his gut. He tossed a few bills onto the bar, more than enough for a drink he didn't want. "Thanks anyway." He left 'The Rusty Mug' with the same heavy feeling that had accompanied him from the garage. The city felt larger, more impenetrable, than ever before.

His next stop was 'The Blue Note,' a jazz club on the other side of town, a place Mike had gravitated towards when he was feeling particularly introspective, when the rumble of engines wasn't enough to drown out whatever was churning inside him. This place was a different beast entirely. Dimly lit, with plush velvet seating and the smoky, melancholic strains of a live jazz quartet filling the air, it exuded an atmosphere of quiet contemplation. Here, the patrons were more subdued, their conversations interspersed with the soulful wail of a saxophone.

Joe found a quiet corner booth and ordered a whiskey, letting the amber liquid burn its way down his throat. He watched the musicians, their faces lost in their art, their instruments weaving a tapestry of sound that spoke of longing and lost love. He knew Mike appreciated this kind of raw, unvarnished emotion, the kind that couldn't be fixed with a wrench. He also knew Mike had a few friends in this scene, people he'd sometimes mention in passing, musicians or artists who shared his appreciation for the finer, more ephemeral things in life.

He caught the eye of a young woman with vibrant purple hair who was nursing a drink at the bar. She had the kind of observant gaze that suggested she saw more than most. Joe made his way over, the click of his boots on the polished floor cutting through the ambient music.

"Excuse me," Joe began, trying to keep his voice steady. "I'm looking for someone. Mike Donovan. He sometimes comes here."

The woman tilted her head, a slight frown creasing her brow. "Mike Donovan? Yeah, I think I've seen him. A mechanic, right? Always looked a bit out of place, but he had a good vibe."

A surge of adrenaline coursed through Joe. "You've seen him recently?"

She hesitated, her eyes scanning the room as if searching for a phantom. "Maybe a few weeks ago. He was talking to Silas. You know Silas?" She gestured towards a man sitting alone at a small table, his face half-hidden in shadow, a well-worn guitar case resting against his chair. Silas looked like he'd walked straight out of a blues album cover – lean, weary, with eyes that held a deep, knowing sadness.

Joe thanked her and made his way to Silas's table. Silas looked up as Joe approached, his expression one of weary resignation.

"You looking for Mike?" Silas asked, his voice raspy, like gravel on a country road.

Joe's heart leaped. "You know him? You've seen him?"

Silas nodded slowly, a faint smile playing on his lips. "Yeah, Mike's a good guy. Came here to escape the noise, I guess. We'd talk, sometimes. About… stuff. Life. The mechanics of it all, I guess, just in a different way." He took a slow sip of his drink. "Haven't seen him in a while, though."

"When was the last time?" Joe pressed, his voice laced with a desperate urgency.

Silas rubbed his chin thoughtfully. "Hard to say exactly. Maybe… two, three weeks ago? He seemed… agitated. Like he was wrestling with something big. Said he needed to clear his head, get away from everything."

"Get away from everything? What did he mean by that?"

Silas shrugged, his gaze drifting towards the stage where the saxophonist was now playing a particularly mournful melody. "He didn't say. Just that he had to make a decision. Something that would change everything." Silas's eyes met Joe's, and in their depths, Joe saw a reflection of his own fear. "He paid me back a loan, you know. Said he might be gone for a while, but he'd be in touch."

"He paid you back? That's… that's not like Mike. He's always been good with money, but he wouldn't just disappear without telling me." The words felt like ash in Joe's mouth. A loan? What loan?

"He seemed pretty determined," Silas continued, his voice low. "Like he had a plan. Said he was going to find… peace, or something like that. Sounded a little crazy, to be honest. But Mike… he could always surprise you."

Joe felt a cold dread creeping into his bones. Silas's words, cryptic as they were, painted a picture of a man on the precipice of something drastic. Peace? A plan? It sounded like a prelude to a vanishing act, not a temporary absence. He thanked Silas, his mind racing. He had a name, a vague timeline, and the unsettling feeling that Mike hadn't just walked away from the garage, but from his entire life.

The following days were a blur of frantic searching. Joe visited every place he could think of that Mike might frequent. He spoke to old friends, former colleagues, even casual acquaintances. Most offered the same frustratingly vague answers: "Haven't seen him," "He's been quiet lately," or the ever-unhelpful, "He's probably just off somewhere." Each encounter was a small victory if it yielded a sliver of information, but mostly they were just dead ends, reinforcing the terrifying reality that his brother was becoming a ghost, an apparition that was rapidly fading from existence.

He found himself drifting through the city's underbelly, the places where hope went to die and secrets festered. He visited pawn shops, his stomach churning at the thought of Mike pawning something valuable, something that could be used to fund an escape. He asked at bus stations and train depots, his mind conjuring images of Mike boarding a train with a one-way ticket to oblivion. He even found himself lurking around the edges of the city's less reputable districts, the dark alleys and backstreets that whispered of desperation and illicit deals. But everywhere he went, he was met with the same wall of silence, the same averted gazes.

One particularly bleak afternoon, he found himself standing outside a small, run-down apartment building on the outskirts of town. Mike had a friend who lived there, a guy named Leo, a musician who was as down on his luck as Silas. Joe had been hesitant to approach Leo, knowing he was unreliable and often lost in his own world of drugs and bad decisions. But the desperation was a potent motivator.

The building itself looked like it was slowly crumbling into the earth. Graffiti adorned the brickwork, and the air reeked of damp and decay. Joe climbed the creaking stairs to the third floor, his heart pounding a heavy rhythm against his ribs. He knocked on Leo's door.

After a long moment, the door creaked open, revealing a man who looked as worn and weathered as the building itself. Leo's eyes were bloodshot, his face gaunt, and his clothes were stained and rumpled. He clutched a half-empty bottle of cheap liquor.

"Joe? What are you doing here?" Leo's voice was a slurred mumble.

"I'm looking for Mike, Leo," Joe said, trying to keep his voice even. "Have you seen him?"

Leo blinked slowly, as if processing the question through a thick fog. He took a swig from the bottle. "Mike? Uh… yeah, maybe. He came by a while back. Said he needed to lay low for a bit."

"Lay low? From what?" Joe's voice was sharp.

Leo waved a dismissive hand. "Don't know, man. He was… jumpy. Kept looking over his shoulder. Said he had some trouble he needed to deal with." He squinted at Joe. "He left me some cash. Said to tell you… that he's sorry. And that he'll make it right. Eventually."

Joe felt a surge of anger mixed with a profound sense of betrayal. "Cash? What kind of cash? And sorry for what?"

"Just… cash," Leo said evasively, taking another long drink. "Look, man, I don't know what's going on. Mike's a good guy, but he's got his own demons, you know? We all do." He leaned against the doorframe, his gaze unfocused. "He said he was going somewhere… somewhere quiet. Away from all of it."

"Where, Leo? Where did he go?" Joe's voice was barely a whisper.

Leo just shook his head, a vacant smile spreading across his face. "Don't know, man. He just… vanished. Like a magic trick."

Joe turned away, the weight of the world pressing down on him. Leo's words, coupled with Silas's cryptic remarks, painted a disturbing picture. Mike hadn't just left; he had orchestrated his own disappearance. He had actively sought to sever all ties, to erase himself from their lives. The thought was a bitter pill to swallow. It wasn't just about the garage anymore; it was about the utter dissolution of their brotherhood, the shattering of their shared history. Each dead end, each evasive answer, was a confirmation of his worst fears. Mike wasn't lost; he was gone. And the city, with its endless labyrinth of streets and its countless anonymous faces, seemed to conspire to keep him that way, swallowing him whole into its indifferent maw. Joe was left with nothing but the echoes of his brother's laughter and the chilling silence of his absence, a silence that was becoming more deafening with each passing day.

## Unearthing Small Clues

The stale air of 'The Rusty Mug' still clung to Joe's jacket, a faint but persistent reminder of another dead end. He'd spent the better part of the next day retracing his steps, not just physically, but mentally, replaying every mumbled word, every averted glance. The bartender's practiced indifference, the flicker of something in the purple-haired woman's eyes at The Blue Note, Silas's weary pronouncements – they were like scattered puzzle pieces, none fitting neatly into place. But the pieces were there, glinting faintly in the pervasive gloom of his investigation.

His next foray into the city's underbelly led him to a greasy spoon diner near the docks, a place Mike had once mentioned grabbing a late-night burger after a particularly grueling repair. The diner was a relic, its chrome faded, its booths patched with duct tape, and the air thick with the smell of fried onions and despair. Joe slid into a vinyl booth, the springs groaning in protest, and ordered a coffee, black. He watched the bartender, a woman with tired eyes and a perpetual frown etched onto her face, polish the counter with a damp rag. She looked like she'd seen it all, and then some.

"Looking for someone," Joe began, his voice rough from lack of sleep and too much worry. He pulled out the same crumpled photo of him and Mike. "Mike Donovan. My brother."

The bartender glanced at the photo, her expression unreadable. She didn't take it, just peered at it from a distance. "Donovan," she repeated, her voice flat. "Can't say I recognize the name. Lots of faces come and go through here." She gestured vaguely with her chin towards the grimy window overlooking the street. "Especially lately."

"Lately?" Joe's ears perked up. "What do you mean, lately?"

She shrugged, a weary movement of her shoulders. "Just… more people. New faces. Guys who don't look like they belong around here. Hard types. Always talking low, looking over their shoulders." She paused, her gaze drifting to a corner booth where two burly men were hunched over their plates, their conversation a low, rumbling murmur. "Saw your brother, though. Yeah. A few weeks back. He was in here. With them."

Joe's heart hammered against his ribs. "With them? Who are 'them'?"

The bartender hesitated, her eyes darting towards the men in the corner. She leaned in, lowering her voice. "Don't know their names. Just… noticed them. They're not from around here. Rough crowd. Always in a group, dressed the same – dark jackets, clean shaven. Like they're from out of town, or trying to look like it." She took a slow sip of her own lukewarm coffee. "Your brother, he was talking to them.

Seemed… tense. Like he owed them something, or was trying to get something from them."

Joe's mind raced. This was the first concrete lead, however disturbing. Mike, talking to a "rough crowd," looking "tense," appearing to "owe them something." It painted a grim picture, a stark contrast to the brother he knew, the brother who fixed engines and told bad jokes. "Did you hear what they were talking about?"

The bartender shook her head. "Couldn't make it out. They kept their voices down. But he looked… scared, almost. He left with them. Late. Real late."

"Late? How late?"

"Past midnight," she said, her gaze fixed on the window again, as if replaying the scene in her mind. "Pulled up in a dark sedan. Not a fancy car, but clean. Sleek. Not the kind of car you see parked around here normally."

Joe felt a cold dread seep into him. A dark sedan. Unfamiliar individuals. It all felt like a scene from one of his own grim novels, but this was his life, his brother. He thanked the bartender, leaving a generous tip that she accepted with barely a nod. As he walked out of the diner, the grimy street seemed to hold a new, sinister significance. The "rough crowd," the late-night meetings, the dark sedan – these weren't the actions of a man simply seeking a change of scenery.

He then remembered Mrs. Gable, the elderly woman who lived across the street from the garage, a woman who spent most of her days tending to her small, meticulously kept garden. She had a reputation for noticing everything that went on in their quiet neighborhood, a benevolent neighborhood watch of one. Joe had avoided her so far, not wanting to burden her with his anxieties or have to explain Mike's absence. But now, any lead, no matter how small, was worth pursuing.

He found her on her porch, watering a pot of vibrant red geraniums. She looked up as he approached, her eyes, magnified by thick glasses, crinkling at the corners.

"Joseph, dear! What a surprise," she said, her voice surprisingly robust. "Haven't seen you out and about much these past few days. Everything alright?"

Joe managed a weak smile. "Just… busy, Mrs. Gable. You know how it is." He hesitated, then decided to be direct. "I was wondering if you'd seen anything… unusual lately. Around the garage. My brother, Mike."

Mrs. Gable put down her watering can, her brow furrowing in thought. "Mike? Yes, I've seen him. Saw him leave a few nights ago, actually. Very late. Couldn't have been before midnight, the moon was still high."

Joe's breath hitched. "Leave? Did you see who he was with?"

She nodded slowly, her gaze turning distant. "Yes, I did. A couple of men. They were waiting for him outside. Two of them. They got into a car. A dark one. I couldn't see much, the streetlights are so poor on this end of the block." She paused, her lips pursing. "They didn't look like… well, like folks who'd be doing business with Mike. They were… different. Stern faces. They got in the car, and Mike followed them. He didn't look like himself, Joseph. He looked… hurried. And a little… worried, maybe."

The description, though vague, mirrored the bartender's account. A dark car, late at night, unfamiliar men, and Mike's hurried, worried demeanor. The pieces were beginning to form a disturbing pattern. It wasn't just a disappearance; it was an abduction, or at least a departure under duress. The thought sent a fresh wave of panic through him.

"Did you see where they went, Mrs. Gable?" Joe asked, his voice tight.

She shook her head regretfully. "No, dear. They drove off quickly. Towards the main road. I couldn't tell you which direction. I… I didn't think much of it at the time, you see. I just assumed he had some late-night customers. But now you mention it…" Her voice trailed off, and Joe saw a flicker of concern in her eyes.

He thanked her profusely, the gratitude genuine but tinged with a growing dread. He walked away from her neat little house, the image of Mike getting into that dark car with those strangers burned into his mind. It was no longer about finding a brother who'd walked away; it was about finding a brother who had been taken, or had been forced to flee. The ledger's numbers, the financial troubles that had been dogging them, suddenly seemed like a far more sinister backdrop than he had initially realized. Had Mike gotten himself into something deep, something that had finally caught up with him?

The next few days were a relentless grind. Joe revisited the few people who might have known Mike better than most – old friends from his younger days, a couple of mechanics he used to socialize with at car shows. He sifted through the dregs of Mike's social circle, the conversations often circular, filled with platitudes and the same frustrating lack of concrete information.

One of these conversations was with Frankie "The Fink" Finnegan, a man whose life seemed to revolve around fixing cars and fixing problems, often of the less-than-legal variety. Frankie ran a chop shop out of a disused warehouse down by the industrial yards. Joe hadn't spoken to Frankie in years, not since they'd had a falling out over a job that had gone sideways. But desperation made him swallow his pride.

He found Frankie amidst a skeletal remains of a vintage muscle car, his hands stained with grease, a cigarette dangling from his lips. Frankie greeted him with a gruff nod, his eyes assessing Joe as if he were a piece of machinery to be diagnosed.

"Joe. Long time no see," Frankie drawled, wiping his hands on a greasy rag. "What brings you to my humble abode? Come for a part?"

"No, Frankie. I'm looking for Mike," Joe said, getting straight to the point. "My brother."

Frankie's eyes narrowed slightly. "Mike? Haven't seen him. Not in months."

"Are you sure, Frankie? He sometimes used to… come around. To talk business, maybe." Joe was fishing, trying to see if Frankie's known association with the shadier side of automotive might have intersected with Mike's recent troubles.

Frankie chuckled, a dry, rasping sound. "Business with Mike? He was always too clean for my taste. Stuck to his engines, his honest work. Not like some of us." He took a drag from his cigarette. "But…

actually, now that you mention it… I did see him a few weeks back. Saw him talking to some guys. Looked like they were arguing."

Joe leaned forward, his heart pounding. "Arguing? What were they arguing about?"

"Couldn't hear," Frankie admitted, flicking ash onto the concrete floor. "But it looked heated. And the guys he was talking to… they weren't the usual type. They had that look. The kind that says 'don't mess with me'." Frankie gestured vaguely with his cigarette. "They were parked across the street from your shop, late one night. Mike went out to meet them. Looked like he was trying to smooth things over, but they weren't having it. Then they drove off, and Mike went back inside. Seemed pretty shaken up after that."

"What kind of guys, Frankie?" Joe pressed, his voice a low growl.

"Hard faces. Dressed sharp, but not in a good way. Like they were trying too hard. And they had this… vibe about them. Like danger was their business card." Frankie squinted, trying to recall more details. "One of them had a scar. A thin one, right across his cheek. Looked like he'd had a close call with a knife."

The scar. Joe clung to that detail like a lifeline. A tangible characteristic in a sea of vagueness. It was another piece of the puzzle, a physical identifier that made the shadowy figures feel a little more real, and a lot more terrifying. "Did you see the car they were in?"

Frankie thought for a moment. "Yeah, I think so. Dark. A sedan. Nothing flashy, but definitely not a beat-up clunker. Like I said, sharp. Expensive, probably."

The dark sedan again. It was a recurring motif, a symbol of the unknown force that had entered Mike's life. The argument, the shaken demeanor, the meeting with these "hard face" men – it all pointed towards a conflict, a debt, or a threat that Mike had been desperately trying to manage.

Joe left Frankie's warehouse with a heavy heart. The fragments were coalescing into a picture he didn't want to see. Mike, his meticulous, honorable brother, entangled with dangerous people. The ledger's implications, the mounting debts, were no longer just accounting errors; they were likely the direct cause of his brother's predicament. He had to understand the nature of this entanglement, to figure out what Mike had done or owed to attract such dangerous attention.

He spent the next few days poring over the garage's financial records again, looking for any anomalies, any unusual transactions that might explain the source of Mike's problems or the cause of his disappearance. He found nothing immediately obvious, no large, unexplained withdrawals that might have been used to pay off a debt or buy silence. But the sheer volume of work, the increasing number of late nights Mike had been putting in, suggested a strain that went beyond the usual ebb and flow of their business.

He also started looking at Mike's personal belongings, his small apartment above the garage. He rummaged through drawers, closets, and the clutter of a life lived at a fast pace. He found bills, unopened junk mail, and the usual detritus of single living. But tucked away in a shoebox at the back of his brother's closet, beneath old photographs and ticket stubs, Joe found something that made his blood run cold.

It was a small, worn leather-bound notebook. Not a ledger, but a personal journal. Mike had never been one for writing things down, not in this way. Joe's hands trembled as he opened it. The pages were filled with Mike's familiar, hurried script, but the tone was different. There was a desperation in the entries, a fear that was palpable even in the neat, precise handwriting.

The entries began about six months ago, detailing a series of "difficult" clients and "unusual requests." Then, the language grew more guarded, referencing "investments" and "opportunities" that promised to resolve their financial woes quickly. Mike wrote about meeting with "new associates," people who could "make things happen." He described a growing unease, a feeling of being watched, and a sense of regret that he hadn't just stuck to the honest work.

One entry, dated about three weeks prior, was particularly chilling. It read: "They're getting impatient. The pressure is immense. I told them I needed more time, but they don't understand. Or they don't care. I made a mistake, Joe. A terrible mistake. I've put us in danger. I have to… I have to fix this. I have to make them go away."

Joe's hands were shaking so badly he could barely hold the notebook. This was it. This was the confession he had been dreading, the confirmation that Mike had willingly stepped into a dangerous world, perhaps in an attempt to save their business, but ultimately digging himself into a hole he couldn't escape. The "new associates" were the "rough crowd," the men with the "hard faces" and the "scar."

Another entry, from just a few days later, was even more cryptic: "The plan is in motion. It's risky, but it's the only way. I have to disappear for a while. Let them think… Let them think I'm gone. Then I can start again. From scratch. I'll contact you when it's safe, Joe. I promise."

Disappear? Let them *think* he was gone? The notebook offered a twisted explanation for his brother's vanishing act. Mike hadn't been taken; he had staged his own disappearance, a desperate gamble to escape the very people who were now hunting him, or who he believed were hunting him. The fear of their own financial ruin had driven Mike to make a deal with the devil, and now the devil was demanding payment.

Joe closed the notebook, the worn leather cool against his clammy skin. He finally had a semblance of understanding, a horrifying narrative taking shape. Mike, overwhelmed by debt and pressure, had sought help from dangerous individuals. This had escalated, and now, fearing for his life or freedom, he had decided to vanish, to go into hiding, leaving Joe to deal with the fallout. The worry, the tension Mrs. Gable and Frankie had observed, it all made a terrible kind of sense.

But the notebook offered no answers about *where* Mike had gone, or *how* he planned to make them "go away." It was a breadcrumb trail leading to a precipice, and Joe was left standing at the edge, the wind howling in his ears, the vast unknown stretching out before him. He knew, with a sickening certainty, that his search had just become infinitely more dangerous. He wasn't just looking for a lost brother anymore; he was looking for a brother who was actively trying to outrun a deadly threat. And he had a chilling premonition that those "new associates" wouldn't be easily fooled by Mike's disappearing act. They would be looking for him too, and if they found Joe looking, they might see him as a loose end, or worse, a bargaining chip.

## The Silence of the Streets

The ringing of the phone was a jolt, sharp and unwelcome, in the suffocating stillness of the garage. Joe flinched, his hand instinctively reaching for the receiver, only to freeze halfway. It had been days – or was it weeks now? – since he'd last heard Mike's voice. Each unanswered call, each unreturned message, had chipped away at his hope, leaving behind a raw, exposed nerve of dread. The initial frantic energy of the search had long since dissipated, replaced by a dull ache, a gnawing emptiness that settled deep in his gut. The city, which had once been a tapestry of shared memories and familiar streets, had transformed into a vast, indifferent labyrinth, a place where people could simply... vanish. The silence from Mike wasn't just an absence of sound; it was a crushing weight, a testament to the growing certainty that his brother was truly gone, swallowed whole by the anonymity of urban life.

He let the phone ring, its insistent clamor a cruel mockery of his burgeoning despair. Each ring hammered home the reality: Mike wasn't going to pick up. He wasn't going to stride into the garage, a sheepish grin on his face, with some improbable excuse for his absence. The notebook, Mike's desperate confession of a "terrible mistake" and a plan to "disappear," had offered a terrifying explanation, but it had also severed any remaining thread of easy connection. If Mike was actively hiding, then Joe's frantic attempts to reach him were not only futile but potentially dangerous, a beacon that could draw unwanted attention. The notebook had been a breadcrumb, yes, but it led to a precipice, not a comforting reunion.

Joe sank onto a stool, the cold metal a shock against his worn jeans. The garage, usually alive with the hum of machinery and the scent of oil, felt like a tomb. Dust motes danced in the shafts of weak sunlight slanting through the grimy windows, illuminating the stillness. He could almost feel the phantom presence of Mike, the echo of his laughter, the way he'd whistle off-key when he was focused on an engine. These memories, once a source of comfort, now served only to amplify the ache of his absence. He ran a hand over the workbench, the smooth, worn wood cool beneath his fingertips. Mike's tools were still laid out neatly, as if he'd just stepped away for a moment. A half-finished cup of coffee sat beside them, a pale, stagnant film on its surface. It was a snapshot of a life interrupted, a narrative abruptly cut short.

The days had bled into one another, marked not by progress, but by a relentless erosion of hope. He'd revisited the diner, the bartender's impassive face offering no new information, just a weary shrug and a repetition of "lots of faces come and go." He'd driven by Mrs. Gable's house, but she hadn't been on her porch, and he hadn't had the heart to bother her again. Even Frankie "The Fink," who'd always been a reliable source for the city's less savory whispers, had offered nothing but a grim shake of his head and a muttered, "Some guys just disappear, Joe. That's how it is." The scar on the cheek of one of the men Frankie had described – a detail that had once seemed so significant – now felt like a ghost, a phantom limb of a lead that had gone cold.

He remembered the initial surge of adrenaline, the sharp focus that had propelled him through those first few days. He'd been operating on pure instinct, fueled by fear and a desperate need to find his brother. He'd chased down every whisper, every half-remembered detail, piecing together a narrative of danger and deceit. But now, the adrenaline had faded, leaving behind a profound exhaustion. The city, once a familiar playground, had become a menacing entity. Its alleys seemed darker, its crowds more anonymous, its sheer scale a constant reminder of how easily someone could be lost. He felt like a man shouting into a void, his voice swallowed by the indifferent roar of the metropolis.

The financial records lay scattered across the garage's small office desk, a testament to his fruitless efforts. He'd spent hours poring over them, hoping for a hidden clue, a forgotten transaction that might shed light on the depth of Mike's troubles or the identity of his associates. But the numbers offered no solace. They spoke of mounting debts, of desperate measures taken to keep the garage afloat, but they didn't reveal the faces of the men Mike had been dealing with, nor the precise nature of the "deal" that had apparently gone so wrong. The notebook had confirmed Mike's involvement with dangerous people, but it had also removed him from the realm of a simple missing person, placing him in the far more perilous category of someone in hiding from powerful enemies.

He picked up the notebook again, his fingers tracing the worn leather. Mike's words – "They're getting impatient," "The pressure is immense," "I made a mistake, Joe. A terrible mistake." – echoed in his mind. This wasn't the Mike he knew, the pragmatic mechanic who could fix anything with an engine. This was a man driven to the brink, desperate enough to gamble with his life and freedom. The thought of Mike orchestrating his own disappearance, of deliberately severing ties, was a bitter pill to swallow. It felt like a betrayal, even though he understood the fear that must have driven it.

He looked out the window, his gaze unfocused. The street was quiet, the usual lunchtime bustle absent. Or perhaps it was just his perception, his mind now attuned to the absence of sound, the lack of reassuring normalcy. He thought about the people who might have seen something, the neighbors, the regulars at the local bars and diners. But even if they had, what could they say? "Saw him leave with some guys." "Looked worried." Vague, unhelpful observations that offered no real direction. The city was a place of fleeting interactions, of transient encounters, and Mike, in his desperate attempt to escape, had become another ghost in its crowded anonymity.

The crushing weight of uncertainty pressed down on him. This wasn't just about finding Mike anymore; it was about understanding what had happened, about uncovering the truth behind his brother's vanishing act. And the truth, he suspected, was far darker and more dangerous than he had initially imagined. He was no longer just a worried brother; he was an investigator, driven by a grim determination to piece together the fractured fragments of Mike's last days, to understand the forces that had driven him into hiding, and to hope, against all odds, that he would find him alive. The silence from Mike had become the loudest sound in his life, a deafening testament to his brother's absence and the dangerous path he had taken. And Joe knew, with a chilling certainty, that this silence was only the beginning of a much longer, and potentially much more perilous, journey. He was still standing at the precipice, the wind howling, the unknown stretching out before him, and the only certainty was the gnawing fear that Mike's plan to disappear might have been too good, too complete. The city, with its endless streets and anonymous faces, was a perfect place to vanish, and Joe had the terrifying feeling that his brother had found exactly that. He was a ghost now, and the living had no way of finding a ghost. The silence was his brother's shield, and it was Joe's prison.

# Chapter Four
# Six Months of Silence

## The Empty Space Where Mike Should Be

The relentless march of time had done little to soften the edges of Joe's grief, nor had it offered any semblance of closure. Six months. The number felt obscene, a mockery of the years of shared laughter, weathered crises, and unspoken understanding that had defined his relationship with Mike. It had been half a year since the phone had last rung with his brother's familiar, off-key whistle accompanying the dial tone, half a year since the scent of oil and sawdust had been anything but a painful reminder of what was lost. The auto shop, 'Mike & Joe's Reliable Repairs,' remained a mausoleum of their shared dream. Its corrugated metal doors were sealed tight, the once vibrant signage faded and peeling, a testament to a business abruptly halted, a life irrevocably interrupted. Dust had claimed the interior, an uninvited guest that had settled on every tool, every workbench, every inch of floor space where they'd once toiled side-by-side. The windows, once gleaming, were now milky with accumulated grime, obscuring the life that had once pulsed within, turning the familiar structure into an opaque, unreadable presence on the street. Joe drove past it every day, a ritualistic pilgrimage that offered no solace, only a deepening of the hollow ache in his chest. It was a physical manifestation of the void Mike's absence had carved into his life.

His own apartment, the small, cluttered space that had once vibrated with the low hum of their shared existence, felt similarly hollowed out. The phantom echoes of Mike's voice, his boisterous laugh, the clatter of his tools being set down on the kitchen counter after a late-night tinkering session, were more pronounced now than they had been in the immediate aftermath of his disappearance. It was as if the silence, having permeated every corner of the garage, had finally seeped into the very walls of his home, amplifying the emptiness. He'd stopped tidying Mike's side of the small shared closet, the clothes still hanging there a silent, accusing presence. It felt disrespectful, almost a betrayal, to disturb them, to pretend that the space wasn't still, in some fundamental way, Mike's. The unread mail piled on the small table by the door, mostly bills and junk, held a morbid fascination for Joe. He'd long ago stopped checking Mike's voicemail, the number now a phantom limb he couldn't quite bring himself to sever. The few messages from those early days, frantic calls from concerned friends and bewildered customers, had long since faded into a desolate landscape of unheard pleas and unanswered questions. Now, the inbox was a barren wasteland, a digital tombstone marking the end of communication.

The initial frenzy of the search, the desperate chasing of leads that had felt so vital in those first weeks, had long since evaporated, leaving behind a residue of exhaustion and a gnawing, persistent dread. The notebook, Mike's cryptic confession of a "terrible mistake" and a desperate plan to "disappear," had been a double-edged sword. It offered a terrifying rationale, a justification for the inexplicable vanishing act, but it had also slammed the door shut on any hope of a simple reunion. If Mike had orchestrated this, if he was actively hiding, then Joe's efforts were not only futile but potentially dangerous, a beacon that could draw unwanted attention to them both. The city, once a familiar canvas of shared memories, had morphed into an indifferent, sprawling labyrinth, a place where even the most tangible of presences could simply... cease to be.

Joe found himself trapped in a monotonous loop of routine, a stark contrast to the unpredictable chaos of the days following Mike's disappearance. His days were now marked by a dull, persistent ache, a phantom limb sensation that throbbed with the tangible absence of his brother. He'd tried to re-establish some semblance of normalcy, to force his life back onto its old tracks, but the tracks themselves had been warped, the landscape irrevocably altered. He'd gone back to his part-time construction job, the physical labor a welcome distraction, a way to channel the restless energy that still coursed through him. But even there, the camaraderie of the crew, the casual banter, felt distant, filtered through the lens of his own private sorrow. He was present, but not entirely there, his mind perpetually drifting back to the unanswered questions, the ghost of his brother.

He'd spent hours poring over Mike's financials, a futile attempt to unearth some hidden clue, some forgotten transaction that might shed light on the depth of his brother's troubles. The records painted a grim picture: mounting debts, a precarious struggle to keep the garage afloat, a constant battle against the tide of economic hardship. But they offered no names, no faces, no concrete evidence of the dangerous circles Mike had apparently fallen into. The notebook's vague allusions to "pressure" and "impatience" were all he had to go on, fragile threads leading into a darkness he couldn't fully comprehend. The scar on the cheek of one of the men Frankie "The Fink" had described – a detail that had once seemed so significant, so potent – now felt like a faded echo, a phantom limb of a lead that had gone cold.

The silence was the most oppressive element. It wasn't merely an absence of sound; it was a tangible entity, a suffocating blanket that smothered any flicker of hope. Each unanswered call, each unreturned text message, had been a small death, a confirmation of his growing certainty that Mike was truly gone, swallowed whole by the vast, indifferent anonymity of the city. He remembered the initial surge of adrenaline, the sharp, almost manic focus that had propelled him through those first few weeks. He'd been a man possessed, driven by a primal need to find his brother, to pull him back from whatever abyss he had stumbled into. He'd chased down every whisper, every half-remembered detail, piecing together a fragmented narrative of danger and deceit. But the adrenaline had long since faded, leaving behind a profound, bone-deep exhaustion. The city, once a familiar playground, had transformed into a menacing entity, its alleys darker, its crowds more anonymous, its sheer scale a constant, overwhelming reminder of how easily someone could be lost. He felt like a man shouting into a void, his voice absorbed by the indifferent roar of the metropolis.

He'd revisited the diner where Mike often ate, the bartender's perpetually bored expression offering no new information, just a weary shrug and a repetition of the same dismissive phrase: "Lots of faces come and go, you know?" He'd even driven by Mrs. Gable's house, the kindly old woman who lived down the street from the garage, but she hadn't been on her porch, and he hadn't had the heart to bother her again, to inflict his own misery on her quiet existence. Frankie "The Fink," a man whose life revolved around the city's underbelly, had offered nothing but a grim shake of his head and a muttered, "Some guys just disappear, Joe. That's how it is. The city's got a way of swallowing people whole." The words, once intended as a grim pronouncement, now felt like a prophecy.

He clung to the small victories, the routine tasks that tethered him to reality. He still made his coffee each morning, the familiar ritual a small anchor in the vast sea of his uncertainty. He still bought groceries, even though his appetite had diminished to a shadow of its former self. He even forced himself to go through the motions of maintaining the garage, a futile attempt to keep the memory of their shared life alive, even as the dust thickened and the silence grew. Each day was a battle against despair, a quiet war waged in the empty spaces where Mike should have been. The silence wasn't just an absence of Mike; it was an absence of everything that had made life feel real, vibrant, and meaningful. It was the quiet that settled when a vibrant melody abruptly stopped, leaving only the ringing in your ears. And that ringing, for Joe, was the constant, unending sound of Mike's disappearance.

## The Lingering Fear of the West

The sharp, almost manic clarity that had fueled Joe's desperate search in the initial weeks had long since dissipated, replaced by a creeping, insidious dread that coiled in his gut like a serpent. Six months. The number itself had begun to feel like a physical weight, pressing down on his chest, constricting his lungs. It was a stark, unyielding testament to the gnawing reality that his brother, his flesh and blood, was still gone. The frantic energy that had propelled him through the city's labyrinthine streets, chasing down every phantom lead, every whispered rumor, had been replaced by a weary resignation. The adrenaline had long since burned out, leaving behind the cold, hard ash of uncertainty. He found himself trapped in a relentless cycle of replaying conversations, dissecting every word, every inflection, of their last argument. It had been a petty squabble, something about a misplaced tool, a careless remark about a customer's car — the kind of insignificant bickering that brothers engage in daily. But now, those innocuous exchanges were twisted and distorted in his memory, re-contextualized as potential omens, missed signals that he'd been too blind, too preoccupied, to recognize.

He'd lie awake at night, the silence of his apartment amplified by the relentless whirring of his own thoughts. Had Mike's casual mention of needing "a little extra cash" been a veiled cry for help? Had his brother's unusually guarded demeanor the last time they'd spoken been a sign of something far more sinister than mere fatigue? Joe agonized over these questions, picking at the scab of his guilt, convinced that he'd somehow missed the crucial signposts, the subtle indicators that would have alerted him to the precipice Mike was teetering on. He imagined their last conversation replaying on an endless loop, each word a tiny, sharp shard of glass, capable of inflicting further pain. He saw Mike's face, etched with a worry Joe hadn't registered at the time, his eyes holding a depth of concern that had been completely lost on Joe amidst his own trivial frustrations. The memory felt like a physical blow, a constant reminder of his perceived failure as a brother. He'd always prided himself on his intuition, his ability to read

Mike, to sense his moods, but now, that very intuition felt like a cruel joke, a bitter testament to his blindness.

The city, once a familiar tapestry of shared memories, had transformed into a menacing, unpredictable entity. The evening news, once a distant hum of civic affairs, had become a constant barrage of grim reports, each story of a mugging, a hit-and-run, a violent crime, feeding the insidious fear that was slowly consuming him. He'd find himself flinching at sudden noises, his gaze snapping towards shadowy alleyways, his mind conjuring phantom threats lurking around every corner. He'd read about a body discovered in the industrial district, another in the murky waters of the river, and his stomach would clench with a sickening dread, the unspoken question hanging heavy in the air: was that Mike? The sheer anonymity of the city, its vastness and its indifference, had become the ultimate horror. It was a place where people could simply vanish, swallowed whole by the concrete and the crowds, leaving behind nothing but a void and a lingering sense of dread.

He'd tried to engage with the few people who still remembered Mike with any clarity, seeking some shared understanding, some flicker of reassurance. But the conversations were strained, punctuated by awkward silences and forced smiles. Mrs. Gable, their elderly neighbor, had offered him a plate of cookies, her eyes brimming with a pity that felt more like an accusation. "Such a good boy, your brother," she'd murmured, her voice raspy with age. "Always so polite." Her words, meant to comfort, only deepened Joe's despair. Polite boys didn't just disappear. Polite boys didn't leave behind a trail of unanswered questions and a brother consumed by a fear that bordered on madness. Frankie "The Fink," whose world revolved around the city's murky underbelly, had been even less helpful. He'd met Joe at their usual dive bar, the air thick with stale beer and cigarette smoke, and had offered a grim nod. "Look, Joe," Frankie had said, his voice low and gravelly, "some guys get tangled up. Things happen. You gotta be careful who you owe, who you cross. The city's a tough place, and it don't forgive mistakes." Frankie's words, meant to be a pragmatic assessment, had only served to confirm Joe's deepest fears. What kind of mistake had Mike made? What kind of people had he entangled himself with?

The fear wasn't a singular, easily definable emotion; it was a complex, multifaceted beast that gnawed at him relentlessly. It was the fear of the unknown, the terrifying abyss of not knowing what had happened to Mike. It was the fear of guilt, the gnawing suspicion that he could have, should have, done more. It was the fear of loss, the crushing weight of accepting that Mike might truly be gone, irrevocably, permanently. And beneath it all, a darker, more primal fear began to take root: the fear that Mike had gotten himself into something so deep, so dangerous, that even Joe, his own brother, couldn't pull him out. He pictured Mike, trapped, injured, or worse, and the images were so vivid, so horrifying, that he had to physically force himself to shake his head, to push them away. The gnawing dread was a constant companion, a shadow that clung to him in every moment, transforming the ordinary into the potentially catastrophic.

He'd find himself staring at the phone, willing it to ring, to burst the suffocating silence with the familiar, off-key whistle that had always heralded Mike's call. But the silence persisted, a deafening roar in the absence of sound. He'd scroll through his contacts, Mike's name a painful, stark reminder of what was missing, a ghost in the digital ether. He'd even found himself calling Mike's old number, a desperate, almost involuntary act, only to hear the automated voice informing him that the number was no longer in service. Each failed attempt, each dead end, chipped away at the fragile edifice of hope he'd been desperately trying to maintain. The notebook, Mike's cryptic scrawl about a "terrible mistake" and a plan to "disappear," no longer offered a sliver of possibility; it now seemed like a chilling premonition, a blueprint for his own erasure.

The uncertainty was the most corrosive element of all. It was the constant doubt that ate away at his resolve, the insidious whisper that perhaps Mike had simply walked away, intentionally severing all ties. But that thought, while offering a perverse kind of relief from the more violent possibilities, was almost equally unbearable. It implied a betrayal, a deliberate abandonment of their shared life, their bond. Joe couldn't reconcile that image with the Mike he knew – the loyal, if sometimes reckless, brother who would have faced anything head-on, who would never have simply vanished without a word. This internal conflict, this wrestling with conflicting possibilities, only amplified the lingering fear, trapping him in a psychological no-man's-land where every thought was a double-edged sword.

He remembered their childhood, the shared secrets whispered in the dark, the fierce loyalty that had always bound them. Mike had been his protector, his confidant, his partner in crime and in life. And now, he was simply… gone. The absence was a gaping wound, a constant ache that no amount of time or distraction could truly heal. The initial shock had given way to a deeper, more profound sorrow, a sorrow laced with the chilling certainty that Mike had been caught in something far beyond their understanding, something that had ultimately consumed him. The fear wasn't just about finding Mike; it was about finding out what had happened to him, and the truth, Joe suspected, was a grim, terrifying prospect. The city, with its endless possibilities for both discovery and oblivion, held its secrets close, and Joe felt increasingly like a man lost in its unforgiving embrace, desperately searching for a brother who might have already been swallowed whole by its insatiable hunger. The silence from Mike had become a tangible entity, a heavy shroud that enveloped Joe's life, and with each passing day, the fear of the worst grew stronger, more insistent, a chilling premonition that the silence would never be broken by anything other than the cold, hard finality of despair. The lingering fear was no longer a possibility; it was a suffocating certainty, a chilling whisper that the worst had already happened. He felt it in the marrow of his bones, in the tightness in his chest, in the ever-present ache behind his eyes. Mike was gone, and the silence was his epitaph. He could feel the narrative of their lives diverging, Mike's story ending abruptly, violently, in the shadowy corners of the city, while Joe was left to navigate the desolate landscape of its aftermath, forever haunted by the questions that would never be answered.

## Navigating the City's Underbelly

The city, once a vibrant symphony of his life, had devolved into a discordant cacophony of shadows and whispers. Six months. The words themselves had become a dull, persistent ache, a constant reminder of the void Mike's absence had carved into Joe's existence. The initial frenetic energy, the wild-eyed pursuit of phantom leads, had long since been leached away, replaced by a grim, methodical immersion into the city's forgotten corners. Joe had become a phantom himself, drifting through its underbelly, a silent observer in a world where secrets were currency and survival was a fragile art. His search had taken him to places he'd never imagined, to the frayed edges of society where the light struggled to penetrate and trust was a luxury few could afford.

His days were a monotonous circuit through a landscape of faded paint and flickering neon. Dive bars, their air thick with the mingled scents of stale beer, cheap liquor, and desperation, became his impromptu intelligence hubs. He'd sit hunched over a counter, nursing a lukewarm drink, his eyes scanning the faces around him, searching for any flicker of recognition, any subtle tell that might betray a connection to his missing brother. These were places where reputations were built on grit and guarded by suspicion. The men and women who frequented these establishments operated on a different set of rules, a code of silence and self-preservation. Information, if it existed at all, was traded in hushed tones and wary glances, a commodity parceled out with extreme prejudice. Joe had learned to navigate this labyrinth of veiled intimations, to decipher the language of averted eyes and the subtle shifts in body language that spoke volumes.

He'd learned to present himself as a man adrift, a casual observer rather than a desperate brother. A few well-placed questions about any newcomers to the neighborhood, any unusual activity, were met with blank stares or dismissive shrugs. But occasionally, a bartender with tired eyes and a knowing smirk, or a patron nursing a drink in a dimly lit booth, would offer a sliver of something more. It was never a direct answer, never a clear lead. Instead, it was a cryptic remark, a half-finished sentence, a pointed finger towards another shadowed corner of the city. "Heard there was some trouble down by the docks a while back," a grizzled man with a faded tattoo snaking up his arm might grumble, his gaze fixed on the condensation of his glass. "Some new faces. Looked like they meant business." Or a weary waitress, her smile plastered on, might lean in conspiratorially, "Funny you ask. There was a guy, looked a bit like you said, asking around a few weeks ago. Seemed… on edge." These were the crumbs Joe meticulously collected, the fragments he pieced together in the solitary confines of his apartment, hoping to construct a semblance of truth from the scattered debris.

The alleyways, slick with grime and smelling of decay, were another grim extension of his search. They were the city's forgotten arteries, pathways trodden by those seeking to avoid the prying eyes of the law or the casual notice of passersby. Here, deals were struck, information exchanged, and sometimes, lives were irrevocably altered. Joe would walk these narrow passages, the towering brick walls pressing in on him, his senses on high alert. He'd learned to distinguish the furtive rustle of movement from the scuttling of rats, the low murmur of voices from the distant city hum. He'd encounter men with eyes that held no reflection, their faces hardened by a life lived on the fringes. They were the gatekeepers of this hidden world, their silence a formidable barrier. To them, Joe was an anomaly, an outsider intruding on their carefully constructed anonymity.

He approached each encounter with a calculated caution, a silent acknowledgment of the inherent danger. He'd learned to read the subtle cues of this world: the averted eyes that signaled a refusal to engage, the guarded smiles that masked a deeper wariness, the unspoken rules of survival that dictated every interaction. His own vulnerability was a weapon he dared not reveal, a chink in his armor that could be exploited with devastating ease. Each conversation was a careful dance, a tightrope walk between extracting a sliver of truth and revealing his own desperate pursuit. He'd ask about Mike indirectly, weaving his questions into seemingly casual inquiries about local happenings or potential job opportunities. "Seen anyone new around here lately?" he might venture, his voice deliberately neutral. "Guy who might be looking for some… discreet work?" The responses varied wildly. Some ignored him completely, their faces impassive masks. Others offered outright hostility, a gruff warning to mind his own business.

But there were those who, for a price, or perhaps a fleeting moment of connection, would offer a glimpse behind the curtain. These were often men who'd seen too much, who understood the precariousness of their existence and saw a flicker of shared desperation in Joe's eyes. He'd pay for information, not with cash directly – that would be too easily traced and could invite unwanted attention – but with favors, with a willingness to listen, with the unspoken promise of discretion. He learned that loyalty in this world was a fleeting commodity, bought and sold on the fly. He met a pawn shop owner, a man named Sal, whose shop was a dimly lit repository of forgotten lives and ill-gotten gains. Sal had a knack for remembering faces, for piecing together fragments of conversations overheard from the desperate souls who pawned their possessions. Joe would frequent his shop, ostensibly looking for tools or old electronics, but his real quarry was information.

"Anything new, Sal?" Joe asked one afternoon, his voice low as he examined a tarnished silver locket.

Sal, wiping down the counter with a stained cloth, grunted. "Same old story, Joe. People needing cash, pawning memories. But yeah, a few weeks back, a fella came in. Looked jumpy. Sold a cheap watch, real fast. Kept looking over his shoulder." Sal paused, his eyes narrowing as he met Joe's gaze. "Said his name was… Mikey. Sounded familiar. Asked if I'd heard any buzz about… odd jobs. Said he needed to make a clean break."

Joe's heart gave a familiar, painful lurch. "Mikey? What did he look like?"

Sal shrugged, the movement conveying a practiced indifference. "Average. Brown hair, bit of a stubble. Nothing remarkable. But he had this look, you know? Like he was running from something. Or someone." He leaned in, lowering his voice. "Said he was heading out of town. Didn't say where, though. Just needed to disappear for a while."

Disappear. The word echoed the cryptic entry in Mike's notebook, the chilling phrase that had become Joe's obsession. "A clean break." Was this the same Mike? Could it be? The uncertainty was a constant torment, a perpetual shadow that clung to him. He knew Mike could be impulsive, prone to sudden decisions, but disappearing without a word, without even contacting him, felt alien to the brother he knew.

He pressed Sal further. "Did he mention anyone? Anyone he was meeting, or anyone he was trying to avoid?"

Sal shook his head. "Nah. He was quick. In and out. Paid cash for the watch, barely glanced at the offer. Just wanted to be gone. Seemed desperate, like I said. But that's not my business, Joe. You know me."

Joe did know him. Sal was a survivor, and survival in this city often meant knowing when to look away, when to feign ignorance. Joe understood. He left the shop with a renewed sense of urgency, the brief flicker of a potential lead quickly overshadowed by the vastness of the unknown. He started frequenting the bus depots and train stations, observing the faces, listening to snippets of conversations. He'd scan the departing passengers, his eyes searching for a familiar profile, a gait that might belong to his brother. He'd linger in the waiting areas, the air thick with the transient hopes and anxieties of travelers, imagining Mike amidst the anonymity, a ghost slipping through the cracks.

He also ventured into the seedier districts, the areas where illicit activities were more openly conducted, where the shadows held more than just the absence of light. He spoke to street vendors who saw everything and said nothing, to small-time hustlers who operated in the gray areas of the law, to the night owls who seemed to possess an innate understanding of the city's hidden rhythms. Each encounter was a careful negotiation, a test of his resolve and his ability to blend in. He discovered a network of informal information brokers, men who traded in whispers and rumors, their loyalty as fluid as the city's ever-shifting tides. They operated out of back rooms of forgotten shops, from park benches in the dead of night, their exchanges conducted with the furtive urgency of spies.

One such contact, a wiry man named 'Whispers' who earned his moniker by rarely speaking above a murmur, met Joe in the cramped confines of a dimly lit laundromat. The rhythmic hum of the washing machines provided a constant, low-level distraction, a sonic veil for their clandestine conversation. Whispers, his eyes darting nervously from the spinning clothes to Joe, spoke in clipped sentences.

"Heard you're looking for someone," Whispers began, his voice barely audible above the machinery. "Similar to you. Your brother."

Joe nodded, his gut tightening. "That's right."

"Heard he was into something… heavy. Not just a little bit of fast cash. This was bigger. Nasty business." Whispers picked at a loose thread on his jacket. "Made a mistake. A big one. Owed people who don't forget."

"What kind of mistake?" Joe's voice was tight, strained.

Whispers looked around, his gaze lingering on the glass door of the laundromat. "Don't know the specifics. Just that it involved… something valuable. Something someone wanted very badly. And your brother, he… he didn't play by the rules. Got in too deep, too fast." He paused, a hint of genuine concern finally flickering in his eyes. "They're not the forgiving type, Joe. They'll look for him. And if they find him… well." He left the implication hanging in the air, a chilling testament to the danger.

"Did he mention where he was going?" Joe's question was a desperate plea.

Whispers shook his head. "No. Not to me. But I heard whispers… about a place out of the city. A quiet place. Where people go to… get away from things. Might be worth checking out. But be careful, Joe. This is a dangerous game you're playing. You're not built for this."

Joe felt a cold dread settle in his stomach. The casual dismissal of his presence, the subtle warning – it was all a stark reminder of his outsider status in this world. He was a man driven by love and desperation, armed with a dwindling sense of hope, trying to navigate a treacherous landscape populated by those who operated on instinct, on survival, on a profound understanding of the city's dark heart. He had no real allies here, only temporary conduits of information, their willingness to help bought with a transactional cynicism that was as disheartening as the silence itself.

He continued his rounds, his focus sharpening, his senses honed by months of relentless searching. He learned to recognize the subtle differences between the casual patron of a bar and the man nursing a drink with a purpose, the weary shopkeeper and the one whose eyes held a glint of something more, something knowing. He started to notice the patterns, the unspoken connections that bound these disparate elements of the city's underbelly together. He saw how information flowed, not in a direct line, but in a convoluted web of favors, debts, and mutual understandings. He realized that to find Mike, he couldn't just ask questions; he had to become a part of this hidden ecosystem, to understand its unspoken language and its unwritten laws.

He spent hours poring over old city directories, tracing the history of businesses that had long since shuttered, searching for any potential link, any forgotten connection that might have once involved Mike. He visited community centers in the neighborhoods Mike had frequented, not for comfort, but for clues, for the chance encounter with someone who might have seen something out of the ordinary. He started to build a mental map of the city's forgotten spaces, the abandoned warehouses, the derelict factories, the forgotten docks – places where secrets could be buried, and where a man could disappear without a trace. These were the places that whispered Mike's name, the desolate landscapes that held the echoes of his potential presence.

His own life had become a testament to the corrosive nature of uncertainty. Sleep offered little respite, his dreams often populated by fragmented images of Mike, by scenarios of violence and despair that mirrored his waking fears. The notebook, once a fragile beacon of hope, had become a chilling artifact, its cryptic words a constant torment. He'd trace the words with his finger, 'terrible mistake,' 'disappear,' trying to infuse them with a meaning, a direction, that remained stubbornly elusive. He was adrift in a sea of possibilities, each one more terrifying than the last. Was Mike a victim? A perpetrator? Had he simply run? The questions gnawed at him, leaving him hollowed out, a shell of the man he once was.

The city, once a familiar stage for his life, had become an adversary, a vast, indifferent entity that seemed determined to keep its secrets locked away. But Joe was no longer deterred by its silence. He had become a part of its underbelly, a shadow among shadows, driven by a brotherly love that refused to yield, a stubborn refusal to let Mike's story end in the anonymity of the city's unforgiving embrace. He knew the risks, he understood the danger, but the alternative – the suffocating weight of never knowing – was a far greater terror. He was a man on a mission, his quest etched into the very fabric of his being, a grim determination burning in his soul. The city's underbelly was his new reality, and he would navigate its treacherous depths until he found the answers he so desperately sought, or until he too was swallowed whole by its insatiable hunger. He was a hunter, a ghost, a brother lost in the concrete jungle, his every step a testament to the enduring power of familial bonds in the face of overwhelming despair.

## Dead Ends and False Hopes

The city, a labyrinth of broken promises, had become Joe's unwilling accomplice in his Sisyphean quest. Each dawn brought with it a renewed, albeit fragile, hope, a desperate belief that today might be the day. But the city, in its infinite capacity for indifference, consistently offered only more dead ends and the bitter taste of false hope. The supposed sighting, relayed with hushed urgency by a jittery informant Joe had met in the echoing bowels of a disused subway station, had evaporated like mist in the harsh morning light. The man described – tall, gaunt, with a distinctive scar above his left eyebrow – had indeed been seen boarding a late-night bus headed south. Joe, fueled by a surge of adrenaline that momentarily eclipsed the gnawing fatigue, had tracked down the bus company, bribed a dispatcher for passenger manifests, and spent an agonizing day cross-referencing names. The man on the manifest, a traveling salesman named Arthur Jenkins, bore no resemblance to his brother beyond the vaguest of descriptions. Arthur Jenkins, when finally located through sheer persistence, was a mild-mannered accountant with a receding hairline and a penchant for floral shirts, his alibi for the night in question meticulously documented by his wife. Joe's brief flicker of elation had guttered out, leaving behind only the acrid smell of disappointment.

Then there was the cryptic message. A crumpled note, slipped under his apartment door by an unseen hand, contained only a street name and a time: "Elmwood Avenue, midnight." Joe had arrived early, the deserted street bathed in the sickly yellow glow of distant streetlights. He'd waited, the silence amplifying the frantic thrumming of his own heart. Minutes bled into an hour, then another. The only movement was the scuttling of a rat across the asphalt and the rhythmic creak of a loose sign swinging in the faint breeze. The message, it turned out, was a cruel prank, a piece of anonymous malice designed to torment him. He'd learned later, through a hesitant whisper from a regular at a dive bar he frequented, that the note had been a drunken dare, a joke among a group of bored teenagers who'd found a morbid amusement in his increasingly desperate search.

The landscape of his informants had become a gallery of rogues and liars. There was "Silas," a street preacher with eyes that burned with an unsettling fervor, who'd claimed Mike had joined a clandestine religious sect operating in the city's forgotten industrial zones. Silas had painted a picture of Mike finding solace, of a spiritual awakening. Joe, clinging to any narrative that offered a glimmer of his brother's well-being, had followed Silas's trail into a labyrinth of abandoned warehouses, the air thick with the scent of rust and decay. He'd found only a handful of desperate souls huddled around a flickering bonfire, their faces gaunt and their pronouncements rambling and nonsensical. Silas himself was nowhere to be found, his proclaimed spiritual mission seemingly abandoned as quickly as it had begun.

Another contact, a former petty thief named "Lucky" Lou, notorious for his ability to procure anything from stolen electronics to fabricated identification, had offered a far more sinister account. Lou claimed Mike had become embroiled in a high-stakes poker game, losing a significant sum to a notoriously ruthless syndicate. He'd described Mike's mounting debt, the veiled threats, the desperate attempts to flee. Lou had even provided a fabricated address, a rundown tenement building in the city's grittiest district, claiming Mike had been seen there, seeking refuge. Joe had braved the treacherous streets, the air thick with the stench of refuse and despair, only to find the building condemned, its windows boarded up, its inhabitants long gone. Lou, when Joe confronted him again, had merely shrugged, a greasy grin spreading across his face, and admitted he'd "confused" Mike with someone else, his casual disregard for Joe's pain a stark testament to the moral bankruptcy of his world.

The sheer weight of these repeated betrayals, these dashed hopes, was beginning to erode Joe's resolve. Each dead end was not just a setback; it was a fresh wound, a reopening of the raw grief that lay beneath the surface of his outward composure. The relentless pursuit, the constant vigilance, the immersion in the city's underbelly – it was a corrosive process that was taking a severe toll on his mental and emotional resilience. He found himself increasingly irritable, his patience worn thin by the constant barrage of misinformation and evasion. Sleep offered little solace, his dreams a chaotic tapestry of fleeting glimpses of Mike, interspersed with distorted faces of the liars and deceivers he'd encountered, their mocking laughter echoing in the silence of his waking hours.

The physical toll was also becoming undeniable. The meager meals he forced down, often consisting of stale sandwiches grabbed from street vendors or lukewarm coffee gulped down in lonely diners, were insufficient to sustain him. His once-familiar routines had dissolved, replaced by a grueling, all-consuming search that left him perpetually exhausted. His apartment, once a sanctuary, now felt like a sterile cage, a place where he retreated only to sleep and to stare, unseeing, at the city's indifferent skyline. He'd catch his reflection in the grimy windows – his eyes hollowed, his face gaunt, a stranger staring back at him, consumed by an all-encompassing grief and a desperate, fading hope.

He knew, with a chilling certainty, that he was teetering on the brink. The constant exposure to danger, the emotional drain, the gnawing uncertainty – it was a potent cocktail that threatened to shatter his carefully constructed composure. He had to find a way to remain grounded, to not let the despair consume him entirely. He would often retreat to the anonymity of the public library, not for research, but for the quiet, the order, the brief respite from the chaos of his own life. He'd lose himself in the silent turning of pages, the hushed reverence of the place a stark contrast to the clamor of the streets. It was there, amidst the towering shelves of forgotten stories, that he sometimes found a brief, fragile calm, a reminder that other lives, other narratives, existed beyond his own agonizing quest.

But the city always beckoned him back, its secrets still whispering in the shadows, its silence still holding the echo of his brother's voice. The dead ends were not reasons to stop; they were merely detours on a road that had no discernible end. He had to believe that somewhere, beyond the labyrinth of lies and the crushing weight of disappointment, there was a truth waiting to be unearthed. He had to believe that Mike was out there, waiting to be found, and that his relentless, soul-crushing search, however futile it sometimes felt, was the only path forward. The false hopes were painful, the dead ends demoralizing, but the thought of giving up, of accepting the silence as the final word, was a prospect far more terrifying than any of the city's hidden dangers. He would continue to chase the phantom, to decipher the whispers, to navigate the treacherous currents of the city's underbelly, clinging to the stubborn, almost irrational, conviction that he would find Mike, or at least, the truth of what had happened to him. The path was littered with broken glass, but Joe kept walking, his gaze fixed on the unseen horizon, his spirit battered but not yet broken.

## The Fading Image of His Brother

The persistent hum of the city, once a comforting thrum of life, had morphed into a dull, incessant ache behind Joe's eyes. Six months. Six months of chasing ghosts, of navigating the city's labyrinthine alleys and its equally tangled human networks, and the only tangible thing he'd acquired was a profound sense of weariness. But it wasn't just the physical exhaustion that was taking its toll; it was the insidious erosion of memory itself. Mike, his brother, the anchor of his childhood and the constant presence in his early adulthood, was becoming a phantom not just in his physical absence, but in Joe's own mind.

He'd found himself staring at old photographs, the glossy surfaces of the prints offering a fragile tether to a past that felt increasingly distant. There was one, taken at a long-forgotten family picnic, of Mike grinning, his eyes crinkled at the corners, a half-eaten sandwich clutched in his hand. Joe would trace the outline of his brother's smile, trying to conjure the sound of his laughter, that distinctive, booming laugh that could fill a room and chase away any lingering shadows. But the sound wouldn't come. It was like trying to recall a melody heard long ago, the notes dissolving before they could fully form. The image was there, sharp and clear, but the auditory essence, the very *sound* of Mike, was slipping through his fingers.

He'd started listening to old voicemails, his phone a shrine to a life that was rapidly becoming abstract. Mike's voice, once a familiar comfort, now felt like a recording from another era, a disembodied echo. He'd play them on repeat, straining to catch the nuances, the subtle inflections that had once been as familiar as his own heartbeat. There was the exasperated sigh when Joe had messed up a recipe, the conspiratorial whisper when they were planning a surprise for their parents, the genuine warmth when he'd offered advice about a girl Joe was crushing on. But even these recordings, once imbued with so much life, were starting to sound… flat. The digital fidelity couldn't quite capture the rasp in his brother's throat after a late night, or the way his voice would lift when he was genuinely excited about something. The more he listened, the more he felt like he was trying to reassemble a shattered vase, each fragment precious, but the original form forever lost.

The harsh realities of his search were a constant, corrosive force, actively working to overwrite the loving memories of their shared past. The encounters with Silas and Lucky Lou, the dead-end leads and the outright betrayals, had injected a cynicism into Joe's worldview that was bleeding into his recollections of Mike. He found himself questioning everything, even the idealized versions of his brother he'd held onto. Had Mike

*really* been that carefree? Had their childhood bond been as unbreakable as he remembered, or was he just projecting his own desperate need for connection onto a past that was more complicated than he allowed himself to admit? The addiction that had consumed Mike, the desperation that had led him to disappear, these were ugly truths, and they threatened to stain the untarnished portrait Joe had meticulously constructed in his mind.

He'd tried to combat this internal erosion by creating a physical memorial. He'd cleared a shelf in his small apartment, arranging a curated collection of mementos. There was a faded concert ticket from a band they'd both loved, a chipped mug they'd shared countless breakfasts from, and, of course, the photographs. He'd even dug out a dusty cassette tape from their teenage years, a recording of them attempting to cover a song they'd heard on the radio, their off-key harmonies a testament to their youthful exuberance and their utter lack of musical talent. He would touch these objects, hoping to reignite the spark of recognition, to force his mind to recall the context, the emotion, the sheer

*presence* of Mike. But sometimes, when he looked at the collection, it felt less like a tribute and more like an exhibit of a stranger. The objects were there, but the spirit, the intangible essence of his brother, felt increasingly elusive.

The city, too, seemed to conspire against his efforts. Every street corner, every dimly lit bar, every anonymous face he encountered carried the potential for a new lead, a fresh sighting, a fragment of truth. But it also carried the weight of his increasingly desperate search, the constant exposure to the city's underbelly, its desperation and its deceit. This immersive dive into the grim reality of Mike's potential fate was leaving him raw, his emotional defenses worn thin. The bright, innocent memories of his brother were like delicate watercolors, and the harsh solvents of his current existence were causing them to bleed and fade, their sharp outlines blurring into a muddy indistinctness.

He remembered a specific argument they'd had a few years back, a petty disagreement about something he couldn't even recall now. He remembered Mike's frustration, the way he'd run a hand through his hair, a gesture Joe had always found endearingly familiar. He remembered the heat of the moment, the sharp words exchanged. But the details were fuzzy. What had the argument been about? What had been the precise words? He could picture the scene, the setting – their shared apartment, the late afternoon light slanting through the blinds. But the emotional resonance, the specific cadence of their voices, the exact nature of their disagreement – these were becoming elusive, like trying to grasp smoke.

The fear of forgetting Mike entirely was a new and terrifying dimension to his grief. It was a colder, more abstract fear than the immediate worry for his brother's safety. The thought that the man who had been such a fundamental part of his life could become nothing more than a collection of faded images and fragmented memories was almost unbearable. He felt a desperate need to anchor himself, to solidify the past before it dissolved completely. He started carrying a small notebook, not for jotting down leads, but for writing down memories. He'd sit in quiet corners of parks or late at night in his apartment, forcing himself to recall specific moments: the taste of the pizza they'd shared after their first high school football game, the silly nicknames they'd had for their teachers, the sheer terror of a thunderstorm they'd weathered together in their childhood treehouse. He wrote it all down, a frantic attempt to create a bulwark against the encroaching tide of forgetfulness.

He'd found himself scrutinizing strangers on the street, not just for a physical resemblance, but for a shared mannerism, a fleeting expression that might echo Mike. A tilt of the head, a way of shrugging, a particular stance – anything that might trigger a deeper, more visceral memory. But often, the flicker of recognition would prove to be a false alarm, a cruel trick of the light or a misfiring of his own desperate hope. These moments of perceived connection, only to have them snatched away, were more disheartening than the outright rejections he'd grown accustomed to.

The addiction was a particularly difficult aspect to reconcile with his memories. Mike, in his healthier days, had been impulsive and sometimes reckless, but he'd also been fundamentally good, kind, and fiercely loyal. How could the same person succumb to the destructive grip of addiction? Joe wrestled with this dissonance, the image of his brother battling his demons a stark contrast to the carefree kid he remembered. He found himself trying to compartmentalize: the brother he remembered fondly, and the brother who had fallen into the shadows. But the lines were blurring, the addiction becoming inextricably linked to the very essence of his brother's absence. It was a painful transformation, a redefinition of the man he loved, forced upon him by circumstances he couldn't control.

He'd started sketching again, something he hadn't done since his college days. He'd buy cheap sketchpads and charcoal pencils, and he'd try to draw Mike from memory. The lines were often hesitant, the proportions awkward. He'd get frustrated, crumpling page after page, the charcoal smudging his hands like the dirt and grime of his ongoing search. But he persisted, driven by an almost primal urge to capture his brother's likeness before it faded entirely. The sketches were imperfect, a far cry from the vibrant reality of his memories, but they were tangible proof that Mike had existed, that he had a face, a form, a presence that Joe was fighting to preserve.

The irony wasn't lost on him. He was searching for his brother in the physical world, chasing leads and informants, but he was also engaged in an equally desperate, internal search – a battle to keep the essence of Mike alive within himself. The vibrant, laughing brother of his youth was slowly being eclipsed by the image of a man lost to addiction and disappearance, and the fading of those cherished memories was a betrayal of a different, more profound kind. It was a betrayal not by Mike, but by time, by circumstance, by the sheer, unforgiving passage of days.

He caught himself using phrases Mike used to say, little idioms and turns of phrase that had become so ingrained in his own speech that he barely noticed them. Sometimes, he'd hear himself speak and a chill would run down his spine, a sudden awareness that he was becoming a conduit for his brother's lost voice, a living repository of his mannerisms. It was a strange comfort, a macabre form of connection, but it also highlighted the profound emptiness left by Mike's absence. He was carrying fragments of his brother within him, but it was a hollow echo, a pale imitation of the original.

The search was a relentless, consuming force, and it was demanding a steep price. It was not just the physical and emotional toll; it was the slow, agonizing erasure of his own past, the blurring of the vivid hues of his shared history with Mike. He was fighting a two-front war: one against the external forces that had taken his brother, and another against the internal tide of forgetfulness that threatened to swallow the very memory of the man he was trying to save. The image of his brother was fading, but Joe's resolve, though battered and weary, remained, a stubborn ember glowing in the encroaching darkness, fueled by the desperate need to remember, and to find

# Chapter Five
# A Whispered Lead

## A Shady Informant's Offer

The stale air of "The Rusty Mug" clung to Joe like a second skin, a potent cocktail of cheap whiskey, cigarette smoke, and the indefinable funk of desperation. It was a dive bar that catered to the city's fringes, a place where shadows clung to corners and secrets were traded for the price of a drink. Joe nursed a lukewarm beer, its bitterness a fitting accompaniment to the gnawing emptiness in his gut. Six months. Six months of dead ends, of chasing shadows in the labyrinthine underbelly of this sprawling metropolis, and the only thing he'd managed to solidify was the relentless ache behind his eyes. His brother, Mike, was a phantom, not just in his absence, but increasingly in Joe's own mind, the vivid hues of their shared past fading like old photographs left too long in the sun. He'd started listening to old voicemails, trying to recapture the cadence of Mike's voice, the easy laugh that had once filled their small apartment, but even those digital echoes were starting to sound hollow, like recordings from another life. The addiction that had consumed Mike was a stain he couldn't scrub from his memories, a grim truth that threatened to overwrite the carefree kid he'd grown up with. He'd even taken to sketching Mike from memory, the charcoal smudging his fingers like the grime of his relentless, fruitless search, a desperate attempt to anchor the fading image before it dissolved completely. The irony was not lost on him: he was searching for his brother in the physical world, but also engaged in an internal battle to keep Mike's essence alive within himself, a fight against the encroaching tide of forgetfulness.

The bartender, a hulking man with forearms like oak trunks and a perpetually bored expression, slapped Joe's empty glass down, the gesture more of a dismissal than a service. Joe caught his eye, a silent question passing between them. The bartender grunted, a barely perceptible nod towards a booth tucked away in the darkest recess of the bar. A figure sat there, hunched over a drink, their face obscured by the low brim of a worn fedora and the perpetual haze of smoke.

Joe's instinct screamed caution, a primal hum beneath the weariness. This was not the kind of place you stumbled into by accident if you were looking for the straight and narrow. This was a place where paths diverged, where those seeking solace, or escape, or something far more illicit, tended to congregate. But Mike, in his increasingly desperate final months, had been straddling that line, teetering on the precipice of a world Joe was only just beginning to understand. And if there was even the slimmest chance that this figure in the booth held a piece of that puzzle, Joe had to take it.

He pushed himself away from the bar, the stool scraping a protest against the grimy floor. Each step towards the booth felt heavier than the last, as if the very air in The Rusty Mug was thick with unspoken warnings. The man in the booth didn't look up until Joe was almost upon him, and then, slowly, deliberately, he raised his head.

The informant. Joe had heard whispers of him, a ghost in the city's rumor mill, a man known only by a moniker Joe couldn't quite recall at that moment, something about a bird, perhaps? A crow? Or maybe a raven? It didn't matter. What mattered were the eyes, ancient and knowing, that seemed to have witnessed every transaction, every betrayal, every whispered promise and every broken dream that had ever passed through these four walls. They were eyes that had seen too much, and in their depths, Joe saw a reflection of his own burgeoning cynicism.

The man's lips curved into a smile, not a warm, inviting one, but a thin, predatory slash that promised trouble. It was a smile that had seen opportunities in desperation, a smile that understood the currency of secrets. He gestured with a bony hand, a silent invitation to sit.

"Joe, is it?" the man rasped, his voice like gravel being churned in a cement mixer. He didn't wait for a confirmation. "Heard you've been asking around. Asking about your brother. Mike."

The directness of it, the casual mention of Mike's name, sent a jolt through Joe. It was a jolt of hope, sharp and unexpected, quickly followed by a cold dread. This man, whoever he was, knew. And knowing in this city often came with a price.

"You know him?" Joe asked, his voice tighter than he intended. He slid into the worn vinyl seat opposite the informant, the cracked material sticking uncomfortably to his leg. The booth was upholstered in a dark, indeterminate color that had probably once been red, now faded and stained by years of spilled drinks and forgotten confessions.

The informant took a slow sip of his drink, his gaze never leaving Joe's face. "Know *of* him," he corrected, the smile still playing on his lips. "Heard the name. Heard he'd… misplaced himself. A lot of people misplace themselves in this city, son. Especially when they owe. Or when they're owed." He let the words hang in the air, a delicate dance of insinuation.

"Misplaced himself?" Joe repeated, the phrase sounding euphemistic, almost polite, a stark contrast to the grim reality he was wrestling with. "He disappeared. Six months ago. I'm trying to find him."

The informant leaned back, the springs of the booth groaning in protest. He reached into his jacket pocket, his movements economical and precise, and produced a crumpled pack of cigarettes. He offered one to Joe, who instinctively shook his head. The informant lit his own cigarette, the flare of the match illuminating his sharp features for a brief, fleeting moment. He took a long drag, the smoke curling upwards, obscuring his face once more.

"Disappeared," the informant echoed, exhaling a plume of blue-grey smoke. "A word with many meanings in this town. Sometimes it means they're lying low. Sometimes it means they've been *made* to disappear. And sometimes," he paused, tapping ash from his cigarette onto a small, metal tray that served as an ashtray, "it means they've finally caught up with themselves."

Joe's jaw tightened. He was tired of riddles, tired of veiled threats and cryptic pronouncements. He wanted answers, not literary allusions. "Look," he said, his voice low and urgent, "if you know something, anything, just tell me. I'm not afraid of what I might hear."

The informant chuckled, a dry, humorless sound. "Oh, but you will be, son. This path you're treading… it isn't a paved road with pleasant scenery. It's a back alley, slick with things you don't want to step in. And the further you go, the darker it gets." He took another drag, his eyes glinting in the dim light. "But I do know this. Your brother, Mike. He was running with a… certain crowd. A crowd that likes to operate out of the warehouse district. Down by the docks. You know the place?"

The warehouse district. Joe's mind flashed to the skeletal silhouettes of derelict buildings against the perpetually grey sky, the lingering smell of brine and decay, the rusting hulks of ships that hadn't sailed in years. It was a no-man's-land, a place the city tried to forget, and a place where people could vanish without a trace.

"I've been there," Joe admitted, his voice barely a whisper. He'd walked the perimeter, peered through broken windows, felt the oppressive silence that seemed to emanate from the very bricks and mortar. But he hadn't dared to venture too deep, hadn't known who or what to look for.

"Good," the informant said, a hint of approval in his tone. "Because that's where the whispers about Mike are coming from. He was involved in something. Something that made certain people… uneasy. He was trying to make a quick buck, I reckon. Thought he was smarter than the rest of them. But in that part of town, being smart isn't enough. You gotta be lucky. Or you gotta be ruthless."

Joe's hand clenched into a fist under the table. He pictured Mike, his impulsive nature, his willingness to take risks that always seemed to backfire. Had he finally pushed his luck too far? Had he crossed the wrong people? The image of Mike, the brother who had once taught him to ride a bike, who had held his hand through childhood nightmares, was now intertwined with the grim reality of the docks, with the shadowed figures who operated in the city's underbelly.

"What kind of crowd?" Joe pressed, trying to keep his voice steady. He could feel his heart hammering against his ribs, a frantic drumbeat against the oppressive silence of the booth.

The informant leaned forward, lowering his voice conspiratorially. The smoky veil around him seemed to deepen, his features becoming more indistinct, his words more resonant with a sense of danger. "Think... people who deal in things that aren't supposed to be dealt in. Think... muscle. Think... secrets. They like to keep things quiet. And if Mike made too much noise, or if he tried to play them, well..." He let the implication hang, a palpable threat in the air.

"And you know this?" Joe's gaze was fixed on the informant's face, searching for any flicker of deception, any hint that this was just a wild goose chase designed to extort money or worse.

The informant gave another slow, deliberate sip of his drink. "Let's just say I have ears in places where other people have blind spots. And the whispers I've been hearing about your brother... they're not good ones. He was asking questions too, you see. Questions that weren't his to ask. And that's a dangerous game to play."

"What questions?" Joe demanded, leaning in. The weariness that had settled into his bones seemed to recede, replaced by a surge of adrenaline, of urgent, desperate need.

"That's where it gets... complicated," the informant said, his eyes narrowing. "And that's where my offer comes in. Information like this... it doesn't come free. This is the kind of knowledge that can get a man killed. Or worse." He gestured vaguely with his cigarette. "You want to know more, you want me to point you in the right direction, you're going to have to pay. And it isn't going to be with pocket change."

Joe swallowed, the lump in his throat making it difficult to speak. He knew this was coming. He'd expected it. But the gravity of the informant's words, the palpable sense of danger they conveyed, still hit him with the force of a physical blow. He had very little money left. His savings were dwindling, eaten away by weeks of dead-end investigations, bar tabs, and the sheer cost of existing while chasing a ghost.

"How much?" Joe asked, his voice rough.

The informant smiled again, a slow, appraising look. "Let's talk about what you're willing to do. What you're willing to risk. Because this isn't just about money, Joe. This is about stepping into the dark. And once you're in, it's hard to find your way back out." He leaned closer, his voice dropping to a near-inaudible murmur, the words a dangerous whisper that promised both salvation and ruin. "Mike was getting tangled up with some very unsavory characters, characters who don't like loose ends. And it sounds like your brother might have become a rather large loose end."

The informant's words hung in the smoky air, a chilling premonition of the path ahead. Joe's mind reeled. The warehouse district. Unsavory characters. Loose ends. It painted a grim picture, a far cry from the comforting memories of his brother he was fighting so hard to preserve. The vague allusions, the veiled warnings – they were designed to intimidate, but they also ignited a desperate spark of hope. This was the first real lead, the first concrete direction, however fraught with peril.

"What do you want?" Joe asked again, his voice raw with a mixture of fear and determination. The image of Mike's face, now tinged with the shadows of the docks and the whispers of danger, was a constant ache in his mind, a stark reminder of the stakes. He was prepared to pay, to risk, to do whatever it took. The thought of forgetting Mike entirely, of letting his brother's memory fade into an indistinguishable blur, was a more terrifying prospect than any of the dangers the informant hinted at.

The informant leaned back, his eyes glinting. "Let's just say, I have a certain… interest in seeing certain matters resolved. And if you can help me with that, then perhaps I can help you find your brother. Or at least, find out what happened to him. It's a two-way street, you see. You scratch my back, I scratch yours. But remember, son," he added, his gaze hardening, "in this particular part of town, sometimes the scratching turns into tearing."

He took a final, lingering drag from his cigarette, then stubbed it out with a decisive motion. He pushed himself up from the booth, his movements still unnervingly fluid and precise. "Think about it, Joe. The warehouse district. Ask around there. Discreetly. You'll find what you're looking for. Or what's looking for you."

With that, the informant turned and walked away, disappearing into the smoky labyrinth of The Rusty Mug as silently as he had appeared. Joe watched him go, the man's parting words echoing in the oppressive silence of the booth. He was left with a name, a place, and a gnawing sense of dread. The lead was a precarious one, offered by a man who dealt in shadows and secrets, a man whose smile promised more trouble than solutions. But it was a lead nonetheless. And in his desperate quest to find Mike, Joe knew he had to follow it, no matter how dark or dangerous the path might be. The city, in its vast, indifferent sprawl, had just handed him another piece of the puzzle, a piece stained with the grime of the docks and the chilling certainty that his search was leading him into ever-deeper waters, waters that threatened to drown not only his brother, but his own fragile hope. The memory of Mike, the brother he fought so hard to keep alive in his mind, was now inextricably linked to the grim realities of this underbelly, and Joe felt a cold certainty that the journey ahead would test the very fabric of those precious recollections. He had to know. He had to find out what happened to Mike, and the informant's veiled offer, however dangerous, was the only flicker of light in the encroaching darkness. He pushed the beer bottle away, the metallic tang on his tongue a stark reminder of the bitter reality he now faced. The warehouse district awaited.

## The Name of a Neighborhood

The informant's gravelly voice, amplified by the echoing silence of the booth, finally deposited the name into Joe's consciousness like a poisoned seed. It wasn't a name whispered in hushed tones of respect, nor was it a place marked on any tourist map. It was a label, spat out with a mix of contempt and weary familiarity, a place that had long since been written off by the city's clean-cut facade: the Iron Triangle. Joe felt a cold dread seep into his bones, a visceral reaction that had nothing to do with the chill of the bar and everything to do with the reputation that preceded the name. The Iron Triangle. Even the words conjured images of rusted metal, of decay, of a place where hope went to die.

He'd heard of the Iron Triangle, of course. Everyone in the city had. It was the urban legend whispered in hushed tones by parents to warn their children, the dark smudge on the city's otherwise polished reputation. It was a district carved out of forgotten industrial land, a labyrinth of decaying factories, boarded-up tenements, and streets that seemed to bleed into one another, each one darker and more desolate than the last. It was a place where the law held little sway, a haven for the desperate, the addicted, and the criminal. It was the antithesis of everything Mike had represented to Joe, the carefree, optimistic younger brother who, despite his struggles, had always carried a flicker of light.

"The Iron Triangle?" Joe repeated, the words catching in his throat. He'd spent months chasing ghosts, sifting through the detritus of Mike's last days, but he'd always steered clear of this particular cesspool. It was too raw, too close to the bone of his worst fears. The informant's confirmation, delivered with a shrug of indifference, felt like a punch to the gut.

The informant nodded, taking a slow drag from his cigarette. "That's the word. Down by the old rail yards. You know it?"

Joe did. He'd skirted the edges of it once, on a particularly grim errand that had taken him to the city's fringes. Even from a distance, the atmosphere had been palpable – a heavy, oppressive shroud that seemed to stifle any semblance of life. He remembered the skeletal remains of factories, their broken windows like vacant eyes staring out at nothing, the pervasive stench of something foul, something metallic and decaying. It was a place that actively repelled normalcy, a district that had seemingly been designed to swallow people whole.

"I've seen it," Joe admitted, his voice tight. He couldn't bring himself to say he'd

*been* there, not in any meaningful way. He'd always maintained a safe distance, a healthy fear of what lurked within its poisoned heart. But now, the informant's words had painted a terrifyingly clear picture: Mike, his vibrant, messy, but ultimately loving brother, had likely plunged headfirst into this abyss.

"And your brother," the informant continued, his voice unnervingly calm, "he was seen asking questions in the Triangle. Asking about… certain shipments. Certain people. The kind of people who don't like outsiders poking their noses where they don't belong." He gestured with his cigarette again, a vague sweep of the hand that encompassed the entire grimy room. "He was looking for a score, maybe? Or maybe he'd stumbled onto something bigger than he could handle. In the Triangle, both usually end up the same way."

Joe's mind raced, trying to reconcile the image of his brother with the informant's grim prognosis. Mike, with his youthful exuberance and his penchant for bad decisions, but still fundamentally good at heart. Had he truly been drawn into the vortex of the Iron Triangle, into the clutches of people who dealt in vice and violence? The thought was almost unbearable. He remembered Mike's easy laughter, his terrible jokes, the way he'd always been there to pick Joe up when he stumbled. Now, that image was being overlaid with the dark, suffocating reality of the Iron Triangle.

"Shipments?" Joe asked, his voice barely above a whisper. He tried to keep his expression neutral, to project a calm he didn't feel. He needed more. He needed to understand what Mike had been involved in, what had brought him to this godforsaken corner of the city.

The informant leaned forward, his eyes, like chips of obsidian, glinting in the dim light. "Things that move in the dark, Joe. Things that keep the city running, but not the kind of things they teach you about in school. Drugs, maybe. Weapons. Or maybe something else entirely. Mike was a curious kid. And curiosity, as they say, can get you killed, especially in a place like the Triangle." He paused, letting the weight of his words settle. "He was asking about routes, about who was moving what, and more importantly, who was getting paid. That's a dangerous line of inquiry for anyone, but for someone who didn't belong… well, it's a death wish."

Joe felt a knot tighten in his stomach. He'd always known Mike had his demons, his struggles with addiction that had cast a long shadow over their lives. But this… this sounded like something far more sinister than a personal battle. This sounded like Mike had been caught in the crosshairs of organized crime, a pawn in a game he likely didn't understand.

"How do you know this?" Joe asked, his gaze locked on the informant's face, searching for any tell, any hint of a fabricated story. He'd paid enough for this information, and he wasn't about to be strung along by a con artist.

The informant offered a wry, mirthless smile. "I have… associates. People who keep their ears to the ground. The Triangle is a tight-knit community, in its own twisted way. News travels fast. And when someone like your brother starts making waves, asking questions that are none of his business, people notice. They talk. And my associates… they listen." He took a slow, deliberate sip of his drink, as if savoring the moment. "They heard Mike's name. They heard he was asking about the 'Iron Serpent' – that's what some of the players call the main distribution network in that area. And they heard he was getting too close."

The 'Iron Serpent.' The name itself was chilling, evoking an image of a vast, unseen entity, coiled and deadly, operating beneath the surface of the city. Joe felt a surge of anger, a hot, protective rage that momentarily pushed back the fear. Mike had never deserved this. He was a victim, caught in a web far larger and more dangerous than he could have ever imagined.

"Who are these people?" Joe demanded, his voice hardening. He needed names, faces, anything to latch onto. The vague descriptions, the metaphorical pronouncements, were wearing thin.

The informant held up a hand, a gesture of caution. "Names are a luxury, Joe. And in the Triangle, luxury is a concept best left at the city limits. But I can tell you this: they're the kind of people who deal in consequence. They don't leave loose ends. And if Mike was a loose end… well, you can guess what happened." He leaned back again, the worn leather of the booth groaning. "But maybe he wasn't. Maybe he saw an opportunity. Maybe he thought he could play them. In the Triangle, that's usually where the real trouble starts."

Joe's mind was a whirlwind of conflicting emotions. The informant's words painted a grim picture, a terrifying descent into a world of organized crime that felt a million miles away from the life he and Mike had shared. Yet, there was also a sliver of a possibility that his brother, in his desperation, had tried to turn the tables, to profit from the very darkness that was consuming him.

"What if he wasn't a loose end?" Joe pushed, his voice hoarse with a mixture of hope and desperation. "What if he was trying to get out? Or trying to get help?"

The informant's gaze was unblinking. "People don't just 'get out' of the Triangle, Joe. Not without paying a hefty price. And help… well, help usually comes in the form of someone looking to exploit your weakness. Mike was vulnerable. And in a place like that, vulnerability is an invitation for disaster." He crushed his cigarette out in the ashtray. "But if you're determined to go down that road, to find out what happened… you'll need to go there yourself. You'll need to ask the right questions, to the right people. And you'll need to be careful. Very careful. Because the people who operate in the Triangle… they're not forgiving."

Joe felt a wave of exhaustion wash over him, the weariness of months of fruitless searching crashing down. But beneath the exhaustion, a new resolve was hardening. He couldn't let Mike disappear into the anonymity of the Iron Triangle without a fight. He couldn't let his brother's memory be buried under the weight of a nameless crime in a forgotten district.

"How do I find these 'right people'?" Joe asked, his voice firm. He had the name of the district, the grim confirmation of where Mike's path had likely led him. Now, he needed the next step, the thread that would lead him through the maze of the Iron Triangle.

The informant gave him a look that was almost pitying. "That, my friend, is the million-dollar question. You don't just walk up to someone and ask about the 'Iron Serpent.' You gotta listen. You gotta observe. You gotta show them you're not afraid, but also that you're not stupid. There are certain… establishments, places on the fringes of the Triangle, where information might be exchanged. Bars, gambling dens, back rooms. Places that look welcoming, but aren't. Places where the veneer of normalcy is thin, and the rot underneath is palpable."

He paused, his gaze sweeping over Joe's weary face. "But you asked about the name of the neighborhood. You got it. The Iron Triangle. Now, if you want more than just a name, if you want me to give you a starting point, well, that's going to cost you. And this time," he added, his eyes narrowing, "it's going to cost you more than just cash." The implied threat, the unspoken offer of services rendered in exchange for something more significant than money, hung in the air, a chilling promise of the compromises Joe might have to make. The Iron Triangle, the name itself was a confirmation of his worst fears, and the informant's veiled pronouncements only solidified the terrifying reality that Mike's descent had led him into a world from which there was often no return. The weight of that realization settled upon Joe, heavy and suffocating, like the very air of the district he now had to confront.

## Retracing Mike's Last Steps

The informant's words, a grim echo in the cavernous silence of the bar, had branded the Iron Triangle onto Joe's consciousness. It was no longer a nebulous urban myth but a tangible destination, a foul-smelling nexus where his brother's vibrant spark had likely been extinguished. The name itself, the 'Iron Triangle,' was a suffocating blanket of dread, but it was also a thread, however thin and sharp, leading him out of the suffocating fog of not knowing. Now, the real work began, the grim, meticulous, soul-crushing task of piecing together the final days of a life he had desperately tried to save, a life that had apparently spiraled into a pit he could barely comprehend.

Joe left the bar with the informant's pronouncements ringing in his ears, the stench of stale beer and desperation clinging to him like a shroud. The city, usually a familiar tapestry of light and shadow, now seemed to pulse with a hidden, malevolent energy, a subtle hum that he'd never noticed before, but which now felt undeniably linked to the Iron Triangle. He found himself instinctively looking at the faces of passersby, wondering if any of them carried the weight of that forgotten district, if any of them were part of the unseen network the informant had so cryptically described.

His first instinct, a desperate clinging to the familiar, was to revisit the places he'd already scoured. He drove back to the cramped apartment Mike had rented, the stale air within now feeling even more oppressive, charged with the unspoken tragedy that had unfolded there. He ran his hands over the worn surfaces, searching for any new detail, any overlooked clue that the informant's words might illuminate. He pulled out the box of Mike's belongings again, sifting through the detritus of his brother's life with a renewed, almost frantic intensity. The cheap posters, the half-read books, the crumpled ramen wrappers – they were all so achingly ordinary, so utterly at odds with the dangerous underworld they now suspected him of inhabiting.

He spread out the handful of photos he had of Mike. There he was, grinning, arms slung around Joe's shoulders at a summer barbecue, his eyes bright with the easy optimism Joe had always envied. Another showed him at his college graduation, a hopeful, slightly bewildered look on his face as he clutched his diploma. Joe stared at these images, trying to reconcile the vibrant young man captured in them with the informant's description of a curious kid delving into the dangerous currents of the Iron Triangle. Had Mike's descent been gradual, a slow erosion of his youthful idealism, or had it been a sudden, catastrophic plunge? The thought of Mike, once so full of life, getting tangled in "certain shipments" and "certain people" sent a fresh wave of nausea through him.

He spent hours hunched over the few pieces of technology Mike had left behind. A battered flip phone, its battery long dead, and a cheap, prepaid laptop that had clearly seen better days. He'd already tried to access them, but without passcodes or a clear understanding of Mike's digital habits, it had been a fruitless endeavor. Now, armed with the knowledge that Mike had been asking about the "Iron Serpent," Joe approached them with a different mindset. He wasn't just looking for casual browsing history; he was searching for any flicker of communication, any encrypted message, any hint of contact with the shadowy figures operating in the Triangle.

He managed to get the phone to power on after a lengthy charge. The contact list was a familiar roll call of friends, family, and a few names he didn't recognize, some with cryptic alphanumeric identifiers. He scrolled through the call logs and text messages, his heart sinking with each passing minute. There were plenty of calls to friends, texts arranging meetups, even a few frantic messages from Joe himself during periods when Mike had gone off the grid. But nothing that directly pointed to the Iron Triangle, nothing that explicitly mentioned shipments or the Serpent. The digital breadcrumbs were sparse, and the ones that were there were maddeningly vague. He found a series of deleted texts, the timestamps suggesting they were sent in the weeks leading up to Mike's disappearance. With a surge of adrenaline, he tried to recover them, but the phone's primitive system offered little in the way of sophisticated data recovery. He managed to salvage fragments: "…meeting at…" "…need the package…" "…trust no one…" These cryptic snippets only deepened the mystery, hinting at clandestine dealings and a growing sense of paranoia.

The laptop proved to be an even tougher nut to crack. It was password-protected, and none of the usual suspects – birthdays, pet names, significant dates – worked. Joe spent a frustrating afternoon trying every combination he could think of, his frustration mounting with each failed attempt. He even tried to access the browsing history directly from the hard drive, a crude method that required him to physically connect the laptop to his own computer. The results were a jumble of sports websites, music streaming services, and a few searches for local bars and clubs. Nothing that screamed 'organized crime.' But then, buried deep within the cached files, he found a series of searches related to shipping manifests and port authority records. The searches were sporadic, spanning several weeks, and often followed by queries about specific company names that sounded vaguely industrial, names that might be fronts for illegal operations. One particular search query, flagged with a timestamp from the week before Mike vanished, simply read: "trucking companies with routes to the old shipyard." The old shipyard. Joe knew exactly where that was. It was on the periphery of the Iron Triangle, a decaying monument to the city's industrial past, now a haven for less savory activities.

He spent the next few days retracing Mike's physical steps, trying to overlay the informant's new information onto the ghost of his brother's movements. He revisited the dive bar where Mike had been seen arguing with someone a few weeks before he disappeared. This time, he didn't just ask the bartender if he'd seen Mike; he showed them a photo, pointedly asking if Mike had been seen with anyone "involved in shipping" or "talking about deliveries." The bartender, a gruff man with a permanently unimpressed expression, shook his head. "Look, pal, I told you, I see a lot of faces. If he wasn't causing trouble, I don't remember him." Joe pressed, "Did he talk about anything unusual? Anything about, say, cargo or transportation?" The bartender shrugged. "Maybe. Everyone talks about something. But nothing stuck out. He was a regular, quiet enough. Paid his tab." The lack of concrete leads was like a physical ache.

He returned to the pawn shop where Mike had reportedly sold some of his possessions to make quick cash. The owner, a wiry man with shifty eyes, was initially evasive. But when Joe mentioned the informant's description of Mike asking about "shipments," the man's demeanor shifted. He hesitated for a beat, then admitted, "Yeah, he was in here a few times. Sold a few things. Nothing unusual. He seemed… distracted, maybe. Jittery. Asked if I knew anyone who moved 'product.' I told him I just sell old electronics and guitars, man. That isn't my scene." The mention of "moving product" sent a jolt through Joe. It was more specific than just vague shipments; it hinted at drugs, or perhaps something more.

Joe also drove out to the area near the old rail yards, the heart of the informant's description of the Iron Triangle. He parked his car a few blocks away, the silence of the deserted streets punctuated only by the distant drone of traffic and the rustling of unseen vermin. The skeletal remains of factories loomed against the bruised twilight sky, their broken windows like vacant eyes staring out at a forgotten world. The air was thick with the metallic tang of decay and something else, something acrid and chemical. It was a place that seemed to actively resist any intrusion of light or life. He walked, cautiously, observing the few dilapidated buildings that still showed signs of occupancy, the shuttered storefronts bearing the faded ghosts of former businesses. He saw a few figures moving in the shadows, their movements furtive, their faces obscured by the gloom. He felt exposed, a stark anomaly in this forgotten landscape.

He found himself drawn to a small, dimly lit bar on the edge of the district, a place that looked like it had been transplanted from another, grimmer era. It was the kind of establishment the informant had vaguely alluded to, a place where the veneer of normalcy was paper-thin. The sign above the door, barely legible, read "The Rusty Anchor." The air inside was thick with cigarette smoke and the cloying scent of cheap whiskey. A handful of patrons, mostly men with weathered faces and hard eyes, nursed their drinks in silence, their conversations hushed and guarded. Joe slid into a booth at the back, ordering a beer he didn't want, and began to observe. He scanned the room, his gaze lingering on the faces, searching for any flicker of recognition, any hint that Mike had been here, or that anyone here knew something about him.

He noticed a man at the bar, his back to Joe, who seemed to be the center of a quiet, almost imperceptible buzz. The man was talking to the bartender, his voice low but animated. Joe strained to listen, catching only fragments. "…the usual route… no hiccups… but the new consignment…" Joe's heart pounded. "Consignment" was another word that fit the informant's narrative. He watched as the bartender nodded, his expression unreadable. Joe made a mental note of the man's rough appearance – dark hair, a scar above his left eyebrow. He looked like the type who wouldn't shy away from asking tough questions, or from giving them.

He stayed for another hour, nursing his beer, feeling the oppressive atmosphere of the place seep into his bones. He saw a couple of men exchange a small, wrapped package discreetly near the restrooms. He noticed a group in a corner booth engaged in what looked like a tense negotiation over a deck of cards. The Iron Triangle wasn't just a place; it was a network, a web of interactions and transactions that operated beneath the surface of the city. And Mike, in his desperation or his curiosity, had clearly stepped into its deadly embrace.

Joe's investigation was a painstaking process of elimination, of sifting through mountains of mundane details in the hope of finding one critical piece of the puzzle. He re-examined Mike's phone records, this time looking for any calls made to or received from numbers that were unknown to him, or that had been recently disconnected. He found a few such instances, short calls to numbers that were no longer in service. He tried to trace them, using online databases and public records, but the numbers were too old, too ephemeral, lost in the churn of disposable technology.

He revisited Mike's social media profiles, though he knew it was a long shot. Mike hadn't been overly active online in the months leading up to his disappearance, his posts becoming increasingly sparse and fragmented. But Joe scrolled through the comments sections of his older posts, looking for any interactions that seemed out of character, any cryptic messages that might have been overlooked. He found a few exchanges with usernames he didn't recognize, comments that were dismissive or vaguely menacing. One commenter, under the handle "Shadow Broker," had repeatedly posted cryptic warnings to Mike, telling him to "stay in his lane" and that "some doors should remain closed." The timing of these comments, appearing in the weeks before Mike's disappearance, was chilling. Joe tried to look up "Shadow Broker," but the profile was long gone, scrubbed from the digital landscape.

The informant had mentioned Mike asking about "routes" and "who was moving what." Joe tried to conceptualize this, to think like Mike might have. If Mike was looking for information, where would he get it? Who would he trust? The informant had suggested certain establishments, places on the fringes. The Rusty Anchor was one. But there had to be others. Joe started researching the history of the Iron Triangle, looking for old industrial sites, defunct warehouses, anything that might have served as a hub for illicit activities in the past. He found old newspaper articles about smuggling operations, about organized crime syndicates that had once thrived in the area. He cross-referenced these historical hotspots with the informant's vague directions, trying to map out Mike's potential movements.

He decided to focus on the old shipyard. It was a desolate, sprawling complex of decaying docks and rusting cranes, a stark reminder of a bygone era of prosperity. Joe drove there during the day, the harsh sunlight illuminating the extent of the decay. He walked through the crumbling structures, the silence broken only by the screech of gulls and the groan of stressed metal. He found evidence of recent activity – tire tracks in the mud, discarded cigarette butts, even a half-eaten sandwich on a rusty workbench. It was clear that people still used this place, perhaps for meetings, perhaps for clandestine exchanges.

He spoke to a few of the transient individuals who frequented the area, the homeless and the down-and-out who saw the shipyard as a temporary refuge. They were wary, their answers clipped and evasive. Most claimed not to have seen anything, or anyone, unusual. But one old man, his face a roadmap of hardship, spoke of seeing a young man, "looked like he had money on him, but scared too," talking to a couple of men in a beat-up panel van near one of the main loading docks a few weeks ago. The description, though vague, sent a tremor of recognition through Joe. The timing, the location, the young man's demeanor – it all fit. The old man described the panel van as nondescript, dark blue or black, but couldn't recall the license plate or any other details.

Joe realized he was essentially trying to recreate a ghost's path. Mike had been a ghost in the Iron Triangle, moving through its shadows, asking questions that were dangerous to ask. Joe's task was to become a detective of shadows, to illuminate the darkness that had swallowed his brother. The painstaking process of retracing Mike's last steps was yielding fragmented clues, whispers of movement and communication, but nothing concrete enough to grasp. The informant had given him a name, a place, a direction. Now, Joe had to find the people who inhabited that space, the ones who held the answers, the ones who were part of the deadly network that had likely claimed his brother's life. The weight of the task pressed down on him, a heavy, suffocating burden, but beneath it, a flicker of fierce determination ignited. He wouldn't stop until he found out what happened to Mike, no matter how deep into the rot he had to go.

## A Glimmer of Recognition

The Iron Triangle. The name itself had become a physical weight in Joe's chest, a dense, suffocating mass that made each breath a conscious effort. He'd walked its periphery, felt its oppressive atmosphere clinging to him like the city's perpetual grime, but now, armed with the informant's whispers, he was venturing deeper into its decaying heart. He drove slowly, the familiar urban sprawl gradually giving way to a more desolate, skeletal landscape. Dilapidated warehouses, their brickwork crumbling like ancient teeth, stood as silent sentinels to a forgotten industrial age. The air grew heavier, thick with the metallic tang of rust and the underlying, acrid stench of neglect. This was where Mike had been, where his brother's curiosity had led him, a terrifying descent into a world Joe was only beginning to comprehend.

He parked a few blocks from the main artery of the Triangle, a street that seemed to bleed the life and color from the surrounding blocks. The buildings here were a uniform shade of grim, their facades scarred by time and indifference. Graffiti, not the vibrant, artistic kind, but aggressive, territorial scrawls, marred every available surface. He stepped out of the car, the sudden silence after the engine's hum unnerving. The sounds of the city were muted here, replaced by a low, guttural hum that seemed to emanate from the very ground beneath his feet – the ceaseless, unseen activity of the Triangle. He pulled his collar up, a futile gesture against the chill that had nothing to do with the temperature.

His objective was simple, yet impossibly daunting: to find the places Mike had frequented, to see what he had seen, to feel what he had felt. The informant had spoken of specific landmarks, of a certain kind of establishment that catered to those who operated in the shadows. Joe's first stop was a corner store, a grimy, fluorescent-lit box that seemed to be perpetually half-closed, its windows opaque with dust and grime. He pushed open the door, a tinny bell announcing his arrival to an audience of one – a hunched figure behind a scratched counter, his face obscured by the low-hanging gloom. The air inside was stale, a cloying mix of cheap detergent and something vaguely unpleasant, like forgotten fruit left to rot.

Joe bought a bottle of water, the transaction silent, punctuated only by the clink of coins. He scanned the aisles, his eyes searching for any clue, any echo of Mike's presence. He saw rows of dusty canned goods, cheap cigarettes, and lottery scratch cards. It was a universal tableau of urban decay, but here, in the Triangle, it felt charged with a different kind of significance. He remembered Mike's fleeting mention of stopping at a corner store for a late-night snack, a casual detail that now resonated with a chilling familiarity. Could this be it? The vacant stare of the shopkeeper offered no answers, his eyes flicking over Joe with a practiced indifference that suggested he'd seen a thousand men like him, all searching for something that was best left unfound.

He left the store, the bell's jingle a jarring sound in the oppressive quiet. He continued his slow walk, his senses on high alert. He passed a row of apartment buildings, their fire escapes rusted and skeletal, like grasping claws against the drab brickwork. The windows were mostly dark, but here and there, he saw slivers of light, glimpses of lives lived behind drawn curtains, lives that were likely as steeped in the Triangle's grim reality as the streets themselves. He noticed one particular building, a four-story structure with peeling paint and a gaping hole where a window should have been on the third floor. A young woman, her face gaunt and her eyes hollow, stood on the stoop, staring blankly at the street. Her posture, the way she held herself – a slump of weary resignation – struck Joe with a jolt of recognition. It was the same defeated stance he'd seen in Mike in the weeks before he disappeared, that subtle but profound erosion of hope. It was a look he'd tried to fight, a look he'd desperately wanted to pull his brother back from. Was Mike's presence here the cause or the consequence of such despair?

The informant had also mentioned a specific bar, a dive that served as a waypoint for those navigating the Triangle's treacherous currents. Joe found it nestled between a boarded-up laundromat and a derelict auto repair shop. The sign, a faded neon outline of a cracked martini glass, flickered intermittently, casting a sickly green glow onto the cracked pavement. The name, "The Last Drop," was etched into the grimy glass of the door. This felt like a pivotal point, a place where connections were made, where information, or perhaps something far more dangerous, was exchanged.

He pushed open the door, the sudden influx of noise and light a harsh contrast to the street. The air inside was thick with the smell of stale beer, cheap tobacco, and something else, something vaguely metallic that Joe couldn't quite place. The lighting was dim, cast by bare bulbs and a few sputtering neon signs behind the bar. The patrons were a grim collection of faces, etched with hardship and suspicion. Men with worn leather jackets, women with eyes that had seen too much, all seemed to exist in their own private pockets of isolation within the crowded room. Joe felt like an intruder, his clean clothes and his palpable unease marking him as an outsider.

He found a stool at the far end of the bar, ordering a whiskey, his hand trembling slightly as he reached for the glass. He nursed the drink, his gaze sweeping across the room, trying to absorb every detail, every interaction. He saw men huddled in booths, their conversations conducted in hushed tones. He saw the bartender, a burly man with a shaved head and a permanent scowl, moving with practiced efficiency, his eyes missing nothing. Joe focused on his brother's memory, trying to overlay it onto the scene before him. Had Mike sat here? Had he met someone here? The informant had said Mike had been asking questions, probing the edges of the Triangle's secrets. This was the kind of place where such inquiries could be met with either information or a swift, brutal silencing.

He noticed a group of men in a corner booth, their body language tense. They were leaning in, their voices low, but Joe could sense the undercurrent of aggression. One of them, a heavily built man with a shaved head and a thick gold chain, gestured emphatically, his words lost in the ambient noise. Joe felt a prickle of unease, a primal instinct warning him to be cautious. These were not the casual drinkers he was used to seeing. These were men who belonged here, men who understood the unwritten rules of the Triangle.

He caught the bartender's eye, catching his attention with a subtle nod. "Looking for someone," Joe began, his voice carefully neutral. "Young guy, maybe mid-twenties, dark hair, usually wore a beat-up leather jacket. Name's Mike." He slid a photograph of Mike across the polished wood, a picture of his brother smiling, his eyes full of a life that seemed impossibly distant now. The bartender picked up the photo, his expression unreadable as he studied Mike's face. He held it for a long moment, his gaze drifting from the photo to Joe, then back again. The silence stretched, each tick of the bar clock amplified in Joe's ears.

Finally, the bartender grunted, a noncommittal sound. "Seen a lot of faces. This place... people come and go. They isn't always memorable." He slid the photo back, his movements casual, but Joe detected a subtle shift in his demeanor. A flicker of recognition, perhaps? Or just the practiced deflection of someone who knew how to keep his head down. "He ask about anything in particular?" Joe pressed, his voice tight with anticipation. The bartender wiped down the counter with a stained rag, his eyes still fixed on the task. "Just drinks. Like everyone else. Now, you want another one, or are you just here to ask questions?"

Joe understood. The bartender wasn't going to volunteer information. He was part of the Triangle's ecosystem, a silent observer who traded in secrets only when it served his purpose. Joe paid for his drink, his mind racing. He needed to approach this differently. He couldn't just ask direct questions; he had to be like Mike, subtly probing, looking for the cracks in the facade. He left The Last Drop, the weight of his unfulfilled quest pressing down on him.

As he walked back towards his car, he noticed a group of men gathered on a street corner, their presence casual but watchful. They were loitering, leaning against a graffiti-covered wall, their eyes scanning the sparse traffic. One of them, a man with a prominent scar across his cheek, met Joe's gaze for a moment, a flicker of something unreadable in his eyes before looking away. It was a glance that felt like an assessment, a silent question: 'Who are you, and what are you doing here?' Joe felt a prickle of unease, a sense of being observed, categorized. These were the inhabitants of the Triangle, the people who knew its rhythm, its dangers.

He found himself drawn to a derelict apartment building, its façade a canvas of decay. The informant had mentioned Mike had been seen around places like this, looking for information. Joe walked past it, peering into the dark recesses of the entranceway. The air inside was thick with the smell of damp and mildew. He saw a few shadows moving within, figures that melted back into the darkness as he approached. He recognized the same defeated energy he'd seen in the young woman on the stoop earlier, the same hollowed-out look that had become so tragically familiar. It was as if the very air of the Triangle leeched the spirit from its inhabitants.

He remembered another detail the informant had mentioned: Mike's growing paranoia, his increasing isolation. He'd withdrawn from Joe, his calls becoming shorter, his explanations more vague. Joe had attributed it to stress, to whatever personal demons his brother was battling. Now, he knew better. Mike had been entangled in something dangerous, something that had made him look over his shoulder, something that had likely led him to these very streets, these very buildings.

He drove through the neighborhood again, the layout of the streets beginning to feel disturbingly familiar. He saw a specific fire hydrant, its paint chipped and rusted, standing sentinel on a street corner. He recalled seeing it in a blurry background shot of one of Mike's earlier, more casual social media posts, a post about a spontaneous walk he'd taken. The connection was tenuous, almost absurd, but it sent a shiver down his spine. Had Mike been documenting his descent, unknowingly leaving breadcrumbs for Joe to follow?

He passed a small park, its playground equipment rusted and broken, a stark symbol of neglected childhoods. A couple of rough-looking teenagers were sitting on a bench, their faces impassive as they watched the sparse traffic. Their presence, their watchful stillness, felt out of place, almost staged. Joe felt a growing sense of dread, a chilling realization that the faces he was seeing, the places he was passing, were not just random elements of urban decay. They were nodes in a network, a network that Mike had somehow become a part of.

He saw a group of men gathered outside a dilapidated storefront, what might have once been a bakery or a butcher shop, now sealed with corrugated metal. They were talking amongst themselves, their voices low and conspiratorial. As Joe drove by, one of them turned his head, his gaze locking with Joe's for a brief, intense moment. There was no animosity in the look, no overt threat, but there was an undeniable recognition, a silent acknowledgment of Joe's presence as an outsider in their territory. It was a look that said, 'We see you. We know you don't belong.'

The entire neighborhood seemed to pulse with a hidden current, a silent undercurrent of activity that Joe was only just beginning to perceive. The informant's words, once vague and cryptic, were now coalescing into a tangible, terrifying reality. The Iron Triangle wasn't just a geographical location; it was a state of being, a world unto itself, and Mike, in his quest for something, had stepped into its suffocating embrace. Joe felt a growing certainty, a cold, hard knot in his stomach. He was on the right track. He was seeing what Mike had seen, walking where Mike had walked, and the disturbing familiarity of it all was both terrifying and galvanizing. He wasn't just looking for a missing brother; he was uncovering a truth, a dark, twisted truth that was slowly, inexorably, revealing itself to him in the desolate streets of the Iron Triangle. He gripped the steering wheel tighter, his knuckles white. He had to keep going, had to push deeper into this suffocating labyrinth, for Mike, for himself, for the answers that lay buried within the Triangle's grim embrace.

## The Inevitable Plunge

The informant's words, a patchwork of half-truths and veiled warnings, had become an insistent siren call, drawing Joe deeper into the warren of the Iron Triangle. Each snippet of information, however fragmented, was like a single thread pulled from a vast, tangled tapestry, hinting at a larger, more sinister design. He knew, with a certainty that settled cold and heavy in his gut, that stepping further into this decaying labyrinth was a gamble with his own safety. The air itself seemed to hum with unspoken threats, a palpable tension that clung to the crumbling facades and the furtive glances of the few figures he saw lurking in the shadows. Yet, the image of Mike's hopeful, then increasingly desperate, face was a constant, burning ember, igniting a resolve that flickered defiantly against the encroaching darkness. The fear was a persistent companion, a gnawing anxiety that whispered of unseen dangers, of men who operated by a different code, a code written in blood and desperation. But the need to find his brother, to unravel the mystery that had consumed him, was a force more potent than any apprehension. He straightened his shoulders, the fabric of his jacket rustling with the decisive movement, and with each measured step deeper into the heart of this forgotten district, his determination solidified. The abstract fear began to coalesce into a tangible understanding of the risks, and with that understanding came a grim acceptance. He was walking into the lion's den, armed with little more than a whispered lead and a brother's memory, but he was walking nonetheless.

He followed the informant's directions, a convoluted path that wound through narrow alleys choked with overflowing dumpsters and past the skeletal remains of abandoned vehicles. The main thoroughfare of the Triangle, which he'd glimpsed earlier, was merely a gateway; the true depth of its rot lay in these forgotten arteries. The buildings here were even more derelict, their windows boarded up or shattered, their brickwork stained with the effluence of decades of neglect. Graffiti, scrawled in thick, defiant strokes, dominated every available surface, a crude map of territorial claims and resentments. Joe kept his eyes down, his senses on high alert, trying to blend in, to become just another shadow in this already shadowy landscape. He noticed a group of men huddled in a doorway, their faces obscured by the deep recess, their conversation a low murmur that was swallowed by the general hum of the district. They didn't acknowledge him, but Joe felt their eyes on his back, a silent assessment that made the hairs on his neck prickle. He imagined Mike navigating these same desolate corridors, his curiosity a dangerous beacon in this suffocating darkness.

The informant had mentioned a specific intersection, a place where the whispers often coalesced into more concrete, albeit still dangerous, information. It was a corner where three streets converged, creating a small, desolate plaza dominated by a defunct neon sign that once advertised a long-gone pawnshop. The sign, a broken halo of flickering red, cast an intermittent, malevolent glow on the grimy asphalt. Joe reached the intersection, his heart thudding a little faster. This was it. This was the nexus, the point where the threads of Mike's disappearance seemed to converge. He stopped, feigning an interest in the crumbling façade of a building opposite the pawnshop, his gaze sweeping over the area. He saw a lone figure standing near the defunct sign, a man silhouetted against the faint light. He was nondescript, his features indistinct in the gloom, but there was an air of watchful stillness about him that drew Joe's attention. Was this the next step? Another informant? Or something more sinister?

Joe decided to approach indirectly. He crossed the street, his footsteps unnervingly loud in the stillness, and walked towards a small, shuttered newsstand a few yards away. He pretended to scan the faded advertisements plastered on its side, his peripheral vision focused on the man by the sign. The man didn't move, his posture rigid, his gaze seemingly fixed on the ground. Joe took a deep breath and stepped closer to the newsstand, his hand reaching out as if to touch one of the peeling posters. He cleared his throat, a deliberate, casual sound.

"Rough neighborhood," Joe said, his voice carefully modulated to sound weary rather than suspicious.

The man by the sign turned his head, slowly, deliberately. Joe still couldn't make out his features clearly, but he saw the glint of eyes in the faint light. The man didn't respond immediately. The silence stretched, punctuated by the distant wail of a siren, a sound that seemed to belong to another world entirely.

Finally, the man spoke, his voice a low rasp, like gravel shifting. "Depends on who you are and what you're looking for."

Joe felt a jolt of recognition, a subtle shift in the man's tone that echoed the informant's earlier words. This was it. He was being tested. "Just trying to find my way," Joe replied, keeping his tone light. "Lost my bearings a bit. This place… it's a maze."

The man chuckled, a dry, humorless sound. "That's putting it mildly. Most people don't get lost here by accident. They come here on purpose." He paused, and Joe could feel the man's gaze assessing him, dissecting him. "You don't look like you belong here. Too clean."

Joe forced a smile, a practiced ease that felt alien on his face. "Trying not to. Just a wrong turn. Heard there might be some work around here, odd jobs." He knew this was a flimsy pretext, but it was all he had. "My brother… he used to talk about this area. Said there were opportunities if you knew where to look." He risked mentioning Mike, a calculated gamble.

The man remained silent for a long moment, his stillness unnerving. Joe braced himself, wondering if he had misread the situation, if he had just stepped into a trap. Then, the man shifted his weight, his eyes briefly flicking towards Joe's face, a more direct look this time.

"Brother, huh?" the man rasped. "What kind of opportunities was he looking for?"

Joe's pulse quickened. "I don't know, exactly. He was… looking for something. Asking questions, I think. About people who… operate differently." He chose his words carefully, trying to mimic the coded language he suspected was common currency here. "Heard he might have spent some time around here."

The man let out another dry chuckle. "People ask questions all the time. Most of 'em end up learning the hard way that some doors are best left closed." He took a step closer, and Joe instinctively tensed. The man was a few inches shorter than Joe, but there was a coiled energy about him, a latent strength that suggested he was far more dangerous than his unassuming appearance implied. "What's his name?"

"Mike. Mike Davies." Joe handed the man the photograph he'd taken earlier, the one of Mike smiling, radiating a life that seemed impossibly distant now. The man took the photo, holding it carefully, his gaze fixed on Mike's face. The flickering neon sign cast shifting shadows across his features, making them impossible to discern.

The man studied the photograph for a long time, the silence stretching taut between them. Joe watched his face, searching for any sign, any flicker of recognition. It was like watching a stone statue, so devoid of expression was the man's face. Then, he handed the photograph back.

"Yeah, I might have seen him," the man said, his voice still a low rasp, but with a subtle shift in its timbre. "He was… looking for information. Asking about things he shouldn't have been." He paused, then added, almost as an afterthought, "He had a habit of talking to the wrong people."

Joe felt a surge of adrenaline, a mix of triumph and dread. He had a lead, a confirmation. Mike had been here, he had been asking questions. "The wrong people? Who are the wrong people?" Joe asked, his voice tight with urgency.

The man shook his head slowly. "That's not information I give away for free, friend. Not to someone who just wandered in off the street." He met Joe's gaze, his eyes glinting in the dim light. "You want to know more, you gotta show you're serious. You gotta show you're willing to get your hands dirty."

Joe understood. The Iron Triangle didn't offer its secrets lightly. "What do I need to do?" he asked, his voice firm.

The man gave a slow, deliberate nod. "There's a place. A backroom. Not for everyone. But if your brother was asking questions, he might have ended up there. Or someone who knows what he was looking for might be there." He gestured with his chin towards a narrow alleyway to their left, a dark chasm between two towering, derelict buildings. "You go down there. Second door on the right. Looks like nothing. But inside… inside, you might find what you're looking for."

Joe hesitated for only a moment. The informant had warned him that this part of the investigation would be dangerous, that he would have to navigate a world of suspicion and violence. He had to trust this man, or at least the information he was providing. The thought of Mike, lost and possibly in danger, propelled him forward.

"Thank you," Joe said, his voice low.

The man simply grunted, turning his back and resuming his stoic vigil by the defunct sign. Joe didn't linger. He walked towards the alleyway, the oppressive darkness seeming to swallow him whole as he entered. The air grew thick with the stench of decay and something else, something chemical and acrid. The sounds of the street faded, replaced by the drip of unseen water and the scurrying of unseen creatures. He counted the doors, his heart pounding against his ribs. One, two. He reached for the doorknob, a rusted piece of metal that felt cold and slick under his touch.

He pushed the door open, and the immediate assault on his senses was almost overwhelming. The air was thick with the smell of stale cigarettes, cheap liquor, and a pervasive dampness that clung to everything. The light was minimal, emanating from a few bare bulbs hanging precariously from the ceiling, casting long, distorted shadows. The room was small, sparsely furnished with mismatched tables and chairs, most of them scarred and stained. A few men sat at the tables, their faces impassive, their eyes betraying a weary cynicism. They didn't look up as Joe entered, but he felt their awareness of his presence, a subtle shift in the room's equilibrium.

He stood just inside the doorway, letting his eyes adjust to the gloom, trying to gauge the atmosphere. This felt different from the bar, more intimate, more clandestine. It was a place where conversations were held in hushed tones, where alliances were forged and broken in the shadows. He saw a figure emerge from a back room, a man who fit the description the informant had given of the 'gatekeeper' for this particular establishment. He was a wiry man, with sharp features and eyes that darted around the room with unnerving speed. He approached Joe, his expression unreadable.

"You lost?" the man asked, his voice smooth, almost silken, a stark contrast to the gravelly tones of the man outside.

Joe met his gaze, trying to project a confidence he didn't feel. "I'm looking for someone. My brother. Mike Davies." He repeated the name, the photograph of his brother a clear image in his mind. "He was asking questions around here. Someone said I might find information in here."

The man's eyes narrowed slightly, a flicker of something that might have been recognition. "Mike Davies," he repeated, the name rolling off his tongue with a practiced detachment. "He was asking about… certain things. Things that don't concern outsiders."

"He's my brother," Joe insisted, his voice gaining a touch of desperation. "I need to know what happened to him. He's been missing for weeks."

The man stepped closer, his voice dropping to a near whisper. "This is not a place for family reunions. This is a place for business. And Mike Davies was dabbling in business that was far too dangerous for him." He looked Joe up and down, his gaze lingering on Joe's clean clothes, his unscarred hands. "You don't look like the type to ask these kinds of questions. You look like you have a life, a good one. You should turn around and go back to it."

Joe's jaw tightened. "I can't. I won't. Whatever he was involved in, I need to understand it. I need to find him." He took a step forward, his resolve hardening. "Tell me what you know."

The man smiled, a thin, humorless baring of teeth. "Knowledge has a price. And the price for what Mike was digging into… it's steep. It's not just money. It's loyalty. It's about knowing when to keep your mouth shut and when to speak. And it's about knowing who to trust." He paused, his eyes locking with Joe's. "Are you ready to pay that price?"

Joe looked around the dimly lit room, at the shadowy figures at the tables, at the man before him who held the keys to whatever twisted world his brother had stumbled into. He thought of Mike's last voicemail, the fear in his voice, the urgent plea for help that had come too late. The fear was still there, a cold knot in his stomach, but it was now overshadowed by a burning need for answers, a desperate hope of finding his brother alive. He knew he was stepping further into the darkness, further from the life he knew, but he had already committed himself.

"Yes," Joe said, his voice firm, cutting through the oppressive silence of the room. "I'm ready."

The man's smile widened, a predatory gleam in his eyes. "Good. Because Mike… he didn't just disappear. He got tangled. And the deeper you dig, the more tangled you'll become. Welcome to the Iron Triangle." He gestured towards a door at the back of the room, a door that was slightly ajar, revealing a sliver of even deeper darkness beyond. "Your brother's story starts behind that door."

# Chapter Six
# Into the Lion's Den

## The Atmosphere of Fear

The air in the Iron Triangle was a physical weight, pressing down on Joe's chest, making each breath a conscious effort. It wasn't just the stagnant, cloying smell of decay, of damp rot and unseen waste, that choked him. It was the palpable tension, a silent, unseen current that ran through the very marrow of this place. Every boarded-up window was a blind eye, every patch of peeling paint a scar that spoke of neglect and something far more sinister. Graffiti, a chaotic tapestry of defiant slogans and territorial claims, bled across brickwork and corrugated iron, a visual cacophony that mirrored the unseen disharmony of the district. Joe felt it like a physical touch, a constant, unnerving awareness that he was an intruder, a foreigner in a land where the rules of engagement were written in a language he was still struggling to comprehend.

His own presence here felt like a glaring anomaly. His clothes, though rumpled from the journey, were still too clean, too new. His gait, though he tried to mimic the hesitant shuffle of the few other figures he'd seen, was probably too purposeful. He was a bright splash of color in a palette of muted greys and browns, a discordant note in a symphony of hushed desperation. Each passerby, a ghost in the periphery, seemed to hold a silent judgment, their furtive glances not necessarily hostile, but laced with a deep-seated caution that spoke volumes. They moved with a practiced economy of motion, their eyes constantly scanning, assessing, calculating. Joe found himself doing the same, his senses on hyperdrive, trying to decipher the subtle cues, the unspoken warnings that seemed to hang in the very air.

He saw them then, a small knot of men loitering in a recessed doorway, their faces obscured by the deep shadow cast by an overhanging, crumbling cornice. They weren't engaged in conversation, their stillness more unsettling than any boisterous activity might have been. Their stillness was a predator's stillness, a patient waiting that sent a shiver down Joe's spine. He averted his gaze, forcing himself to focus on the cracked pavement ahead, on the overflowing bin that spilled its foul contents onto the already stained concrete. He imagined Mike, his brother, his eager, inquisitive brother, walking through these same streets, his youthful optimism a beacon in this suffocating gloom. Had he felt this same prickle of unease? Had he recognized the danger, or had it simply enveloped him, a slow, insidious trap?

The informant had described the Iron Triangle as a place that "grinds you down," and Joe was beginning to understand what he meant. It wasn't just the physical decay, the crumbling infrastructure, the pervasive smell of neglect. It was the psychological erosion, the constant drip-drip-drip of apprehension that wore away at a person's resolve. Every shadow seemed to stretch and writhe with imagined threats, every distant sound – a car backfiring, a dog barking, a siren wailing somewhere in the vast, indifferent city – was amplified, distorted, imbued with a sinister significance. Joe found himself jumping at his own shadow, his muscles tensed, his breath catching in his throat at the slightest provocation. He was a tightly wound spring, ready to snap, his every nerve ending screaming a silent warning.

He reached the intersection the informant had spoken of, the desolate plaza dominated by the skeletal remains of a neon sign. The faded red lettering, advertising a long-forgotten pawnshop, flickered intermittently, casting an eerie, disjointed glow on the grimy asphalt. It was a morbid beacon, a dying ember in the heart of this forgotten district. Joe stopped, feigning an interest in the grimy storefront across the plaza, his peripheral vision a wide-angle lens capturing every movement, every subtle shift in the oppressive atmosphere. He saw him then, the solitary figure by the defunct sign, a silhouette against the weak, intermittent light. The man's stillness was unnerving, a watchful calm that contrasted sharply with the general air of furtive unease that permeated the Triangle. He was a statue carved from shadow, his presence radiating a quiet authority, an unspoken understanding of the rules of this grim domain.

Joe knew, with a chilling certainty, that this was his next contact. The informant had promised a stepping stone, and this man, with his unnerving stillness, looked every bit the part. He was an enigma, his features lost in the gloom, but his posture, the way he held himself, spoke of a coiled readiness, of a man who belonged in this place, who understood its language. Joe's heart hammered a frantic rhythm against his ribs, a drumbeat of fear and anticipation. He had to approach, but how? A direct confrontation felt too risky, too likely to provoke suspicion. He needed to play the part, to be just another lost soul in this labyrinthine district, even as his every instinct screamed at him to be cautious, to be prepared for anything. The fear was a cold, creeping tide, but beneath it, a flicker of grim determination was starting to burn. He was closer now, closer to finding out what had happened to Mike. He just had to navigate this treacherous path, one careful step at a time. The Iron Triangle was a lion's den, and he was about to step deeper into its maw.

## Asking the Unspoken Questions

The solitary figure by the defunct neon sign remained an unmoving sentinel, an island of stillness in the restless tide of the Iron Triangle. Joe's gaze flickered from the man to the ground, his hands shoved deep into his pockets, mimicking the posture of someone lost, or perhaps waiting for a different kind of transaction. He couldn't just walk up and ask about Mike. The informant's warning, delivered in a hushed, raspy whisper, echoed in his mind: "They don't talk. Not to strangers. Not to anyone who isn't part of the fabric."

Joe took a deep, steadying breath, the acrid air doing little to calm his nerves. He needed to be subtle, to weave his questions into the existing tapestry of conversation, or lack thereof. He started by observing. The man by the sign was a study in quiet vigilance. His coat was dark, nondescript, blending with the encroaching dusk. His face, when he turned it slightly, was a map of hard living, etched with lines that spoke of sleepless nights and grim decisions. Joe saw no overt threat, but there was an undeniable aura of capability, a coiled watchfulness that suggested this wasn't a man to be trifled with.

He moved away from the plaza, his footsteps unnaturally loud on the broken concrete. He passed a small, grimy storefront, its windows plastered with faded posters advertising long-gone music acts. A man sat slumped on a stool just inside, nursing a dark liquid in a thick glass, his eyes fixed on nothing in particular. Joe paused, feigning interest in the peeling paint of the shop front. He considered approaching, but the man exuded an aura of profound disinterest, a man who had seen too much to be bothered by anything new.

Instead, Joe gravitated towards a narrow alleyway where two figures stood hunched over, their heads bent close, engaged in what looked like a hushed, urgent exchange. Their voices were low murmurs, swallowed by the general hum of the district. Joe slowed his pace, his ears straining. He couldn't make out words, but the body language was clear: furtive, secretive. This was the kind of interaction the informant had warned him about – the whispered dealings that formed the invisible currency of the Iron Triangle.

He decided to try a different tack. He saw a woman with a shopping trolley, overflowing with plastic bags, making her way slowly down the street. Her face was gaunt, her eyes hollow, but there was a resilience in her determined stride. Joe fell into step a respectful distance behind her, his own pace mirroring hers. He waited until she stopped to adjust a precariously balanced bag.

"Excuse me," Joe began, his voice intentionally softer, less intrusive. "I'm looking for someone. My brother. His name is Mike. Have you, by any chance, seen him around here?"

The woman's head snapped up, her eyes, previously dull, now sharpened with suspicion. Her gaze swept over Joe, taking in his slightly out-of-place attire, his general air of being an outsider. A flicker of something – annoyance, perhaps, or a deep-seated weariness – crossed her face.

"Mike?" she echoed, her voice gravelly. She didn't answer the question directly. Instead, she tightened her grip on the trolley handle. "This isn't a place for looking for lost brothers, mister. This is a place where things get lost, and they tend to stay lost."

Her words were a wall, a polite but firm dismissal. Joe sensed that pushing further would be met with an even greater wall of silence. He offered a small, apologetic smile. "I understand. It's just… he might have gotten mixed up in something. He's not from around here."

The woman gave a short, sharp laugh that held no humor. "Nobody's really *from* here, mister. We all just end up here." She gave her trolley a decisive tug and resumed her slow, steady progress, leaving Joe standing alone once more, the weight of her words settling upon him. "Things get lost."

He watched her go, a knot of unease tightening in his stomach. The silence wasn't just a lack of noise; it was an active participation in the district's secret-keeping. It was a shield, a defense mechanism against the intrusion of the outside world. Every averted gaze, every curt reply, was a brick in the wall that separated the inhabitants of the Iron Triangle from those who sought to understand it.

Joe moved on, his strategy shifting. Direct questions were a dead end. He needed to become an observer, a silent witness. He found a relatively clean bench on a wider street, a place where he could watch the ebb and flow of the district's inhabitants without appearing too conspicuous. He saw men in worn work clothes heading home, their faces etched with fatigue. He saw women with children, their expressions a mix of worry and determination. And he saw the others, the ones who seemed to exist in the shadows, their movements fluid and unhurried, their eyes holding a different kind of awareness.

He noticed a small group gathered near a corner shop, their conversation a low rumble that periodically punctuated by sharp bursts of laughter. They seemed more relaxed than the others, more at ease with their surroundings. Joe decided to approach, but not with a direct question. He waited until he was closer, then deliberately stumbled, catching himself on a nearby lamppost.

"Whoops, nearly took a tumble there," he muttered, more to himself than anyone else, but loud enough to be heard. He then turned to the group, a rueful smile on his face. "This pavement's a real hazard, isn't it?"

One of the men, a burly individual with a grizzled beard and tattoos snaking up his arms, turned a quizzical eye on Joe. "You isn't from around here, are you?" It wasn't a question that demanded an answer.

"Just passing through," Joe replied, keeping his tone light. "Trying to get my bearings. It's quite a maze, this place." He paused, then added, as if a thought had just occurred to him, "Actually, while I'm here, I was wondering if anyone's seen a young bloke. Bit of a dreamer, my brother. Goes by the name Mike. Bit too curious for his own good, if I'm honest."

The burly man's expression didn't change. He looked at Joe for a long moment, his gaze assessing. Then, he turned back to his companions, resuming their conversation as if Joe had never spoken. The silence that followed was deafening, more so than the outright refusal from the woman with the trolley. This was a different kind of dismissal – one of complete erasure. Joe was invisible, his words meaningless.

He felt a surge of frustration, a primal urge to grab someone, to shake them until the information spilled out. But he knew that would be his undoing. He forced himself to breathe, to acknowledge the futility of his approach. He was an outsider, speaking a different language, even when he thought he was speaking their words.

He retreated, his mind working furiously. The informant had mentioned a bar, "The Rusty Mug," a place where "deals got made and secrets got spilled, if you knew who to ask." It was a long shot, but it was the only lead he had left in this immediate vicinity. He walked in the direction he'd been told, the Iron Triangle unfolding before him in ever-more-intricate patterns of decay and desperation.

The Rusty Mug was exactly as described – a low-slung building with a flickering neon sign that seemed to hum with a life of its own, casting an unhealthy orange glow on the surrounding grimy brickwork. Inside, the air was thick with the smell of stale beer, cheap tobacco, and something vaguely metallic, like old blood. The patrons were a mixed bag, but all bore the unmistakable stamp of the district. Joe's entrance caused a ripple of mild interest, quickly subsiding as he found a seat at the far end of the bar, away from the main cluster of activity.

The bartender, a hulking man with a shaved head and a scarred eyebrow, wiped down the counter with a slow, deliberate motion. He didn't greet Joe, but his eyes, when they met Joe's in the grimy mirror behind the bar, held a silent question. Joe ordered a whiskey, his voice deliberately low.

"Rough night?" the bartender grunted, sliding the glass across the counter.

"Just trying to navigate," Joe replied, taking a sip of the harsh liquid. It burned its way down, but it was a welcome distraction from the gnawing anxiety. He waited for a beat, then, keeping his voice casual, he asked, "I'm looking for information, really. About someone. My brother, Mike. He's… he was looking for work. Might have passed through here."

The bartender's hand paused in its wiping motion. His eyes narrowed slightly, but his expression remained impassive. He gave a slow shake of his head. "This isn't a job agency, pal. People come and go. Don't keep tabs."

Joe felt a familiar prickle of frustration, but he held it in check. He tried a different approach, one that was more about observation than direct questioning. He looked around the bar, letting his gaze linger on a few of the more hardened-looking patrons. He saw one man, nursing a drink alone at a table, his face half-hidden by the brim of a worn cap. There was something about his stillness, his guarded posture, that drew Joe's attention. He reminded Joe of the man by the defunct sign earlier.

Joe finished his drink, the burn of the whiskey doing little to alleviate the cold dread in his gut. He still hadn't learned anything substantial about Mike. He had only confirmed what he already suspected: the Iron Triangle was a place of omerta, a community bound by unspoken rules of silence. He needed to dig deeper, to find a crack in the facade, a chink in the armor of their collective discretion. He left the Rusty Mug, the oppressive atmosphere of the Iron Triangle seeping into him, a persistent, unwelcome guest. The night was young, and his search for answers had only just begun. He knew he couldn't afford to be discouraged. Mike wouldn't be. Joe's resolve hardened with each unanswered question, each averted gaze. He had to keep going. He had to find out what happened to his brother, no matter how deep into the lion's den he had to venture. The unspoken questions were the loudest, and Joe was learning to listen to their silence. He knew that somewhere within this maze of decay and distrust, a flicker of truth lay hidden, waiting for someone persistent enough to uncover it. He just hoped he was that someone. The weight of the Iron Triangle pressed down on him, but he refused to buckle. He would find a way to ask the unspoken questions, and he would find a way to hear the answers, even if they were whispered in the darkness.

## Encountering Familiar Faces

The Iron Triangle was a notoriously tight-lipped place, a labyrinth of suspicion where trust was a currency rarer than clean water. Joe had walked into this territory armed with little more than a gnawing worry and a name. His initial attempts at inquiry had been met with the impenetrable wall of the district's silence, a collective shrug that spoke volumes about their reluctance to engage with outsiders. He'd learned to read the subtle cues: the quickening of a pace, the averted gaze, the curt dismissal that was more eloquent than any shouted refusal. Now, however, a new strategy was forming, born from the sheer necessity of his mission. He wasn't looking for casual conversation anymore; he was looking for patterns, for the tell-tale signs of those who operated within the district's underbelly, the very individuals his informant, a ghost himself, had warned him about.

He'd been told to look for the 'made men,' the guys who weren't just users or low-level runners, but those who had carved out their own small empires within the sprawling mess of the Iron Triangle. These were the ones who knew things, the ones who, if approached correctly, might offer a sliver of information. Joe hadn't seen them yet, not clearly. He'd seen faces that hinted at a harder life, eyes that held a dangerous glint, but nothing concrete, no definitive markers that screamed 'dealer,' 'enforcer,' or 'kingpin.' He was still sifting through the noise, trying to isolate the signal.

He found himself drifting towards a small, open-air market that had sprung up between two derelict buildings. It wasn't a place for fresh produce; rather, it was a swap meet for the district's detritus. Stolen electronics, dubious pharmaceuticals, and a general assortment of goods that had clearly passed through many hands were laid out on stained blankets and upturned crates. It was here, amidst the haggling and the hushed transactions, that Joe's informant's descriptions began to coalesce into recognizable figures.

The first one he saw was a man the informant had called 'Silas.' Silas was described as being stocky, with a perpetual sneer and a habit of fiddling with a cheap, silver chain around his neck. Joe spotted him arguing with a younger, wiry individual over what looked like a bundle of sealed plastic baggies. Silas's voice was low, a gravelly growl that carried an undercurrent of menace, even when discussing what appeared to be a petty dispute. He had a scar that ran from his left eyebrow down to his cheekbone, a stark white line against his olive skin. Joe had seen that scar in a mental snapshot provided by his informant, a quick sketch of a face that held no compassion. Silas's hands, thick and calloused, gestured aggressively, and Joe watched as the younger man eventually relented, shoving the baggies into his own pocket and disappearing into the crowd. Silas, unmoved, resumed his casual surveying of the market, his eyes scanning the faces that passed, a predator's awareness in every flick of his gaze. Joe felt a knot of apprehension tighten in his gut. This was the kind of power his informant had warned him about – the quiet authority wielded by those who profited from the district's despair.

He didn't approach Silas directly. That would be a rookie mistake, a surefire way to end up like the countless other lost souls he'd glimpsed in this neighborhood. Instead, Joe melted back into the flow of the market, his eyes now searching for other familiar specters. He'd been given names, but more importantly, he'd been given archetypes, behavioral patterns that acted as signposts. He was looking for the subtle indicators of command, the subtle ways these individuals differentiated themselves from the flotsam and jetsam of the Iron Triangle.

Then he saw her. 'Lola.' The informant had described her as a woman who moved with an almost predatory grace, her presence commanding attention even when she said nothing. She was younger than Silas, perhaps in her late twenties, with sharp features and eyes that seemed to miss nothing. She was dressed in a way that was subtly out of sync with the general attire of the district – a fitted leather jacket, dark jeans, and boots that looked too expensive for this environment. Lola was surrounded by a small entourage, two burly men who stood guard on either side of her, their faces impassive, their stances radiating a quiet threat. She was engaged in conversation with a man who looked desperate, his hands clasped tightly in front of him as he pleaded his case. Lola listened, her head tilted slightly, an expression of cool appraisal on her face. Joe caught snippets of their exchange, words like "payment," "short," and "consequences." Lola didn't raise her voice; her authority was conveyed through a steely calm, a measured tone that brooked no argument. When the man finally nodded, a look of defeated resignation on his face, Lola gave a curt nod to one of her guards, who then produced a small, unmarked vial from his pocket and handed it to the supplicant. Joe watched the transaction unfold with a growing sense of dread. This wasn't just about drugs; it was about control, about the systematic exploitation of vulnerability.

He continued his silent observation, his senses on high alert. The Iron Triangle was a dense ecosystem, and he was beginning to discern the apex predators. He saw a man known only as 'The Professor,' a nickname earned for his meticulous approach to his illicit trade. The Professor wasn't physically imposing, but his reputation preceded him. He was said to be the source of the purer, more potent strains of whatever was circulating in the district. Joe spotted him standing near a stall selling chipped ceramic figurines, seemingly examining a faded Madonna with a critical eye. The Professor was older, his greying hair thinning on top, but his eyes, sharp and intelligent, darted constantly, taking in everything. He wore a worn tweed jacket, a stark contrast to the utilitarian clothing of most of the people around him. He wasn't dealing directly, not in the open. Instead, he was engaged in what appeared to be a low-voiced conversation with a man who was clearly one of his distributors, a man Joe recognized from a previous brief encounter – the one who had practically ignored him when he'd asked about Mike. The distributor, a wiry man with greasy hair and a nervous twitch, kept glancing over his shoulder. The Professor, meanwhile, remained unnervingly calm, his hands clasped behind his back, the picture of detached intellectualism even in this den of desperation.

Joe felt a chill creep up his spine. These were the people who would know about Mike, or at least about what happened to him. They were the ones who held the threads of the district's economy, the ones whose decisions dictated the lives and deaths within these grimy streets. Their presence was a constant, unsettling reminder of the pervasive nature of the drug trade, a web that ensnared everyone, from the hardened dealers to the desperate users. He saw the reflection of their trade in the vacant stares of passersby, in the hunched shoulders of those who shuffled through the streets, their lives reduced to the pursuit of the next fix. It was a grim, suffocating tableau, and the faces of Silas, Lola, and The Professor were the key players in this tragic drama.

He needed to find a way to approach them, to extract information without becoming a target himself. His informant had

provided a crucial piece of advice: "They respect strength, but they despise weakness. And they
*never* want to be seen as needing help. If you go to them, you go as an equal, or better yet, as someone who *has* something they want." Joe didn't have drugs or money to offer. What did he have? He had a story, a reason for being there that was rooted in his own desperate search.

He noticed Silas moving away from the market, heading towards a more secluded alleyway that ran between a boarded-up pawn shop and a crumbling apartment building. The alley was dark, its entrance partially obscured by overflowing dumpsters. This was clearly Silas's territory, a place where he could conduct business away from the prying eyes of the general populace. Joe's heart pounded in his chest. This was it. A chance to get closer, to observe, perhaps even to engage.

He waited for a few minutes, letting Silas disappear into the gloom. Then, taking a deep breath, Joe began to walk towards the alley. He kept his movements casual, his gaze fixed on the cracked pavement in front of him, as if he were simply navigating the treacherous terrain. He reached the mouth of the alley and paused, peering into the shadows. He could hear the low murmur of voices, Silas speaking to someone.

He edged further in, his senses on high alert. The stench of decay was stronger here, mingling with the sharp, chemical odor of something burning. He hugged the wall, his body tensed, ready to retreat or defend. He could now see Silas standing with another man, a gaunt figure whose skeletal frame and sunken eyes screamed addiction. The man was clearly agitated, his hands trembling as he reached out towards Silas.

"Just give me what I need, Silas," the gaunt man pleaded, his voice reedy and desperate. "Just a little bit. I'll get you the money, I swear."

Silas chuckled, a harsh, guttural sound. "You always swear, Benny. And you always come up short. What makes you think tonight's any different?" He gestured with his chin towards the baggies he held. "These isn't for promises, Benny. They're for cash. Cold, hard cash."

Benny fumbled in his pockets, producing a few crumpled bills. Silas barely glanced at them before sneering. "That won't even buy you a sniff. You owe me. And you owe me big."

Joe watched, his own desperation a mirror to Benny's. He saw the subtle shift in Silas's posture as Benny continued to beg, a slight straightening of the shoulders, a tightening of the jaw. It was a display of dominance, a ritual of power. Benny eventually broke down, tears streaking through the grime on his face, pleading for just one hit, just enough to take the edge off. Silas, unmoved, finally tossed him a single, small packet, a gesture of almost cruel magnanimity. "Don't let me see your face again until you've got what I'm owed," Silas growled, turning his back on the grateful, yet still utterly broken, Benny.

As Silas began to walk further down the alley, Joe saw his opportunity. He stepped out from his hiding place, deliberately making a slight noise as his shoe scraped against loose gravel. Silas stopped, his head snapping around, his eyes narrowing in the dim light. He didn't see Joe clearly at first, just a silhouette emerging from the shadows.

"Who's there?" Silas's voice was a low growl, laced with suspicion.

Joe emerged fully into view, keeping his hands visible and his posture non-threatening. "Just passing through," he said, his voice deliberately calm. "Didn't mean to intrude."

Silas took a step back, his body tensing, his eyes now fixed on Joe with a predator's calculation. He was assessing the threat, his mind already running through potential scenarios. "You're not from around here," Silas stated, his tone flat, accusatory. It wasn't a question.

"No," Joe admitted, keeping his gaze steady. "I'm looking for someone. My brother. Name's Mike. He's… he's been missing for a few days. Last I heard, he might have been headed this way, looking for work." He paused, then added, a touch of weariness in his voice, "He's not the most street-smart, my brother."

Silas's expression remained unreadable, but Joe detected a subtle shift in his posture, a loosening of the coiled tension. He was no longer purely defensive; he was evaluating. "Mike, huh?" Silas repeated, the name rolling off his tongue like a foreign object. "Ain't heard that name. Lots of guys looking for work around here. Most of 'em end up finding something they didn't bargain for." He took a step closer, his eyes scanning Joe's face. "You looking for trouble, or just answers?"

Joe met his gaze, his own eyes holding a quiet determination. "Just answers," he replied. "And if I find trouble, I'll deal with it." He decided to risk a more direct question, a calculated gamble. "He might have gotten involved with something… dangerous. You know, drugs, that sort of thing. Wouldn't be the first time he'd made bad choices."

Silas let out a short, rasping laugh. "Drugs are the only currency some people understand around here, pal. So yeah, chances are he got involved. Whether he's still breathing because of it, that's another question entirely." He paused, his gaze lingering on Joe's face, a flicker of something unreadable in his eyes. "You got anything to offer me for my time and information? 'Cause my memory isn't free."

Joe's mind raced. He didn't have money, but he had something else. His informant had also mentioned Silas had a penchant for rare, vintage vinyl records, a surprising hobby for a man of his profession. Joe had a hunch, a shot in the dark. "I might have something," Joe said, his voice carefully neutral. "Something that might interest you. I'm a collector, of sorts." He decided to play it coy. "Heard you have an ear for good music."

Silas's eyes narrowed slightly, a spark of curiosity igniting in their depths. "What kind of music?" he asked, his tone shifting, becoming marginally less hostile.

"The kind that tells a story," Joe replied, sensing he might have struck a nerve. "The kind that's hard to find." He decided to press his advantage, carefully. "Heard you might be the man to ask about certain… transactions. Not just the ones you're famous for, but maybe other kinds of exchanges, too. Information for… favors."

Silas stared at Joe for a long moment, his gaze piercing, trying to decipher Joe's intentions, his capabilities. The gaunt man, Benny, had long since stumbled away, a ghost consumed by his addiction. The alley was now just the two of them, the oppressive silence broken only by the distant hum of the city. Joe felt the weight of Silas's scrutiny, the unspoken challenge hanging in the air. This was the critical juncture, the moment when his approach would either lead to a breakthrough or a dead end, or worse. The Iron Triangle was a place where missteps had severe consequences, and Joe knew he was walking a razor's edge. He could feel the eyes of Silas on him, reading him, judging him, and for the first time since entering this grim district, Joe felt a cold dread that had nothing to do with his brother and everything to do with the man standing before him. He had encountered a familiar face, and now he had to navigate the treacherous currents of its acquaintance.

## A Glimpse of the Past

The alley, once a conduit to the elusive Silas, had proven to be a dead end, at least for now. Silas had offered no concrete information about Mike, only veiled threats and a dismissive wave of his hand that clearly communicated Joe's presence was no longer welcome. Joe had retreated, the acrid smell of desperation clinging to him like the city's perpetual grime. He was back in the labyrinth, the silence of the Iron Triangle as oppressive as ever. He'd learned that approaching these individuals directly, armed with nothing but a worried brother's plea, was akin to walking into a bear's den with a butter knife. Respect, his informant had stressed, was earned, not demanded. And in this place, respect often came in the form of leverage, of shared interests, or of a shared history. Joe had neither.

He found himself drifting, the initial surge of adrenaline from his encounter with Silas giving way to a dull ache of frustration. The afternoon sun, what little of it managed to pierce the smog-choked sky, cast long, distorted shadows that seemed to writhe with unspoken histories. He passed boarded-up storefronts, their windows clouded with neglect, and apartment buildings that sagged under the weight of their own decay, their brickwork stained with years of rain and pollution. The air was thick with the metallic tang of exhaust fumes and a pervasive, underlying odor of damp concrete and something vaguely organic, like overripe fruit left to rot.

His informant had mentioned a place, a bar called 'The Rusty Mug,' describing it as a neutral ground, a place where people came to forget, to connect, or to conduct business away from the harsh glare of the street. It was a hub, he'd said, a place where the threads of the Iron Triangle's operations often converged. Joe hadn't seen it yet, but the description had lodged itself in his mind, a potential anchor in the swirling chaos of the district.

He rounded a corner, the street opening up slightly into a small, grimy square. And there it was. The Rusty Mug. The sign above the door was faded, the once-bold lettering now a ghost of its former self, scratched and peeling. The building itself was a hulking, low-slung structure, its brick facade blackened with soot, the windows dark and opaque, like vacant eyes. A few neon beer signs flickered weakly behind the glass, casting an eerie, intermittent glow. The entrance was a heavy, scarred wooden door, its paint long since surrendered to the elements. The air around it hummed with a low, constant thrum, a mixture of distant traffic noise and the muffled sounds emanating from within.

Joe hesitated for a moment, a familiar knot of apprehension tightening in his stomach. This was it. The den. The place where the whispers turned into conversations, where the solitary predators sometimes congregated. His informant had advised caution, had warned him that while The Rusty Mug was a nexus, it was also a place where you could easily become a target if you weren't careful. "They don't like strangers asking too many questions," he'd said. "Especially not about things that don't concern them."

He took a deep breath, steeling himself. He wasn't here for casual observation anymore. He was on a mission, and every day that passed without a trace of Mike was a day lost. He pushed the door open, the hinges groaning in protest, and stepped inside.

The immediate impression was one of sensory overload, a jarring assault on the senses after the relative quiet of the street. The air was thick with the cloying haze of stale cigarette smoke, so dense it seemed to coat the back of his throat. Dim, yellow light emanated from a few bare bulbs hanging from the ceiling, casting long, dancing shadows that distorted the faces of the patrons. The dominant color scheme was a depressing palette of worn wood, chipped linoleum, and peeling paint, all contributing to an atmosphere of pervasive neglect. The low murmur of conversation was punctuated by the occasional raucous laugh, the clink of glasses, and the tinny, distorted wail of a blues song from a poorly maintained jukebox in the corner.

The bar itself was a long, dark expanse of polished wood, scarred with countless rings from spilled drinks and the careless placement of glasses. Behind it, a harried-looking bartender, his apron stained and his eyes weary, moved with practiced efficiency, slinging drinks with a speed born of long hours and a clientele that rarely waited patiently.

Joe scanned the room, his eyes darting from face to face. The patrons were a motley crew, a cross-section of the Iron Triangle's inhabitants. There were men in work-worn clothes, their faces etched with fatigue and hard living. There were younger men, their eyes darting nervously, their postures coiled with an almost animalistic tension. And there were women, some sitting alone at tables, their expressions unreadable, others huddled in conversation with the men, their laughter sharp and brittle. The overall impression was one of weariness, of lives lived on the fringes, where the pursuit of solace, however fleeting, was a constant endeavor.

He'd been warned about looking too obviously like he was searching, like an outsider on the prowl. So, he affected an air of casual indifference, walking towards the bar and sliding onto a stool, his gaze sweeping over the room without lingering. He ordered a whiskey, the cheapest available, and nursed it slowly, his senses still on high alert, absorbing the ambient details of the establishment.

He noticed several small groups clustered at tables, their conversations hushed and intense. He saw men whose faces bore the tell-tale signs of having spent too much time in the sun and too much time making bad decisions, their skin leathery and their eyes clouded. He saw younger men, their swagger a thin veneer over a palpable nervousness, their hands always in motion, fiddling with a cigarette, tapping a glass, or running a hand through their hair.

Then, his gaze snagged on a table in the far corner, partially obscured by a pillar. It was a group of men, perhaps four or five, all with the hard, weathered faces that Joe was beginning to associate with the district's more entrenched operators. They were laughing, their voices low and rough, and their attention was focused on one of their number, a man who was gesturing animatedly.

Something about the man's build, the way he held himself, struck a chord of recognition deep within Joe. It was a fleeting impression, a ghost of a memory, but it sent a jolt of adrenaline through his system, momentarily eclipsing the weariness and the gnawing anxiety. He squinted, trying to get a clearer view through the smoky haze. The man was speaking, his head tilted, his hand occasionally reaching for a glass of amber liquid. Joe couldn't make out his features clearly, not from this distance, not through the oppressive atmosphere of the bar. But there was a familiar intensity in his posture, a certain way he seemed to command the attention of the others, that resonated with something he knew, something he desperately wanted to be true.

Could it be? Was it Mike? The thought was a desperate, fragile thing, easily crushed by the harsh realities of this place. Mike had been struggling, yes. He'd fallen into bad company, made poor choices. But this… this was a level of grit, of hardness, that Joe hadn't fully grasped until he'd stepped into the Iron Triangle. Could his brother have truly become one of *them*?

He held his breath, trying to focus, to discern any distinguishing marks, any familiar gesture. The man's face was in profile, and the lighting was terrible, but there was a set to his jaw, a slight curve to his brow, that was unsettlingly familiar. Joe's heart pounded against his ribs, a frantic drumbeat against the dull roar of the bar. He wanted to get closer, to get a better look, but the fear of drawing attention, of making a mistake, held him captive on his stool.

The group at the table seemed to be engaged in a heated discussion, their voices rising and falling. Joe strained to hear, to catch any fragment of conversation that might offer a clue. He saw one of the men at the table, a burly individual with a shaved head and a scar across his left eye, laugh heartily at something the man Joe suspected might be Mike had said. The man in question then leaned forward, his voice dropping, and the others leaned in to listen, their expressions serious.

It was then that Joe noticed something else. A subtle gesture. The man he suspected was Mike reached up and ran his fingers through his hair, a habit that was so distinctly Mike. He did it absentmindedly, as if lost in thought, or perhaps trying to recall something. Joe had seen that gesture a thousand times. It was the way his brother often fidgeted when he was thinking deeply about something, a nervous tic that had always been part of his charm.

A cold dread washed over Joe, mixing with a surge of desperate hope. It was too much of a coincidence. The posture, the way he commanded attention, and now that familiar gesture. It had to be him. Or, at the very least, it was someone who knew what had happened to him. These were the kinds of men who held the keys, who saw the comings and goings, who knew the whispers of the district. If Mike had been here, if he'd gotten involved in whatever mess had led to his disappearance, these were the men who would know.

He took another sip of his whiskey, the burn in his throat doing little to quell the growing unease. He couldn't approach them directly. Not here. Not now. He was an outsider, and they were clearly a tight-knit group, entrenched in the district's operations. He needed a plan, a way to get closer, to gather more information without becoming a target himself. His informant's words echoed in his mind: "They respect strength, but they despise weakness. And they never want to be seen as needing help. If you go to them, you go as an equal, or better yet, as someone who has something they want."

Joe didn't have much, but he had his wits. He needed to observe, to learn their patterns, their routines. He watched as the group at the corner table finished their drinks and began to disperse, one by one. The man Joe believed to be Mike stood up last, exchanging a few more words with the remaining men before turning and heading towards the back of the bar, presumably towards a restroom or an exit.

Joe waited until the man had disappeared from view, then he slid off his stool. He paid for his drink, his hands steady despite the tremor that ran through him. He knew he couldn't let this opportunity slip away. He had seen a ghost, a flicker of hope in the suffocating darkness of the Iron Triangle. Now, he had to find out if it was real.

He decided to take a calculated risk. He wouldn't follow the man directly, not yet. Instead, he would linger, try to glean more information from the remaining patrons, from the bartender, perhaps even from the empty tables and the lingering scent of their conversations. The Iron Triangle was a maze, but Joe was slowly, painstakingly, beginning to map its corridors. The sighting, however brief, however uncertain, had renewed his resolve. He was closer now, he felt it. He just had to play it smart, and the next move, he knew, would have to be precise, deliberate, and perhaps, very dangerous. He needed to find a way to insert himself into the periphery of their world, to become a shadow of a shadow, and listen. The night was still young, and the secrets of the Iron Triangle were only just beginning to reveal themselves. He finished his whiskey, the taste bitter and metallic on his tongue, a fitting prelude to the night's uncertain unfolding. He left the bar, the smoky air clinging to him, and stepped back into the grimy embrace of the district, his eyes scanning the shadows with a renewed intensity. He was looking for Mike, but he was also looking for his own way in.

## The Point of No Return

The smoky haze of The Rusty Mug had clung to Joe's clothes, a greasy testament to the grim reality he'd just inhaled. The fleeting glimpse of a figure that might have been Mike was a siren song in the suffocating darkness of the Iron Triangle, a fragile hope that had solidified into a desperate certainty. He hadn't found concrete answers, not yet, but he'd found the first whisper of truth: Mike was here. And "here" was a place where innocence withered and survival was a constant, bloody negotiation. The boy he knew, the brother he remembered, was likely buried beneath layers of hardened experience, shaped by the unforgiving currents of this district. The thought was a cold shard of ice in his gut, but it also ignited a stubborn ember of resolve. There was no turning back.

Joe exited the bar, the night air, though still thick with the city's perpetual grime, felt cleaner than the oppressive atmosphere within. The Iron Triangle wasn't just a geographical location; it was a state of being, a descent into a world governed by its own brutal, unwritten laws. To navigate this labyrinth, to find Mike and perhaps save him, Joe knew he had to shed his former skin. He had to become a chameleon, blend into the shadows, and learn to read the subtle, often dangerous, language of the streets. His previous attempts, driven by earnest concern and a naive hope for straightforward answers, had been met with indifference or veiled threats. Silas had made that brutally clear. Direct appeals were a weakness here, a sign of vulnerability that predators like Silas exploited. Respect, his informant had emphasized, was a currency earned through leverage, shared interests, or a history forged in the crucible of this place. Joe possessed none of these.

He walked with a newfound purpose, his eyes no longer scanning the crowd with the frantic desperation of a lost soul. Instead, they began to trace the patterns of the district, to observe the flow of movement, the subtle interactions that spoke volumes. The alleyways, once just routes to a potential source of information, now seemed like arteries of this organism, each leading to different organs of its illicit operations. The boarded-up storefronts weren't merely signs of decay; they were potential fronts, hiding places, points of transaction. The apartment buildings, sagging under their own weight, were roosts for those who operated in the twilight, their lives as precarious as the structures they inhabited.

He needed a new approach, one that acknowledged the fundamental truth of the Iron Triangle: information was power, and power was gained through strategic positioning, not brute force. His informant, a ghost of a man who operated in the shadows of these same streets, had been the one to whisper about The Rusty Mug. He hadn't just pointed Joe towards a location; he'd offered a glimpse into a philosophy of survival. "You don't barge in," the man had rasped, his voice like dry leaves skittering across pavement. "You become part of the scenery. You watch. You listen. And you wait for the right moment to make your move. Nobody here trusts anyone who announces their arrival."

Joe drifted, his senses heightened, absorbing the ambient details like a sponge. He noticed the shift changes of the street patrols, the subtle nods exchanged between individuals who passed each other on the street, the way certain doorways seemed to draw more attention, more lingering glances, than others. He saw a man with a deep scar across his cheek lean into a parked car, a brief exchange of what looked like an envelope, and then the car drove off, leaving the scarred man to melt back into the anonymity of the street. These were the transactions of the Iron Triangle, the silent commerce that fueled its existence.

His mind kept returning to the man at the corner table, the unsettling familiarity of his posture, the way he gestured, the unconscious habit of running a hand through his hair. It was a gamble to assume it was Mike, a desperate leap of faith. But the alternative – that Mike had simply vanished without a trace, swallowed whole by the city's indifference – was a far more terrifying prospect. He had to believe there was a thread to pull, a connection to be made. If that man wasn't Mike, he was someone who knew Mike, someone who could lead Joe to him.

He found himself near a small, dimly lit pawn shop, its window display a chaotic jumble of tarnished silver, outdated electronics, and chipped porcelain figurines. The proprietor, a thin, sharp-eyed man with a perpetually furrowed brow, sat behind a counter cluttered with paperwork and small, glassine bags of assorted items. Joe had learned from his informant that these establishments, while seemingly innocuous, often served as informal clearinghouses for information, places where goods changed hands and whispers were exchanged alongside desperate pleas for cash.

Joe entered, the small bell above the door announcing his presence with a tinny jangle. The air inside was stale, a mix of dust, old paper, and the faint scent of mothballs. He browsed the meager offerings, his eyes not on the items themselves, but on the proprietor, trying to gauge his demeanor, his level of engagement with the outside world. The man watched him, his gaze sharp and assessing, the way a hawk watches a field mouse.

"Looking for something in particular?" the proprietor asked, his voice flat and toneless.

Joe picked up a tarnished pocket watch, its hands frozen at ten past two. "Just… browsing," he replied, his voice deliberately casual. "Thinking of picking up a little something. Times are tough."

The proprietor grunted, a sound that conveyed neither agreement nor disagreement. "Times are always tough for some folks. For others, well, it's just another Tuesday." He gestured vaguely at a shelf of old photographs. "Seen a lot of faces come through here. A lot of stories, too. Most of them end the same way. Someone needing a quick bit of cash for something they shouldn't have had in the first place."

Joe's ears perked up. This was the opening. He needed to be careful, to frame his question in a way that sounded like idle curiosity, not a desperate search. "I hear this part of town has a… colorful cast of characters," Joe said, turning the pocket watch over in his hand. "Always wondered what kind of stories end up here."

The proprietor's eyes narrowed slightly. He was a professional listener, Joe realized, adept at sifting through noise for any hint of genuine inquiry. "Colorful? Depends on your definition. Most of them are just trying to get by. Some are trying to get ahead, no matter the cost." He paused, his gaze drifting towards the street outside. "Seen a few fellas lately, talking about… opportunities. Big ones."

Joe's heart gave a lurch. "Opportunities? What kind of opportunities?"

"The kind that don't ask too many questions," the proprietor said, his tone shifting, becoming even more guarded. He wiped his hands on his apron, a deliberate, delaying tactic. "Look, pal, I sell what people need to sell. I don't ask why. And I don't need to know who's asking for who. It's bad for business."

Joe understood. He wasn't going to get a direct answer here. But he had confirmed that there was activity, that people were talking about "opportunities." This was the language of the Iron Triangle. These weren't random acts of desperation; they were coordinated efforts, often with significant risk and reward. He needed to find the source of these discussions, not just the places where the echoes of them could be heard.

He purchased the pocket watch for a few dollars, the transaction feeling less like a purchase and more like a down payment on information. As he left the pawn shop, the proprietor's words echoed in his mind: "Some are trying to get ahead, no matter the cost." And the image of the man at The Rusty Mug, his confident posture, his command of attention, resurfaced with renewed intensity. What if Mike had been trying to get ahead? What if he'd gotten caught in one of these "opportunities"?

The afternoon was beginning to bleed into evening. The sky, previously a hazy gray, now took on a bruised, purplish hue. The streetlights flickered on, casting pools of sickly yellow light onto the grimy sidewalks. Joe knew he couldn't just wander aimlessly. He needed to establish a more direct connection to the people he suspected might know something about Mike. Silas had dismissed him, but the men at the corner table in The Rusty Mug were different. They were the ones who *belonged* to this world, not outsiders looking in.

He thought about the informant's advice again. "Leverage." What leverage could he possibly have? He had no muscle, no deep pockets, no reputation in this district. But he had his brother. And that, he realized, was his only leverage. He had to make himself valuable, or at least, indispensable.

His mind drifted back to his own world, to the life he'd left behind before this descent into the Iron Triangle. He'd been a mechanic, a good one. He knew engines, he knew how things worked, how to fix them when they broke. It was a skill, a tangible asset. Could that be his entry point?

He continued his walk, his senses still on high alert, but now with a more focused intent. He passed a small, grimy garage, its bay doors rolled up, revealing a dimly lit interior where a lone figure was wrestling with the engine of a battered pickup truck. The clang of metal on metal, the hiss of compressed air, the acrid smell of oil and exhaust – it was a familiar symphony to Joe. He paused, watching the mechanic, a stout man with grease permanently etched into the lines of his hands, struggle with a stubborn bolt.

Joe approached the open bay, the sound of his footsteps on the concrete echoing slightly. The mechanic looked up, his expression one of weary annoyance. "Can I help you?" he asked gruffly, wiping his hands on an equally greasy rag.

"Just admiring your work," Joe said, his voice low and steady. "Looks like a tough one."

The mechanic grunted. "It's always the ones you can't see. The ones buried deep. This one's got a screw loose, alright. And not in the way I like." He gestured with his chin towards the engine. "This bolt here, it's seized tighter than a drum. Tried everything. Heat, penetrating oil… nothing's budging it."

Joe stepped closer, his eyes examining the bolt. He recognized the problem immediately. "You're using the wrong wrench," he said, almost without thinking. "You need a torque multiplier, or at least a good impact wrench with the right socket. That's a fine-thread bolt, and you're just rounding off the head with brute force."

The mechanic blinked, his annoyance momentarily replaced by a flicker of surprise. He looked at the bolt, then back at Joe, his gaze more curious now. "A torque multiplier? You know your stuff, huh?"

"Used to fix engines for a living," Joe said, a small, almost involuntary smile touching his lips. It was a strange feeling, to be back in his element, even in this desolate landscape. "What's the problem with the truck?"

"This old girl's been sitting here a week," the mechanic replied, his voice losing some of its gruffness. "Owner's desperate to get it back on the road. Says it's… important." He hesitated, a subtle shift in his demeanor that Joe, now attuned to the district's coded language, immediately picked up on. "Important delivery to make. Down the south side."

South side. That was in the direction of where Silas operated, where the more volatile elements of the Iron Triangle tended to reside. "Delivery, huh?" Joe said, his mind already racing. "Maybe I can help. I've got a knack for those stubborn bolts."

The mechanic eyed him for a long moment, a calculating look in his eyes. "You in the market for work?"

"Looking for opportunities," Joe said, echoing the proprietor's words, making the connection. "Like everyone else." He held the mechanic's gaze. "If you need a hand, and the price is right, I'm your man. And maybe, just maybe, you might have heard of someone… someone who disappeared. A younger guy, goes by the name Mike."

The mechanic's expression didn't change, but there was a subtle tightening around his eyes. He gestured towards the engine bay. "You think you can get that bolt off?"

Joe nodded. "Give me twenty minutes."

He worked with a quiet intensity, his hands moving with a practiced efficiency that belied his emotional turmoil. He found the right tools, assessed the situation, and with a few precise maneuvers, managed to loosen the seized bolt. The mechanic watched him, impressed.

When the bolt finally came free with a satisfying pop, the mechanic let out a low whistle. "Well, I'll be damned. You're good. Real good." He extended a greasy hand. "Name's Gus."

Joe shook it firmly. "Joe."

"So, Joe," Gus said, leaning against the side of the truck, the grease rag now tucked into his back pocket. "You mentioned an opportunity. And a missing person. Let's talk about what you're looking for, and what you're offering."

This was it. The point of no return. He had stepped further into the maze, not as a lost stranger, but as someone offering a skill, a potential solution. He was no longer just searching for Mike; he was actively seeking to insert himself into the machinery of the Iron Triangle, to become a cog, however small, in its operations. The risk was immense. One wrong move, one misspoken word, and he could become another face in the crowd of forgotten souls that populated this district. But the chance, however slim, of finding Mike, of uncovering the truth, was a risk he was now willing to take. He had no other choice. He had to become part of the scenery, and Gus, with his grimy garage and his "important deliveries," was a thread he could now begin to pull. The night was still young, and the Iron Triangle was slowly revealing its secrets, one greasy bolt, one whispered word, at a time. He was no longer just Joe, the concerned brother. He was Joe, the mechanic, the man who could fix things, and who was now beginning to understand that to fix things in this world, you first had to get your hands dirty. Very dirty indeed.

# Chapter Seven
# Unraveling the Truth

## A Key Witness Emerges

The sticky residue of cheap coffee still clung to Joe's fingertips, a faint reminder of the hours spent nursing a single cup at the counter of "The Daily Grind." The diner was a relic, a worn-out beacon in the encroaching gloom of the Iron Triangle, its Formica tables scarred with the history of countless hurried meals and hushed conversations. For three days, Joe had been a fixture here, a silent observer amidst the ebb and flow of dockworkers, night-shift laborers, and the ever-present undercurrent of the district's less savory inhabitants. He'd perfected the art of looking busy, of appearing lost in thought, all while his senses strained to catch any echo of the brother he was desperately searching for. He'd learned to differentiate between the forced camaraderie of the regulars and the furtive glances of those who had something to hide. His earlier attempts to solicit information had been met with a wall of practiced indifference, a collective shrug that spoke volumes about the unspoken rules of this place. But today, something felt different. A shift in the air, perhaps, or a subtle change in the rhythm of the diner that signaled an opportunity.

Her name was Maria, and she was as much a part of The Daily Grind as the perpetually brewing coffee pot. Her movements were economical, her smile polite but distant, the kind that came from years of deflecting unwanted attention. Joe had noticed her observing him, a flicker of recognition in her eyes each time he'd subtly steered the conversation towards the young man he was looking for. He'd described Mike in detail – his height, the nervous way he chewed on his lip, the faded tattoo of a bird on his wrist that Joe himself had helped him get. Maria had always offered a polite, noncommittal nod, a fleeting acknowledgment that he was being heard, but nothing more. Until today.

He'd just finished his third lukewarm coffee, the bitter taste a familiar companion, when Maria approached his booth. She didn't serve him directly, instead choosing to wipe down the adjacent table with a practiced, almost absentminded, air. Her voice, when it finally came, was a low murmur, barely audible above the clatter of plates and the drone of the overhead fluorescent lights. "You're looking for a ghost," she said, her eyes meeting his for a fraction of a second before darting back to her task.

Joe's breath hitched. This was it. The ice was finally breaking. He kept his voice steady, betraying none of the frantic hope surging within him. "I'm looking for my brother," he replied, his gaze fixed on her. "He's been gone a while."

Maria continued her work, her movements a little more deliberate now. She placed the damp cloth on the counter, then turned to face him, leaning against the counter, her arms crossed. The weariness in her eyes was palpable, a deep-seated fatigue that spoke of too many late nights, too many hard truths witnessed. "He comes in here sometimes," she admitted, her voice still low, as if sharing a secret. "Always keeps to himself. Sits over there," she nodded towards a corner booth, the same one Joe had focused on during his stakeout. "Orders coffee, sometimes a sandwich. Doesn't stay long."

Joe's heart hammered against his ribs. He'd been right to focus on that booth, right to believe that someone here would know something. "You've seen him? Recently?"

Maria sighed, a soft exhalation that seemed to carry the weight of all the unspoken stories within the diner's walls. "Last week, I think. Maybe the week before. It's... it's not good, what I've seen." Her gaze flickered down to the worn counter again, her fingers tracing an invisible pattern. "He looks... different. Thinner. And his eyes... they're not the same eyes I remember."

Joe felt a cold dread creep into his stomach. He knew what she meant. The spark, the youthful optimism he remembered in Mike's eyes, had likely been extinguished long ago. "What do you mean, 'not the same'?" he prompted, his voice tight.

"Lost," Maria said simply. "Like he's looking for something he'll never find. And he's always with... someone. Or looking for someone." She hesitated, a subtle tension entering her posture. "There's a man he meets with sometimes. Sits in the car outside, waits for him. Dark sedan. Tinted windows. Mike goes out, they talk for a minute, then Mike's back inside, looking even worse than before."

"Who is this man?" Joe pressed, the image of a shadowy figure in a dark car conjuring a familiar unease. "Do you know him?"

Maria shook her head. "Never seen his face clearly. He stays in the car. But Mike... Mike looks scared when he sees him. And he owes him. I can tell. The way he fumbles with his wallet, the way he avoids eye contact. It's clear as day."

Joe's mind immediately went to Silas, to the kind of men who operated in the shadows of the Iron Triangle, men who dealt in favors and debts that could never truly be repaid. "This man," he began, choosing his words carefully, "is he one of the... dealers in this area? Someone Mike might owe money to?"

Maria's expression tightened. She glanced around the diner, her eyes scanning the few remaining patrons. Even in the relative anonymity of the diner, the fear of being overheard was a palpable thing in the Iron Triangle. "I don't know names," she whispered, leaning in closer. "But I've seen Mike getting his... fix. From a guy who hangs around the docks. Name's Rat. Everyone knows Rat. He's a bad one. Ruthless. Doesn't care who you are, if you owe him, he'll come for you. And Mike... Mike owes him a lot."

The name "Rat" sent a shiver down Joe's spine. He'd heard whispers of him from his informant, a low-level enforcer who had a reputation for extreme violence and a particular fondness for exploiting the desperation of others. The thought of Mike, his younger brother, caught in Rat's web, was almost unbearable. "How do you know Mike owes him?"

"Mike's been coming here more and more," Maria explained, her voice a low, steady cadence. "He used to be… different. Had a job, I think. But then… things changed. He started missing days. Coming in looking rough. And he started asking for money. Small amounts at first, from the regulars who'd known him longer. But then… it got worse. He'd be twitchy, agitated. Always looking over his shoulder. And I saw him with Rat a few times, down by the old warehouse district. Rat would give him something, and Mike would give him cash. Whatever he had. It wasn't a friendship, Mr…" she trailed off, waiting for him to supply his name.

"Joe," he supplied, his voice a low rumble.

"Joe. It wasn't a friendship. It was a transaction. A transaction with no happy ending for Mike." She pushed herself away from the counter, her gaze hardening with a flicker of anger. "He's digging his own grave, that boy. And Rat is holding the shovel."

Joe leaned back in the booth, the worn vinyl cool against his back. The pieces were starting to fit together, forming a picture that was both horrifying and disturbingly familiar. Mike's struggles with addiction, his tendency to fall into bad company – these were demons Joe had hoped he had left behind in their childhood. But the Iron Triangle had a way of resurfacing old wounds, of amplifying existing vulnerabilities. "How bad are the debts, Maria?" he asked, his voice barely a whisper. "Do you have any idea?"

Maria gave a short, humorless laugh. "Bad. Very bad. You see the way he carries himself? The fear in his eyes? That's the look of a man who knows he can't pay. He's been trying to borrow from everyone. And when they say no, he gets desperate. I've seen him trying to pawn things he shouldn't have. His watch, a chain… I think he even tried to sell the jacket his mother gave him. The one with the blue lining."

Joe flinched. He remembered that jacket. A gift from their mother on his eighteenth birthday, a small comfort against the harshness of the world. The thought of Mike pawning it for a fix, for whatever Rat was supplying him, was a gut punch. "He's been here... recently? When was the last time you saw him?"

"Like I said, last week, maybe the week before," Maria repeated, her brow furrowed in concentration. "He seemed... more desperate than usual. Kept asking if anyone had seen his... friend. The one in the dark sedan. Said he needed to talk to him about a big score. Something that would clear his slate. He was excited, almost manic. But also terrified. A strange combination."

A big score. The phrase hung in the air, heavy with unspoken implications. Joe knew that in places like the Iron Triangle, "big scores" rarely meant legitimate opportunities. They usually involved risk, violence, and a disregard for the law. "A big score," Joe repeated, his mind racing. "Did he say what it was?"

Maria shook her head. "He was too agitated to be coherent. Just kept muttering about getting out, about finally being free of Rat. But you could see the fear. He was running on fumes, Joe. And Rat... Rat doesn't let people out easy. Not ever." She paused, her gaze sweeping across the diner once more. "You need to be careful, Joe. Rat is not someone you want to cross. He's got people. Lots of people. And they're all as bad as he is, if not worse."

Joe nodded, his jaw tight. He understood the danger. Maria was risking a lot by talking to him. Her quiet confession, her willingness to break the silence, was an act of immense courage in this unforgiving district. "Thank you, Maria," he said, his voice rough with emotion. "You've... you've helped me more than you know. Is there anything else? Anything at all you can remember?"

Maria thought for a moment, her gaze distant. "There was one other thing. A few weeks ago, before all this started getting really bad. He came in here, looking for something. He'd lost something. I didn't know what. He was tearing up the place, under the tables, in the booths.

He was so frantic. I asked him what he was looking for, and he just said… 'the key.' Said he'd dropped it. And that it was important. Very important."

The key. Joe's mind flashed back to the small, nondescript apartment Mike had rented before he disappeared. A place Joe had searched meticulously, finding nothing out of the ordinary. But what if he'd missed something? What if "the key" wasn't a literal key, but something else? A piece of information? A contact? The possibilities were endless, and each one felt like another potential lead, another piece of the puzzle that was slowly, agonizingly, coming together.

He paid for his coffee, leaving a generous tip on the counter. Maria met his gaze, a silent understanding passing between them. She knew he was walking into a dangerous situation, and he knew he was indebted to her. As he stepped out of The Daily Grind, the evening air felt cooler, heavier, as if the weight of Maria's words had settled upon the district. He had a name – Rat. He had a motive – Mike's mounting debts and his desperate search for a way out. And he had a new clue – the elusive "key." The path ahead was still shrouded in darkness, but for the first time since he'd entered the Iron Triangle, Joe felt a flicker of genuine direction. He wasn't just wandering anymore; he was hunting. And he knew, with a chilling certainty, that the hunt was about to get very dangerous. He needed to find Rat, and he needed to find out what "big score" Mike had been so desperate to be a part of. The Iron Triangle was a maze, but he was beginning to find the threads, and he wouldn't stop pulling until he found his brother.

## The Dealers Shadow

The waitress, her face etched with a weariness that went beyond the long hours, leaned in, her voice dropping to a near-whisper, a stark contrast to the diner's usual low hum. "You're looking for your brother, you said?" Her eyes, a deep, bruised shade of brown, flickered nervously towards the entrance, as if expecting trouble to walk through the door at any moment. "He's been in here. A few times. Always with that… that look in his eyes. Like a cornered animal."

Joe's gut clenched. He'd seen that look before, in Mike's reflection after a bad night, a fleeting glimpse of the desperation that gnawed at him. "He's in trouble, isn't he?" Joe asked, his voice barely audible. "Who's he dealing with?"

The waitress, whose name tag read 'Brenda', hesitated, her gaze fixed on the grimy linoleum floor. She picked at a loose thread on her apron, her movements betraying a deep-seated apprehension. "There's a man," she began, her voice almost swallowed by the ambient noise of the diner. "Everyone knows him. He's like... like a shadow that stretches over this whole district. They call him Silas."

The name hung in the air, heavy and suffocating. Silas. Even the sound of it was like a cold draft, a chilling premonition. Joe had heard whispers of Silas before, hushed conversations among the dockworkers and the street vendors, always spoken with a mixture of fear and reluctant respect. Silas was the kingpin of the Iron Triangle's underbelly, the architect of its despair, the man who held the reins of the illicit trade that had ensnared so many.

"Silas?" Joe repeated, the name tasting like ash in his mouth. "What do you know about him?"

Brenda wrung her hands, her knuckles white. "He's... he's not just a dealer, Joe. He's a puppeteer. He finds the ones who are weak, the ones who are already falling, and he pulls them in. He doesn't just sell them drugs; he sells them a way out. A promise of escape. And then he traps them. Makes them owe him. For everything. For their lives." She looked up, her eyes meeting Joe's, a raw plea in their depths. "He's got a network. People who watch for him, who bring him the lost souls. And your brother... he's exactly the kind of person Silas preys on."

Joe's mind raced, piecing together Brenda's words with the fragmented information he'd gathered. Mike's increasing desperation, his erratic behavior, the hushed mentions of debts—it all pointed to Silas's insidious grip. This wasn't just a matter of drug dealing; this was a systematic exploitation of addiction, a cruel business built on the ruins of broken lives.

"How does he do it?" Joe asked, his voice tight with a mixture of anger and a growing sense of dread. "How does he keep them indebted?"

"It's a cycle," Brenda explained, her voice growing steadier as she spoke of something she clearly understood, even if it terrified her. "He'll front them a little. Just enough to keep them coming back. Then he'll offer them a way to 'earn' more, a way to pay him back by doing… favors. Small things at first. Running messages, watching a corner. But it escalates. Before they know it, they're deeper than they ever imagined. They're doing his dirty work, and they're still owing him. And if they try to get out? Silas doesn't forget. He doesn't let go."

Joe's jaw tightened. He pictured Silas, a man of calculated cruelty, a predator in human form, orchestrating the downfall of vulnerable individuals like his brother. He imagined Mike, lost and desperate, falling prey to Silas's manipulative charm, trading his freedom for a temporary reprieve from his addiction. The thought was a bitter pill to swallow.

"He's dangerous," Brenda stated, her voice barely above a whisper. "He has a reputation for being… thorough. He doesn't leave loose ends. And the people who work for him are just as bad. Or worse. They're the muscle. The ones who make sure Silas's word is law."

Joe knew this was a dangerous path he was walking. Silas was not some petty street thug; he was a force, a respected and feared figure in the Iron Triangle's ecosystem. To confront him, to even get close to him, would be akin to walking into the lion's den. But the image of Mike, trapped in Silas's web, fueled a fierce determination within him. He couldn't let his brother be consumed by this darkness.

"Where can I find him?" Joe asked, his voice steady despite the turmoil churning inside him. "Where does Silas operate?"

Brenda hesitated, her eyes widening slightly. "He doesn't have one single spot, Joe. He moves around. But his… his headquarters, you could say, is usually around the old cannery down by the docks. That's where he meets with his lieutenants, where the real deals go down. But be careful. Very careful. Silas has eyes everywhere. If he knows you're looking for him, asking questions… it won't end well."

The cannery. A derelict monument to a bygone era, now a hub of illicit activity. Joe had heard of it, a place where the shadows were thickest and the law rarely dared to tread. It was the heart of Silas's operation, the viper's nest he needed to infiltrate.

"Does Silas know Mike?" Joe pressed, needing to understand the extent of his brother's entanglement. "Has he dealt with him directly?"

Brenda nodded slowly, her gaze distant, recalling a specific memory. "I saw them talking, once. A few weeks back. Mike was desperate. He was begging Silas for something. For money, I think. Silas just stood there, calm as you please, and then he said something to Mike that made him shrink. Like a kicked dog. Silas just watched him, that cold smile on his face, and then he turned and walked away. Mike looked... broken. Like he'd just sold his soul."

The image was stark, brutal. Silas, exuding an aura of power and control, while Mike, his younger brother, was reduced to a pathetic plea. It confirmed Joe's worst fears. Silas wasn't just a supplier; he was a tormentor, deriving a twisted pleasure from the suffering of those he enslaved.

"And the people who work for him?" Joe continued, his mind already formulating a plan, a dangerous, desperate gamble. "Who are they? Do you know any names?"

Brenda shook her head. "They're a rough crowd, Joe. Just... street thugs. Thugs who do Silas's bidding. I've heard names thrown around, but I don't know them. I don't want to know them. They're all just... extensions of Silas. His shadow. And if you get in Silas's way, you'll have to deal with them first." She looked at him, her expression a mixture of pity and fear. "You're not from around here, are you? You don't understand how this place works. Silas is the law in the Iron Triangle. And he doesn't play fair."

Joe understood. He understood the pervasive fear, the unspoken rules, the hierarchy of power that governed this desolate district. Silas was at the apex, a figure of almost mythical menace, his influence woven into the very fabric of the Iron Triangle. Getting information about him, let alone confronting him, would be a perilous undertaking.

He thanked Brenda for her help, leaving a more substantial tip this time, a silent acknowledgment of the risk she had taken. As he stepped back out into the grimy twilight, the weight of Brenda's words settled heavily upon him. Silas. The name echoed in his mind, a siren call to a dangerous confrontation. He knew, with a chilling certainty, that his search for Mike had just entered a far more perilous phase. He wasn't just looking for a missing brother anymore; he was stepping into the shadow of a man who wielded power through fear and addiction, a man who would stop at nothing to maintain his iron grip on the Iron Triangle. The cannery, Silas's domain, loomed in his thoughts, a dark and foreboding destination. He had to go there. He had to find Silas. And he had to get Mike out, before Silas's shadow consumed him completely. The path was fraught with danger, but the stakes were too high to turn back. He would face Silas, the puppeteer, and he would unravel the truth, no matter the cost.

## Mike's Deepening Entanglement

Joe sat back in the booth, the lingering taste of stale coffee a fitting metaphor for the bitter revelations swirling in his mind. Brenda's words, initially a desperate whisper, had bloomed into a chilling narrative, a testament to the suffocating grip Silas held over the Iron Triangle, and more specifically, over Mike. He replayed the waitress's descriptions, not just of Silas, but of the cyclical nature of his control, the insidious process of drawing the vulnerable in, offering a fleeting illusion of escape, and then tightening the noose of debt. It wasn't just about drugs anymore; it was about a systematic dismantling of a person, a deliberate reduction to servitude.

The image Brenda had painted—Mike, begging Silas for something, anything, his desperation a visible stain—gnawed at Joe. He saw not the brother he remembered, the one who dreamt of grease-stained hands and the roar of a tuned engine, but a broken man, a shadow of his former self, reduced to a supplicant. The auto shop, that shared dream they'd nurtured since childhood, felt like a cruel mirage now, a phantom of a life that Mike, and by extension Joe, had lost. The thought of Mike, not just using, but actively participating in Silas's sordid enterprise, was a gut punch. The idea of him being a "runner" or a "courier" wasn't a stretch; it fit the pattern of escalation Brenda had described. A desperate man, needing money, finding a way to "earn" it from Silas, a way that inevitably led deeper into the mire.

He leaned forward, his elbows on the sticky Formica tabletop, and pulled out the worn notebook and pen he always carried. He started jotting down keywords, fragments of conversations he'd overheard in the past weeks, memories that now clicked into place with horrifying clarity. The hushed tones, the averted gazes, the sudden silences when he entered certain rooms – they weren't just the ambient noise of the Iron Triangle; they were the sounds of a hidden machinery grinding away, powered by fear and addiction. He remembered a conversation he'd had with an old timer down at the docks, a man named Sal, who'd been unusually cagey when Joe had asked about Mike's whereabouts. Sal had muttered something about "owing the wrong people," about "getting mixed up in something heavy." At the time, Joe had dismissed it as drunken ramblings, but now, Sal's words felt like pieces of a larger, more sinister puzzle.

He recalled another instance, a few weeks prior, when he'd been walking past a derelict warehouse near the waterfront, a place usually buzzing with unseen activity. He'd heard shouting, angry and guttural, followed by the distinct thud of something heavy hitting the ground. He'd peered through a broken window, his heart hammering against his ribs, and seen two men, rough-looking, their faces hard and impassive, dragging a third man, limp and seemingly unconscious, into the back of a nondescript van. He hadn't recognized the victim, but the aggression, the cold brutality of the scene, had stayed with him. Could that have been Mike? Or someone else caught in Silas's web? Brenda's description of Silas's enforcers, his "muscle," the ones who ensured his word was law, flashed in his mind. They were the extensions of Silas, the instruments of his will.

The waitress had mentioned Silas operating out of the old cannery. Joe tried to visualize it, a hulking, rusting skeleton of a building against the bruised evening sky. He'd passed it countless times, a place avoided even by the bravest souls in the neighborhood, a symbol of decay and forgotten industry. Now, it was transformed in his mind's eye, not just a derelict structure, but the nerve center of his brother's impending doom. The thought of Silas's "lieutenants," his inner circle, meeting there, planning their next moves, sending their pawns out into the city's underbelly, sent a shiver down his spine.

He remembered Mike's last visit to his apartment, a week before he disappeared. Mike had seemed agitated, his eyes darting around as if expecting someone to burst through the door. He'd asked Joe for money, more than Joe could reasonably afford, and when Joe had pressed him, asked what it was for, Mike had stammered, "Just… stuff. Debts, man. It's getting out of hand." He'd refused to elaborate, his usual openness replaced by a guardedness that had unnerved Joe. Mike had always been an open book, his joys and his struggles laid bare. This new secrecy, this palpable fear, was a terrifying departure.

Joe also recalled a brief, almost dismissive encounter with a known associate of Silas, a wiry, shifty character named Frankie "Fingers." Frankie usually operated on the fringes, doing odd jobs for Silas, acting as a low-level informant. Joe had run into him outside a dimly lit bar on the edge of the Iron Triangle. Frankie had seen Joe approaching and had quickly ducked into an alley. When Joe had called out to him, Frankie had emerged, his face pale, his eyes wide with a fear that seemed disproportionate to Joe's presence. "You gotta be careful, man," Frankie had rasped, not even meeting Joe's gaze. "Silas… he don't like people asking questions. Especially not about his runners. They're important to him." Frankie had then scurried away, disappearing into the labyrinthine streets before Joe could press him further. At the time, Joe had thought Frankie was simply scared of drawing attention to himself. Now, he understood. Frankie had been part of the information network, a cog in Silas's surveillance machine, and Joe's questions had threatened to expose not just his own activities, but Mike's.

The dream of the auto shop. It wasn't just a dream; it was a symbol of escape, of a legitimate future, of hard work and honest reward. Joe remembered showing Mike the blueprints they'd sketched out, the worn advertisements for auto parts they'd clipped from magazines. Mike had been so excited, his eyes alight with a future that was finally within reach. Now, that future was a distant, shattered memory, replaced by the grim reality of Mike's entrapment. Joe's own commitment to that dream, his willingness to sacrifice and save, felt almost naive now, a stark contrast to the brutal pragmatism of Silas's world. He was no longer just trying to find his brother; he was trying to extricate him from a sophisticated criminal enterprise that preyed on the very essence of human frailty.

He flipped through his notebook, the scribbled words forming a disturbing pattern. Mike wasn't just dabbling; he was deeply enmeshed. The "favors" Brenda mentioned – running messages, watching corners – they were the initial steps, the gentle tugs on the leash that eventually became an unbreakable chain. Joe imagined Mike, with his inherent loyalty and perhaps a misplaced sense of obligation, agreeing to these small tasks, seeing them as a temporary means to an end, a way to clear his debts and get back to his life. But Silas wouldn't allow that. Silas thrived on perpetual indebtedness, on keeping his assets in a state of constant vulnerability and dependence.

The realization settled upon Joe with the crushing weight of certainty: Mike wasn't lost in the conventional sense. He hadn't simply wandered off the path. He had been actively recruited, manipulated, and ultimately, enslaved. He was a pawn, not a player, in Silas's dangerous game, his addiction expertly exploited to ensure his compliance and continued service. The depth of Mike's entanglement meant that simple intervention, a plea for him to come home, would likely be futile, perhaps even dangerous. Silas wouldn't just let a valuable asset walk away. He would deploy his enforcers, his network of informants, to ensure his control remained absolute.

Joe's gaze drifted to the window, the diner's fluorescent lights casting a sickly yellow glow on the rain-slicked street outside. The world beyond the diner's grimy windows seemed unchanged, oblivious to the grim drama unfolding within the lives of its inhabitants. But Joe knew better. He knew that beneath the surface of everyday life in the

Iron Triangle, a relentless war was being waged, a war fought in the shadows, on the streets, and within the minds of those caught in its unforgiving grip. And Mike, his brother, was right in the thick of it, a casualty of a system designed to break him.

He closed his notebook, the soft click echoing in the relative quiet of the booth. The vague unease he'd felt upon entering the diner had transformed into a cold, hard resolve. He couldn't afford to be sentimental, to dwell on what might have been. He had to focus on the present, on the brutal reality of Mike's situation. He had to understand the full extent of Mike's involvement, not just as a user, but as an active participant in Silas's criminal network. The information Brenda had provided, combined with his own memories and observations, painted a grim picture, but it was a picture that finally gave him a clear target. He knew where he had to go, who he had to face, and the stakes involved. This wasn't just about saving Mike; it was about dismantling the very system that had ensnared him, a system built on exploitation and fear. The road ahead was dangerous, fraught with peril, but the thought of Mike trapped in Silas's web, his dreams extinguished and his life systematically dismantled, spurred Joe onward. He had to unravel this truth, piece by painstaking piece, and in doing so, he hoped to find a way to bring his brother back from the brink. The dream of the auto shop might be a distant memory, but the fight for Mike's life, and perhaps for his own redemption, had just begun. He needed more information, more names, more connections. He needed to understand the hierarchy, the key players in Silas's operation. Who were Silas's lieutenants? Who were the people Mike reported to, the ones who collected his debts and dictated his tasks? He needed to dig deeper, to peel back the layers of deception and fear, and expose the rotten core of Silas's empire. He stood up, leaving the half-finished coffee behind, the weight of his mission a tangible burden. The Iron Triangle, and its shadowy kingpin, awaited.

## A Trail of Betrayal

The cryptic pronouncements of the informant, Brenda, had been a starting point, a harsh, unwelcome illumination of the abyss his brother had fallen into. Now, with the foundation of Mike's entrapment laid bare, Joe found himself sifting through the wreckage, not just for the architect of his brother's downfall, but for anyone who might have aided and abetted him. The word "betrayal" echoed in his mind, a chilling whisper that grew louder with each passing hour. It wasn't just Silas, the predatory kingpin, that gnawed at him, but the possibility of someone closer, someone within their shared orbit, someone who had known Mike's vulnerabilities, his dreams, his desperate need for escape, and had weaponized them.

He found himself replaying every interaction, every casual conversation with people from Mike's periphery. Old friends, acquaintances from the garage, even the faces of those who frequented the same dimly lit bars Mike had started to haunt. Had anyone seen an opportunity in Mike's struggles? Had anyone offered him a poisoned chalice disguised as a helping hand? The informant's vagueness about who had initially "pointed Mike in Silas's direction" had always felt deliberate, as if she knew more than she was letting on, or perhaps, as if the betrayal was so deep, so personal, that naming names was too painful to bear. Joe understood that pain. The thought of a trusted confidante, someone Mike had confided in, someone who had seen his desperation and instead of offering solace, had steered him towards Silas, was a sickness in his gut.

He thought of Marco, Mike's oldest friend from their childhood. Marco, who had always been a bit envious of Mike's natural talent with engines, his innate charisma. Marco, who had a penchant for gambling, always chasing the next big win, often falling short. Could Marco, drowning in his own debts, have seen Mike as a lifeline, not to save, but to exploit? Joe remembered a time, years ago, when Marco had tried to rope Mike into a shady import-export scheme that had nearly landed them both in serious trouble. Mike had been wary, had seen the danger, but Marco had been persistent, weaving tales of quick money and easy living. Mike had ultimately refused, but the seed of desperation, the allure of a shortcut, had been planted. Had Marco, years later, found a more sinister way to profit from Mike's vulnerabilities? Had he, perhaps, seen Silas as the ultimate shortcut, a means to both clear his own slate and secure a cut from Silas's operation by delivering a new, compliant pawn? The idea was almost too repulsive to contemplate, yet it fit the grim narrative that was unfolding. Marco had the access, the shared history, and a history of questionable judgment when his own needs were on the line.

Then there was Sylvie, the ex-girlfriend who had a notoriously volatile relationship with Mike. She'd always been attracted to the rougher edges, the danger that sometimes clung to Mike, but she'd also been possessive, prone to dramatic outbursts. Had she, in a fit of pique, or perhaps a misguided attempt to control Mike, fed Silas information about his whereabouts, his habits, his vulnerabilities? Joe remembered a particularly nasty breakup, where Sylvie had threatened to make Mike's life a living hell if he ever left her again. It had seemed like drunken hyperbole at the time, the typical melodrama of their relationship. But what if she had taken it a step further? What if, out of spite or a twisted sense of revenge, she'd used her knowledge of Mike's secret struggles with drugs, his mounting debts, to feed Silas the information he needed to reel Mike in? Silas was known for his network of informants, people who worked for him in exchange for favors, protection, or, as Brenda had hinted, a cut of the profits. Sylvie, with her intimate knowledge of Mike's life, could have been an invaluable asset to Silas, an inside source feeding him the precise intel needed to orchestrate Mike's downfall. The thought of her being complicit, her anger weaponized against the man she once claimed to love, sent a cold dread through Joe.

Joe also considered the possibility of a more subtle betrayal, one born not of malice or greed, but of misguided paternalism or a desperate attempt to "help." He thought of some of Mike's older friends, men who had known him since he was a kid, men who had seen him falter before. Perhaps one of them, seeing Mike's life spiraling out of control, his addiction a gaping wound, had made a deal with Silas. Maybe they believed they were protecting Mike, giving him a structured way to deal with his problems, a way to pay off his debts under Silas's "supervision." It was a twisted logic, a self-deception that allowed them to sleep at night while Mike was being systematically destroyed. But even this thought was a bitter pill. To betray a friend, even with the intention of helping, was still a betrayal.

He tried to recall any recent interactions, any odd behavior from people who were usually reliable. Had anyone been unusually eager to know where Mike was, or what he was up to? Had anyone seemed overly sympathetic, offering money or drugs that, in retrospect, might have been an attempt to keep him indebted and compliant with Silas? He remembered a few weeks before Mike disappeared, a casual encounter with an old acquaintance from the auto shop, a guy named Sammy "The Shank" Russo. Sammy had always been a low-level player in the Triangle, a hanger-on, more bark than bite. Joe had bumped into him outside a pawn shop, and Sammy had seemed uncharacteristically nervous, his eyes darting around. He'd mumbled something about Mike owing "some heavy hitters" and that it would be best if Mike kept his nose clean and did what he was told. At the time, Joe had dismissed it as Sammy's usual paranoia, his tendency to get caught up in the general fear that permeated the Triangle. But now, the words took on a different hue. Sammy, a petty criminal himself, might have been an unwitting informant, or worse, an active participant in setting Mike up, perhaps for a promised reward from Silas, or even just to curry favor with the neighborhood's new power broker. Sammy's fear might not have been about his own skin, but about the repercussions of failing to deliver Mike to Silas.

The informant, Brenda, had been vague about the specifics of *how* Mike had first come into contact with Silas. She'd alluded to him being "introduced," to someone "connecting the dots." Joe now wondered if that "someone" wasn't Silas's goon squad, but a familiar face, a voice Mike trusted. The thought was a corrosive acid, eating away at his memories. He recalled Mike mentioning a new "business opportunity" he was looking into, something that could solve all his financial woes. He'd been cagey about the details, but he'd seemed genuinely excited, hopeful. Joe had dismissed it as another one of Mike's schemes, a pipe dream that would inevitably fizzle out. But what if that "opportunity" had been a carefully constructed trap, laid by someone Mike knew and trusted? What if that person had received a commission, a percentage of whatever Mike was forced to do for Silas, a finder's fee for delivering a new recruit?

The complexity of Silas's operation, as described by Brenda, suggested a network far more intricate than a simple drug dealer. It was about control, about exploiting vulnerabilities, about building an empire on the backs of broken people. And for that, Silas would need more than just muscle; he'd need ears and eyes, people who could identify potential recruits, who could assess their weaknesses, and who could facilitate their induction into his world. Joe's gut told him that such a system would rely heavily on insider information, on the quiet complicity of those who knew the neighborhood, who knew its people, and who knew their struggles.

He pictured Mike, naive and desperate, confiding in a friend about his financial troubles, his burgeoning addiction. He imagined that friend, perhaps seeing a way out of their own troubles, or simply driven by a cold, calculating self-interest, making a call, sending a text, arranging a meeting. The betrayal wouldn't have been a dramatic act of violence, but a quiet, insidious conversation, a whispered suggestion that led Mike down a path from which there seemed no return. The thought of someone he knew, someone who might even be a friend of his own, being responsible for this, was a betrayal of a different order, a violation of the unspoken code of loyalty that, however fragile, still existed in pockets of the Iron Triangle.

Joe realized he couldn't afford to let sentimentality cloud his judgment. He had to approach every acquaintance with a critical eye, to question every motive, to be prepared for the possibility that someone he trusted might have been involved. The informant had provided him with a framework, but the details, the specific threads of betrayal that had led Mike into Silas's clutches, were still missing. And Joe suspected those details would be the hardest to uncover, hidden behind masks of normalcy and feigned ignorance. He had to dig deeper, to look beyond the obvious enforcers and the drug kingpins, and examine the shadows, the quiet whispers, the seemingly innocuous connections that might have paved the way for Mike's descent. The search for his brother had become a quest not just for a lost soul, but for a truth stained with the bitter taste of betrayal. He knew that uncovering this would be the most painful part of his journey, a confrontation with the darkest aspects of human nature, and perhaps, a confrontation with someone he once considered a friend.

He remembered a conversation he'd had with a bartender down at "The Rusty Mug," a place Mike occasionally frequented before his disappearance. The bartender, a burly man with a perpetually weary expression, had mentioned Mike being seen with a new crowd, guys who seemed "too slick" for the usual regulars. He'd also mentioned, almost as an afterthought, that Mike had been asking around about a specific kind of high-end auto part, something rare and expensive, the kind that would require a significant outlay of cash. At the time, Joe had thought Mike was just looking for a good deal for a project car. But now, it hit him like a ton of bricks. Silas's operation, as Brenda had described, often involved more than just drugs; it was a diversified enterprise, and Mike, with his knowledge of cars, could have been utilized for more than just running errands. Could he have been tasked with sourcing stolen parts, or perhaps acting as a fence for stolen high-performance vehicles? If so, who had steered him towards that line of work? Who had identified his skills and his financial desperation as a perfect combination for Silas's nefarious purposes? The bartender's casual observation now seemed like a crucial breadcrumb, a hint of a deeper involvement that went beyond simple drug use and petty tasks.

Joe's mind raced, trying to connect the dots, to identify anyone who might have had access to both Mike and Silas's network, and a motive to facilitate the connection. He thought of people who had recently come into money, who had suddenly acquired new cars or moved into better apartments. Such changes were rarely subtle in the Iron Triangle, and any sudden improvement in fortune often came under scrutiny. Had anyone from Mike's circle benefited from his downfall? Had anyone seen Mike as a stepping stone, an easy mark to exploit for their own advancement within Silas's organization, or even simply to get out from under Silas's thumb themselves by delivering someone else?

The informant's words about Silas "rewarding loyalty and usefulness" kept replaying. Usefulness could come in many forms. It could be muscle, it could be an informant, or it could be someone who identified and brought in new talent. Joe's gaze fell on a faded photograph on his desk – a group of him and Mike with their old crew from the neighborhood. Faces he hadn't thought about in years. Were any of them still around? Had any of them fallen in with Silas? The Iron Triangle had a way of chewing people up and spitting them out, but it also had a way of retaining its own, of pulling people back into its orbit, often through coercion or the promise of power.

He needed to retrace Mike's steps, not just physically, but socially. Who had he been talking to in the weeks leading up to his disappearance? Who had he been seen with? Brenda had mentioned Mike's growing desperation, his increasing reliance on drugs to cope. This made him more susceptible, more likely to trust anyone who offered a solution, however illicit. Joe remembered Mike's strained relationship with his estranged father, a man who had always been absent, a man who had offered little guidance and even less support. Could his father, in some twisted attempt to reconnect or perhaps to absolve himself of past failures, have made contact with Mike, only to steer him towards Silas, seeing it as a form of "tough love" or a way to get Mike "sorted out"? It was a long shot, a desperate theory, but in the absence of any other solid leads, Joe felt compelled to consider every possibility, no matter how painful. The desire to find Mike, to understand what had happened, was pushing him to confront the darkest corners of his own relationships and memories. He knew that the truth, however ugly, was the only path forward.

## The Looming Confrontation

The weight of Brenda's words, the chilling confirmation of Mike's entanglement with Silas, settled over Joe like a shroud. The shadows he'd been probing, the whispers of betrayal he'd been chasing, were coalescing into a single, terrifying entity: Silas Thorne. He was no longer an abstract threat, a name spat by a desperate informant. Silas was the architect of Mike's ruin, the puppeteer pulling the strings of his brother's addiction and despair. And Joe knew, with a certainty that chilled him to the bone, that gathering information was no longer enough. He had to face Silas.

The thought sent a tremor through him, a visceral reaction to the sheer, unadulterated danger the man represented. Silas Thorne was more than a kingpin; he was a malignancy that had spread its tendrils throughout the Iron Triangle, feeding on desperation and fear. His reputation preceded him like a foul odor – a man who dealt in broken lives, who saw vulnerability not as a human failing, but as an opportunity for exploitation. To walk into Silas's world was to step into a viper's nest, a place where survival was a privilege, not a right, and where every smile could hide a blade.

Joe's mind replayed Brenda's description of Silas's operation. It wasn't just about pushing drugs; it was a sophisticated, multi-faceted enterprise built on a foundation of control and coercion. Silas offered a twisted semblance of order, a brutal hierarchy that promised escape from the chaos of the streets, but delivered only a more insidious form of enslavement. And Mike, in his desperate state, his judgment clouded by addiction and mounting debts, had stumbled right into the maw of that operation. He was a pawn, a disposable asset in Silas's grander schemes. The thought ignited a fire in Joe's gut, a fierce, protective rage that warred with the primal instinct for self-preservation.

He couldn't afford to be reckless. He was a single man against a well-oiled machine, a hunter against a predator who knew every inch of his territory. Brenda had been clear: Silas was ruthless, paranoid, and utterly unforgiving. He operated from a fortified compound, shielded by layers of loyalty, fear, and brute force. Getting to him wouldn't be a matter of kicking down a door; it would require precision, intelligence, and a deep understanding of Silas's operations.

Joe spent days meticulously piecing together what little he knew. He revisited the informants, pressing them for any detail, any nuance about Silas's routines, his habits, his weaknesses. He haunted the fringes of Silas's known territory, observing, listening, trying to glean any scrap of information that might provide an advantage. He noted the increased presence of Silas's enforcers, their hulking frames a constant, menacing reminder of the power they wielded. He saw the fear in the eyes of the locals, the way conversations hushed and gazes averted whenever Silas's name was even whispered.

He considered the possibility of enlisting help, but who? The police were too compromised, too entangled in the Triangle's rot to be reliable. The few honest cops he knew were either too far removed from the situation or too overwhelmed to offer any tangible assistance. His own circle was small, and dragging anyone else into this mess felt like a death sentence. This was his burden to bear, his fight to wage.

The plan began to crystallize, not in a grand, decisive moment, but in a series of calculated steps, each one fraught with peril. He knew he couldn't go in guns blazing. Silas wouldn't be caught off guard by a frontal assault. He needed an opening, a way to penetrate the defenses without triggering an immediate, overwhelming response. And that opening, he suspected, lay not in brute force, but in the very human elements that Silas so readily exploited: desperation, greed, and the desperate need for an escape.

He started by focusing on the periphery, the outer layers of Silas's operation. Brenda had mentioned Silas's reliance on a network of informants, people who fed him information in exchange for favors or protection. These were the loose threads Joe could potentially pull. He remembered Sammy "The Shank" Russo, the nervous low-level player Joe had encountered. Sammy's fear, his rambling warnings about Mike needing to do what he was told, now seemed less like paranoia and more like a genuine, albeit terrified, insight into Silas's methods. Sammy was a nobody, a sycophant, but perhaps he was also a terrified pawn himself, someone Silas could easily manipulate or dispose of. If Joe could get to Sammy, perhaps he could gain a small leverage, a crack in Silas's armor.

Joe sought out Sammy in the usual haunts, the grimy dive bars and pawn shops that served as informal meeting places for the Triangle's underbelly. He found him nursing a cheap whiskey in a corner booth of a dimly lit establishment called "The Lucky Seven." Sammy's eyes, already small and beady, widened with a mixture of recognition and dread when he saw Joe approach.

"Joe? What are you doing here, man?" Sammy's voice was a reedy whisper, his hand instinctively reaching for the glass.

"Just looking for someone who knows things, Sammy," Joe said, his voice deliberately low and steady. He slid into the booth opposite Sammy, ignoring the man's visible discomfort. "Someone who might have seen something. Someone who might have heard something about my brother."

Sammy swallowed hard. "Mike? Look, man, I don't know nothin'. Silas… he keeps his circle tight."

"Tight, but not invisible, Sammy," Joe pressed, his gaze unwavering. "Brenda mentioned you were around. Said you had a few words for me a while back. About Mike owing some people."

Sammy's face paled. He fidgeted, his eyes darting towards the exit. "That was… that was just talk, man. You know how it is in this neighborhood. People talk."

"They talk, and sometimes they listen, Sammy. And sometimes, they tell," Joe countered, leaning forward. "Silas seems to have a lot of people talking for him. People who benefit from him, people who owe him. People who might be looking for a way to get out from under his thumb, maybe? Or maybe just looking for a way to get ahead." He let the words hang in the air, observing Sammy's reaction.

The glint in Sammy's eyes, however fleeting, told Joe everything he needed to know. Sammy was scared, yes, but he was also looking for an out. The possibility of leverage was there, a faint shimmer of hope in the oppressive darkness.

"Look, man," Sammy began, his voice even more strained, "Silas… he isn't someone you mess with. He's got eyes everywhere. He knows who's talking, who's thinking about talking. You don't want to be on his radar."

"And you do?" Joe's question was a subtle probe, a calculated risk. "You seemed pretty worried about Mike owing people. Worried enough to warn me, in your own way."

Sammy finally broke eye contact, staring intensely at the condensation on his glass. "It's… it's complicated, Joe. Mike, he got himself into something deep. Deeper than you think. And Silas… Silas always finds the ones who are hurting, the ones who need something. He's a damn magnet for lost causes."

"And who pointed him towards Mike, Sammy?" Joe's voice was a low growl. "Who 'introduced' Mike to Silas's 'opportunity'?"

Sammy flinched. "I can't, man. I just… I can't. If Silas thinks I'm talking to you…" He trailed off, the unspoken threat hanging heavy between them.

Joe pushed a folded twenty-dollar bill across the table. It was a pittance, but in this context, it was a lifeline, a bribe, a desperate offer of protection. "This is for your time, Sammy. But if you know something, anything, that could help me find my brother, you owe it to him. You owe it to yourself. You don't want to be just another one of Silas's lost causes, do you?"

He left Sammy sitting there, a coiled spring of fear and indecision. Joe knew he hadn't gotten a confession, not yet. But he had planted a seed of doubt, a flicker of hope for Sammy, and a sliver of information about the subtle ways Silas operated. Silas didn't just use muscle; he used fear, debt, and the desperate hope for a better life.

The strategy began to shift from direct confrontation to infiltration, a slow, dangerous dance around the edges of Silas's operation. Joe needed to understand how Silas controlled his network, how he identified his targets, and how he ensured their compliance. Brenda had mentioned Mike's involvement in sourcing rare auto parts. This was a detail that had nagged at Joe. It wasn't the kind of thing Mike would typically get involved in, unless there was a significant profit motive, or a strong incentive, or perhaps, a direct order from Silas.

He returned to the bartender at "The Rusty Mug," a man named Gus, who had a knack for casual observation and a willingness to talk for a price. Gus had mentioned Mike asking about a specific, expensive auto part. Joe needed to know what that part was, and more importantly, who else had been asking about it, or who might have been facilitating such transactions.

"Gus," Joe said, sliding onto a stool and ordering a whiskey, "that guy Mike I asked about last week… the one asking about the car parts. You remember what kind of parts he was looking for?"

Gus wiped down the bar with a slow, deliberate motion. "Yeah, Mike. He was asking about some high-end stuff. Turbochargers, performance engines… the kind of parts you don't find on your average sedan. Real niche market. Expensive."

"And who else was asking about that kind of stuff?" Joe probed. "Anyone new in town? Anyone who suddenly seemed flush with cash?"

Gus pursed his lips, his gaze drifting towards the street outside. "Funny you ask. There's been a few new faces around. Guys who don't belong here, really. Drive the flashy cars, wear the slick clothes. They come in here sometimes, looking for information, looking for muscle, or just looking to flash their cash. Heard a couple of 'em talking about 'imports' and 'special orders.'"

"Imports?" Joe's ears perked up. "What kind of imports?"

"Cars, man. High-end stuff. Not just parts, but whole damn vehicles. Heard whispers about them being moved through here, specially modified, then shipped out. Silas's boys are involved, no doubt. They're always looking for ways to diversify, I guess."

This was it. This was the connection. Mike's knowledge of cars, his expertise with engines, was being weaponized by Silas. He wasn't just a drug mule; he was a facilitator, a specialist in Silas's illicit automotive trade. And the people asking about the parts were likely Silas's buyers, or his intermediaries. Joe needed to know who these new faces were.

He spent the next few days staking out "The Rusty Mug" and other watering holes frequented by Silas's crew. He wasn't looking for a direct confrontation, but for reconnaissance, for identifying key players, for mapping out the network. He saw them: men with the unmistakable air of casual menace, their eyes scanning, their conversations guarded, their loyalty bought and paid for. He started to recognize a few faces from Brenda's descriptions, the lieutenants, the enforcers, the men who ran Silas's dirty work.

One man, in particular, caught his attention. A sharp-dressed individual with a predatory smile and eyes that missed nothing. Brenda had referred to him as "Silas's right hand," a man named Marco Varelli. Not Marco, his brother's childhood friend, but a different Marco. This Varelli was known for his intelligence, his ruthlessness, and his uncanny ability to anticipate Silas's needs. Varelli was the kind of man who could orchestrate a complex operation, who could identify a valuable asset like Mike and integrate him into Silas's burgeoning automotive racket.

Joe's focus narrowed. If he could somehow get close to Varelli, if he could exploit Varelli's ambition or his greed, he might gain access to Silas himself. But Varelli was not going to be found in a dive bar; he operated on a higher level, in the cleaner, more clandestine corners of Silas's empire.

Brenda had also mentioned Silas's compound, a fortified estate on the outskirts of the Triangle, rumored to be a fortress of sorts, heavily guarded and virtually impenetrable. It was the heart of Silas's operation, the place where he conducted his business, where he kept his most valuable assets, and where he likely held Mike, or at least knew his current whereabouts. Getting to that compound was the ultimate objective, the final, most dangerous step.

Joe knew he couldn't go in alone. He needed a plan that was more than just a desperate gamble. He needed to understand the compound's layout, its security protocols, the routines of its guards. He started by mapping out the perimeter from a distance, observing the comings and goings, the shift changes, the blind spots. He also began researching Silas Thorne himself, delving into his past, looking for any cracks, any vulnerabilities, any leverage he might have. He learned that Silas had risen from the ashes of a rival gang, that he was known for his meticulous planning and his ability to exploit every opportunity. He also learned that Silas was a creature of habit, a man who thrived on control, and that any disruption to his routine could create an opening.

He remembered the informant Brenda's cryptic comment about a "special delivery" that was due to arrive at the compound within the next week. If he could intercept that delivery, or somehow gain access to it, he might be able to get inside. It was a long shot, a dangerous proposition, but it was a lead, a potential pathway into the lion's den.

The days leading up to this "special delivery" were a blur of heightened tension and meticulous preparation. Joe felt the familiar knot of adrenaline tighten in his stomach, a constant companion on this perilous journey. He knew this was it. The culmination of his investigation, the point of no return. He had gathered enough information, enough whispers and inklings, to form a rudimentary plan. The confrontation with Silas was no longer a vague possibility; it was an impending reality. He understood the immense risks involved. One misstep, one moment of hesitation, and it would all be over. But the thought of Mike, lost and broken, fueled his resolve. He had to do this, for Mike, for himself, for the semblance of justice that still held meaning in the grimy streets of the Iron Triangle. He was walking into the heart of the storm, and he had to be ready for whatever lay within.

# Chapter Eight
# The Secret Unveiled

### Infiltrating the Dealers Circle

The hum of the city was a low thrum against Joe's senses, a constant reminder of the life pulsing through the Iron Triangle, a life he was increasingly becoming a part of, albeit through its underbelly. He'd spent the better part of the last week shedding the skin of the concerned brother and donning the hardened shell of a man looking for a different kind of service. It was a performance, a carefully constructed illusion, but one he believed would grant him an audience with the unseen puppeteer. His strategy hinged on a single, undeniable truth: Silas Thorne didn't just deal in narcotics; he dealt in solutions, however illicit, for those who operated outside the law. And Joe, with his inherited knowledge of engines and a carefully cultivated air of desperate ambition, was about to present himself as just such a solution.

He started small, scouting the periphery of Silas's known operations, the sort of places where loose ends were tied up, or rather, where new connections were forged. The Rusty Mug had been a good start, providing him with a sliver of insight into the automotive undercurrent of Silas's empire. Now, he needed to escalate. He focused on a less frequented watering hole, "The Grindstone," a place known for its clientele who dealt in more specialized, less visible transactions. Here, the talk wasn't about stolen goods or petty scams, but about discreet modifications, untraceable vehicle conversions, and the lucrative business of moving sensitive cargo. It was a world Joe knew intimately, thanks to his father's legacy.

He entered The Grindstone on a Tuesday afternoon, the kind of slow day that invited conversation but discouraged scrutiny. The air was thick with stale cigarette smoke and the metallic tang of cheap beer. Joe took a seat at the bar, nursing a lukewarm coffee, his eyes scanning the room with an attentiveness that belied his casual posture. He'd practiced the lines in his head a hundred times, refining the persona: a man down on his luck, but with a skillset that could still command a price. He needed to project an image of competence, of discretion, and most importantly, of a shared understanding of how the world truly worked beneath the veneer of legality.

The bartender, a burly man with forearms like tree trunks and a perpetual scowl, eventually sidled up to him. "You new around here?" the man grunted, not unkindly, but with a professional assessment.

Joe met his gaze, offering a tight, almost imperceptible nod. "Just looking to see if there's work for someone with my hands." He let his gaze drift to his own calloused palms, a subtle signal. "I'm good with engines. Real good. The kind of good that can make things… run better. Quieter. Faster."

The bartender grunted again, wiping down a glass. "Silas got a lot of mouths to feed, and a lot of vehicles to keep running. What kind of 'better' are we talking about?"

This was the opening. Joe leaned in slightly, lowering his voice. "The kind that doesn't attract attention. The kind that can carry things. Or the kind that can outrun whatever's chasing it." He paused, letting the implication hang in the air. "Heard he's got a need for specialized work. Stuff that can't go through the usual channels. Stuff that requires… finesse."

The bartender's eyes narrowed, a flicker of interest in their depths. "Finesse. Silas likes finesse. But he also likes results. And he doesn't pay for talk."

"I don't talk," Joe replied, his voice hardening, shedding the last vestiges of his civilian demeanor. The anger that had been simmering beneath the surface began to surface, a controlled burn. "I do. My old man… he taught me how to make anything run like a dream. Or disappear into thin air. He ran a garage, back in the day. Clean on the outside, but he knew how to grease the right wheels." He was weaving a narrative, a backstory that resonated with the unspoken language of their world. His father's reputation, tarnished but still a known commodity in certain circles, served as a subtle credential.

"Your old man?" The bartender's expression shifted, a subtle recognition dawning. "Heard of him. Good with his hands, they said."

"He was," Joe confirmed, a grim satisfaction in his voice. "And I inherited it. Look, I'm not looking to get involved in the… day-to-day. I'm looking for a specific kind of job. Something that requires discretion. Something that pays well for a skilled hand." He pictured Mike, his brother, lost in the web Silas had spun. The thought fueled his resolve. "I heard Silas has a bit of a… logistics problem. Things that need to be moved, modified, made… invisible. I can help with that."

The bartender studied him for a long moment, his gaze dissecting Joe's every expression. He was weighing the risk, assessing the potential reward. "You talk about 'modifications,' 'invisible.' You talk about more than just oil changes and tune-ups."

"I do," Joe stated plainly. "I can make a car undetectable. I can outfit it for specific purposes. Special compartments. Reinforced chassis. Whatever Silas needs. I heard he's got a… growing need for transportation solutions." He was deliberately vague, letting Silas's presumed network fill in the blanks. The mention of "logistics problem" and "transportation solutions" was a nod to Brenda's earlier hints about Silas's expanding operations, possibly involving the movement of contraband beyond just drugs.

A slow smile, a predator's smile, spread across the bartender's face. "You're a bold one. Coming in here, talking like this."

"I'm a man who needs to work," Joe said, his voice steady, unwavering. "And I hear Silas is a man who values talent, regardless of how it's presented. I'm not asking about his business. I'm offering a service. A service that, I'm told, is in high demand." He was pushing, but carefully, not overplaying his hand.

The bartender let out a short, sharp laugh. "High demand, alright. Silas isn't afraid to get his hands dirty, and he isn't afraid to pay for someone who can clean up his messes, or create new ways to make them. You got a specific idea of what you can do?"

Joe decided to offer a concrete, but deniable, example. "I've been looking at some of the modified vehicles that have surfaced recently. The ones with the specialized fuel injectors, the upgraded suspension systems… the kind that could carry a significant payload without raising suspicion. I can replicate that. Improve it, even. Make them capable of longer hauls, of evading standard detection methods. And I can do it discreetly. No traceable parts, no signatures. Clean work." He was referencing the specialized automotive modifications that might be used for smuggling, hinting at his ability to facilitate such operations.

He watched the bartender closely. The man's eyes flickered with a recognition that went beyond mere curiosity. This was the language Silas's people understood – efficiency, discretion, and a certain level of sophisticated criminality.

"You saying you can make a car disappear into traffic?" the bartender asked, a hint of genuine interest replacing his gruff exterior.

"I can make it a ghost," Joe confirmed. "Or I can make it a bullet. Depends on what Silas needs." He leaned back, letting the weight of his words settle. He was offering his skills not just as a mechanic, but as a craftsman of illicit transportation, a creator of tools for Silas's operations.

The bartender seemed to consider this, his gaze drifting towards a back room, an area Joe had noted earlier with a reinforced door. "Silas likes to know who he's dealing with. He likes to vet his… contractors. Takes a while."

"I've got time," Joe said, pulling out a crisp fifty-dollar bill and sliding it across the bar. "And I've got skills. Tell him… tell him Joe from the old garage is looking for a serious project. One that requires a certain… specialized touch." He deliberately used the familial connection to his father's business, a subtle hint of legitimacy and reputation within the shadows.

The bartender pocketed the money with a nod. "Joe from the garage. Got it. I'll pass it along. But don't hold your breath. Silas moves at his own pace."

"I'm not going anywhere," Joe replied, his voice laced with a quiet determination. He knew this was just the first step, a carefully placed gamble. He hadn't gotten any direct information about Mike, not yet. But he had established himself as a potential asset, a craftsman with specialized, illicit skills. He had created an opening, a crack in the wall of Silas's guarded world. He'd also begun to subtly alter his own presentation. The slightly too-tight clothes, the forced swagger, the way he held himself – it was all a conscious effort to shed the image of the grieving brother and project an aura of someone who understood the transactional nature of this world, someone who wasn't afraid to get their hands dirty.

Over the next few days, Joe continued his subtle immersion. He frequented The Grindstone, always ordering the same thing, always observing, always projecting the same image of quiet competence and availability. He made sure to be seen, but not to be overly eager. He let the whispers of Silas's needs filter through the bar's grapevine, absorbing snippets of conversations about discreet transport, modifications for specific… 'shipments,' and the occasional mention of needing vehicles that could withstand unusual stress. He even overheard a hushed conversation about a particular shipment of rare auto parts, the very type Mike had been reportedly involved with, needing specialized containment and a quick, untraceable transfer.

He used his own knowledge to his advantage, occasionally dropping seemingly casual remarks to the bartender about specific engine modifications that would be ideal for covert operations. He spoke of reinforcing chassis to carry heavier loads, of advanced exhaust baffling systems to reduce noise signatures, of custom-built fuel tanks that could be easily disguised or repurposed. He was speaking their language, demonstrating a depth of knowledge that Silas would undoubtedly find valuable. His aim was to make himself indispensable, a craftsman whose skills were too specialized and too useful to be ignored.

One evening, as he was about to leave The Grindstone, the bartender called him over. "Got a message for you, Joe from the garage," he said, his tone significantly less gruff. He handed Joe a small, folded piece of paper. "Someone wants to talk to you about a 'project.' Said it's urgent."

Joe's heart hammered against his ribs. This was it. The bait had been taken. He unfolded the paper. It contained only a time and a location: an abandoned warehouse on the industrial edge of the Triangle, a place known for its isolation and its anonymity. The message was terse, impersonal, and exactly the kind of communication Silas Thorne would employ.

He knew, with a certainty that sent a shiver down his spine, that this was his first direct step into the lion's den. He wasn't just gathering information anymore; he was actively seeking the source of his brother's pain. The meticulous planning, the persona adoption, the carefully chosen words – it had all led to this clandestine meeting. He had to be ready for anything. He had to be more than just a brother looking for his lost sibling; he had to be a craftsman, a specialist, a man who understood the brutal calculus of this world, and who was willing to play the game to its dangerous conclusion. The shadows were deepening, and Joe was walking right into them, armed with nothing but his skills and a desperate hope for answers. He felt a grim satisfaction as he pocketed the note. He was finally getting closer to the truth, but he knew this was only the beginning of a much more dangerous game. The skills he was offering were precisely the skills Silas would use to further his own empire, and Joe was about to become an unwitting participant in its expansion, all in the hopes of finding his brother.

## The Network of Exploitation

The air in the abandoned warehouse hung thick and cloying, a potent cocktail of damp concrete, stale oil, and something acrid that Joe couldn't quite place – the lingering scent of desperation, perhaps. He'd arrived an hour before the time stipulated on the crumpled note, a habit ingrained from years of anticipating mechanical failures and the need for swift, decisive action. The silence here wasn't peaceful; it was a heavy, expectant void, punctuated only by the drip of unseen water and the scuttling of unseen things. Joe found a shadowed alcove, blending into the decay, his senses on high alert. He wasn't just a mechanic anymore; he was a ghost in the machine, observing the gears grind.

When they arrived, it wasn't with the swagger of men in charge, but with the furtive movements of those who understood the value of invisibility. Two men, their faces obscured by the gloom and the low-brimmed caps pulled low over their eyes, entered first, their movements fluid and economical, like predators casing their territory. They spoke in hushed, clipped tones, their words swallowed by the vastness of the space. Joe strained to hear, his focus sharpening, but their dialogue was a series of almost inaudible murmurs, punctuated by the clink of keys and the rustle of fabric.

Then, Silas Thorne. He moved with a deliberate, almost regal slowness, a stark contrast to the nervous energy of his associates. There was an aura about him, a coiled intensity that seemed to vibrate in the very air. He didn't need to shout to command attention; his presence alone was enough. Joe watched as Thorne surveyed the space, his eyes – sharp, assessing, and utterly devoid of warmth – sweeping over every shadowed corner. He was a man who understood leverage, who knew how to acquire and maintain control through a complex web of obligation, fear, and opportunity.

The conversation that followed was a masterclass in veiled threats and calculated incentives. Joe, hidden in his sanctuary of shadows, absorbed it all. They were discussing vehicles, modifications, and shipments, the same coded language he'd been learning, but now he was hearing it directly from the source. He heard Thorne's voice, a low rumble that carried an unnerving authority. "We need those units running cleaner, quieter. No loose ends. The buyer is… particular about discretion. And the payload? It needs to be secured. No surprises."

Joe's blood ran cold as he realized the conversation wasn't just about moving drugs. The mention of "units" and "payload" hinted at something far more complex, a diversified operation far beyond the simple narcotic trade he'd initially suspected. He saw one of Thorne's men, a gaunt individual with eyes that darted nervously, approach Thorne with a small, leather-bound ledger. Thorne took it, flipped through it with practiced speed, his lips tightening at something he read. He then casually tossed the ledger to the gaunt man. "Your numbers are off. Again. You know what happens when the numbers don't add up, don't you?"

The gaunt man flinched, his voice a reedy squeak. "Mr. Thorne, sir, it's just… the girls. They… they're a difficult asset to manage. They require… upkeep. And the risks… the risks are higher."

The word "girls" landed like a physical blow. Joe's gut twisted. This wasn't just about illicit cargo; this was about human lives, reduced to inventory. He saw Thorne laugh, a dry, rasping sound that held no humor. "Upkeep? Risks? They're commodities, aren't they? And commodities have a market value. If they're costing too much, we adjust the… inventory. Understand?" He gestured to the gaunt man's own pale, drawn face. "You're looking a little pale yourself. Maybe you need some… adjustments. To your own finances."

Joe felt a surge of icy rage. This was it. This was the true horror of Silas Thorne's empire. It wasn't just the drugs, the stolen goods; it was the systematic dehumanization, the reduction of people, particularly women, to mere tools, to disposable assets in a ruthless economic equation. He saw Thorne's men exchange nervous glances, their fear palpable. They were cogs in a machine, and Thorne was the unforgiving operator.

He watched as Thorne discussed modifications for a fleet of vans, the specifications chillingly precise. Reinforced bulkheads, hidden compartments, sophisticated tracking jammers – all designed for efficient, untraceable transport. Joe's mind, the mechanic's mind, cataloged the details, recognizing the ingenuity and the sheer criminality of the adaptations. He was witnessing the creation of instruments of exploitation, vehicles built to move not just illicit goods, but people, likely unwillingly.

The conversation then shifted to the recruitment of new personnel. Thorne spoke dismissively of loyalty, emphasizing instead utility and disposability. "We need fresh faces. Hungry ones. The kind who won't ask too many questions, who'll do what they're told. And if they can't deliver, we find someone else. The Triangle is full of people eager for a way out, even if it's just a different kind of cage."

Joe saw the gaunt man nod, his eyes fixed on the floor. "We've been looking into some of the newer arrivals. Those from out of state. They're less… connected. Easier to control."

"Excellent," Thorne's voice purred. "Find them. Offer them a chance. A chance to belong. A chance to escape their past. But make sure they understand the terms. This isn't charity. It's an investment. And we expect a return."

Joe's breath hitched. He thought of Mike. Was this how his brother had been drawn in? Offered a false sense of belonging, a promise of escape, only to be trapped in a cycle of exploitation? The thought was a corrosive acid, burning through his carefully constructed calm. He saw the casual way Thorne discussed human trafficking, the sheer banality with which he treated the lives of those he ensnared. It was a calculated system, built on the vulnerability of the desperate. The network wasn't just about logistics and mechanics; it was a human-harvesting operation.

He saw Thorne finalize a deal with one of his men, a nod of assent that sealed a transaction involving a shipment of… something… that needed to be moved swiftly and unseen. "Get it done. And make sure the… packaging is intact. No damage. We can't afford to lose the quality." The implication was clear, and Joe's stomach churned. He realized the depth of Thorne's depravity. He wasn't just a crime lord; he was a predator, meticulously orchestrating the suffering of the vulnerable for profit.

As the meeting drew to a close, Thorne's gaze swept over the warehouse again, a flicker of unease crossing his face. "This place… it's too exposed. Find me something more secure for the next… inventory transfer." He clapped one of his men on the shoulder, a gesture that was more of a threat than camaraderie. "And make sure the new recruits understand their value. If they think they can walk away, remind them of the cost."

Joe waited until the sounds of Thorne and his entourage had faded into the night, the heavy silence of the warehouse descending once more. He stayed for a long time, the images replaying in his mind, each one a further indictment of Silas Thorne. He had seen the machinery of exploitation up close, and it was far more horrific than he had ever imagined. The addicts were not just users; they were currency. The young women were not just victims; they were commodities. And Mike, his brother, was caught somewhere in this horrifying ecosystem, a pawn in Thorne's ruthless game.

Stepping out of the shadows, Joe felt the grit of the warehouse floor beneath his worn boots. He hadn't spoken a word, hadn't revealed his presence, but he had gained something more valuable than any overheard conversation: a visceral understanding of the monstrous scale of Silas Thorne's enterprise. It wasn't just about illegal goods; it was about the systematic crushing of human spirits, the commodification of lives. His resolve hardened into an unyielding obsidian. He wasn't just looking for his brother anymore; he was looking to dismantle this entire network of exploitation, piece by agonizing piece. He had glimpsed the true face of Silas Thorne's operation, and it was a face of utter, chilling inhumanity. The mechanical expertise he possessed was now to be weaponized against this very system, a silent war waged in the shadows of the Iron Triangle. The knowledge he'd gained was a dangerous burden, but it fueled a fire within him, a conviction that he could, and he must, do something to stop this. He knew the risks were astronomical, but the alternative— letting his brother and countless others remain trapped in Thorne's web—was unthinkable. He had to find a way to leverage his skills, his father's legacy, and his own desperate courage to chip away at this edifice of suffering, to expose the rot at its core and bring it all crashing down. The next step would require more than just observation; it would demand action, however covert, however perilous.

## A Devastating Revelation

The stale, metallic tang of the warehouse still clung to Joe's clothes, a grim perfume of his recent reconnaissance. He'd driven back to his workshop, the familiar hum of the engine a strange comfort after the oppressive silence he'd endured. The words Silas Thorne had uttered, casual as a dismissal, replayed in his mind, each one a shard of ice lodging itself deeper into his gut. "The girls… they're a difficult asset to manage." "Upkeep? Risks? They're commodities, aren't they?" "If they're costing too much, we adjust the… inventory." Joe had always known Thorne was a monster, but witnessing the chillingly detached language with which he discussed human lives, the reduction of desperate souls to mere line items on a ledger, had been a visceral shock. It wasn't just about drugs or stolen goods; it was a meticulously constructed system of human exploitation, a grotesque economy built on the desperation of others. And Mike… his brother was enmeshed in it, a pawn in Thorne's ruthless game.

He'd kept his presence a secret, a phantom in the shadows, but the knowledge he'd gleaned was a heavy, suffocating cloak. He'd seen the modifications Thorne was planning for the vehicles, the reinforced compartments, the jamming technology – not just for smuggling contraband, but for the efficient, untraceable transport of unwilling cargo. The "payloads" Thorne spoke of, the "packaging" that needed to be intact, the "quality" that couldn't be lost – it painted a horrifying picture that transcended mere criminal enterprise. It was a business built on the systematic dehumanization of people, particularly women, their lives commodified and traded for profit. The casual brutality, the sheer banality of Thorne's evil, gnawed at him.

Back in the sterile familiarity of his workshop, surrounded by the ordered chaos of tools and spare parts, Joe tried to piece together the fragmented clues. Thorne's operation was far more extensive than he'd initially conceived. It was a vast network, weaving through the Iron

Triangle, preying on the vulnerable, offering false promises of escape and belonging. He thought of the "recruits" Thorne mentioned, the "hungry ones," the "easier to control" individuals from out of state. Was this how Mike had been drawn in? Offered a way out, a chance to finally get on his feet, only to find himself trapped in Thorne's suffocating web? The thought was a bitter poison, turning his stomach.

He spent the next few days in a fog of grim determination. Sleep offered little respite, his dreams haunted by the cold, calculating eyes of Silas Thorne and the faceless, unheard cries of his victims. He meticulously reviewed every scrap of information he'd managed to gather, cross-referencing whispers from the street with the coded language he'd overheard. He pored over old schematics, tracing potential routes, identifying vulnerabilities in the seemingly impenetrable logistical chain Thorne had established. His mechanical mind, trained to find the flaw, the weak point, was now focused on a far more devastating target: Thorne's empire of exploitation.

The breakthrough, when it came, was not a dramatic confrontation but a quiet, almost insignificant detail unearthed from a stack of discarded invoices he'd managed to pilfer from a small, nondescript warehouse Thorne used as a front. Among the usual manifests for auto parts and industrial lubricants, he found a series of meticulously itemized receipts for what appeared to be specialized medical supplies – sedatives, restraints, and a particular brand of high-strength tranquilizer. The quantities were staggering, far exceeding anything that could be justified for legitimate medical purposes. But it was the notation on the final receipt that truly stopped Joe's breath. Scribbled in Thorne's own distinctive, angular handwriting, beneath a list of sedatives and restraints, was a single, chilling phrase: "Mike R. – special requisition. Final payment due upon completion of transfer."

The words hit Joe with the force of a physical blow, knocking the air from his lungs. *Mike R.* Special requisition. Completion of transfer. The implications were immediate, sickeningly clear. It wasn't just that Mike was involved in Thorne's operation; it was that he was a *part* of it, a tool being prepared for some grim purpose. The medical supplies, the restraints – they weren't for Thorne's workers or his enforcers. They were for the unwilling cargo, the "commodities" Thorne so casually discussed. And Mike was somehow involved in their procurement or administration.

His mind raced, piecing together the horrifying puzzle. Was Mike being forced to administer these drugs? To prepare these "units" for transfer? The idea that his own brother, the man he'd once taught to change a tire, was now complicit in such unspeakable acts, was almost unbearable. The special requisition confirmed his deepest fears: Mike wasn't just a victim of Thorne's manipulation; he was being actively utilized, his skills, whatever they had become, were being weaponized against innocent people. The debt Thorne alluded to in the warehouse – was it a debt Mike owed, or a debt that was being *collected* through his forced participation?

Joe felt a wave of nausea wash over him. He remembered Mike's increasingly erratic behavior in the months leading up to his disappearance, the secretive phone calls, the furtive glances. He'd dismissed it as Mike struggling to make ends meet, falling into bad company. But now, the pieces clicked into place with a sickening finality. Mike had been drawn into Thorne's web, perhaps initially with promises of easy money, then coerced, threatened, and finally, used. The revelation was more devastating than any violence Thorne could inflict. It wasn't just that his brother was in danger; it was the dawning horror that Mike might be actively contributing to that danger for others.

He sifted through the other invoices, his hands trembling. Another set of receipts detailed the purchase of advanced tracking devices, the same kind used in high-security cargo, alongside specialized signal jammers. These weren't for Thorne's usual smuggling routes; these were for precision movements, for cargo that needed to be monitored and controlled with absolute certainty. And then, another note, this time on a manifest for a shipment of vehicle parts: "Mike R. – oversight required for transfer protocol. Ensure all units remain offline until designated drop point." Transfer protocol. Units. The words echoed the chilling language Thorne used to describe the enslaved individuals he trafficked.

The truth was a corrosive acid, eating away at Joe's resolve, yet simultaneously hardening it. Mike wasn't just being held captive; he was an active, albeit coerced, participant in Thorne's human trafficking operation. The "special requisition" was a clear indication that Thorne viewed Mike as a valuable, albeit compromised, asset. He was being used to manage the human cargo, to ensure their compliance, their silence, and their ultimate delivery. The thought of Mike, his own flesh and blood, being forced to subdue and transport innocent women and girls, was a torment beyond anything Joe could have imagined.

He needed more. He needed to understand the extent of Mike's involvement, the nature of the "transfer protocol" he was overseeing, and, most importantly, how to get his brother out without becoming another casualty of Thorne's ruthlessness. The casual mention of "girls" and "upkeep" in the warehouse, combined with the medical supply receipts, painted a grim picture of Thorne's barbaric business model. Mike was caught in the middle, a captive performing the role of captor.

Joe felt a deep, gnawing sense of betrayal, not just by Thorne, but by circumstances, by the system that had created this desperate situation for his brother. He remembered their father, a man who had taught him the value of honesty and hard work, of protecting those weaker than yourself. How would his father have viewed Mike's current predicament? The questions burned in Joe's mind, fueling a desperate need to rectify this horrific situation, to pull Mike back from the precipice of complicity.

He meticulously documented every detail, every receipt, every cryptic note. This was more than just proof of Thorne's depravity; it was a roadmap to Mike's subjugation, a chilling testament to how deeply his brother had been ensnared. The medical supplies, the restraints, the tracking devices – they were the tools of Thorne's trade, and Mike was being forced to wield them. The revelation was a devastating confirmation of Joe's worst fears, painting a clearer, more horrific picture of Mike's situation than he had ever dared to imagine. It wasn't just a debt or a misguided association; it was active participation in a crime that chilled him to the bone. Mike was complicit, not by choice, but by Thorne's brutal coercion. The path forward was fraught with danger, but Joe knew he couldn't stand idly by. He had to find a way to expose Thorne, to free his brother, and to dismantle this monstrous enterprise, no matter the personal cost. The secret unveiled was not just about Thorne's crimes; it was about the shattering realization that his own brother was entangled in the very machinery of suffering he was determined to destroy.

## The Deeper Consequences

The stark revelation of Mike's complicity, however coerced, was a bitter pill for Joe to swallow. It transmuted his quest from a simple rescue mission into something far more complex, far more dangerous. The "special requisition" for Mike, the overseeing of "transfer protocols" – these weren't isolated incidents. They were threads in a much larger tapestry of corruption that Joe was only beginning to perceive. He'd focused so intently on his brother, on rescuing Mike from Silas Thorne's clutches, that he'd inadvertently overlooked the broader implications of Thorne's enterprise. The Iron Triangle wasn't just a place where desperate people went to disappear or find illicit work; it was a fertile ground for Thorne's brand of predatory capitalism, a system that preyed on the very fabric of the community.

Joe returned to his workshop, the retrieved invoices spread out on his workbench like a morbid hand of cards. He meticulously re-examined every detail, his mechanical mind searching for patterns beyond the immediate. The medical supplies, the tracking devices, the sedatives – they spoke of control, of suppression, of a chilling efficiency in managing unwilling human assets. But it was the subtle indicators, the periphery details, that began to paint a more unsettling picture. He noticed repeated transactions with a small, regional pharmaceutical distributor, a company whose usual clientele consisted of local clinics and veterinarians. The sheer volume of Thorne's orders, however, far exceeded any legitimate need. This wasn't just about procuring supplies; it was about manipulating the supply chain itself, potentially diverting or hoarding resources meant for legitimate medical purposes.

He started tracing the origins of these suppliers, cross-referencing them with local business directories and public records. Most were legitimate, small businesses struggling to stay afloat in a tough economy. But one name kept reappearing: a company called "Haven Consulting." Thorne's invoices listed Haven Consulting as a provider of "logistical support" and "personnel management" for his operations. On the surface, it sounded innocuous, a professional service. But Joe, keenly aware of Thorne's deceptive nature, felt a prickle of unease. He dug deeper, finding that Haven Consulting was a shell corporation, a phantom entity with no discernible physical presence or publicly listed employees. Its registered address was a post office box, and its listed directors were a series of placeholder names that appeared and disappeared with unnerving regularity. This wasn't just about Thorne; it was about the infrastructure that enabled him, the layers of obfuscation that allowed his vile business to thrive.

The realization dawned slowly, like a bruise spreading across his consciousness: Thorne's operation wasn't a standalone criminal enterprise. It was, in all likelihood, deeply embedded within the community. The sheer scale of the operation, the specialized equipment, the seemingly legitimate suppliers – these things required a certain level of access, a tacit approval, or at the very least, a willful ignorance from individuals in positions of authority. He thought of the local police force, the city council, the community leaders he'd always assumed were figures of integrity. Were they complicit? Or were they simply blind, their vision clouded by the sheer pervasiveness of Thorne's influence?

Joe remembered conversations he'd had with Mike in the months leading up to his disappearance. Mike had been desperate, drowning in debt from a gambling addiction that had spiraled out of control. He'd spoken vaguely of a "big opportunity," a way to "get ahead," but had been evasive about the details. Joe had dismissed it as the hopeful rambling of a man trying to escape his own failures. Now, he saw those desperate pleas in a new, horrifying light. Mike wasn't just addicted; he was a target. Thorne and his ilk preyed on individuals like Mike, on their weaknesses, their desires, their desperation. They offered a false sense of belonging, a way out, only to ensnare them in a web of debt and coercion.

The "girls" Thorne had referred to, the "commodities" he spoke of so casually – Joe's mind kept returning to that chilling language. He'd initially assumed it referred to sex trafficking, a grim reality that was unfortunately all too common. But the scale of the operation, the specialized medical supplies, the "transfer protocols" – it suggested something even more horrific. What if Thorne was involved in something far more systematic, more insidious? What if the "inventory" he managed wasn't just about coercion and forced labor, but something even more profound, more disturbing? The thought sent a shiver down his spine, a cold dread that had nothing to do with the chill of the workshop.

He started looking at the community with a fresh, jaundiced eye. He thought of the families who had lived in the Iron Triangle for generations, the working-class people who had always been overlooked, undervalued. He remembered the whispers of families struggling to make ends meet, of children going hungry, of a pervasive sense of hopelessness that permeated certain neighborhoods. Was Thorne's operation a symptom of this societal decay, or was it a cause? Was he not only exploiting individuals but also actively contributing to the disintegration of families, preying on the vulnerable and leaving a trail of broken lives in his wake?

Joe recalled a specific incident from his childhood, a family friend who had suddenly disappeared, leaving behind a wife and two young children. The official explanation had been that he'd "run off," but Joe's father had always suspected something more sinister. At the time, Joe had been too young to understand the implications. Now, he wondered if that family friend had been another victim of Thorne's network, another soul swallowed by the shadows of the Iron Triangle. The thought that Thorne's predatory reach extended back years, ensnaring generations, was almost too much to bear.

He painstakingly cataloged every name, every address, every transaction that seemed even remotely suspicious. He realized that his mission had expanded exponentially. It wasn't just about rescuing Mike; it was about exposing Silas Thorne and the entire network that supported him. It was about shining a light into the darkest corners of the Iron Triangle and revealing the rot that had taken root. He understood now that Mike's addiction and disappearance were not isolated incidents, but symptoms of a larger societal illness, a pervasive corruption that had allowed Thorne to flourish.

The medical supply receipts, in particular, nagged at him. The specific tranquilizers, the quantities, the stated purpose – they suggested more than just subduing victims. They hinted at preparation, at conditioning, at a chillingly systematic approach to control. What if the "special requisition" for Mike wasn't just about him assisting in transfers, but about him being a conduit, a handler for individuals who were being drugged, manipulated, and transported like so much chattel? The sheer dehumanization inherent in Thorne's operation was staggering.

He began to consider the possibility of collusion with corrupt officials. The seemingly effortless movement of goods, the lack of overt law enforcement intervention – it all pointed to a system that was either deliberately blind or actively involved. He thought of the local district attorney's office, known for its tough stance on street crime, yet seemingly oblivious to the larger, more insidious operations festering beneath the surface. Was it incompetence, or something far more deliberate? The thought that the very institutions meant to protect the community were either unwilling or unable to act was a bitter indictment.

Joe felt a surge of anger, a righteous fury that burned through his despair. He had to act. He couldn't let Thorne continue to exploit the vulnerable, to shatter families, to turn his brother into an accomplice in his vile trade. The evidence he had gathered was a powerful weapon, but it needed to be wielded strategically. He couldn't just storm Thorne's compound; he needed to dismantle the entire network, brick by painstaking brick.

He meticulously pieced together the timeline of Mike's descent, correlating it with Thorne's known activities. Mike's gambling debts had escalated dramatically around the same time Thorne's operations in the Iron Triangle had begun to expand. It was a grim confirmation of his suspicion: Thorne had likely identified Mike as a vulnerable target, an easy mark, and had slowly, systematically drawn him into his web. The "opportunity" Mike had spoken of was a gilded cage, a promise of salvation that had instead led to utter damnation.

The implications of Thorne's operation being so deeply entrenched sent a cold shiver down Joe's spine. It meant that his fight wouldn't be confined to a single warehouse or a single street. It would be a battle against a system, against corruption, against the very apathy that allowed such darkness to fester. He knew he couldn't win this alone. He needed allies, people who were also being wronged, people who had also suffered at Thorne's hands. But finding them, trusting them, would be another challenge entirely. In the Iron Triangle, trust was a rare and precious commodity, often bought and sold like any other illicit trade.

He spent hours poring over the invoices and receipts, his brow furrowed in concentration. He was looking for connections, for vulnerabilities, for anything that could be used to bring Thorne down. The "special requisition" for Mike was a clear indication of Thorne's control, but it also suggested a potential point of leverage. If Mike was being used, perhaps he could be turned. Perhaps there was a sliver of the brother Joe remembered, buried beneath the layers of coercion and despair, who could be reached.

The medical supplies were particularly disturbing. The mention of specific tranquilizers and sedatives implied a level of expertise, a medical knowledge that Thorne likely didn't possess himself. This pointed to another layer of complicity, perhaps a corrupt doctor or a rogue nurse providing Thorne with the means to control his "cargo." Joe wondered if Haven Consulting played a role in this as well, acting as an intermediary for these illicit medical supplies. The shell corporation was a linchpin, a central hub for Thorne's network of deception.

He realized that his understanding of Thorne's operation had evolved significantly. It wasn't just about stolen goods or drug trafficking. It was about the systematic exploitation and commodification of human lives, the creation of a shadow economy built on misery and despair. Mike was not just a pawn; he was a cog in a much larger, more sinister machine. And Joe was now determined to dismantle that machine, piece by agonizing piece, even if it meant confronting the deepest, darkest secrets of his own community. The revelation of Mike's entanglement had opened his eyes to a far more pervasive sickness, a rot that extended far beyond his own family and threatened to consume the entire Iron Triangle. His fight had just begun, and the stakes were higher than he had ever imagined.

## The Personal Stake

The stark reality of Mike's involvement, however manufactured, hit Joe with the force of a physical blow. It wasn't just about rescuing his brother anymore; it was about unraveling a conspiracy that had clearly burrowed deep into the heart of their community. The seemingly innocuous "special requisition" for Mike, the meticulous oversight of "transfer protocols" – these weren't isolated incidents. They were integral components of a far larger, more insidious operation orchestrated by Silas Thorne. Joe had been so consumed with the singular goal of pulling Mike out of Thorne's suffocating grip that he had, in his tunnel vision, failed to grasp the sheer scale of Thorne's enterprise. The Iron Triangle wasn't merely a place where the desperate sought refuge or illicit employment; it had become a breeding ground for Thorne's predatory capitalism, a system that systematically exploited the very foundations of their shared existence.

Back in the familiar, grease-scented confines of his workshop, Joe spread the retrieved invoices across his workbench. They lay there like a grim tableau, a stark testament to Thorne's clandestine activities. His methodical mind, accustomed to diagnosing mechanical failures and rebuilding intricate engines, now sifted through a different kind of mechanism – one fueled by corruption and human suffering. The medical supplies, the sophisticated tracking devices, the potent sedatives – each item whispered of control, of suppression, of a chillingly efficient methodology for managing unwilling human assets. But it was the subtler details, the peripheral anomalies, that began to coalesce into a far more disturbing narrative. He noticed a recurring pattern of transactions with a small, regional pharmaceutical distributor. This company, as far as Joe could tell from his initial research, typically catered to local clinics and veterinary practices. The sheer volume of Thorne's orders, however drastic, vastly exceeds any conceivable legitimate necessity. This wasn't just about acquiring supplies; it was about the manipulation of the entire supply chain, a calculated diversion and hoarding of resources that should have been accessible to the community for genuine medical purposes.

His investigation led him down a rabbit hole of cross-referenced business directories and public records, tracing the origins of these suppliers. Most were legitimate, small enterprises struggling against the relentless economic tide. Yet, one name surfaced with unsettling frequency: "Haven Consulting." Thorne's invoices consistently listed Haven Consulting as a provider of "logistical support" and "personnel management" for his various operations. On the surface, the description was blandly professional, seemingly innocuous. But Joe, acutely aware of Thorne's capacity for deception, felt a growing unease. Further digging revealed Haven Consulting to be a phantom entity, a mere shell corporation with no discernible physical presence or publicly listed employees. Its registered address was a post office box, and the names of its listed directors shifted with an almost spectral regularity, appearing and disappearing like phantoms in the bureaucratic ether. This wasn't solely about Thorne's direct actions; it was about the intricate infrastructure that facilitated them, the layered obfuscation that allowed his vile business to fester and flourish.

The dawning realization was slow, like a bruise blooming across his consciousness, spreading an inky stain of dread. Thorne's operation wasn't an isolated criminal venture. It was, with a terrifying degree of certainty, deeply embedded within the fabric of their community. The sheer magnitude of the operation, the specialized equipment, the veneer of legitimacy presented by his suppliers – all of it hinted at a level of access, a tacit approval, or at the very least, a deliberate, willful blindness from individuals in positions of authority. He found himself replaying conversations with local law enforcement, with members of the city council, with community leaders he had always regarded as pillars of integrity. Were they complicit in this rot, or were they simply oblivious, their vision clouded by the pervasive, insidious influence Thorne wielded?

Joe's mind drifted back to the fragmented conversations he'd had with Mike in the months preceding his disappearance. Mike had been adrift, drowning in a sea of debt stemming from a gambling addiction that had spiraled catastrophically out of control. He'd spoken in vague, almost hopeful terms of a "big opportunity," a chance to "get ahead," but had become evasive when pressed for details. At the time, Joe had dismissed it as the desperate rationalizations of a man trying to escape his own failures. Now, those hushed confessions took on a horrifying new dimension. Mike wasn't just battling an addiction; he had become a target. Thorne and his ilk preyed on individuals like Mike, exploiting their vulnerabilities, their desires, their sheer desperation. They offered a deceptive promise of belonging, a fabricated pathway to salvation, only to ensnare them in an inescapable web of debt and coercion.

The chilling language Thorne had used – referring to the "girls" and the "commodities" with such callous detachment – echoed in Joe's mind. He had initially interpreted it as a grim reference to sex trafficking, a brutal reality tragically prevalent in many urban centers. But the sheer scale of Thorne's operation, the sophisticated medical supplies, the cold efficiency of the "transfer protocols" – these elements suggested something far more systematic, far more insidious. What if Thorne's business extended beyond coercion and forced labor, venturing into something even more profound, more disturbing? The mere possibility sent a tremor of cold dread through him, a visceral reaction that had nothing to do with the chill in his workshop.

He began to view his own community through a new, jaundiced lens. He thought of the families who had been rooted in the Iron Triangle for generations, the working-class people who had consistently been overlooked, their contributions undervalued. He remembered the hushed whispers of families struggling to put food on the table, of children going to bed hungry, of a pervasive, suffocating sense of hopelessness that seemed to settle over certain neighborhoods like a perpetual fog. Was Thorne's operation a symptom of this societal decay, or was it actively contributing to it? Was he not only exploiting individuals but also systematically dismantling families, preying on the most vulnerable and leaving a devastating wake of broken lives?

A poignant memory surfaced from his childhood: a family friend, a man Joe had admired, had vanished without a trace, leaving behind a distraught wife and two young children. The official story had been that he had simply "run off," but Joe's father had always harbored a deep suspicion of something far more sinister. At the time, Joe had been too young to comprehend the gravity of such implications. Now, a chilling question echoed in his mind: could that family friend have been another victim of Thorne's sprawling network, another soul irrevocably lost to the encroaching shadows of the Iron Triangle? The thought that Thorne's predatory reach might extend back years, ensnaring multiple generations, was almost unbearable.

With painstaking precision, Joe began to meticulously catalog every name, every address, every transaction that even remotely hinted at impropriety. He understood now that his mission had undergone a radical transformation. It was no longer solely about extracting Mike from Thorne's clutches; it was about exposing Silas Thorne and the entire corrupt ecosystem that propped him up. It was about forcing a harsh, unflinching light into the darkest corners of the Iron Triangle, revealing the deep-seated rot that had taken root. Mike's addiction and subsequent disappearance were not isolated incidents, but rather symptoms of a pervasive societal illness, a systemic corruption that had allowed Thorne to thrive unchecked.

The medical supply receipts, in particular, continued to gnaw at him. The specific tranquilizers, the alarmingly large quantities, the deliberately vague stated purpose – they suggested far more than mere incapacitation. They hinted at a chilling level of preparation, of conditioning, of a systematic approach to dehumanization and control. What if the "special requisition" for Mike wasn't simply about his assistance in facilitating transfers, but about him acting as a conduit, a handler for individuals who were being systematically drugged, manipulated, and transported like inanimate cargo? The sheer, unadulterated dehumanization inherent in Thorne's entire operation was staggering, a monstrous perversion of human decency.

He started to seriously consider the undeniable possibility of collusion with corrupt officials. The seemingly effortless movement of illicit goods, the conspicuous absence of overt law enforcement intervention – it all pointed towards a system that was either willfully ignorant or actively complicit. He thought of the local district attorney's office, a body known for its aggressive stance on petty street crime, yet inexplicably oblivious to the larger, more insidious operations festering beneath the surface. Was this a failure of competence, or something far more deliberate and sinister? The notion that the very institutions established to safeguard the community were either unwilling or unable to act was a bitter, damning indictment of their integrity.

He acknowledged that his entire understanding of Thorne's operation had undergone a profound and unsettling evolution. This wasn't merely about stolen goods or some localized drug trafficking ring. It was about the systematic, industrialized exploitation and commodification of human lives, the creation of a vast shadow economy built upon the bedrock of misery, despair, and broken dreams. Mike was not merely a pawn in Thorne's ruthless game; he had become an unwitting cog in a much larger, far more sinister and pervasive machine. And Joe, fueled by a potent mix of grief and righteous fury, was now irrevocably determined to dismantle that machine, piece by agonizing piece, even if it meant confronting the deepest, darkest secrets that lay buried within his own community. The horrifying revelation of Mike's entanglement had ripped away a veil, exposing him to a far more pervasive sickness, a deep-seated rot that extended far beyond the confines of his own family and threatened to consume the entirety of the Iron Triangle. His fight, he knew with absolute certainty, had only just begun, and the stakes were immeasurably higher than he had ever dared to imagine. The weight of this knowledge settled upon him, a crushing burden that made every breath feel like a struggle. His identity as a brother, once a source of uncomplicated love and protection, now felt terrifyingly fragile, twisted into a desperate quest for redemption and retribution. The legacy of his family, a legacy of hard work and community pride, now felt like a precarious tightrope he was being forced to walk, with the abyss of his brother's fate yawning below. He wasn't a soldier, nor a detective; he was simply a man staring into the abyss of his own making, forced to reconcile the brother he loved with the stranger he had become, all while carrying the heavy mantle of his family's past and the perilous uncertainty of their future. The personal stake was no longer just about Mike; it was about his own soul, his own humanity, and the very survival of everything he held dear. The confrontation, he knew, was not just inevitable; it was the only path forward.

# Chapter Nine
# Confrontation

## The Trap is Set

The flickering fluorescent lights of the abandoned warehouse hummed a discordant lullaby, casting long, dancing shadows that seemed to writhe with a life of their own. Joe stood in the cavernous space, the stale air thick with the metallic tang of rust and something else... something vaguely organic, like decay. His hands, calloused and ingrained with the grease of a thousand engine repairs, felt strangely alien as he adjusted the concealed microphone clipped to the inside of his jacket. Every rustle of his clothes, every breath he took, felt amplified, a deafening roar in the oppressive silence. He was a mechanic, not a spy, a man who understood the predictable mechanics of an engine, not the unpredictable, volatile machinery of human malice. Yet here he was, a lone cog in a much larger, far more dangerous contraption, about to engage directly with the architect of his brother's downfall.

He had spent the last forty-eight hours in a state of heightened, almost hyper-vigilant awareness, a blur of late-night calls, clandestine meetings in dimly lit diners, and hours spent hunched over his workbench, poring over the damning evidence he'd painstakingly unearthed. The invoices, the supplier lists, the phantom addresses – they were all pieces of a monstrous puzzle, and now he was about to force the final, crucial piece into place. The plan, if one could call such a desperate gamble a "plan," had coalesced with a chilling, almost inevitable logic. He had used the very vulnerabilities Thorne exploited to bait his trap. He'd contacted Marcus "The Serpent" Bellwether, a fixer known throughout the underbelly of the city for his discretion and his uncanny ability to procure anything, or anyone, for the right price. Bellwether, a man whose eyes held the cold, calculating gleam of a predator, had been surprisingly amenable, his price a hefty percentage of whatever Thorne was willing to pay for the "special delivery" Joe was supposedly offering. The "delivery" itself was a carefully constructed ruse, a shipment of high-grade pharmaceuticals that Joe claimed to have intercepted from a rival operation. It was a dangerous lie, a tightrope walk over an abyss, but it was the only currency Thorne understood: illicit goods and profitable transactions.

Joe had chosen this particular warehouse for its isolation, its anonymity, its utter lack of history or significance. It was a blank slate, a void where Thorne's avarice could meet its match. He'd arrived an hour before the scheduled meeting, meticulously checking the perimeter, his senses on high alert for any sign of surveillance, any anomaly in the otherwise unremarkable urban decay. He'd felt a profound sense of irony as he'd scanned the rusted metal beams and broken windows. This was a place where things were discarded, forgotten, deemed useless. It was a fitting stage for Thorne's inevitable downfall.

His heart hammered against his ribs, a frantic, trapped bird beating its wings against the confines of his chest. He ran through the mental checklist again, a litany of desperation. The backup transmitter he carried in his pocket, the discreet burner phone, the small, sturdy wrench he kept tucked into his waistband – crude tools, perhaps, against the sophisticated network Thorne commanded, but they were all he had. He'd confided in no one, not his family, not even his closest friends. This was a solo operation, a burden he had to carry alone. The thought of putting anyone else in danger, of implicating another soul in this sordid affair, was a risk he couldn't afford to take.

He closed his eyes, forcing himself to breathe, to channel the quiet focus he employed when coaxing a stubborn engine back to life. It was about precision, about understanding the intricate workings of the mechanism and applying the right pressure, the right leverage. Thorne was the mechanism, and Joe had spent weeks dissecting his operations, identifying the pressure points, the hidden vulnerabilities. He knew Thorne was arrogant, supremely confident in his invincibility, his ability to manipulate and control every situation. That arrogance was Joe's greatest asset.

He'd rehearsed the conversation a hundred times in his head. He wouldn't show fear, wouldn't betray the panic churning within him. He would be calm, professional, even a little dismissive. He needed Thorne to underestimate him, to see him as just another desperate businessman, another pawn in his game. The revelation of Mike's involvement, the detailed accounting of Thorne's exploitation of the vulnerable, would be his opening salvo, his gambit to gain the upper hand. He would present it not as an accusation, but as a business proposition, a cautionary tale of risks and liabilities that Thorne, the shrewd businessman, would surely appreciate.

The sound of an approaching vehicle, a low rumble that vibrated through the concrete floor, shattered the fragile quiet. Joe's muscles tensed, his body instinctively preparing for the inevitable confrontation. He pressed himself against a stack of decaying crates, the rough wood scratching against his jacket. The engine noise grew louder, closer, finally cutting out with a jarring finality. Footsteps echoed in the vast space, heavy, deliberate, accompanied by the murmur of voices. Thorne was here.

Joe's breath hitched. He could see Thorne now, a hulking silhouette emerging from the gloom, flanked by two burly guards, their faces impassive, their eyes scanning the surroundings with practiced vigilance. Thorne himself seemed to radiate an aura of predatory power, his expensive suit a stark contrast to the grimy surroundings, his voice a low, resonant growl that carried easily through the air.

"You're late, Joe," Thorne said, his voice devoid of any warmth, laced with an undercurrent of impatience. "And I don't appreciate being kept waiting."

Joe stepped out from behind the crates, his hands held loosely at his sides, a carefully cultivated semblance of nonchalance masking the tremor that threatened to betray him. "Traffic was a bitch," he replied, his voice deliberately flat, betraying none of the adrenaline coursing through his veins. "You know how it is around here."

Thorne's lips curled into a semblance of a smile, a predatory baring of teeth that sent a fresh wave of unease through Joe. "I'm more interested in the merchandise you've brought, Joe. Let's see if it's worth the inconvenience."

Joe gestured towards a tarp-covered pallet he'd strategically placed near the center of the warehouse. "It's all there. As agreed. High-grade, untraceable. Enough to keep your operation running smoothly for a good long while." He kept his gaze steady, meeting Thorne's unnerving stare. He could feel the weight of the guards' gazes, the silent, omnipresent threat they represented.

"Good," Thorne said, nodding to one of his men, who approached the pallet and began to pull back the tarp. "Because I'm not a man who tolerates… deviations from the plan." His eyes, dark and unreadable, bored into Joe. "Especially not from people I've helped."

The words hung in the air, a subtle, veiled threat that Joe refused to acknowledge directly. "We all have our… arrangements, Silas," Joe said, his tone shifting subtly, a new edge creeping into his voice. He'd decided on his opening gambit, the calculated risk that could either win him the game or lose him everything. "But I've been doing some thinking. About the liabilities involved. About the risks inherent in certain… unsavory partnerships."

Thorne's head tilted, a flicker of curiosity in his eyes. "Liabilities? What are you talking about, Joe?"

"I'm talking about your extensive use of… distressed assets," Joe continued, his voice low and measured. "Your reliance on individuals with… compromised backgrounds. People like my brother,

Mike." He saw Thorne's expression tighten, the casual veneer beginning to crack. "I've seen the invoices, Silas. The requisitions. The transfer protocols. It's all there. Every transaction, every diversion of resources. And it paints a very clear picture."

He saw the guards shift, their hands instinctively moving towards their belts. Joe didn't flinch. He knew this was the moment, the precipice.

"What picture is that, Joe?" Thorne's voice was dangerously soft, a predator's purr.

"The picture of a man who's built an empire on the backs of the desperate," Joe said, his voice gaining strength, resonating with a newfound conviction. "A man who preys on addiction, on vulnerability, on the very people this community is supposed to protect. I know about the medical supplies, Silas. The sedatives. The conditioning. I know what you're doing to those girls, to those families."

Thorne's face contorted, the mask of calm finally shattering, replaced by a cold, unadulterated fury. "You think you can come into my territory, threaten me with some half-baked conspiracy theory, and expect to walk away with a profit?" he spat, his voice rising in volume. "You're a fool, Joe. A desperate, deluded fool."

"I'm not here to threaten you, Silas," Joe countered, his gaze unwavering. "I'm here to make you an offer. An offer you can't refuse. Because I have something you don't want anyone to know about. I have proof. Proof that could bring this entire operation down. Proof that could put you away for a very long time." He paused, letting the weight of his words sink in. "And I'm willing to forget it all. For a price."

He watched Thorne's eyes, searching for any flicker of weakness, any hint of capitulation. Thorne's guards had fanned out, surrounding Joe, their menacing presence a palpable pressure. Joe felt a bead of sweat trickle down his temple, the tension in the air thick enough to choke on. This was it. The ultimate gamble. He had laid his cards on the table, the raw, unvarnished truth of Thorne's depravity. Now, he waited to see if the devil himself would fold. The silence stretched, taut and suffocating, punctuated only by the distant wail of a siren, a mournful sound that seemed to underscore the grim reality of the world they inhabited. Joe braced himself, his knuckles white, his breath held tight, ready for whatever hell Thorne was about to unleash. He had walked into the lion's den, and now, he had to face the beast. The trap was set, and whether he was the hunter or the prey remained to be seen.

## Facing Th Architect of Ruin

The air in the warehouse hung heavy, not just with the usual scent of damp concrete and neglect, but with a palpable tension, a charged stillness that preceded a storm. Joe felt it in his bones, a prickling awareness that sharpened his every sense. He stood in the vast, echoing space, a solitary figure dwarfed by the cavernous emptiness and the looming silhouettes of Thorne's enforcers. His heart, a frantic drum against his ribs, was a testament to the precariousness of his position. He was a mechanic, a man whose hands were accustomed to the predictable, tangible reality of engines, thrust into a game of shadows and deceit where the stakes were his brother's life and his own.

Silas Thorne emerged from the deeper recesses of the warehouse, not walking so much as gliding, an embodiment of predatory grace. He was a man who exuded an almost casual menace, his expensive tailored suit a stark contrast to the grimy, industrial landscape. The two hulking guards flanking him were less individuals and more extensions of Thorne's will, their impassive faces and coiled tension a silent, potent warning. Thorne's eyes, dark and unnervingly steady, met Joe's across the expanse of the decaying space. There was no surprise in them, no apprehension, only a cold, calculating assessment.

Thorne's laughter, when it finally came, was a harsh, grating sound that echoed like a death knell in the vast space. It was devoid of mirth, laced instead with a chilling amusement that sent a fresh wave of dread through Joe. "An offer," Thorne repeated, his voice regaining a measure of its earlier control, though the fury still simmered just beneath the surface. "You come into my warehouse, under the guise of a transaction, and then you attempt to extort me? With what? Some poorly organized files you probably stole from a low-level clerk?" He gestured dismissively at the documents spread out on the pallet. "You overestimate your own importance, Joe. And you underestimate mine."

"These aren't just files, Silas," Joe said, his voice firm, refusing to be cowed. He knew Thorne was attempting to regain control, to dismiss the evidence as insignificant. He had to counter that, to press his advantage. "They're a detailed accounting of every dirty dollar, every life you've manipulated. They show how you prey on the desperate, how you turn their pain into your profit. And they show how you used my brother, Mike, like a pawn in your sick game." The mention of Mike's name was a calculated risk, a raw nerve he was willing to prod. He saw Thorne's jaw clench, a flicker of something that might have been anger, or perhaps just irritation, crossing his face.

"Mike is a troubled individual," Thorne said, his tone dismissive. "He came to me. He needed help. And I provided it."

"You provided him with a drug habit that's killing him!" Joe's voice rose, the carefully constructed calm threatening to shatter. He clenched his fists, fighting to regain composure. He had to stay focused, to play Thorne's game. "And you used his desperation to funnel your illicit product, to launder your dirty money. These records prove it. They detail the transfers, the falsified prescriptions, the dead drops. They show you systematically dismantling lives, starting with my brother's."

Thorne took a slow, deliberate step towards Joe, his guards fanning out wider, their presence a tangible, menacing force. "You think you're the only one with information, Joe?" Thorne's voice was low, a dangerous purr. "You think you can waltz in here, armed with what you believe is damning evidence, and dictate terms? I know about your little… side hustle. Your attempts to build your own network. Your brother, Mike, he was quite forthcoming about your aspirations."

Joe's breath hitched. Thorne knew about his attempts to gather information, his clandestine meetings with Bellwether. The information flow was more complex, more dangerous, than he had realized. He felt a chill creep up his spine, the realization that Thorne was always several steps ahead, always anticipating his moves.

"Mike was… misguided," Joe said, choosing his words carefully. "He was looking for a way out, and you exploited that. But he's still my brother, Silas. And I won't stand by while you destroy him." He gripped the small, sturdy wrench he kept tucked into his waistband, a primitive, yet comforting weight. It was a tool, a symbol of his trade, a reminder of his own capabilities.

"Destroy him?" Thorne chuckled, a dry, humorless sound. "I offered him a path. A way to numb the pain. A way to feel something other than the crushing weight of his own failures. That's more than you ever did for him, isn't it, Joe? You, the responsible older brother, always lecturing, always judging." Thorne's eyes narrowed, his gaze piercing. "Tell me, Joe, when was the last time you truly understood what Mike was going through? When was the last time you offered him solace, not just sermons?"

The words struck Joe like a physical blow. Thorne was hitting below the belt, preying on his guilt, his regrets. He knew Thorne was masterful at this, at turning people's weaknesses against them. But he wouldn't break. Not now.

"That's none of your business, Silas," Joe retorted, his voice strained. "My relationship with my brother is between me and him. Your involvement, your exploitation, that's what matters here. And I have the proof to expose it all." He gestured again to the documents, his resolve hardening with each passing second. "This isn't just about Mike anymore. This is about every life you've touched, every family you've shattered. These records are your downfall."

Thorne stepped closer, his gaze unwavering, his presence overwhelming. Joe could smell the expensive cologne he wore, a sharp, artificial scent that did little to mask the underlying predatory aura. "You think these papers can hurt me?" Thorne sneered. "These are just words on paper, Joe. Easily dismissed. Easily explained away. You're a mechanic, Joe. You fix broken things. You don't understand the intricacies of power, of influence. You don't understand how easily a narrative can be controlled."

He reached into his inner jacket pocket, and for a terrifying moment, Joe's heart leaped into his throat. But Thorne produced not a weapon, but a slim, high-end smartphone. He unlocked it with a practiced flick of his thumb, the screen glowing in the dim light.

"You see, Joe," Thorne said, his voice laced with a chilling calm, "I've been anticipating this. I've had my own sources, my own... informants. And they've been very busy. They've been compiling a rather interesting dossier on you. Your little meetings with Bellwether. Your attempts to gather evidence. And, of course, your own past indiscretions. Nothing that can't be explained away, perhaps, but enough to cause significant... inconvenience. Enough to make certain people question your motives. Your credibility."

Joe felt a cold dread seep into his veins. Thorne had played him, had anticipated his every move, his every desperate strategy. He had walked into Thorne's meticulously laid trap, and now he was caught, the walls closing in. The proof he thought was his trump card was, in fact, just another piece in Thorne's larger, more intricate game.

"What do you want, Silas?" Joe asked, his voice barely a whisper, the fight draining out of him, replaced by a grim resignation. He knew he had lost. The odds had always been stacked against him, and Thorne, with his cunning and his vast resources, had once again proven to be the superior player.

Thorne's smile widened, a triumphant, avaricious glint in his eyes. "What do I want, Joe? I want you to understand your place. I want you to realize that you're playing in a league far beyond your understanding. And I want you to deliver that shipment of pharmaceuticals you mentioned earlier. Intact. Untouched. And then, you will disappear. You will go back to fixing cars, and you will never, ever speak of this again. If you do," Thorne paused, his gaze hardening, "then this dossier I have on you, and the details of your little meeting with Bellwether, will find their way to the right ears. And it will be very... unpleasant for you."

Joe stared at Thorne, the harsh reality of his situation sinking in. He had gambled everything, and he had lost. His brother was still in Thorne's clutches, and Joe was now beholden to him, a puppet dancing on Thorne's strings. The incriminating documents, the evidence he'd risked everything to obtain, were now worthless. He had traded one form of leverage for another, a far more dangerous kind.

He looked at the documents, the painstakingly gathered proof of Thorne's depravity, and felt a profound sense of defeat. They represented not justice, but a precarious truce, a fragile deal struck with the devil himself. He was a mechanic, and Thorne was the architect of ruin, and in this twisted, brutal game, the architect had emerged victorious. The weight of his failure settled upon him, heavy and suffocating. He had come seeking justice, seeking to expose Thorne and save his brother, but he had only managed to entangle himself further in the darkness. Thorne, with his calculated ruthlessness, had once again proven to be the master manipulator, the true architect of his own survival, and Joe, the unwitting pawn, was left to pick up the shattered pieces of his idealism.

## A Battle of Wills and Words

Joe met Thorne's icy gaze, his own burning with a mixture of defiance and despair. The air crackled with unspoken threats, each word a calculated thrust in a duel far more dangerous than any physical brawl. Thorne, exuding an aura of supreme confidence, leaned back against a stack of crates, his posture a blatant display of his perceived dominance. "You misunderstand, Joe," Thorne began, his voice smooth as polished obsidian, yet carrying the cold edge of a predator. "I'm not trying to manipulate you. I'm offering you a pragmatic solution. A way out of this mess you've so enthusiastically dug for yourself."

Joe scoffed, a harsh, guttural sound that bounced off the concrete walls. "A way out? You call this a way out? You call trapping my brother, poisoning this whole damn community, and then expecting me to play nice a solution? You're a parasite, Thorne. A sickness. And these," Joe gestured to the documents scattered on the pallet, the tangible proof of Thorne's depravity, "are the diagnostics. The ugly truth you've been trying to bury."

Thorne's lips curved into a thin, mirthless smile. "Always so dramatic, Joe. Such a romantic. You see things in black and white, don't you? Good versus evil. Hero versus villain. The world isn't that simple. It's about survival. It's about taking what you need, when you need it, from those who are too weak to hold onto it." He pushed himself off the crates, his movements fluid and deliberate. "Your brother, Mike, he understood that. He was desperate. He saw an opportunity. And I gave it to him. I gave him purpose."

"You gave him a monkey on his back!" Joe's voice was raw, laced with years of suppressed grief and anger. He could feel the tremor in his hands, the desperate urge to lash out, to shatter the smug composure Thorne wore like a second skin. "You saw his weakness, his addiction, and you exploited it. You fed it. You turned him into your errand boy, your mule, your fall guy. And for what? So you could line your pockets with blood money?"

"He's alive, isn't he?" Thorne countered, his gaze unwavering, as if daring Joe to dispute that simple, brutal fact. "He's got a roof over his head, food in his stomach. He's contributing. Many people in his situation don't even have that. You preach about morality, Joe, but where were you when he was truly at his lowest? Where was your brotherly concern then? Was it drowned out by the ringing of your tools, by the predictable rhythm of your life?"

The words struck Joe with the force of a physical blow. Thorne's accusation, laced with a twisted kernel of truth, landed with brutal accuracy. He had been distant, caught up in his own work, his own life, failing to see the depth of Mike's struggle until it was too late. The guilt gnawed at him, a familiar ache he had carried for years. But Thorne's attempt to weaponize that guilt was despicable.

"That doesn't give you the right to ruin him!" Joe's voice cracked. "That doesn't give you the right to poison an entire city! These documents," he pounded a fist against the pallet, the sound sharp and defiant, "they show everything. The kickbacks, the falsified medical records, the bribes to officials. They show how you manipulated the system, how you preyed on the vulnerable. You're not a businessman, Thorne. You're a predator."

Thorne chuckled, a low, guttural sound that seemed to vibrate in Joe's chest. "And you, Joe, are a naive fool. You think these papers can touch me? You think some petty bureaucrat will have the courage, or the inclination, to act on them? I have friends in high places. I have influence. I can make these inconvenient truths disappear with a few phone calls. Just like I can make your brother disappear, permanently, if you continue to be… uncooperative."

The veiled threat hung in the air, heavy and suffocating. Joe felt a cold dread seep into his bones, the stark reality of his predicament crashing down on him. He had come here armed with what he believed was irrefutable evidence, a weapon to dismantle Thorne's empire. But Thorne, with his chilling foresight and ruthless pragmatism, had already anticipated him, armed with his own arsenal of threats and manipulation. The game had changed, and Joe was suddenly acutely aware of how outmatched he was.

"You think I'm afraid of you?" Joe's voice was surprisingly steady, a testament to the desperate resolve that had propelled him this far. He met Thorne's gaze, refusing to flinch, refusing to show the fear that clawed at his insides. "I've seen what you do, Thorne. I've seen the wreckage you leave behind. Mike is just one of many. Those girls you… condition… their families. They deserve justice. And I'm going to get it for them, no matter what you do."

"Justice," Thorne scoffed, a derisive curl of his lip. "An abstract concept. A luxury for the naive. What matters is power, Joe. Control. And I have both. You, on the other hand, have very little. You have your righteous indignation, your misplaced sense of heroism, and a few pieces of paper that will get you nothing but trouble. You're a mechanic, Joe. You fix broken engines. This is a different kind of machinery you're dealing with, and you're not qualified to operate it."

He took another step, closing the distance between them, his presence an almost suffocating weight. Joe could smell the expensive, cloying scent of Thorne's cologne, a stark contrast to the grime and decay of the warehouse. "Let me explain something to you, Joe," Thorne continued, his voice dropping to a conspiratorial whisper, though the menace within it remained palpable. "You came here with a plan. A foolish, ambitious plan. But I have a counter-plan. Your brother has information too, you see. Information about your own little ventures. Your attempts to gather intelligence on my operation. Your meetings with certain… unsavory characters. People who, if they knew you were cooperating with the authorities, would have very strong opinions about your continued existence."

Joe's blood ran cold. Thorne knew about Bellwether. He knew about his attempts to gather more evidence, to build a case against him. He had been playing Joe like a pawn on a chessboard, anticipating his every move, setting a trap with meticulous precision. The documents he'd so carefully compiled, the leverage he thought he possessed, was now rendered virtually useless. Thorne held all the cards, and Joe had walked willingly into his hand.

"What do you want, Thorne?" Joe's voice was hoarse, the fight draining out of him, replaced by a grim, crushing sense of defeat. He had gambled everything, and he had lost. His brother remained a captive of Thorne's machinations, and Joe was now inextricably bound to his fate.

Thorne's grin stretched, a chilling, avaricious spark igniting his gaze. "What's my objective, Joe? It's to impress upon you your insignificance. To hammer home that you're a mere pawn in a grander strategy. And I require the complete, unblemished delivery of that pharmaceutical consignment you so carelessly procured. Once that's accomplished, you'll vanish. You'll retreat to your workshop, to your instruments, and this entire affair will be erased from your memory. Any deviation, any impulse towards heroism, will result in the exposure of every compromising detail I possess – and I assure you, Joe, that's a considerable ledger. Your prior transgressions, your entanglement with Bellweather, your futile endeavors to thwart my plans… all will be broadcast, causing immense reputational harm. To you. To your sibling. To anyone you hold dear."

Joe stared at Thorne, the weight of his failure crushing him. He had sought justice, sought to expose the monster preying on his brother and his community. Instead, he had become a pawn in Thorne's twisted game, a bargaining chip in a high-stakes transaction.

The incriminating documents, the proof of Thorne's crimes, were no longer a weapon for justice, but a precarious shield, a desperate pact with the devil himself. He was a mechanic, a man who understood the tangible mechanics of machines, but he was utterly outmatched by the invisible, corrupt machinery Thorne commanded. The hope that had fueled him, the righteous anger that had sustained him, began to flicker, replaced by the cold, suffocating reality of his surrender. He had walked into the lion's den seeking to slay the beast, only to find himself on the menu. The harsh, unforgiving reality of Thorne's power had been laid bare, and Joe, stripped of his leverage, was left to contemplate the devastating cost of his defiance.

Thorne, the puppet master, had once again proven his dominance, and Joe, the unwitting player, was left to pick up the shattered pieces of his idealism, the bitter taste of defeat a stark reminder of the brutal truths of their world. The carefully constructed edifice of his plan had crumbled, leaving him exposed and vulnerable in the face of Thorne's calculated ruthlessness. He had sought to dismantle the system, but in the end, he had only managed to entrench himself further within its corrupt framework, a prisoner of his own desperate gambit. The very evidence that was meant to be his salvation had become the instrument of his subjugation, a testament to Thorne's unyielding control. Thorne's laugh, a dry, rasping sound, echoed in the vast emptiness, a chilling validation of his victory.

"A wise choice, Joe,"

Thorne said, his voice laced with a smug satisfaction that grated on Joe's nerves.

"Survival is a virtue, after all. And you, my friend, have just made a very smart decision. Now, about that shipment…"

He gestured with his chin towards the tarp-draped pallet, his eyes glinting with an unmistakable avarice.

"Let's see what you've brought me."

Joe's gaze fell upon the documents, the meticulously gathered proof of Thorne's crimes, and a wave of profound despair washed over him. These papers represented not justice, but a fragile truce, a deal struck with a devil who demanded absolute obedience. He was a mechanic, his hands calloused from honest work, and Thorne was the architect of ruin, the orchestrator of misery. In this brutal, unforgiving arena, the architect had once again emerged victorious.

The weight of his failure settled upon him, heavy and suffocating. He had come seeking to expose Thorne, to save his brother, but he had only managed to bind himself tighter to the darkness. Thorne, with his calculating ruthlessness, had played him masterfully, proving himself to be the ultimate survivor, the true victor in this grim charade. Joe's shoulders slumped, the fight draining from him, replaced by a hollow ache of resignation. He knew, with a chilling certainty, that he had walked into Thorne's trap, and now he was caught, the walls of deceit closing in. The evidence he had risked everything for was now a liability, a weapon Thorne could use against him. His brother remained a captive, and Joe was now Thorne's pawn, his fate dictated by the whims of a ruthless manipulator.

Thorne's pronouncements echoed in the cavernous space, each word a nail in the coffin of Joe's ideals. He had dared to challenge the system, to confront the darkness, and in return, he had been ensnared by it, a testament to Thorne's unassailable power. The stark reality of his compromised position settled upon him, a heavy cloak of defeat. He had stepped onto a battlefield where the rules were unwritten and the stakes were life and death, and in this brutal exchange, Thorne had emerged the undisputed victor. Joe's gaze drifted back to the documents, the damning evidence of Thorne's criminal enterprise.

What had once represented hope and a path to justice now felt like a cruel mockery, a symbol of his own naivete and Thorne's overwhelming control. He had underestimated the depth of Thorne's depravity, the extent of his influence, and the sheer ruthlessness with which he operated. The carefully laid plans, the meticulous research, the desperate courage – all had been met with Thorne's calculated countermoves, leaving Joe exposed and vulnerable. The truth he had unearthed was no longer a weapon, but a burden, a constant reminder of his own powerlessness.

Thorne's presence loomed over him, an embodiment of the corruption that permeated their world, and Joe felt the crushing weight of his own inadequacy. He had sought to be the hero, the one who brought the villain to justice, but he had become something else entirely – a reluctant accomplice, a pawn in Thorne's grand design. The bitter irony of his situation was almost unbearable. He had entered this confrontation with a burning desire for retribution, for the liberation of his brother, but he was leaving with nothing but the chilling realization of his own defeat. Thorne's smug satisfaction was a tangible thing, a testament to his mastery of manipulation and control. Joe knew, with a certainty that chilled him to the bone, that he had been outmaneuvered, outplayed, and ultimately, broken.

The confrontation, which had begun with a flicker of hope, had devolved into a stark display of Thorne's dominance, leaving Joe utterly vanquished. The evidence he held, once his greatest asset, had become his undoing, a stark reminder of the dangerous game he had dared to play. The harsh reality of his compromised position settled upon him like a shroud. Thorne, the architect of ruin, had once again proven his mastery, and Joe, the unwitting pawn, was left to navigate the treacherous aftermath of his own failed rebellion. The weight of his surrender was immense, a crushing testament to Thorne's unyielding power.

## The Truth About Mike's Fate

The air in the warehouse hung thick with the acrid scent of stale chemicals and the metallic tang of old blood, a fitting perfume for the macabre theater Joe had unwillingly entered. Thorne's words, dripping with insincerity, had landed like poisoned darts, each one designed to chip away at Joe's resolve, to drown him in a sea of guilt and despair. But it was Silas, lurking in the periphery of Thorne's predatory orbit, who now held the key to the deepest chamber of Joe's dread. Silas, a man whose very presence seemed to hum with a low, dangerous frequency, had remained largely a silent observer, his eyes, like chips of obsidian, tracking Joe's every tremor of emotion. Thorne had played his part, the charismatic villain orchestrating a symphony of corruption. Now, it was Silas's turn to deliver the final, crushing note.

Thorne, with a final, dismissive flick of his wrist, turned his attention back to the ledger on the pallet, his interest in Joe's emotional turmoil seemingly exhausted. He had presented his terms, laid bare the brutal calculus of their world, and now it was time for the hammer to fall. But before Thorne could resume his charade of business, Silas shifted, a subtle, almost imperceptible movement that drew Joe's gaze. The silence that had settled between the two men was not one of understanding, but of a predator patiently waiting for its prey to reveal its final, desperate weakness.

"You want to know about Mike," Silas's voice, when it finally came, was a low rasp, like stones grinding against each other. It lacked Thorne's polished venom, possessing instead a raw, unfiltered brutality that promised no comfort, no quarter. Joe's breath hitched. He had braced himself for Thorne's cruelty, for his calculated manipulations. But Silas… Silas was different. He was the blunt instrument, the brutal truth delivered without artifice. "Thorne likes to talk. Likes to make it sound like he's doing favors. Giving people purpose, like he said." Silas chuckled, a dry, humorless sound that echoed in the cavernous space. "That's a load of crap, Joe. Thorne doesn't give. He takes. And Mike… well, Mike was a prime candidate for taking."

Joe's heart hammered against his ribs, a frantic drumbeat against the encroaching silence. He forced himself to meet Silas's gaze, to not look away, to demand the truth, no matter how ugly. Thorne, for his part, seemed to find the unfolding drama mildly amusing, a curious diversion before he could return to the more pressing matters of profit and control.

"Mike owed me," Silas continued, his voice devoid of any emotion, as if he were discussing a faulty piece of machinery rather than a human life. "He owed a lot of people. He was deep in the hole. Deeper than a lot of people ever get. Gambling, you know? And other things. Things that cost more than he could ever earn in a lifetime." He paused, letting the words hang in the air, heavy with unspoken implications. "Thorne saw an angle. Mike was desperate. He'd do anything to clear his slate. Thorne offered him a way out. A chance to work off his debt."

Joe felt a flicker of something akin to hope, quickly extinguished by the grim set of Silas's jaw. "Work off his debt? What kind of work?" he managed to choke out, his voice rough, alien to his own ears.

Silas's lips twisted into a sneer. "The kind of work you don't want to know about, Joe. The kind that involves moving product. The kind that involves looking the other way. The kind that makes a man a ghost, even when he's standing right in front of you." He took a step closer, his shadow engulfing Joe. "Thorne doesn't do hand-holding. He uses people. He breaks them. And then he discards them. Mike was good for a while. He was loyal. He was scared. That's a powerful combination when you're controlling the leash."

"But he's alive," Joe said, the words a desperate plea, a desperate hope. He clung to Thorne's earlier statement, to the assertion that Mike was breathing, that he had a roof over his head. Was that all Silas meant? That Mike was simply a tool, a piece on Thorne's chessboard, still in play?

Silas's gaze met Joe's, and in those dark depths, Joe saw not the spark of life, but a chilling emptiness. "Alive?" Silas let out another dry, rasping chuckle. "Sure, Joe. He's alive. In a manner of speaking. He's breathing. His heart's beating. But the Mike you knew? The one who used to come to your garage, smelling of oil and desperation, asking for a loan? That guy… that guy is gone." Silas reached into his jacket, his movements slow and deliberate, and pulled out a small, worn leather wallet. He tossed it onto the pallet, the dull thud a punctuation mark in the oppressive silence. "This was his. Found it in his jacket pocket. Along with a few other things."

Joe's hands trembled as he reached for the wallet. His fingers fumbled with the worn leather, the familiar texture a cruel mockery of the life it once represented. Inside, he found a faded photograph of himself and Mike, younger, happier, standing by his father's old pickup truck. There were a few crumpled bills, a business card for a bar Joe vaguely remembered Mike frequenting, and then, beneath it all, a small, tarnished silver locket. He opened it, his breath catching in his throat.

Inside were two tiny, faded portraits: one of him, the other of a woman Joe didn't recognize. A knot of dread tightened in his stomach.

"What… what is this?" Joe's voice was barely a whisper, the weight of the wallet suddenly immense, crushing.

Silas leaned in, his voice dropping to a conspiratorial tone that sent shivers down Joe's spine. "It's what he was working for, Joe. Thorne made him an offer. A big one. Said he'd clear all his debts, give him a clean slate. All he had to do was one last job. A big one. Delivered some… specialized cargo. For a very discerning client. And he'd be set. Free and clear."

Joe stared at Silas, his mind reeling. Specialized cargo? A discerning client? This was escalating beyond his worst nightmares. "What kind of cargo?" he asked, the question a desperate attempt to anchor himself in something tangible, something he could understand.

Silas's eyes narrowed, a flicker of something unreadable passing through them. "That's where it gets messy, Joe. Thorne's clients… they don't like loose ends. They don't like things that can talk. Or testify. Or identify them." He paused, letting the implication settle. "Mike, he got scared. He realized what he was carrying. He realized who he was delivering it to. And he made a mistake. He tried to run."

The words hit Joe like a physical blow, knocking the air from his lungs. He stumbled back, his hand instinctively reaching for the pallet, for something to steady himself. Thorne, still engrossed in his ledger, let out a soft hum of satisfaction, seemingly oblivious to the unfolding drama, or perhaps, enjoying it from a detached, clinical perspective.

"Run?" Joe repeated, his voice cracking. "He ran from Thorne? From you?"

Silas gave a short, sharp nod. "He thought he could outsmart us. Outsmart Thorne. Silly bastard. Nobody outsmarts Thorne. Nobody gets away clean." He kicked a loose piece of debris, sending it skittering across the concrete floor. "So, the client… they weren't happy. Thorne wasn't happy. When you don't deliver, when you don't follow instructions… there are consequences."

Joe felt a cold dread wash over him, a suffocating wave that threatened to pull him under. He looked at the wallet, at the faded photograph of him and Mike, at the locket containing faces he didn't recognize. These were not the remnants of a man starting a new life. These were mementos from a life violently, irrevocably ended.

"What… what happened to him?" The question was barely a whisper, a confession of his deepest fear. He didn't want to hear the answer. He already knew. He could feel it in the chilling finality of Silas's words, in the utter lack of remorse in his eyes.

Silas's gaze was direct, unflinching. There was no pity, no empathy, only a grim statement of fact. "He's gone, Joe. The client took care of him. Made sure he wouldn't be a problem anymore. Thorne… Thorne just cleaned up the mess. Made it look like he disappeared. Like he ran off. Like he always did when things got tough."

Joe stared at Silas, his mind struggling to process the brutal finality of it all. Mike was dead. Not just gone, not just in debt, but dead. Murdered. And Thorne, Thorne had orchestrated it, had used Mike's desperation, his addiction, as a stepping stone to his own profit, and then, when Mike had become inconvenient, had simply disposed of him. The carefully constructed world Joe had tried to navigate, the world of blackmail and manipulation, suddenly seemed infinitely more horrific, infinitely more devastating.

"No," Joe choked out, shaking his head, a denial that was as much for himself as for Silas. "No, you're lying. Thorne said he was alive."

Silas shrugged, a gesture of utter indifference. "Thorne says a lot of things, Joe. He says them to get what he wants. He wanted you to cooperate. He wanted to keep you compliant. Telling you Mike was alive and well served his purpose. Kept you from going off the deep end, from making a scene. But the truth is, Joe, Mike's gone. And Thorne knew it. He knew it all along."

The revelation hung in the air, a black hole that swallowed all of Joe's remaining hope. The fight drained out of him, leaving him hollowed out, an empty vessel filled with a grief so profound it threatened to consume him. He looked at Thorne, who was now meticulously examining a vial of what looked like liquid, his face impassive, utterly devoid of any human concern. Thorne was a monster, a predator, and Joe had just discovered that his brother had been, quite literally, devoured by him.

"So, this… this shipment," Joe finally managed, his voice a dry rasp. "This was Mike's last job?"

Silas gave a curt nod. "The one that got him killed. And Thorne wants to make sure it gets to the client. No matter what. He's got… leverage on you, Joe. He knows about your little side ventures. He knows about Bellwether. He knows who you've been talking to. And if you don't deliver this shipment, he'll make sure everyone knows. Your brother might be dead, Joe, but Thorne can still hurt you. And everyone you care about."

Joe's gaze fell upon the pallet, upon the meticulously packaged pharmaceuticals. This was what Mike had died for. This was what Thorne was holding over his head. The evidence he had gathered, the hope of exposing Thorne, had been replaced by a chilling ultimatum, a demand to become complicit in the very corruption he had sought to fight. He was no longer a mechanic trying to save his brother. He was a man forced to traffic in death, to become a cog in the machine that had already claimed his brother's life.

## Joe's Moment of Reckoning

The truth about Mike's fate was a brutal, unflinching revelation, stripping away any remaining illusions Joe might have held about his brother's situation. He was not just a victim of circumstance; he was a casualty of Thorne's insatiable greed, a life extinguished to serve the master's purpose. The stark reality of his compromised position settled upon him like a shroud. Thorne, the architect of ruin, had once again proven his mastery, and Joe, the unwitting pawn, was left to navigate the treacherous aftermath of his own failed rebellion. The weight of his surrender was immense, a crushing testament to Thorne's unyielding power. Thorne's smug satisfaction was a tangible thing, a testament to his mastery of manipulation and control. Joe knew, with a certainty that chilled him to the bone, that he had been outmaneuvered, outplayed, and ultimately, broken. The confrontation, which had begun with a flicker of hope, had devolved into a stark display of Thorne's dominance, leaving Joe utterly vanquished. The evidence he held, once his greatest asset, had become his undoing, a stark reminder of the dangerous game he had dared to play.

Silas, sensing the shift in Joe, the collapse of his resistance, took another step closer. His obsidian eyes, which had seemed to hold a flicker of something akin to understanding, now mirrored Thorne's cold pragmatism. "He wasn't just using Mike, Joe. He was grooming him. Like he grooms everyone. He finds your weaknesses, your attachments, and he uses them. Your brother's addiction, his desire for a clean slate, his guilt about the past – Thorne saw it all. He saw a man drowning, and he offered him a life raft, knowing full well it was made of lead." Silas's voice was devoid of emotion, a chilling testament to the desensitization that came with his line of work. "Mike believed Thorne could fix him. He believed he could earn his way back, not just to sobriety, but to respectability. He thought this last job… this was it. The big payday that would set him and anyone he cared about straight."

Joe's gaze flickered to the wallet on the pallet. The faded photograph of him and Mike, younger, carefree, a stark contrast to the grim reality of the present. Mike had always been the one to chase the easy way out, the quick fix, a trait that had both endeared him and exasperated Joe. He remembered countless nights spent pulling Mike out of trouble, bailing him out, listening to his promises of reform. And each time, a piece of Joe's hope had eroded, replaced by a weary resignation. Now, that resignation was a gaping wound, bleeding out any lingering belief in redemption. He had always known addiction was a powerful force, a darkness that could consume a person from the inside out. He had seen its toll on Mike, the hollowed-out eyes, the desperate lies, the stolen possessions. But he had never truly comprehended its ruthlessness, its capacity to extinguish a life, to turn a brother into a commodity to be traded and discarded. Thorne had merely exploited a vulnerability that already existed, a crack in Mike's foundation that addiction had widened into a chasm.

"He… he sold something, didn't he?" Joe's voice was a strained whisper, the question born of a desperate need to grasp at any remaining shred of understanding. The 'specialized cargo' Silas had mentioned, the 'discerning client' – it all pointed to something far darker than simple drug trafficking. Thorne dealt in the volatile, the dangerous, the highly profitable.

Silas nodded, his expression grim. "The client wanted specific compounds. Pharmaceuticals, yes, but not the kind you'd find in a pharmacy. Research chemicals. Some of them are used in the development of… less than legal substances. Others… well, they're dangerous in the wrong hands. They can be weaponized, in a way. The kind of things that can do a lot of damage, quietly." He gestured towards the vials. "Thorne's got a reputation for sourcing hard-to-get, high-purity compounds. He's the middleman for people who don't want their names associated with anything that could trace back to them. Mike was just the mule for this particular delivery. A very expensive, very fragile mule."

Joe's stomach churned. His brother, a mule for potentially dangerous, weaponizable compounds. The image of Mike, frail and desperate, being used in such a capacity was almost more than he could bear. He thought of the locket, the faded portraits of faces he didn't recognize. Was that Mike's attempt to connect with some semblance of normalcy, some anchor to a life he was losing? Or were those faces connected to the client, to the dangerous world Thorne had pulled him into? The questions swirled in his mind, a tempest of grief and accusation.

"And when Mike… when he made the mistake," Joe continued, his voice hardening with a burgeoning anger, "when he tried to run… what exactly did the client do?" He needed to hear it, to have the horror laid bare, to strip away any lingering ambiguity. He braced himself for the answer, his knuckles white as he clenched his fists.

Silas met his gaze, his expression unreadable. "Thorne doesn't get his hands dirty with that kind of thing. He delegates. The client handles the… disposal. They have their methods. Efficient. Thorough. They don't leave loose ends. Mike was carrying their property, and he tried to abscond with it. That's not something anyone overlooks." He paused, a flicker of something that might have been grim satisfaction crossing his lips. "He was found later. Out in the old industrial park. Looked like an overdose. A bad batch. Thorne made sure the story held. That's what he's good at, Joe. Making messes disappear. Making people disappear."

The words hit Joe with the force of a physical blow. An overdose. A convenient cover story. Thorne had orchestrated Mike's death, not with his own hands, but with a cold, calculated arrangement, a neatly packaged lie to mask a brutal truth. Joe felt a surge of primal rage, hot and searing, that threatened to consume him. He wanted to lash out, to smash everything in sight, to inflict some of the pain he was feeling onto Thorne, onto Silas, onto the very fabric of this corrupt reality. But he was trapped, bound by Thorne's leverage, by his own fear.

He looked at the pharmaceuticals, the carefully sealed vials. This was the payload, the product of his brother's demise. Thorne wanted it delivered. Thorne wanted Joe to be complicit. The thought was abhorrent, a betrayal of everything Mike had stood for, even in his compromised state. Mike, for all his flaws, had never been a monster. He had been a victim, lured into darkness by promises of escape, only to be consumed by it.

"You want me to deliver this?" Joe's voice was low, a dangerous growl that held no hint of his earlier despair. "You want me to be the one to hand this over to whoever… whoever killed my brother?"

Silas tilted his head, a predator assessing its prey. "Thorne wants this delivered. And he's made it very clear that you're the one who's going to do it. He's got you by the balls, Joe. Bellwether, your business, your reputation – he can dismantle it all with a few phone calls. And if he's feeling generous, he'll even make sure your brother's name gets dragged through the mud, painting him as a junkie who just ran off." Silas's eyes held Joe's, a silent dare. "The question isn't whether you'll do it, Joe. The question is how you're going to do it. Will you be a broken man, doing Thorne's bidding out of fear? Or will you find some way to turn this into… something else?"

Something else. The words echoed in Joe's mind, a sliver of defiance in the crushing despair. Silas's veiled suggestion, perhaps an unconscious acknowledgment of Joe's resilience, or maybe just another manipulation, sparked a tiny ember of defiance within him. He was trapped, yes. He was compromised, absolutely. But he wasn't broken. Not yet. He looked at the pharmaceuticals, then at Thorne, who was now carefully capping the vial, his expression one of supreme self-satisfaction. Thorne had taken Mike's life, but he wouldn't take Joe's spirit.

He had to accept the truth, the brutal, unforgiving truth about Mike's choices, about his addiction, and about the devastating consequences that had ultimately led to his death. Mike wasn't a hero, and Joe couldn't save him from himself. But Joe could honor his memory. He could refuse to become another tool in Thorne's arsenal. He could find a way to push back, even if it meant walking into the lion's den. The fear was still there, a cold knot in his gut, but it was no longer paralyzing. It was a catalyst, a reminder of what he stood to lose, and what he was fighting for.

"So, Thorne knows about Bellwether," Joe stated, his voice steady, the rage now a cold, controlled burn. "He knows about my contacts. He knows I've been asking questions." It wasn't a question, but a confirmation, a mental inventory of Thorne's leverage.

Silas gave a slight nod. "He knows everything. And he's not afraid to use it. He sees you as a threat, Joe. Someone who's gotten too close. But he also sees you as useful. A mechanic who can fix things. And right now, he needs this shipment fixed and delivered."

Joe's gaze swept over the vials, then back to Thorne. The vials represented Mike's last breath, his final transaction. But they also represented Thorne's vulnerability. If Thorne was so eager for this shipment to reach its destination, then it had to be important. And if it was important, then it was also something Thorne would want to protect at all costs.

"What if," Joe began, his mind racing, piecing together fragments of information, of possibilities, "what if the delivery doesn't go exactly as planned?"

Silas's eyes narrowed, a flicker of interest breaking through his impassive façade. "Thorne doesn't tolerate deviations, Joe. Not from anyone."

"Thorne might not," Joe countered, a dangerous glint in his eyes, "but maybe the client will." He was walking a tightrope, his next words potentially fatal, but the thought of striking back, of turning Thorne's own tactics against him, was a potent draw. He had to accept the reality of Mike's death, but he didn't have to accept Thorne's victory. He had to find a way to bring this monster to justice, even if it meant treading through the very darkness that had consumed his brother. The moment of reckoning had arrived, and Joe, though shaken to his core, was not yet ready to surrender. He had faced the truth, accepted the loss, and now, he had to decide how he would fight back. The path ahead was perilous, fraught with danger, but for the first time since Silas had spoken Mike's name, a grim determination settled over Joe. He would not be a broken man. He would be a force.

# Chapter Ten
# The Reckoning

## The Fallout of the Confrontation

The acrid tang of stale sweat and something metallic, something Joe couldn't quite place, clung to the air, a testament to the violent ballet that had just concluded. He staggered back, the concrete beneath his worn soles a sudden, unwelcome anchor. Silas was gone. The echo of his footsteps, receding into the labyrinthine shadows of the warehouse, was a phantom limb, a phantom threat. Joe's breath hitched, ragged and uneven, each inhale a fresh stab of pain in his side, a visceral reminder of the rough handling he'd endured. The encounter had been brutal, a chaotic blur of desperate action and chilling pronouncements. He hadn't defeated Silas, not by any stretch of the imagination. But he hadn't been utterly broken either. He had fought back, a raw, unreasoning instinct to survive, to push against the suffocating tide of Thorne's machinations. He'd landed a blow, a glancing, desperate strike that had staggered Silas, a momentary victory in a battle he was already losing. The image of Silas's face contorting in surprise, a flicker of genuine pain crossing his otherwise impassive features, was a small, dark comfort. It proved that Thorne's enforcers, like Thorne himself, were not invincible.

The adrenaline, which had coursed through Joe's veins like a lightning strike, began to recede, leaving behind a hollow ache, a profound exhaustion that settled deep in his bones. The warehouse, moments before a theater of desperate struggle, now felt cavernous and empty, the silence amplified by the ringing in his ears. Thorne was still there, his silhouette a dark, unmoving monolith against the harsh glare of the overhead lights. He hadn't intervened, hadn't shown any inclination to aid Silas. Thorne's detachment was a chilling affirmation of Joe's compromised position. He was Silas's problem, and by extension, Thorne's property, to be dealt with as he saw fit. The knowledge gnawed at Joe, a bitter acid in his gut. He was trapped, a fly caught in a spider's web, and the spider was currently preoccupied with its ledger, meticulously calculating the profit derived from his brother's death.

Joe's gaze fell upon the scattered vials, their contents glinting innocently under the artificial light. Mike's final cargo. The instruments of his demise, now thrust into Joe's unwilling hands. The weight of that responsibility was crushing, a tangible force pressing down on his chest, making it difficult to draw a full breath. He thought of Mike, of his easy smile, his hopeful eyes, a lifetime ago. The stark contrast between that memory and the grim reality of the present was almost unbearable. Mike had been caught in Thorne's web, a pawn sacrificed for profit, his addiction a vulnerability Thorne had ruthlessly exploited. And now, Joe was being coerced into becoming an extension of that exploitation, a conduit for the very poison that had killed his brother.

The rough fabric of his jacket scratched against his skin, a physical manifestation of the grime and despair that seemed to permeate this entire operation. He felt exposed, vulnerable, his carefully constructed facade of resilience cracking under the immense pressure. The truths Silas had revealed, the cold, calculated murder of his brother, the depth of Thorne's depravity – it all coalesced into a suffocating nightmare. He had come here seeking answers, seeking justice, but he had found only a deeper descent into the abyss. The confrontation had stripped away any remaining illusions, leaving him with a raw, bleeding wound where his hope used to be.

He looked around the warehouse, his eyes scanning the vast expanse of stacked crates and industrial machinery. Were there others? Silas's crew? Thorne's muscle? The thought sent a fresh wave of adrenaline through him, a primal urge to escape, to disappear into the anonymity of the city's underbelly. But where could he go? Thorne knew about Bellwether, knew about his contacts. He had made that chillingly clear. Every avenue of escape seemed to be blocked, every potential ally tainted or compromised. He was isolated, adrift in a sea of corruption, with only the shattered remnants of his brother's life for company.

He had to think. Panic would be his undoing. Thorne thrived on fear, on control. Silas had seen the crack in Joe's resolve, had witnessed the moment his carefully constructed world imploded. But Silas had also implied a choice, however illusory. "Will you be a broken man, doing Thorne's bidding out of fear? Or will you find some way to turn this into… something else?" The words echoed in the emptiness of the warehouse, a tantalizing, dangerous whisper. Something else. What could that possibly mean? He was no killer, no master manipulator like Thorne. His strengths lay in building, in creating, in fostering legitimate business. But Thorne had twisted those very strengths against him, using Bellwether as leverage.

Joe's gaze drifted back to Thorne. The man was a phantom, a predator cloaked in the guise of a businessman. He operated in the shadows, his influence insidious, his reach seemingly limitless. He was the architect of Mike's destruction, and now he was trying to mold Joe into his next puppet. The thought ignited a spark of defiance, a tiny ember glowing in the vast darkness of his despair. Mike had been a victim, yes, but he had also been Joe's brother. And Joe wouldn't let Thorne desecrate his memory by forcing him to become a willing participant in his twisted games.

He pushed himself away from the cold, unyielding wall, the movement sending a fresh wave of pain through his bruised ribs. He needed to move, to get out of this place, to find a moment of solitude to process the enormity of what had happened. The vials, still carefully arranged on the pallet, seemed to mock him, a silent testament to his captivity. He couldn't leave them behind; Thorne would never allow it. They were his leash, his constant reminder of his obligation. But he also couldn't simply deliver them. That would be a betrayal of Mike, of himself.

He walked over to the pallet, his steps slow and deliberate. He picked up one of the vials, the cool glass a stark contrast to the heat of his palm. He examined the label, the precise, clinical typeface offering no clue to the volatile contents within. These were not mere drugs; these were specialized compounds, research chemicals, potentially weaponized. The implications were chilling. Thorne wasn't just dealing in narcotics; he was trafficking in something far more dangerous, far more insidious. And Mike had been the one to carry it. The irony was a bitter pill to swallow. Mike, who had always been reckless, always seeking the easy way out, had ended up as the mule for weapons of mass destruction, albeit on a molecular level.

Joe turned the vial over and over in his hand, his mind racing. If these compounds were so valuable, so dangerous, then the client who had commissioned them would be just as ruthless, just as determined to protect their investment. Thorne was the intermediary, the facilitator. But the ultimate power, the ultimate threat, lay with the client. And if Joe could somehow disrupt that transaction, expose that client, perhaps then he could strike a blow against Thorne, a blow that would resonate deeper than any physical confrontation.

He glanced at Thorne again. The man was still engrossed in his ledger, his focus absolute. He exuded an aura of unshakeable control, of absolute power. But even the most powerful figures had vulnerabilities. Thorne's obsession with profit, his meticulous attention to detail, his reliance on secrecy – these were all potential chinks in his armor. And Joe, despite his current predicament, still had his wits. He had his understanding of logistics, of supply chains, of the fragile ecosystems of illegal enterprises. He had something Thorne, in his arrogance, seemed to have underestimated: a desperate man with nothing left to lose.

The warehouse began to feel like a cage, its metallic scent a suffocating reminder of his confinement. He needed to leave. He needed to regroup. He carefully placed the vial back on the pallet, his movements deliberate. He couldn't afford to be careless. Every action, every word, was now scrutinized. He looked at the exit, a distant sliver of light in the oppressive gloom. Silas was gone, but Thorne remained. And Thorne was the real danger.

He took a deep breath, trying to quell the tremor in his hands. He had to play Thorne's game, but he would do it on his own terms. He would be a pawn, yes, but a pawn that could disrupt the board. He would be the mechanic who fixed Thorne's shipment, but he would fix it in a way that would unravel Thorne's carefully constructed empire, brick by painstaking brick. The fear was still there, a cold, clammy hand gripping his heart, but it was now tempered by a nascent sense of purpose. He wouldn't let Mike's death be in vain. He would find a way to make Thorne pay, to make him understand the true cost of his greed. The reckoning was coming, and Joe, though he was far from ready, was determined to be a part of it. He just had to survive the immediate aftermath, to escape Thorne's watchful eye and plot his next move. The road ahead was shrouded in darkness, but for the first time since he'd learned of Mike's fate, Joe felt a flicker of something akin to grim resolve. He would not be broken. He would be remade, forged in the fires of grief and betrayal, into something Thorne would never anticipate.

He reached for the vial Thorne had been examining earlier, the one holding the liquid that was supposed to be his next delivery. It felt heavier in his hand now, imbued with a sinister significance. He could feel Thorne's eyes on him, a palpable weight. Thorne hadn't moved from his ledger, but his attention was clearly focused on Joe. The silence stretched, thick with unspoken threats. Joe met Thorne's gaze, a silent challenge passing between them. Thorne offered no reassurance, no guidance, only a silent expectation. Joe was on his own, adrift in a treacherous current, with the very evidence of his brother's murder in his possession. The weight of it was almost unbearable, the responsibility a crushing burden. He had to get out of here, but he also had to be smart. Thorne would be watching his every move. Any overt act of defiance would be met with swift and brutal retribution.

Joe forced himself to take a slow, steadying breath. He couldn't afford to crumble, not now. He had to project an image of compliance, of defeated resignation. Thorne wanted a broken man, a tool to be wielded. Joe would give him that illusion, at least for now. He would play the part of the grieving, terrified brother, forced into a desperate situation. But beneath that mask of despair, a new resolve was hardening, a cold, calculating fury. He wouldn't be a pawn for long. He would find a way to turn the tables. He had to. For Mike.

He carefully picked up the remaining vials, his movements slow and deliberate, as if weighed down by an immense sorrow. He avoided looking at Thorne directly, his gaze fixed on the sterile glass, the chilling symbols of his brother's final transaction. He could feel Thorne's eyes on him, assessing his reaction, gauging his submission. Thorne thrived on this power, on the fear he instilled. Joe refused to give him the satisfaction of seeing him break completely. He would carry this burden, this horrifying legacy, but he would not be defined by it. He would use it as fuel, as a weapon, as a guiding star in the darkness.

Silas's words replayed in his mind: "The question isn't whether you'll do it, Joe. The question is how you're going to do it." Joe had his answer. He would do it in a way that would shatter Thorne's carefully constructed world, a way that would bring justice to Mike, even if it meant walking deeper into the very darkness that had claimed him. He felt a surge of grim determination, a cold, hard resolve settling over him. Thorne had underestimated him, had seen him as a mere mechanic, a disposable asset. But Joe was more than that. He was a brother, a survivor, and now, a man with a score to settle. The immediate fallout of the confrontation had left him battered and bruised, but not defeated. It had ignited a fire within him, a burning desire for retribution that would consume Thorne, Silas, and everyone else involved in his brother's death. He would find a way. He had to.

## Decisions Made in Despair

The oppressive silence of the warehouse pressed in on Joe, each tick of a distant, unseen clock amplifying the turmoil within him. Silas's parting words, laced with a taunt that felt more like a prophecy, echoed in the cavernous space: "The question isn't whether you'll do it, Joe. The question is how you're going to do it." Thorne, a monolithic shadow by the ledger, remained oblivious to the inferno raging in Joe's gut. The vials, cool and clinical on the pallet, were no longer just chemicals; they were the distilled essence of his brother's final act, a terrifying inheritance.

The primary, gnawing uncertainty was Mike. Was he alive? Silas's evasiveness, the hurried, almost panicked retreat, could have meant anything. It could have meant Mike was merely out of Thorne's immediate grasp, a bargaining chip still very much in play. Or, the thought a cold, sharp blade twisting in his side, it could have meant Silas was simply cleaning up loose ends after the job was done, leaving Joe to deal with the bloody aftermath. The possibility, however faint, that Mike was still alive, still breathing, was a siren song, a desperate lure pulling him towards an impossible rescue.

If Mike *was* alive, then what? Thorne held the leash, and Joe knew, with a certainty that chilled him to the bone, that Thorne would use Mike as leverage. Kidnapping Mike wasn't out of the question, a move to guarantee Joe's complete subservience, to ensure the successful delivery of the hazardous cargo. A rescue attempt, however, would be suicide. Thorne's network was vast, his operatives like Silas — dangerous, efficient, and utterly ruthless. To go after Mike would be to walk directly into a carefully laid trap, to become another casualty of Thorne's insatiable greed. The mechanic in him, the part that understood systems and vulnerabilities, screamed caution. But the brother, the one who remembered Mike's infectious laugh, his unwavering loyalty, raged against the cage of pragmatism.

Could he even trust anything Silas had said? Silas was Thorne's man, a tool honed for violence. His words, his apparent surprise at Joe's defiance, could have been an act, a performance designed to manipulate Joe into a state of heightened desperation. The mention of Mike's involvement, the implication that he was more than just a mule, that he was somehow key to Thorne's operation, was a dangerous seed of doubt planted in fertile ground. Joe wanted to believe Mike was a victim, ensnared by circumstance, by his own weaknesses. But the chilling possibility that Mike had willingly participated, that he had been a more active, perhaps even complicit, player in Thorne's sordid enterprise, was a betrayal that cut deeper than any physical blow.

If, God forbid, Mike was truly gone, then the questions shifted, morphing into a different kind of agonizing calculus. Vengeance? Justice? The words felt like ash in his mouth. Vengeance would mean picking up the vials, becoming the instrument of Thorne's will, and then, at the earliest opportunity, turning those tools against Thorne and his ilk. It would be a descent into the same darkness that had consumed Mike, a path paved with blood and regret. He'd be functioning as Thorne's hired gun, a ghost in the machine, and the thought sickened him. Could he even pull the trigger? He was a mechanic, a problem solver, not an executioner. The violence he'd witnessed, the raw brutality of Silas, was a world away from his own experience. To embrace that world, even for retribution, felt like a betrayal of everything he believed in, everything Mike, in his better moments, had aspired to be.

Justice, on the other hand, offered a glimmer of a cleaner path, albeit a far more perilous one. Official channels. The police. He had information, tangible proof of Thorne's illegal activities, the stolen cargo, the implied threat to his own life and the life of his brother. But Thorne's reach was long, his influence pervasive. Could he trust the authorities not to be compromised? Thorne operated in the shadows, but his transactions were substantial, his clients likely powerful. Would a single, unsolicited complaint from a grieving brother, a mechanic with no direct ties to the underworld, be enough to penetrate Thorne's defenses? Or would it simply mark him as a target, exposing him to Thorne's retaliation without offering any real protection? The thought of Silas's brutal efficiency, of Thorne's cold calculation, made the idea of relying on an already strained and possibly corrupted system seem like a fool's errand.

The weight of these decisions settled upon him, a physical pressure in his chest. Each choice was a precipice, and the fall from any of them promised a devastating consequence. If he went after Mike, he risked his own life and likely failed, becoming another statistic. If he pursued vengeance, he risked becoming the monster he fought against. If he sought justice through official channels, he risked being dismissed, ignored, or worse, eliminated. He felt like a man standing at a crossroads in a minefield, with every direction leading to potential detonation.

He looked at his hands. They were calloused, stained with grease and oil, hands that knew how to coax life back into a broken engine, not how to administer death or navigate the labyrinthine corridors of law enforcement. Thorne had spoken of him as a mechanic, a disposable part in his grand, illicit design. And in a terrifying way, Thorne was right. He was a mechanic. But mechanics fixed things. They understood how systems worked, how they could be repaired, or, if necessary, how they could be sabotaged.

The vials. Thorne expected them delivered. That was the immediate task, the tangible obligation. But what if "how" Silas had asked wasn't about *how* Joe would deliver them, but *how* Joe would ultimately deal with them, with Thorne, with the whole damned operation? What if the "how" was about finding a way to dismantle the system, not just fulfill his part in it?

He considered the logistics, his mind instinctively shifting into problem-solving mode. These weren't just drugs; Silas had hinted at something more, specialized compounds, dangerous. Thorne wasn't just a drug dealer; he was a trafficker of something far more volatile. The clients who commissioned such materials would be just as ruthless, just as desperate to protect their investment. Disrupting the delivery, diverting the cargo, exposing the client – that could be a way to hit Thorne where it hurt, not in his pockets, but in his reputation, his meticulously crafted control. It was a long shot, a desperate gamble, but it was a gamble that didn't immediately require him to shed blood or betray his own moral compass.

The thought brought a flicker of something other than despair – a nascent, almost rebellious, pragmatism. He couldn't save Mike with brute force, nor could he defeat Thorne by becoming a mirror of his brutality. But he could, perhaps, exploit Thorne's own system against him. He knew how shipments worked, how supply chains were managed. If he could intercept, reroute, or sabotage this particular delivery, he could create chaos, a disruption that Thorne would be forced to address. It would buy him time, and more importantly, it would force Thorne to reveal more about his operations, about the people he was dealing with.

But the risk was immense. Thorne would discover the tampering, and the retribution would be swift and brutal. He would be directly responsible for Thorne's financial loss, for the exposure of his clients. This wasn't just about survival anymore; it was about actively fighting back, not with fists, but with intelligence and cunning. It was about turning the tools Thorne had given him – his knowledge, his analytical mind – into weapons.

The question of Mike's fate remained the raw, open wound. If Mike was alive, this plan, this disruption, could put him in even greater danger. Thorne would escalate, tighten his grip. Joe would be playing a dangerous game of chess, with Mike's life as the ultimate prize. But if Mike was dead, then this was the only way he could conceive of honoring his memory, of ensuring that his death wasn't just another statistic in Thorne's ledger. It was a choice between two kinds of survival, two kinds of justice, and both were steeped in uncertainty.

He picked up one of the vials again, its cool glass a stark contrast to the heat of his racing thoughts. This was it. The turning point. The decisions made in this moment, in this suffocating silence, would dictate everything that came after. He could either surrender, become the broken man Thorne expected, or he could choose his own path, however perilous. The memory of Mike's face, not the face of a victim, but the face of his brother, flawed but fiercely loyal, flashed in his mind. That memory was his anchor, his true north. He wouldn't let Thorne erase it, wouldn't let him corrupt it. He would find a way to honor it. The road ahead was dark, uncertain, and fraught with danger, but for the first time since the nightmare began, Joe felt a glimmer of control, a fragile sense of agency in a world that had tried to strip him of both. He would not be a passive participant. He would be the wrench in Thorne's carefully calibrated machine. He would be the mechanic who diagnosed the fatal flaw and exploited it. The reckoning had begun, and Joe, despite his fear, was ready to play his part, not as a pawn, but as a catalyst.

## A Call to the Authorities

The weight of the evidence in Joe's hands felt less like a weapon and more like a ticking bomb. The ledger, meticulously detailing Thorne's illicit transactions, was damning. Silas's cryptic threats, coupled with the chilling implication that Mike was more than just a pawn in Thorne's twisted game, painted a stark picture of criminal enterprise. Joe possessed the pieces of Thorne's downfall, the raw materials for a legal takedown. The instinct for self-preservation warred with a burgeoning sense of righteous anger. He could walk into the precinct, lay it all out, and let the system, however flawed, take its course. It was the conventional path, the one society expected, the one that promised a degree of closure, a chance to reclaim a semblance of order in the chaos that had consumed him.

But the specter of Silas loomed large, a constant, gnawing reminder of the brutal reality that governed Thorne's world. Silas, with his cold eyes and unnervingly calm demeanor as he'd delivered his veiled threats, was the embodiment of Thorne's reach. Joe had seen firsthand the efficiency with which Thorne's operations were conducted, the seamless transition from illicit acquisition to the deployment of muscle. This wasn't street-level crime; this was an intricate, sophisticated network, one that had demonstrated a terrifying capacity for silencing opposition. Could he trust that the authorities, when presented with this evidence, would be shielded from Thorne's influence? The thought of Thorne's operatives, like Silas, infiltrating the very institutions meant to uphold justice was not a far-fetched paranoia, but a chillingly plausible scenario.

He pictured himself walking into the local precinct, a greasy mechanic with a story too wild for a police procedural. He'd hand over the ledger, the incriminating vials, the hushed testimony of his brother's last desperate moments. Would they listen? Would they believe him? Or would they see a grieving, potentially unstable individual, clutching at straws? Thorne's influence, Joe suspected, wasn't solely in overt bribery or coercion; it was in the subtle cultivation of relationships, in the quiet placement of allies in positions of power. A complaint from an outsider, a man with no established connections, could easily be dismissed, buried, or worse, used as a warning to Thorne that his operations were being scrutinized.

The potential repercussions were a minefield. If Thorne discovered Joe had gone to the police, the reprisals would undoubtedly be swift and severe. Silas had made it clear that Joe was now entangled, whether he liked it or not. Refusal to cooperate had already earned him a death threat, veiled or not. Going to the authorities would elevate that threat from a potential consequence to a near certainty. He'd be a marked man, his life a ticking clock until Thorne's operatives decided to collect. And it wasn't just him. What about anyone who might have inadvertently helped him, even by remaining silent? What about the faint, lingering hope that Mike was still alive? The police, in their pursuit of Thorne, might inadvertently endanger Mike further, using him as bait or inadvertently revealing his location to Thorne's network.

He considered the alternative, the one that Silas had so artfully presented: compliance. Delivering the vials, playing Thorne's game, and hoping for an opportunity to extract himself, perhaps even to save Mike. But that path felt like a betrayal of his brother, a surrender to the very darkness that had consumed him. It meant becoming complicit, a willing participant in Thorne's poison peddling, his calculated disregard for human life. The mechanic in him recoiled at the thought of being a cog in such a destructive machine. He was meant to fix things, to mend what was broken, not to facilitate the breaking of lives.

The internal debate raged, a relentless storm within the confines of his own mind. Each option presented a terrifying chasm. On one side lay the potential for official justice, a structured, albeit uncertain, path to retribution. On the other lay the grim reality of Thorne's dominion, a world where justice was a foreign concept, and survival depended on ruthless pragmatism and brutal efficiency. He thought of Mike, his brother, a man caught between loyalty and his own demons. If Mike had been coerced, if he was a victim, then reporting Thorne was the only way to honor his memory, to prevent others from suffering the same fate. But if Mike had been a willing participant, then the narrative shifted, and Joe's actions would have different, more complex ramifications.

The very nature of the cargo Thorne was dealing with added another layer of urgency and dread. Silas's mention of specialized compounds, their potential for destruction far beyond mere narcotics, suggested Thorne was dealing with clients who operated on a different, more dangerous, scale. These weren't street-level dealers; they were likely powerful, well-connected entities who would go to extreme lengths to protect their supply chains and their secrets. Exposing Thorne could very well expose them, and their retaliation would be an apocalypse Joe could scarcely fathom.

He ran a hand over the worn leather of his work jacket, the familiar texture a small comfort against the gnawing anxiety. He was a man of tangible problems, of engines that sputtered and transmissions that ground. The intricacies of law enforcement, the labyrinthine corridors of justice, felt alien and unwieldy. He understood the mechanics of a vehicle; he could diagnose a faulty fuel line, recalibrate a carburetor. But the mechanics of Thorne's empire, the intricate web of influence and intimidation, were a dark art, and he was an unwilling apprentice.

He wrestled with the moral implications. Was it cowardly to avoid the direct confrontation, to seek recourse through a system that might be compromised? Or was it pragmatic, a calculated risk assessment that prioritized survival and the potential for a more effective long-term strategy? The image of Silas's smug satisfaction, the unspoken threat in his eyes, was a potent deterrent. Thorne wanted Joe to be a pawn, a tool. To defy him openly, by going to the police, felt like a declaration of war, a move that would strip away any remaining leverage, any possibility of operating from the shadows.

He returned to the ledger, his fingers tracing the precise, almost elegant, handwriting that detailed Thorne's transactions. This was undeniable proof. This, coupled with Silas's own words, constituted a compelling case. But compelling for whom? For a diligent detective who saw a clear path to justice, or for a corrupt official who saw an opportunity to extort Thorne or bury the evidence to protect his own interests? The uncertainty was paralyzing. He was a mechanic, not a detective, not a lawyer, not a whistleblower. His expertise lay in tangible, solvable problems, not in navigating the murky, morally ambiguous landscape of criminal investigations and potential cover-ups.

The thought of involving anyone else, of drawing more people into this vortex of danger, was almost unbearable. He remembered the quiet desperation in Mike's eyes, the fear that had begun to creep in during their last conversation. Had Mike known the extent of Thorne's reach? Had he understood the peril he was in? If Joe went to the police, and Thorne retaliated, it wouldn't just be his life on the line; it would be anyone he confided in, anyone who offered even a sliver of assistance. The weight of that responsibility felt crushing.

He stood there, a solitary figure amidst the sterile, silent expanse of the warehouse, the vials of Thorne's poison glinting under the dim artificial light. The question of whether to involve the authorities wasn't a simple yes or no; it was a complex equation of risk, consequence, and the ever-present, agonizing uncertainty of Mike's fate. It was a decision that would define not only his own actions but the ultimate trajectory of this nightmare. He knew, with a certainty that chilled him, that whatever he chose, the reckoning would be absolute. The only question was whether he would face it armed with the law, or with the same desperate, solitary courage that had led his brother into this abyss. The path of reporting Thorne offered a chance at a clean victory, a triumph of justice, but the whispers of corruption and Thorne's pervasive influence made it a gamble with stakes higher than he could afford to lose. He had to weigh the possibility of bringing

Thorne down against the very real threat of becoming another casualty, another silenced voice in Thorne's meticulously controlled world.

## The Ghost of Mike

The ghost of Mike was a persistent, unwelcome companion. It wasn't a spectral apparition, no sheets and chains or moaning winds. It was subtler, more insidious, woven into the fabric of Joe's thoughts, his actions, his very being. It was the phantom weight of a phone call never made, a question left unasked, a life left to unravel without his intervention. Whether Mike was breathing the same polluted air as Joe, or if his lungs had long since collapsed under the strain of Thorne's poison, the absence, or the profound alteration, was a void that threatened to swallow Joe whole. The ledger, the vials, Silas's veiled threats – they were all tangible elements of Thorne's criminal enterprise, but Mike was the intangible, the emotional core of this entire goddamn mess.

Joe found himself scanning crowds, his eyes instinctively seeking out the familiar slump of Mike's shoulders, the way he used to run a hand through his perpetually messy hair, a nervous tic that had only intensified with his deepening addiction. He'd catch a glimpse of someone with a similar build, a familiar gait, and his heart would lurch, a foolish, hopeful surge followed by a crushing wave of disappointment. Each false alarm was a fresh wound, a reminder of the chasm that had opened between them, a chasm carved by Thorne's calculated exploitation and Mike's own desperate vulnerabilities. He imagined Mike, if he were still alive, a hollowed-out shell of the brother he'd known. The addiction wasn't just a habit; it was a parasitic entity, feeding on Mike's will, his spirit, his very essence. If Joe were to find him, truly find him, what would be left? Would the man he loved, the brother who'd once taught him how to ride a bike, the confidante who'd shared his dreams under the vast, indifferent sky, still exist? Or would he be a stranger, a desperate soul lost in the throes of withdrawal, his eyes vacant, his humanity eroded by the constant craving?

The thought of Mike alive, dependent on Joe for his recovery, was a terrifying prospect. Joe was a mechanic. He fixed engines, not broken people. He understood the mechanics of a faulty carburetor, the intricate dance of gears and pistons. But the delicate, arduous, and often soul-crushing process of addiction recovery was a foreign language, a complex mechanism with no clear manual. He'd witnessed the toll addiction could take, not just on the individual, but on their loved ones. He'd seen families torn apart, bonds fractured beyond repair, all by the relentless grip of dependence. Could he be that person for Mike? Could he endure the relapses, the broken promises, the emotional roller coaster that was the hallmark of recovery? The responsibility felt immense, an almost insurmountable burden. It would require a patience he wasn't sure he possessed, a resilience that felt beyond his current capacity. He imagined himself coaxing Mike into meetings, holding his hand during withdrawal, listening to his confessions without judgment, all while still carrying the weight of Thorne's threat, the knowledge that his brother had been entangled in something so dark, so deadly. It was a future fraught with peril, a road paved with uncertainty and the constant threat of backsliding.

Conversely, the alternative, the chilling possibility of Mike's death, was a void that echoed with unspoken questions. If Mike was gone, then Joe was left with the shattered fragments of their shared history, the ghost of what might have been. The unanswered questions would be the true torment. Why? How? Had he been a victim, a pawn deliberately sacrificed by Thorne? Or had he, in his desperation, made choices that led him down that fatal path? The lack of definitive answers would be a corrosive element, preventing any form of closure, any chance to properly mourn and move on. Joe pictured himself standing over a cold, silent slab, a stranger in a sterile room, identifying a body that was once his brother. The finality of it would be a crushing blow, a testament to Thorne's ruthlessness and the fragile nature of life. He'd be left with the phantom limb of his brotherhood, forever reaching for a connection that was irrevocably severed. The grief would be a constant companion, a shadow that would never truly lift, a reminder of a future stolen, a bond extinguished.

The intricate dance of accusation and justification would play out in his mind for years to come. Had Joe done enough? Could he have seen the signs earlier? Had he been too caught up in his own life, his own work, to notice the subtle shifts in Mike's demeanor, the growing desperation in his eyes? The guilt, if Mike was indeed gone, would be a self-inflicted wound, a constant source of torment. He'd replay their last conversations, dissecting every word, every nuance, searching for clues, for evidence of a deeper pain, a cry for help that he had somehow missed. The ledger and the vials would become symbols of his failure, tangible proof that he had possessed the means to potentially save his brother, but had been too late, too hesitant, or simply too blind.

He would have to learn to navigate a world without Mike's presence, a world where the shared memories, the inside jokes, the unspoken understanding that had defined their bond, were now relegated to the realm of recollection. He'd have to find a way to honor Mike's memory, not by dwelling in the past, but by forging a future that Mike would have been proud of. This would mean confronting Thorne, not just for revenge, but as a testament to the life that had been lost. It would be a solitary fight, a grim pilgrimage fueled by loss and a burning desire for justice. He would carry Mike's ghost with him, not as a burden of guilt, but as a silent, unwavering ally, a reminder of what was at stake.

The duality of Mike's potential fate presented Joe with two equally daunting emotional landscapes. If Mike survived, the challenge would be one of arduous patience and unwavering support, a constant battle against the insidious nature of addiction, a marathon with no guaranteed finish line. Joe would have to become a beacon of hope in the darkness of Mike's struggle, a steady hand to guide him back from the precipice. It would demand a profound shift in Joe's own life, a willingness to sacrifice his own comfort, his own peace of mind, for the sake of his brother. This path offered the possibility of redemption, of rebuilding what had been broken, of reclaiming a lost brother. But it was a path riddled with potential setbacks, with the constant threat of relapse and the emotional toll it would take on both of them.

If Mike was lost, the path would be one of somber remembrance and unwavering pursuit of justice. Joe would have to transform his grief into a weapon, his pain into a driving force. He would carry the weight of Mike's memory, a solemn vow to ensure that his brother's life, and the circumstances of his death, would not be forgotten. Thorne's empire, built on the exploitation of the vulnerable, would have to be dismantled, piece by piece, a monument to Mike's lost potential. This path promised a different kind of catharsis, a sense of closure achieved through retribution, through holding those responsible accountable. It would be a lonely road, marked by sacrifice and the constant specter of danger, but it would be a road paved with purpose, a way to ensure that Mike's story, however tragic, would not be silenced.

In either scenario, the foundation of Joe's existence would be irrevocably altered. The bond of brotherhood, a constant in his life, had been tested to its absolute limit. It had been stretched, strained, and perhaps even broken. Now, Joe had to find a way to adapt, to rebuild, to forge a new understanding of what brotherhood meant in the face of such profound adversity. He had to navigate a future shaped by the presence, or the absence, of the brother he had always known, and in doing so, discover the true strength and resilience of his own character. The ghost of Mike was a reminder of the past, a catalyst for the present, and a haunting premonition of the future, a future Joe would have to face alone, or with a brother irrevocably changed. The choices he made now would not only determine Thorne's fate, but the very essence of his own survival, both physically and emotionally. The reckoning was not just for Thorne; it was for Joe, a profound confrontation with his own limitations, his own capacity for love, loss, and the enduring power of the human spirit. He knew, with a chilling certainty, that whatever happened, the ghost of Mike would forever be a part of him, a silent witness to the trials he had endured and the choices he had made. The mechanics of the situation were complex, but the emotional calculus was brutally simple: he had to find a way to honor Mike, to either save him or avenge him, and in doing so, save himself.

## Consequences for Silas

The air in Silas's penthouse, usually thick with the cloying scent of imported cigar smoke and the subtle aroma of expensive cologne, now carried a different, more acrid odor – the metallic tang of fear. Joe's intrusion, the calculated disruption he'd orchestrated, had been far more effective than a direct assault. It hadn't been about breaking down doors; it had been about systematically dismantling Silas's carefully constructed world, brick by unseen brick. Silas, accustomed to operating from the shadows, to orchestrating his empire through proxies and coded messages, found himself reeling from a direct, unannounced violation of his sanctuary. The security systems, lauded by his technicians as impenetrable, had been bypassed with an almost casual contempt. The discreet cameras that usually offered an unwavering gaze upon his domain had gone dark, their electronic eyes blinded by a phantom touch. The fortified vault, rumored to contain not just illicit earnings but compromising ledgers and personal data, had been accessed, its contents not stolen, but meticulously copied and then subtly, almost tauntingly, replaced.

The immediate aftermath was chaos, a tremor that rippled through the foundations of Silas's criminal enterprise. His lieutenants, men who had sworn loyalty with blood and coin, now found themselves under a harsh, unwelcome spotlight. The information Joe had leaked, anonymously disseminated through encrypted channels to a select few journalists and, more importantly, to certain factions within the law enforcement agencies that had previously turned a blind eye, was a poison that spread with terrifying speed. Suddenly, everyone who had ever benefited from Silas's operations, everyone who had ever facilitated his deals, was under scrutiny. The delicate web of corruption that Silas had spun, a masterpiece of reciprocal blackmail and mutual dependency, began to fray.

For Silas himself, the consequences were swift and brutal. The reputation he had cultivated – a phantom of untouchability, a force of nature that reshaped the city's underbelly to his will – was shattered. The whispers began, insidious and venomous, undermining his authority and planting seeds of doubt amongst his most trusted associates. The very men who had benefited most from his protection now saw him as a liability. The leaked ledgers, detailing illicit transactions, offshore accounts, and the names of complicit officials, were a death sentence for Silas's carefully guarded anonymity. Law enforcement, galvanized by the irrefutable evidence, moved with a speed that belied their usual lethargy. Raids were conducted, not just on Silas's known front businesses, but on the private residences of his inner circle. Arrests were made, and the dominoes began to fall, each one a testament to Joe's calculated execution.

Silas, who had always prided himself on his foresight, found himself blindsided. His informants, his network of eyes and ears that had served him so well, had failed him. Either they had been compromised, or they had simply underestimated the resolve of the man who had infiltrated his empire. The information Joe possessed was too specific, too damning, to be the result of a random act of violence or a minor street informant. This was a targeted strike, a surgical excision that had gone straight for the jugular. Silas could only speculate about the identity of his tormentor, but he knew, with a chilling certainty, that this was no ordinary adversary. This was someone who understood his operations, who knew the chinks in his armor, and who possessed the cold, calculating intelligence to exploit them.

The initial response from Silas was predictable: denial and a furious attempt to regain control. He ordered his remaining loyalists to hunt down the source of the leak, to silence anyone who spoke of the damning information. He vanished from his usual haunts, his opulent penthouse becoming a gilded cage, a place of anxious waiting. The luxury that had defined his existence now felt like a mockery. The silken cushions were too soft, the panoramic views of the city too distant and unattainable. He was a king dethroned, his kingdom crumbling around him, his enemies emboldened by his apparent vulnerability. The paranoia, a constant companion for men in his position, intensified. Every phone call was a potential trap, every shadow a lurking threat. He began to suspect everyone, his most trusted advisors now viewed with suspicion, their every word scrutinized for hidden meaning.

However, the damage was too profound, the evidence too widespread, to be contained. The media, once hesitant to delve too deeply into the city's criminal underbelly for fear of reprisal, now feasted on the scandal. Silas's name, once whispered in hushed tones of fear and respect, was now splashed across headlines, coupled with accusations of drug trafficking, extortion, and murder. The carefully curated image of respectability he had cultivated through legitimate businesses and charitable donations began to crack, revealing the rot beneath. The public, once oblivious or indifferent, now saw him for what he truly was, and the revulsion was palpable.

The law enforcement agencies, spurred by the public outcry and the undeniable evidence, were now compelled to act. The slow, bureaucratic wheels of justice, usually so easily swayed by influence and bribes, found themselves pushed by an unstoppable momentum. Silas's network of complicity, his carefully cultivated relationships with corrupt officials and compliant officers, began to unravel as individuals sought to distance themselves from the sinking ship. Some turned state's evidence, offering up what little they knew in exchange for leniency. Others simply disappeared, melting back into the anonymity they had once so carelessly abandoned.

Silas faced a stark choice: face arrest and a lengthy prison sentence, or flee. The former meant confronting a legal system he had always manipulated, a system that was now, for the first time, truly against him. The latter meant abandoning everything he had built, the empire he had painstakingly constructed over years of ruthless ambition. He paced his penthouse, the expensive rug a soft cushion under his worn soles, his mind a whirlwind of calculations and desperate plans. His resources, though vast, were not infinite, and the net was tightening with alarming speed. Every escape route he considered was fraught with peril, each plan scrutinized by the specter of Joe's actions.

He considered retaliation, a primal instinct to strike back at the one who had brought him low. But who was this elusive figure? Joe was a ghost, a phantom whose motives and identity remained shrouded in mystery. Silas had no leverage, no personal connection to exploit, no easy way to retaliate. He could unleash his remaining enforcers, but with his operations in disarray and his network compromised, such a move would be a desperate gamble, likely leading to further exposure and capture. The calculated precision of Joe's strike left Silas feeling impotent, his usual methods of brute force and intimidation rendered useless.

The consequences, however, were not confined to Silas alone. The ripple effect of Joe's actions extended far beyond the drug lord's immediate circle. The corrupt officials, exposed by the leaked ledgers, found their careers in tatters. Some were forced to resign, their reputations irrevocably damaged. Others faced criminal charges, their carefully constructed lives collapsing under the weight of their transgressions. The city's political landscape, long dominated by Silas's influence, began to shift. New faces emerged, individuals who had been on the periphery, waiting for their opportunity, now found themselves thrust into the spotlight, eager to fill the void left by Silas's downfall.

The streets, too, felt the seismic shift. With Silas's operation severely crippled, a power vacuum emerged. The smaller gangs, the street-level dealers and enforcers who had operated under Silas's umbrella, now found themselves vying for control. Turf wars erupted, a brutal resurgence of violence as ambitious individuals sought to claim Silas's territory. The fragile peace that Silas had enforced, a peace built on fear and control, was replaced by a chaotic free-for-all. The very people Silas had exploited, the addicts and the desperate souls who formed the backbone of his trade, were caught in the crossfire, their lives made even more precarious.

Joe, observing the unfolding events from a distance, felt a complex mix of grim satisfaction and a heavy sense of responsibility. He had achieved his objective, the dismantling of Silas's operation, but the fallout was a tangible, often brutal, reality. He understood that his choices had set in motion a chain of events that would play out in the city's underbelly long after he had left that dangerous territory. The scars left by Silas's empire would not heal overnight, and the void he had created would be filled, one way or another, by forces perhaps as dangerous, if not more so.

Silas's personal fate remained uncertain, a question mark hanging over the city's conscience. Some reports suggested he had managed to slip through the net, escaping the country with a portion of his ill-gotten gains. Others whispered of a clandestine arrest, a hushed-up rendition to some unseen correctional facility. Still others believed he had met a more violent end, a final reckoning meted out by those he had wronged or those who sought to silence him permanently. The truth was, Silas, the architect of so much misery, had become a ghost himself, his presence replaced by the echoing consequences of his actions.

For Joe, the aftermath was a solitary one. He had acted not for glory or for personal gain, but out of a profound sense of duty to Mike, to the life that had been stolen and corrupted. He had navigated the treacherous currents of Silas's empire, not as a participant, but as a surgeon, excising a cancerous growth. The knowledge that his actions had directly impacted Silas's future, that the drug lord's carefully constructed world had been irrevocably altered, was a heavy burden. He had played his part in the brutal, unforgiving calculus of the city's underbelly, and now, he had to live with the knowledge of what that had entailed. The ghost of Mike, though perhaps closer to finding peace in the absence of Silas's direct influence, remained a constant reminder of the sacrifices made, the lives altered, and the enduring, often devastating, consequences of confronting evil. The reckoning had occurred, not just for Silas, but for Joe too, a profound and irreversible transformation forged in the crucible of loss and retribution. He had seen the heart of darkness, and in bringing it to light, he had irrevocably changed his own path, forever marked by the shadows he had dared to confront. The city would continue its brutal dance, but for Joe, the music had changed, the rhythm now dictated by the echo of what he had done, and the quiet, persistent weight of what it all meant.

# Chapter Eleven
# Facing the Aftermath

## Returning to an Empty Shop

The familiar click of the lock echoed in the cavernous space, a sound that had once been a harbinger of welcomed familiarity, of belonging. Now, it was merely a noise, a punctuation mark on a sentence that had long since concluded. Joe pushed the door open, the hinges groaning in protest, a lament for a past that refused to stay buried. The air inside the auto shop was thick and still, a stagnant pool that held the ghosts of a thousand Saturday mornings, of grease-stained hands and shared laughter. Dust motes danced in the slivers of weak afternoon sun that penetrated the grimy windows, illuminated by a light that felt ancient, indifferent to the passage of time and the weight of what had transpired.

He stood on the threshold, the worn linoleum beneath his feet a faded map of his childhood. Every scuff mark, every oil stain, was a memory etched into the very fabric of the place. The 'Closed' sign, a stark white rectangle with bold black lettering, hung precariously from the inside of the glass door. It felt heavier now, not just a testament to the economic realities that had forced its posting, but a shroud, a final, undeniable statement on the dreams that had been nurtured and then brutally extinguished within these walls. It was a symbol of Silas's pervasive reach, a testament to how far the tendrils of corruption had reached, choking the life out of even the most humble of aspirations. This was not just an empty building; it was a mausoleum of lost potential, a monument to a legacy irrevocably tainted.

The scent hit him then, a potent cocktail that was both achingly familiar and profoundly alien. The sharp, metallic tang of motor oil, the faint, lingering aroma of exhaust fumes, the underlying earthiness of tire rubber – these were the scents of his upbringing, the olfactory backdrop to countless hours spent learning the intricacies of engines, the satisfaction of coaxing life back into dormant machinery. But beneath these comforting notes, something else mingled, something acrid and bitter, the unmistakable odor of loss. It was the scent of his parents' dashed hopes, of their tireless efforts to build something honest and good, only to have it systematically dismantled. It was the scent of betrayal, of a system that had preyed on their diligence and ultimately consumed them.

Joe moved deeper into the shop, his footsteps unnervingly loud in the oppressive silence. He ran a hand along the cold, chipped surface of the main workbench, the scarred wood a familiar comfort beneath his fingertips. This was where his father had spent countless hours, his brow furrowed in concentration, the rhythmic tap of his hammer a familiar soundtrack to Joe's youth. He remembered sitting on an overturned bucket, watching his father's hands, thick and calloused but surprisingly nimble, work their magic on a stubborn engine. His father's pride, a quiet, unshakeable dignity, had been as much a part of this place as the tools hanging neatly on the pegboard. Now, those pegboards seemed to mock him, the tools pristine, unused, waiting for a purpose that would never return.

He traced the outline of a particularly deep gouge on the bench, a scar left by a dropped wrench years ago. His father had cursed under his breath, a rare display of frustration, before gently sanding down the rough edges. "Always respect your tools, son," he'd said, his voice rough but kind. "They're like extensions of your own hands, meant to build, not to break." The irony of those words, uttered in this space now emptied and broken, was a bitter pill. Joe's own hands, capable of far more destructive work, were stained with the grime of a different kind of operation, one that had ultimately led him back here, to confront the wreckage.

He walked towards the bays, the cavernous spaces where cars had once been hoisted, their underbellies exposed to the healing touch of mechanics. The air was cooler here, the shadows deeper. He could almost see the spectral outline of the old tow truck, the one his father had painstakingly restored, its chrome glinting in the imagined sunlight. He remembered the thrill of riding shotgun in it, the rumble of its engine a powerful lullaby. Now, the bays were empty, vast, echoing voids. The hydraulic lifts, once gleaming machines of diligent service, stood like skeletal remains, their platforms frozen in mid-air, as if suspended in the very moment the dream had died.

The silence wasn't just the absence of sound; it was a palpable presence, a heavy blanket that suffocated any lingering vestige of warmth. It was the silence of abandonment, of dreams deferred and then extinguished. Joe felt a familiar ache in his chest, a dull throb that had become a constant companion since he'd started this grim undertaking. He had operated in the shadows, orchestrating a symphony of chaos that had brought down a titan. He had wielded information like a weapon, dismantling Silas's empire with surgical precision. And now, the final act of that operation was to return to this hollow shell, this testament to everything that had been lost.

He entered the small office at the back of the shop, the air here even more stale. A thin layer of dust coated the desk, the filing cabinets, the worn leather of his mother's old chair. He remembered his mother sitting here, her face often etched with worry, poring over ledgers, her quiet determination a steady anchor against the rising tide of financial anxieties. She had been the quiet force, the meticulous planner, the one who believed in the power of honest work and fair dealings. Silas, with his insatiable greed and his network of illicit transactions, had preyed on that honesty, twisting it into a tool of his own exploitation.

Joe's gaze fell on a framed photograph on the desk, slightly askew, the glass filmed with dust. It was a picture of his parents on their wedding day, younger, brighter, their faces alight with the promise of a shared future. His mother, in her simple white dress, looked radiant, her hand nestled in his father's. His father, in his best suit, stood tall and proud, his arm around her. It was a snapshot of a life that had been intended, a life built on love and hard work. This was the life Silas had stolen, not just from them, but from him.

He picked up the photograph, his thumb smearing a path through the dust on the glass. The faces in the frame seemed to stare back at him, not with accusation, but with a quiet expectation. He had come here to find closure, to sever the last ties to the past that had been so brutally reconfigured by Silas's machinations. He had exposed Silas, brought down his empire, and in doing so, had, in a way, avenged his parents. But standing here, in the hollow echo of their dreams, the victory felt hollow. It was a brutal, painful kind of catharsis, one that left him feeling more drained than triumphant.

He looked around the office, his eyes scanning the empty shelves, the bare walls. There was nothing left here of value, no physical evidence of the corruption that had seeped into every corner of his family's life. Silas had been meticulous in his dealings, cloaking his illicit activities behind layers of shell corporations and carefully worded contracts. The true damage wasn't in missing assets, but in the shattered lives, the stolen futures, the indcliblc stain on a good name.

Joe walked over to the empty cash register, its drawer hanging open, a silent testament to its last transaction, perhaps his father's final futile attempt to keep the doors open. He remembered the thrill of being allowed to ring up a sale as a child, the satisfying 'cha-ching' of the bell. It was a sound of commerce, of honest work being rewarded. Now, the silence of the empty drawer was a deafening indictment.

He knew he couldn't stay here. This place, once a sanctuary, was now a tomb. It held too many ghosts, too many painful reminders. His mission had been to dismantle Silas's operations, to ensure that no one else would suffer the same fate as his parents. He had succeeded. The information he had leaked, the carefully curated data that painted a damning portrait of Silas's crimes, had been more potent than any weapon. It had ignited a firestorm, consuming the corrupt empire from within. Law enforcement, finally armed with irrefutable evidence, had moved with a swiftness that belied their usual inertia. Arrests had been made, investigations launched, and the city's underbelly, for a brief, shining moment, had been exposed to the harsh glare of accountability.

But the aftermath, as he had learned through his own clandestine operations, was rarely clean. The power vacuum left by Silas's downfall was already being filled by new players, ambitious and ruthless, vying for control of the territories Silas had once commanded. The streets, he knew, would not be peaceful. The cycle of violence and exploitation would continue, merely rebranded under new management. His actions, though aimed at justice, had merely reshaped the landscape of the city's crime, not eradicated it.

He closed the office door behind him, the click even more final this time. He stood back in the main shop, the scent of oil and loss clinging to him. He had done what he had set out to do. He had brought down the man responsible for his family's ruin. He had avenged Mike, his brother, whose life had been snuffed out in the crossfire of Silas's callous ambition. But as he looked around the empty shop, the weight of it all settled upon him. This was the cost of his crusade. This silent, dust-covered auto shop was the ultimate manifestation of that cost.

He walked back towards the entrance, his gaze sweeping across the space one last time. The tools on the pegboard, the worn tire in the corner, the faint outline of an engine block on the floor – they were all relics of a life that had been. His life had been irrevocably altered, forged in the crucible of loss and sharpened by a singular, unwavering purpose. He had emerged from the shadows, a ghost in the machine, to dismantle a kingpin's reign. And now, he was once again a ghost, leaving behind only the lingering scent of oil, the dust of forgotten dreams, and the heavy silence of an empty shop. The 'Closed' sign still hung there, a stark, unwavering declaration. It was a sentence that now echoed within him, a constant reminder of the life that had been, and the life that had been brutally erased. His own path forward was now as unwritten as the clean slate of a freshly wiped engine block, but the indelible mark of this place, and the painful knowledge it contained, would forever be a part of him. The aftermath of Silas's reign had arrived, and for Joe, it had led him right back here, to the silent, somber heart of his own personal desolation.

## Grappling with the Truth

The air in the shop, thick with the ghost of his father's sweat and the tang of oil, now felt suffocating, a physical manifestation of the truth that clung to Joe like a shroud. He'd dismantled Silas's empire, meticulously, ruthlessly. He'd unearthed the rot, exposed the rot, and watched it crumble. But the victory, if it could be called that, was a bitter ash in his mouth. The hollowness of this place, this monument to his family's shattered aspirations, mirrored the hollowness growing inside him. He'd come seeking closure, a definitive end to the reign of terror that had consumed his parents, that had claimed his brother. He'd found that Silas was gone, his reign effectively over. Yet, the true weight of his actions, the profound understanding of what had been lost, was only now beginning to settle. And at the heart of that desolation lay the fractured memory of Mike.

He walked past the empty bays, the skeletal remains of the lifts reaching towards the bruised afternoon sky. He'd imagined a different ending for Mike. A different life. Maybe he'd even envisioned Mike inheriting this place, his hands, like their father's, stained with grease but also with pride. But the reality had been a brutal, drawn-out affair, a slow descent into a darkness that Joe had only glimpsed from the periphery. He replayed it all, a relentless, unwanted reel. The initial promise of Mike's early days – the quick wit, the knack for mechanics that rivaled their father's – had been a beacon. Joe had clung to that image, even as the shadows began to lengthen.

There were nights Joe could still see him, clear as day. Mike, younger, perched on a stool by the workbench, his brow furrowed in concentration as he wrestled with a carburetor. The easy smile he'd flashed Joe when he'd finally coaxed it back to life, a grin that spoke of shared triumph and youthful invincibility. Those were the memories

Joe had guarded, the pristine images he'd refused to let the grime of the world touch. But Silas, and the insidious tendrils of the life he cultivated, had reached into even those guarded spaces. It wasn't a sudden fall, not a single catastrophic event. It was a slow erosion, a gradual chipping away at Mike's spirit, his judgment, his very essence.

Joe's mind drifted back to the whispers he'd overheard, the hushed conversations between his parents that stopped abruptly when he entered the room. The worried glances exchanged, the tight-lipped silences. He hadn't understood then, not really. He'd been too young, too insulated by the routines of school and sports, to grasp the true nature of the rot that was taking root. He remembered the first time he'd seen Mike with the wrong crowd, the subtle shift in his posture, the hard glint in his eyes that hadn't been there before. It had been a fleeting moment, easily dismissed as teenage rebellion, but in retrospect, it was the first tremor, the initial crack in the foundation of their shared reality.

Then came the money troubles. Not just the shop's struggles, but Mike's. The casual requests for loans, the increasingly desperate pleas, the vague explanations of debts owed. Joe, still idealistic, had tried to help, had used his own meager savings, convinced it was a temporary setback, a youthful indiscretion that Mike would eventually outgrow. He'd even confronted Mike once, gently, asking him what was going on. Mike had brushed him off, a flash of anger in his eyes that had startled Joe, followed by a forced, dismissive laugh. "Just a few bad bets, Joey. I'll sort it out. You worry too much."

The truth, Joe now understood, was far more tangled, far more damning. Silas hadn't just offered Mike a way out of his financial woes; he'd offered him a role. A role that appealed to Mike's burgeoning ego, his desire for excitement, his growing resentment of their parents' perceived limitations. Joe replayed a specific conversation, one that had happened a few months before Mike disappeared. They'd been out late, ostensibly to "help a friend" with a car. The friend, Joe now knew, was a low-level dealer connected to Silas's network. Mike had been edgy, his eyes darting nervously. He'd been carrying a small, nondescript package.

"What's that, Mike?" Joe had asked, his voice casual, though a knot of unease was tightening in his stomach.

Mike had flinched, his grip tightening on the package. "Just… stuff. You don't need to worry about it."

"But what is it? Where are you going?" Joe's youthful naiveté had made him persistent, almost an annoyance.

Mike had finally snapped. "It's my life, Joey! Something you wouldn't understand. Something Dad wouldn't understand. Silas… Silas gets it. He gives people a chance. You're just… stuck in the past." The venom in his voice, the raw accusation, had cut Joe to the quick. He remembered feeling a profound sense of alienation, as if his own brother had suddenly become a stranger.

That had been one of the last times Joe had seen Mike lucid, before the addiction truly took hold, blurring the lines between loyalty and necessity, between choice and compulsion. Joe had seen the desperation in Mike's eyes, a desperation fueled by Silas's manipulation and the ever-present lure of the substances that promised escape. He'd also seen Mike's capacity for betrayal, his willingness to use Joe, to lie to him, to protect his secrets, and by extension, Silas's operations.

The betrayal hadn't been a single act, but a series of choices, each one leading Mike further down a path from which there was no easy return. Joe wrestled with the concept of Mike's agency. How much of Mike's fate was a consequence of his own weaknesses, and how much was a direct result of Silas's calculated exploitation? Silas had been a master at identifying vulnerabilities, at preying on insecurity and ambition. He'd seen something in Mike, a desperate yearning for validation, and he'd weaponized it.

Joe's investigation had unearthed fragments, veiled references in encrypted messages, overheard conversations in dimly lit backrooms. Mike had been a courier, a mule, a disposable asset in Silas's vast network. He'd been paid well, enough to feed his habit and impress his associates, but always on Silas's terms, always with the implicit threat of exposure or retribution hanging over him. There were hints of Mike trying to get out, of him attempting to double-cross Silas, perhaps to reclaim some semblance of control, some shred of his former self. That was the most painful thought – that Mike had tried to fight back, and that Silas had crushed him.

The official story, the one he'd pieced together and subtly disseminated to ensure Silas's downfall, was that Mike had met his end during a botched transaction. A drug deal gone wrong, a territorial dispute. It was a convenient narrative, one that neatly explained away Mike's disappearance and death without directly implicating Silas in a way that would have allowed him to evade justice. But Joe knew the truth was murkier. He suspected Mike hadn't just been a victim of circumstance, but of deliberate cruelty. Perhaps he'd been set up, a message sent to anyone else who dared to cross Silas. The precise details of Mike's final moments remained elusive, a void that gnawed at Joe. Had he died alone, terrified, regretting everything? Or had he gone out in a blaze of defiant rage, a final flicker of the brother Joe remembered?

He walked over to the dusty workbench, the same one where he'd run his father's handprint. He traced a deep gouge in the wood, a scar from years ago. His father had smoothed it down with sandpaper, a small act of care. "Always respect your tools, son," he'd said. Mike hadn't respected his tools. He hadn't respected himself. He hadn't respected their father's legacy. And in the end, he hadn't respected Joe.

The harsh realities of addiction, the brutal calculus of betrayal, the unforgiving nature of the city's underbelly – they had all stripped away Joe's youthful optimism. He wasn't the naive kid who'd once believed in the inherent goodness of people anymore. He'd seen the worst, and in his quest for retribution, he'd had to embrace a part of that darkness himself. He'd had to become someone who could navigate those treacherous waters, someone who could make the difficult, often morally ambiguous, decisions required to bring down a man like Silas.

He looked at his own hands, calloused and ingrained with a different kind of grime than the oil that still faintly scented the air. These hands had dealt in information, in strategy, in calculated destruction. They were the hands of a man forged in the fires of loss and revenge. And now, standing in the silent shell of his family's dreams, he had to reconcile that man with the memory of the brother he'd lost. He had to grapple with the man Mike had become, a man consumed by his own demons and manipulated by Silas's wicked influence. And in doing so, he had to confront the man he himself had been forced to become.

The stark contrast between the two paths was stark. Mike had sought escape, a numbing oblivion. Joe had sought justice, a searing clarity. But both had been driven by a need to break free from the constraints of their lives, from the suffocating weight of their circumstances. Mike had succumbed to the allure of easy answers and false promises. Joe had chosen a harder, more solitary path, one that required him to confront the darkness head-on.

He imagined Mike's final thoughts. Were they of his parents, of the life he'd squandered? Or were they of Silas, of the power he'd craved, of the escape he'd pursued? Joe didn't have the answers, and the not knowing was a wound that refused to heal. He had avenged his parents, he had dismantled Silas's operation, but the emotional cost was immeasurable. The act of bringing down Silas had, in a twisted way, brought him face-to-face with the full extent of the damage Silas had inflicted. And that damage extended not just to his parents' business, but to the very fabric of his family, to the lifeblood of his brother.

He walked out of the office, the faint smell of stale air and dust following him. The 'Closed' sign still hung askew, a permanent fixture on a life that was no longer. Joe understood that his own life, too, was irrevocably changed. He had stepped out of the shadows, executed his plan, and now he was left to face the aftermath, not just of Silas's downfall, but of the internal reckoning that followed. The city would continue to churn, new players emerging from the void left by Silas. The cycle of violence would persist, a grim, immutable truth. But Joe's role in that cycle had shifted. He was no longer a participant, but an observer, a witness to the consequences of his actions.

He paused at the entrance, the weak sunlight filtering through the grimy windows casting long, distorted shadows. He had pursued justice with a singular focus, a relentless drive born from pain. He had succeeded in his mission, but the victory was steeped in a profound sorrow. He had brought down a kingpin, but the true battle had been with the demons of his own past, with the fragmented memories of his brother, with the ghost of the life he once knew. The auto shop, once a symbol of aspiration and hard work, now stood as a stark testament to the devastating reach of corruption and the enduring pain of loss. He had grappled with the truth, and the truth was a heavy burden, one that would forever shape the man he had become, and the path that lay ahead. The silence of the shop was not an absence of sound, but a profound statement of what had been irrevocably broken. He was left with the stark reality of Mike's fate, a fate that was a grim tapestry woven from addiction, betrayal, and the cruelties of the city. And as he stepped out into the fading light, Joe knew that the man he had become, in order to confront these truths, was a stranger to the innocent boy who had once learned his trade within these very walls. The confrontation wasn't just with Silas anymore; it was with himself, and the reflection of his brother he saw in the darkest corners of his own soul.

## A Brother's Forgiveness

The silence of the shop was a heavy blanket, muffling the sounds of the city outside, a stark contrast to the storm raging within Joe. He had brought down Silas. He had dismantled the operation, exposed the rot, and for all intents and purposes, avenged his parents. Yet, the victory felt hollow, a brittle shell devoid of the triumph he had envisioned. The true battle, he was beginning to understand, had never been about Silas. It had always been about Mike. The ghost of his brother, once a specter of accusation and pain, had begun to morph into something else entirely, something far more complicated. If Mike was alive – and the gnawing uncertainty of that possibility was a constant thrum beneath the surface of his newfound quiet – then Joe's mission wasn't over. It had merely entered its most agonizing phase.

The thought of Mike's survival, a flicker of hope he had meticulously suppressed, now began to bloom in the barren landscape of his grief. If Mike was alive, not a victim but a survivor, then Joe's journey of vengeance had to pivot. It had to transform into a path of reconciliation, a road paved with the rubble of shattered trust and profound betrayal. This wasn't the clean, definitive victory he'd chased. This was messy, fraught with a vulnerability that made his teeth ache. Forgiveness, he realized, wasn't an act of absolution he could mete out. It was a process, a grueling, painstaking excavation of shared history, of buried love, and of the wreckage left by their individual and collective failings.

He replayed fragments of conversations, moments of camaraderie from their youth, interspersed with the harsh realities of Mike's descent. The easy laughter they'd shared working on cars, the way Mike used to instinctively know what Joe needed before he even asked, the unspoken understanding that passed between them with a mere glance. These were the memories Joe clung to, the pure, untainted remnants of a bond that Silas's poison had tried to eradicate. But then came the other memories: the lies, the evasions, the chilling detachment in Mike's eyes when Joe had tried to reach him. The knowledge that Mike had been complicit, a willing pawn in Silas's game, a participant in the destruction of their family's legacy. How did one forgive that? How did one look past the choices that had led to so much pain, so much loss?

The weight of Mike's potential survival pressed down on him, heavier than any accusation he'd leveled against Silas. If Mike was alive, he wasn't just a victim of circumstance. He was a man who had made devastating mistakes, who had succumbed to the very darkness Joe had fought so hard to conquer. And Joe, the avenger, the meticulous architect of Silas's downfall, now had to grapple with the role of the brother. The brother who could offer solace, but also the brother who had been deeply, irrevocably hurt. The brother who had been lied to, manipulated, and ultimately, abandoned by the very person he had once shared his deepest secrets with.

He imagined walking up to Mike, the words catching in his throat. How would he start? "Hey, remember me? The brother you left behind to deal with all this?" The sarcasm felt like a defense mechanism, a shield against the raw vulnerability of the situation. He knew, with a chilling certainty, that simply saying "I forgive you" wouldn't be enough. Forgiveness, in this context, was an invitation to rebuild, to lay bare the damage, and to try, against all odds, to find a way back to each other. It meant acknowledging Mike's mistakes, not glossing over them, not excusing them, but understanding them within the suffocating grip of addiction and Silas's insidious influence. It meant holding Mike accountable, but not condemning him.

The path to reconciliation would be a minefield. Trust, once shattered, was a delicate thing, easily fractured further. Mike would likely be defensive, perhaps even resentful, haunted by his own shame and the knowledge of how deeply he had wronged Joe. Joe would have to tread carefully, offering support without enabling, offering understanding without condoning. He would have to be patient, infinitely patient, because the scars ran deep, not just on the surface, but in the very core of their relationship. There would be days when the anger would resurface, when the memories of Mike's complicity would threaten to drown out any nascent sense of forgiveness.

He thought of his parents. What would they have wanted? They had loved Mike, fiercely, unconditionally, even as they despaired over his choices. They had mourned him, not just as a son lost to addiction, but as a son lost to Silas's world. If Mike was alive, they would have wanted him found, wanted him helped, wanted him to have a chance at redemption. That, he knew, was the legacy of their love – a capacity for forgiveness that Joe had always admired, and now, had to somehow embody.

The initial steps would be the hardest. Simply finding Mike, if he was indeed still out there, would be a monumental task. Silas's network was vast, and Mike, if he had survived, would likely have vanished into the underbelly of the city, a ghost among ghosts. Joe would have to leverage everything he had learned, every connection, every bit of leverage he had gained in his pursuit of Silas, to locate his brother. And when he found him, he would have to approach him not as an avenger, but as a brother, extending a hand of tentative peace, a silent offering of a chance to start anew.

He knew that the forgiveness wouldn't be instantaneous. It wouldn't be a magical balm that instantly healed the wounds. It would be a gradual process, built on small gestures of trust, on shared conversations that slowly chipped away at the wall of guilt and shame. It would involve witnessing Mike's struggle, perhaps even helping him through it, supporting his efforts to reclaim his life, to build something positive from the ashes of his past. It would require Joe to compartmentalize his own pain, to set aside his justifiable anger, and to focus on the shared humanity that still existed between them, however buried.

The memory of Mike's last coherent words to him – "It's my life, Joey! Something you wouldn't understand" – echoed in the quiet space. Those words had been a chasm between them, a declaration of independence that had felt like a betrayal. Now, if Mike was alive, Joe would have to prove him wrong. He would have to show Mike that he *did* understand, or at least, that he was willing to try. He would have to demonstrate that their shared blood, their shared history, meant something more than the mistakes that had threatened to tear them apart.

There was also the stark reality of Mike's addiction. If Mike was alive, he was likely still battling those demons. Joe couldn't force sobriety upon him, but he could offer a lifeline, a steady hand to guide him through the recovery process. This would require immense strength, not just from Mike, but from Joe as well. He would have to witness the ugliness of addiction, the relapses, the moments of despair, and still maintain his commitment to offering forgiveness and support. It was a daunting prospect, one that would test the limits of his endurance and his capacity for empathy.

He considered the possibility of failure. What if Mike wasn't ready for forgiveness? What if he had been too deeply consumed by his addiction, too hardened by his experiences, to accept Joe's outstretched hand? What if, in his shame, he pushed Joe away, perpetuating the cycle of estrangement? These were valid fears, and they gnawed at Joe, threatening to extinguish the fragile hope that had begun to ignite within him. But the alternative, the continued absence of his brother, the permanent void that Silas's actions had created, was no longer an option he could bear.

Joe realized that true forgiveness wasn't about forgetting. It was about remembering, about acknowledging the past in its entirety, the good and the bad, and choosing to move forward regardless. It was about accepting that people, even those we love most, are capable of profound error, and that growth often comes from the ashes of those errors. It was about understanding that Mike, in his own flawed way, was also a victim of Silas's machinations, a pawn sacrificed in a game of power and control. While this didn't absolve him of his choices, it offered a lens through which Joe could begin to process the pain and extend a measure of grace.

The raw, unvarnished truth was that Joe had sought retribution, not just for his parents, but for himself. He had been consumed by a need to right the wrongs, to balance the scales. But now, standing in the echoing silence of what was left, he understood that the true victory lay not in punishing the perpetrators, but in finding a way to heal the wounds, however deep. And if Mike was alive, then healing had to begin with him, with the fractured remnants of their brotherhood. It was a path fraught with uncertainty, a journey that demanded a complete reimagining of the man Joe had become, and the brother he had lost. The fight against Silas was over, but the fight for Mike, for their shared past and for a possible future, was just beginning. And in that fight, forgiveness wasn't a weakness; it was the only weapon strong enough to forge a new beginning. He had to believe that. He had to hold onto that possibility, even if it meant confronting a pain that was far more profound than any he had yet endured. The weight of expectation, of responsibility, settled upon his shoulders, a burden he would carry with the same grim determination that had guided him through the darkness. The silence was no longer just the absence of Silas; it was the pregnant pause before the arduous work of rebuilding a broken family.

## The Scars of the Search

The city, once a labyrinth of shadows and deceit, now felt like a crucible that had reshaped him. Joe looked at his hands, calloused and scarred, not just from physical altercations, but from the mental and emotional toll of his immersion in the underworld. The relentless pursuit of Silas had stripped away layers of his former self, leaving behind a core of hardened resolve, but also a deep well of weariness. He'd witnessed acts of cruelty that had curdled his stomach, seen desperation twist good intentions into monstrous deeds. Each encounter, each compromise, each moment of doubt had etched itself onto his psyche, leaving an indelible mark. The boy who had walked into this mess, driven by a naive sense of justice, was gone, replaced by a man who understood the intricate, often brutal, mechanics of survival and the devastating cost of moral compromise.

He remembered the first time he had to truly defend himself, the primal fear that had surged through him, the desperate, clumsy movements that had somehow resulted in a victory, albeit a messy one. The adrenaline had been a potent, intoxicating drug, but the aftermath, the cold, dawning realization of what he was capable of, had been far more sobering. He'd had to learn to navigate a world where lines blurred, where loyalty was a currency often traded for survival, and where the enemy could wear the face of a friend. This constant vigilance, this ingrained distrust, was a scar that would likely never fully heal. He found himself scanning crowds, assessing threats, his senses perpetually on high alert, a habit ingrained by the constant proximity of danger. The easygoing nature, the ability to let his guard down, had been a casualty of his journey, a sacrifice he had made to stay alive.

The moral tightrope he had walked had been the most taxing. There were moments when the only path forward seemed to involve dipping his hands into the same murky waters as Silas. He'd had to make choices, calculated risks that had gnawed at his conscience. Was the information he gained worth the methods he employed? Was the greater good served by actions that bordered on the ethically reprehensible? These questions lingered, unresolved, haunting his quiet moments. He'd had to compartmentalize, to compartmentalize ruthlessly, to push down the voice of doubt that whispered that he was becoming the very thing he fought against. This internal conflict, this ongoing battle with his own conscience, had left its own set of invisible wounds. He carried the weight of those decisions, the knowledge that he had crossed lines he could never uncross, a burden that felt heavier than any physical injury.

The addiction, too, had left its mark, not directly on him, but through its devastating impact on his brother. Witnessing Mike's slow, agonizing descent had been a unique form of torture. He had seen the light in Mike's eyes dim, the spark of his personality extinguished by the insatiable craving. He had seen his brother become a stranger, a hollowed-out shell of the person he once was. The helplessness he had felt, the inability to pull Mike back from the brink, was a wound that ran deep, a constant reminder of the powerlessness he'd experienced even as he orchestrated Silas's downfall. The memory of Mike's vacant stare, his desperate pleas, his betrayals – all of it was a tapestry of pain woven into the fabric of Joe's being. These weren't abstract concepts; they were visceral memories, etched into his emotional landscape, shaping his perception of the world and his place within it.

He had learned that the pursuit of justice was rarely a clean, straightforward affair. It was a messy, often brutal undertaking, one that demanded sacrifices and forced individuals to confront the darkest aspects of humanity, including their own. The innocence he once possessed was a distant memory, replaced by a hard-won, somber wisdom. He understood now that the world wasn't black and white; it was a spectrum of grays, and navigating it required a different kind of strength, a resilience forged in the fires of experience. The scars he carried were not just physical reminders of battles fought, but deep psychological imprints of a journey that had irrevocably altered his perception of himself and the world around him. Loyalty, he'd learned, came at a steep price, and the devastating impact of addiction was a destructive force that could shatter lives and families with a terrifying efficiency. These were the lessons he carried forward, the silent testament to the ordeal he had endured, and the profound transformation it had wrought. He was no longer the same person who had begun this quest; the shadows of the underbelly had clung to him, and he suspected they always would. The aftermath wasn't just the absence of Silas; it was the internal reckoning, the quiet acknowledgment of the man he had become.

## Reclaiming His Own Path

The silence of the auto shop, once a familiar comfort, now felt like a tomb. It was the quiet of a battle won, yes, but a battle that had consumed everything in its path, leaving behind a desolate landscape of what-ifs and what-nows. Silas was gone, his network dismantled, his poison purged from the city's veins. But the victory was a hollow echo in the cavernous space, a testament to a war fought on too many fronts. Joe looked at his hands, still bearing the faint scent of motor oil and something darker, something that clung to him like the grime of the underbelly. They were the hands of a man who had done what was necessary, a man who had hunted and fought and bled. But they were also the hands of a man adrift, his purpose extinguished with Silas's last breath.

The auto shop itself, a monument to his father's hard work and his mother's quiet strength, felt like an anchor he no longer had the will to hold. It was his inheritance, yes, but it was also a tangible link to a life that felt increasingly distant, like a photograph fading in the sun. The scent of gasoline and coolant, once the perfume of his childhood, now carried the ghost of his parents, their hopes and dreams inextricably tied to this place. He could see his father, grease-stained and smiling, showing him the intricacies of an engine, his mother bringing them thermoses of coffee, her presence a steady warmth in the often-grimy workshop. But the memories, once a source of solace, now felt like the chains of a life he had outgrown, or perhaps, a life that had been violently ripped away.

Selling it felt like another betrayal, another severing of ties. Yet, keeping it felt like a perpetual penance, a daily reminder of what was lost. The tools, meticulously arranged, the worn leather of the mechanic's stool, the faint scorch marks on the concrete floor – each was a silent witness to a past he couldn't reclaim, a future he hadn't yet dared to imagine. The city outside, a restless organism of steel and glass, pulsed with a life that was both alien and achingly familiar. He had navigated its darkest corners, understood its predatory instincts, and emerged, somehow, intact. But intact wasn't the same as healed. Intact was merely the absence of further damage.

He needed a new direction, a new purpose. The thought was as daunting as the pursuit of Silas had been. For so long, his life had been dictated by the singular, all-consuming goal of avenging his parents and finding Mike. Now, with those objectives, in their own brutal way, met or at least addressed, he was faced with the terrifying prospect of defining himself. Who was Joe, without the shadow of Silas, without the ache of his brother's absence? The question hung in the air, heavy and unanswered. He wasn't just Joe the avenger, or Joe the detective of his own tragedy. He was Joe, a man in his late twenties, with a life yet to be lived, a life that deserved more than the wreckage of the past.

He considered the possibilities, each one a tentative step into an unknown territory. Could he go back to being just Joe, the guy who fixed cars? The thought felt impossibly mundane, a regression after the intensity of his recent experiences. The skills he'd honed, the instincts he'd sharpened, felt wasted on oil changes and transmission repairs. He'd learned to read people, to anticipate danger, to navigate complex networks of information and influence. These weren't skills you picked up in a vocational school. They were forged in the fire of necessity, and they felt intrinsically linked to the man he had become.

Perhaps he could use what he had learned, not for vengeance, but for something constructive. The underworld had taught him about the exploitation, the desperation, the ways in which people could be manipulated and preyed upon. He'd seen firsthand the collateral damage of greed and corruption. There was a whole segment of society, the vulnerable, the forgotten, who were just as susceptible to the machinations of men like Silas, but without the resources or the will to fight back. Could he be a different kind of force in the city? Not a vigilante, not an avenger, but something… else. A protector, perhaps? A quiet bulwark against the encroaching darkness?

The idea, nascent and fragile, began to take root. It wasn't about seeking out trouble, but about being prepared for it, about using his hard-won knowledge to help those who couldn't help themselves. It was about reclaiming his own path, not by retracing the steps of his father, or by being haunted by the ghost of his brother, but by charting a new course, guided by the lessons of his own crucible. He thought of the people he'd encountered during his investigation, the ordinary citizens caught in the crossfire, the ones who had lost everything. They deserved more than just the dismantling of a criminal enterprise; they deserved a chance to rebuild, to live without fear.

He walked through the shop, his movements slow and deliberate, touching the worn surfaces, absorbing the residual energy of the place. This was where his father had poured his life, where his mother had found her quiet joy. It was a legacy, undeniably. But a legacy wasn't a cage. It was a foundation. And from that foundation, he could build something new. He wasn't his father, nor was he Mike. He was Joe, a survivor, a man who had stared into the abyss and refused to blink. And now, he had to find out what that man was capable of, outside the confines of his past.

The notion of selling the shop was still a painful one, but it was becoming less of a surrender and more of a strategic repositioning. He needed capital, yes, but more than that, he needed a clean break, a symbolic shedding of the skin that no longer fit. The money from the sale could be seed money for whatever came next, a financial springboard into the unknown. He envisioned a different kind of operation, perhaps something less tangible than repairing engines, something that dealt with information, with protection, with the subtle, often unseen currents of power that flowed through the city.

He found himself drawn to the quiet hum of the city outside, no longer a place of overt threats, but a vast, complex organism ripe for understanding. He had spent months immersed in its shadows, learning its rhythms, its secret language. Now, he wanted to understand its heart, its needs, its vulnerabilities. He realized that his parents hadn't just left him a business; they had left him a connection to this city, a stake in its well-being. And Mike, in his own twisted way, had shown him the city's capacity for destruction, a warning of the dangers that lurked beneath the surface.

The journey ahead was daunting. It required a shift in perspective, a deliberate act of self-definition. He had to move from a reactive stance – responding to threats, avenging wrongs – to a proactive one, shaping his own future, defining his own purpose. This wasn't about forgetting the past; it was about integrating it, about understanding how the crucible had reshaped him and then channeling that transformation into something meaningful. He had seen the worst of humanity, and he had, at times, participated in it. But he had also seen glimmers of hope, of resilience, of goodness that persisted even in the darkest of times. He wanted to be a part of that goodness, to amplify it, to protect it.

He pictured himself walking away from the auto shop, not with the burden of grief, but with the quiet confidence of a man who had found his footing. The sting of selling his father's legacy would be there, a dull ache beneath the surface, but it would be overshadowed by the excitement of what lay ahead. He would carry the lessons of his parents – their integrity, their hard work, their capacity for love – not as a weight, but as a guiding light. And he would carry the memory of Mike, not as a source of shame or anger, but as a reminder of the fragility of life, the insidious nature of addiction, and the enduring power of the human spirit to seek redemption, even if it was a redemption he himself would have to help forge.

The path of self-discovery wasn't a straight line; it was a winding road, full of unforeseen turns and unexpected obstacles. But for the first time since the darkness had descended, Joe felt a flicker of genuine anticipation, a sense of agency that had been absent for so long. He was no longer defined by what had happened
*to* him, but by what he chose to do *next*. The auto shop, a symbol of his past, was becoming a launching pad for his future. He was reclaiming his own path, not by erasing the past, but by building upon it, brick by painstaking brick, into something new, something entirely his own. The silence of the shop was no longer a tomb; it was the quiet prelude to a life he was finally ready to build. It was time to turn the key in the ignition, not on the familiar rumble of an engine, but on the engine of his own reinvention. He would sell the shop, not as an ending, but as

the beginning of his true journey, a journey where he was not just the son of his parents or the brother of his lost sibling, but simply, irrevocably, Joe. And that, he realized, was a victory far more profound than the one he had already achieved. The dust of Silas's empire had settled, and in its wake, a new landscape was emerging, a landscape that was entirely his to shape. The uncertainty remained, a constant companion, but it was no longer a source of paralyzing fear. Instead, it was the thrilling unknown, the vast expanse of possibility that lay before him, waiting to be explored. He was ready to drive into it, head held high, the past a compass, not an anchor, and the future, a blank canvas.

# Chapter Twelve
# A New Horizon

## The Auction Block

The air hung heavy with a melancholy that was both personal and profoundly public. Joe stood across the street, partially obscured by the shadowed alcove of a closed storefront, the crisp autumn air doing little to cut through the knot of anticipation in his gut. His father's auto shop, a place etched into his very being, was no longer his. Today, it was a commodity, a collection of bricks and mortar and worn-out machinery on an auction block. He'd deliberately chosen to watch from a distance, a silent observer at the dismantling of his own past. The 'For Sale' sign, so stark and jarring against the familiar chipped paint of the garage door, felt like a personal indictment, a definitive statement that his time here, the time of his father and his mother, was unequivocally over.

A motley collection of individuals milled about the property. There were the usual speculators, men in sensible shoes and suits that looked a size too large, their eyes scanning the structure with a detached, calculating gaze. They saw square footage, potential for development, revenue streams. Joe saw the ghost of his father, his broad shoulders hunched over an engine block, the faint smile of satisfaction on his lips as he coaxed life back into a sputtering motor. He saw his mother, her apron dusted with flour from the bakery down the street, bringing him and his father steaming mugs of coffee, her presence a quiet anchor in the often-chaotic world of the garage. He saw the greasy handprints on the walls, the faint, permanent stains on the concrete floor where oil had seeped in over decades, each mark a testament to countless hours of honest work.

A gruff-looking man, presumably the auctioneer's representative, was leading a small group through the interior. Joe could barely make out their movements through the grimy windows, but he imagined them tapping the walls, peering under the lifts, assessing the structural integrity with the same detached efficiency they might apply to a used car. They weren't seeing the memories, the laughter, the quiet pride that had filled this space. They were seeing assets and liabilities. It was a necessary detachment, he knew, a brutal but essential step in his own healing, this act of letting go. It was like watching a loved one enter hospice – the end was inevitable, and the process, however painful, was about preparing for the absence.

He felt a strange sense of calm wash over him, a surrender that was more like acceptance than resignation. This wasn't the end of everything, he reminded himself. It was the end of
*this* chapter, the one that had been dictated by loss and vengeance. Selling the shop, letting it go to the highest bidder, was the final severing of the cords that tied him to that past. It was the physical manifestation of his decision to move forward, to build something new on the foundations of what had been. The money from the sale would be the seed capital for that uncharted territory, a tangible resource to fuel his new direction. He'd spent so long fighting battles he never asked for, defending a legacy that felt both like a birthright and a burden. Now, he was choosing his own fight, his own legacy.

He watched as a younger man, perhaps an aspiring mechanic with dreams of his own, ran a hand along the worn workbench, his expression a mixture of awe and something akin to longing. Joe understood that look. He'd felt it countless times himself, looking up to his father, wanting to emulate his skill, his dedication. But that was then. Now, Joe's skills had been honed in a different forge, tempered by the city's underbelly, by the necessity of survival and the grim pursuit of justice. Those weren't skills you learned by tuning carburetors; they were skills learned by reading faces, by anticipating threats, by navigating the intricate, often deadly, dance of the criminal world.

The auctioneer's voice, amplified by a portable speaker, began to carry across the street. It was a practiced, booming cadence, designed to build excitement, to extract the highest possible price. Joe felt a pang of something close to resentment. How could this man, this stranger, reduce his family's life's work to a series of bids and counter-bids? But then, the resentment subsided, replaced by a quiet resolve. This place had served its purpose for him, for his family. Now, it was time for it to serve a new purpose for someone else. It was the natural order of things, the constant ebb and flow of life and commerce.

The bidding started. Joe listened intently, his gaze fixed on the familiar facade of the shop. The initial offers were hesitant, the numbers tentative. Then, as the auctioneer's energy intensified, so did the bids. He heard numbers that made him wince slightly, numbers that were far beyond what his father would have ever imagined for this humble garage. It was a strange kind of validation, in a twisted way, to see the value that others placed on the physical space, even if they couldn't grasp its deeper significance to him.

He saw a woman, dressed in a sharp business suit, enter the fray, her voice clear and decisive as she placed a bid. She seemed out of place among the rougher, more hands-on types, but her determination was evident. Joe wondered what her plans were for the shop. Would she gut it, turn it into a trendy cafe? Or would she perhaps recognize its potential as a functional space, albeit with a new owner? The uncertainty was a familiar companion, but today, it felt less like a threat and more like an invitation. The future was unwritten, and he was finally holding the pen.

As the bidding escalated, the tension in the air thickened. Each increment was a step further away from the past, a step closer to the unknown future he was determined to forge. He'd been prepared for this day, had mentally rehearsed it, had even, in a morbid way, looked forward to it as a release. And now that it was here, it was both easier and harder than he'd anticipated. Easier because he was ready, he had made peace with the necessity of it. Harder because the sheer finality of the act, the tangible finality of watching it slip away, was a potent emotional force.

He saw the younger man, the aspiring mechanic, shake his head and walk away as the bids climbed past his reach. Joe felt a brief surge of empathy for him, for the dashed dreams. He knew what it was like to have those dreams snatched away. But he also knew that dreams, like engines, could be rebuilt, or replaced with new ones. His own dreams had been shattered and reforged in the fires of loss.

The auctioneer's voice reached a fever pitch. "Going once! Going twice! Sold!"

The finality of that word, "Sold," echoed in the street, amplified by the silence that followed. Joe watched as the woman in the sharp suit exchanged papers with the representative. She turned, a brief, unreadable expression on her face, and walked away, presumably to her new acquisition. Joe stayed put, rooted to his spot across the street, a silent witness to the transfer of ownership. The building that had been the bedrock of his family's existence for so long was now simply a transaction, a closed chapter.

He took a deep, cleansing breath. The air still smelled of exhaust fumes and city grit, but for the first time in a long time, it didn't carry the suffocating weight of the past. It was just air. And he, Joe, was no longer tethered to this place. The sale was more than just a financial transaction; it was a symbolic shedding of skin, a deliberate act of severing ties that had, in their own way, begun to suffocate him. The legacy wasn't gone; it was internalized. The lessons of his father's hard work, his mother's quiet strength, and even the harsh realities Mike had revealed about the city's darkness – these were all a part of him now, indelible markers that would guide his next steps.

He turned away from the shop, not with a sense of loss, but with a quiet, burgeoning sense of possibility. The street stretched out before him, an unknown expanse filled with the promise of what was to come. He hadn't found a new path in the wreckage of Silas's empire;

he had to create it. And the sale of the auto shop, this deeply personal auction, was the official starting pistol for that journey. He was no longer the son of his parents, or the brother of a lost soul, or the hunter of a phantom. He was Joe, a man stepping into his own horizon, carrying the echoes of his past not as chains, but as a compass guiding him toward a future he was finally ready to build. The engine of his reinvention had just been ignited.

## A Difficult Reunion

The city's underbelly, a labyrinth Joe had navigated with a hunter's instinct, offered few havens. Yet, he'd chosen this particular patch of asphalt, a forgotten lot on the edge of the industrial district, for its sheer neutrality. It was a place stripped of personal history, a blank canvas upon which a new, albeit fraught, conversation could be painted. He'd arrived early, the predawn chill still clinging to the air, and watched the sky bleed from bruised purple to a washed-out grey. The rumble of distant traffic was a muted symphony, a constant reminder of the city that pulsed around them, indifferent to the personal drama about to unfold. He checked his watch for the tenth time, the cheap plastic digging into his wrist. Mike was late.

When the beat-up sedan finally materialized from the gloom, a phantom from Joe's past, his gut tightened. It wasn't the sleek, menacing vehicles he was accustomed to encountering in his line of work, but something far more mundane, something that screamed of a life lived on the fringes, of scraped-together resources and constant uncertainty. The car coughed to a halt a few yards away, its engine sputtering a tired protest. The door creaked open, and Mike emerged, not with the swagger Joe remembered, but with a weariness etched into his frame that went beyond physical exhaustion. His shoulders were stooped, his gaze downcast, as if the very act of looking up was too great an effort.

Joe's first instinct was a complex swirl of emotions – a flicker of the old camaraderie, a surge of lingering resentment, and a gnawing, persistent ache of sorrow. Mike looked older, thinner, the lines on his face deeper, carved by something more profound than just time. He was a ghost made flesh, a living testament to the choices they had both made, the paths they had diverged onto. The air between them felt thick, charged with years of silence, of betrayal, of unspoken words that had festered and grown into an insurmountable barrier.

"Joe," Mike's voice was raspy, barely a whisper, as if the sound itself was a painful effort. He stopped a few feet away, his hands shoved deep into the pockets of a worn leather jacket. There was no apology in his tone, no plea for forgiveness, just a simple acknowledgement of his presence.

Joe nodded, his own voice catching in his throat. "Mike." He forced himself to meet his brother's eyes, finding them clouded and unfocused, a stark contrast to the sharp, calculating glint he remembered. "You're late." It was a weak opening, a clumsy attempt to bridge the chasm, but it was all he had.

Mike offered a humorless half-smile, a fleeting twitch of his lips that didn't reach his eyes. "Traffic," he said, the word hanging in the air with all the sincerity of a lie. He kicked at a loose pebble on the ground, his gaze still fixed on the cracked asphalt. "It's always traffic, isn't it?"

Joe didn't respond, letting the silence stretch, heavy with the unspoken question of why they were even here. He'd spent weeks wrestling with the idea of reaching out, of forcing this confrontation. Mike's survival, a fact confirmed by a hushed conversation with a contact who still operated in the shadows, had presented Joe with a stark choice: let the past remain buried, a scar that would never truly heal, or attempt to excavate it, to see if any semblance of their former bond could be salvaged. He'd chosen the latter, driven by a primal need to understand, perhaps even to forgive, the brother who had been both his confidant and his betrayer.

"I sold the shop," Joe stated, cutting through the awkward preamble. The words felt strangely anticlimactic, a casual announcement of a seismic shift in his life.

Mike finally looked up, a flicker of surprise crossing his features, quickly masked by a practiced indifference. "Yeah? Good.

Always was a money pit, that place." He shifted his weight, his stance betraying a nervous energy. "Anything good?"

"Enough," Joe replied, his gaze steady. He saw the flicker of relief in Mike's eyes, a fleeting acknowledgment of the financial lifeline the sale might represent, but he also saw the carefully constructed facade, the practiced deflection that had always been Mike's shield. "Look, Mike, we can't just stand here pretending this is a friendly chat about the weather."

Mike sighed, a ragged sound. "What do you want, Joe?" The question was devoid of emotion, a stark, clinical inquiry.

"I want to know," Joe began, his voice low and steady, each word carefully chosen. "I want to know why. Why you did what you did. Why you disappeared. Why you let me… why you let *us* go through all that." The last words were a raw confession, a vulnerability he rarely allowed himself to express.

Mike's jaw tightened, and he turned away, running a hand through his thinning hair. He seemed to be wrestling with something internally, a battle of his own making. "It's… complicated, Joe."

"Complicated?" Joe's voice rose slightly, a dangerous edge creeping in. "Complicated is a cop out, Mike. You were my brother. You were my partner in… in everything. And then you vanished. You left me to clean up your mess, to deal with the fallout. That's not complicated, that's just cruel."

Mike flinched at the accusation, a genuine pain flashing in his eyes. He turned back, his gaze meeting Joe's, and for a moment, Joe saw a glimpse of the brother he once knew, the one who had shared secrets and dreams under a sky full of stars. "It wasn't like that. Not entirely."

"Then tell me, Mike. What was it like? Because from where I was standing, it looked like you were running. Running from everything, everyone. Running from me." Joe took a step closer, the distance between them shrinking, the charged atmosphere intensifying. "Was it worth it? Whatever you were chasing, whatever you thought you'd gain by cutting us all adrift? Was it worth it?"

Mike's shoulders slumped further, the weight of Joe's words pressing down on him. He took a deep, shuddering breath, and then, in a low, raspy voice, he began to speak. It wasn't a torrent of excuses or elaborate justifications, but a confession, raw and unvarnished, punctuated by long pauses and the occasional choked-back sob. He spoke of the pressure, the debts, the gnawing fear that had consumed him. He spoke of the impossible choices, the desperate measures, the spiraling descent into a world that had promised escape but delivered only further entrapment.

"I was scared, Joe," Mike admitted, his voice barely audible. "So damn scared. They had me. They had leverage, and… and I made a choice. A bad one. The worst one." He looked at Joe, his eyes pleading for understanding, even if he didn't explicitly ask for it. "I thought I was protecting you. By disappearing, by making them think I was gone for good, I thought I was keeping you out of it. Keeping you safe."

Joe listened, his initial anger slowly giving way to a chilling realization. Mike hadn't just abandoned him; he'd made a calculated decision, one born of desperation and fear, but a decision nonetheless. The justification, however flawed, was there, a fragile thread that offered a sliver of connection. "Protecting me? By leaving me to fight your battles? By letting Silas's goons tear through our lives? That's not protection, Mike. That's abandonment."

"I know," Mike whispered, the words a broken confession. "I know how it looked. And I'm sorry. God, Joe, I'm so sorry." The apology, when it finally came, was laced with a lifetime of regret. It wasn't a magic wand that erased the past, but it was a beginning.

Joe studied his brother's face, searching for any sign of deception, any hint of the cunning manipulator he'd once known. But all he saw was a broken man, haunted by his choices. The shared history, the blood that ran in their veins, was a powerful current, pulling them back from the precipice of complete estrangement. "Sorry doesn't fix anything, Mike. It doesn't bring back Dad. It doesn't erase the years of hell I went through."

"I know," Mike repeated, his voice thick with emotion. "But it's all I have to give right now. That, and… and a willingness to try. To make things right, if I can. If you'll let me." He took a hesitant step forward, his eyes fixed on Joe's. "I've been watching you, you know. From a distance. What you've done, what you've become… Dad would have been proud. I'm proud, Joe. Even after… everything."

The unexpected praise, so genuine and unforced, caught Joe off guard. He'd spent so long in the shadows, his actions driven by a need for justice, a burning desire to avenge his family. To hear that his brother, the brother who had betrayed him, saw pride in his journey… it was a complex, deeply affecting moment. It chipped away at the wall Joe had meticulously constructed around his heart.

"Proud of what, Mike? Of the path I took? The one you forced me onto?" Joe's voice was still rough, but the anger had softened into a weary resignation. He realized he couldn't undo the past, couldn't reclaim the innocence they had lost. But perhaps, just perhaps, they could build something new from the ruins.

"Proud of you for surviving," Mike said, his gaze unwavering. "Proud of you for not letting them break you. Proud of you for carrying on, even when… even when I wasn't there." He took another step, closing the remaining distance between them. "I messed up, Joe. Royally. But I'm still your brother. And I want to be a part of your life. If you'll have me."

Joe looked at Mike, at the raw vulnerability in his eyes, and saw not just the betrayer, but the boy he'd once shared secrets with, the partner who had stood by his side through thick and thin, before the darkness had consumed him. The reunion was not a sudden, dramatic embrace, but a fragile, tentative reconnection. It was a recognition that even in the face of profound hurt and betrayal, the bonds of family, however strained, could sometimes endure. He couldn't erase the scars, but he could choose to let them guide him towards a new horizon, one that included the possibility, however faint, of reconciliation.

"I don't know, Mike," Joe admitted, his voice barely a whisper. "I don't know if I can ever fully trust you again. What you did… it changed everything." He paused, the weight of years of pain and resentment heavy in the air. "But I'm not going to leave you standing here like this. Not today." He looked at his brother, a flicker of hope warring with a deep-seated caution. "Let's… let's get some coffee. And we can talk. Really talk. No more hiding, no more running."

Mike's face, illuminated by the nascent dawn, held a look of profound relief. A small, genuine smile finally touched his lips. "Coffee sounds good, Joe. Real good." He gestured towards his beat-up car. "My treat."

As they walked towards the car, the silence between them was different now. It wasn't the heavy, suffocating silence of unspoken grievances, but a contemplative quiet, filled with the unspoken acknowledgment of shared pain and the fragile, burgeoning hope for a different future. The road ahead was uncertain, littered with the debris of their fractured past, but for the first time in a long time, Joe felt a sense of possibility, a quiet understanding that healing, like building something new, was a process, one step, one conversation, at a time. The sale of the shop had been the end of one chapter, but this difficult reunion, this fragile step towards reconciliation, was the true beginning of his new horizon.

## Forging a New Identity

The city, a sprawling organism of concrete and ambition, had always been Joe's battleground. For years, his existence had been inextricably linked to the hum of the shop, the familiar scent of aged wood and polished metal, the steady rhythm of transactions that had become the soundtrack to his life. But the sale, the finality of it, had been more than just a financial transaction; it was an excision, a severing of ties that had bound him to a past he was determined to outgrow. He stood on the precipice of something unknown, a landscape unmarred by the ghosts of his brother's mistakes or the suffocating weight of his father's legacy. The air felt different, lighter, charged with the exhilarating, terrifying possibility of self-definition.

He'd spent days wrestling with the inertia that followed the final handshake, the lingering inertia that threatened to pull him back into the familiar currents of his old life. But the conversations with

Mike, raw and honest as they had been, had also served as a catalyst. Witnessing his brother's brokenness, the genuine remorse etched into his features, had underscored the cyclical nature of despair that Joe was so desperate to escape. He saw in Mike the man he could have become, trapped by circumstances and poor choices, a cautionary tale whispered in the hushed tones of regret. The realization was a cold splash of water, invigorating and stark. He wouldn't be that man. He couldn't be.

The decision to leave the city wasn't born of a sudden impulse, but of a slow, deliberate accumulation of reasons. It was the suffocating familiarity, the constant reminders of what had been lost, the pervasive sense of being an artifact in a place that had moved on without him. He needed a blank slate, a place where the past held no sway, where his name carried no baggage. He wanted to be defined not by what had happened to him, but by what he chose to do next. This wasn't an act of running away, he reminded himself, but a conscious stride towards a new beginning. He was forging a new identity, not from the ashes of his old life, but from the unwritten pages of his future.

He considered a few options, each a potential stepping stone away from the familiar. A small coastal town, its rhythm dictated by the tides rather than the relentless churn of commerce, appealed to him. The salt-laced air, the endless expanse of the ocean, seemed to promise a different kind of peace, a balm for a soul that had weathered too many storms. He also toyed with the idea of heading inland, towards the quiet solitude of the mountains, where the sheer scale of the landscape could dwarf his personal troubles, putting them into a more manageable perspective. But neither of these felt entirely right. They offered escape, but not necessarily reinvention.

The breakthrough came in an unexpected conversation with an old contact, a retired detective named Frank, whose gruff exterior hid a surprisingly insightful mind. They'd met in the sterile quiet of a diner on the outskirts of town, the scent of stale coffee and frying bacon a stark contrast to the polished elegance of his former establishments. Frank, a man who had seen the worst of humanity and emerged with his integrity intact, had listened patiently as Joe, haltingly at first, outlined his predicament.

"You've got a good head on your shoulders, kid," Frank had rasped, swirling the lukewarm coffee in his mug. "And you know how to read people. That's worth more than a thousand degrees in some fancy schools." He'd paused, his gaze sharp and assessing. "Ever think about applying that to something… legitimate?"

The word 'legitimate' hung in the air, a gentle challenge. Joe had always operated in the grey areas, his skills honed in the often-unseen corners of the city's economy. He'd learned to be observant, to anticipate, to piece together fragments of information into a cohesive whole. These were skills, he realized, that could be transferable, adaptable.

"Like what?" Joe had asked, a flicker of curiosity igniting within him.

Frank had leaned back, a slow smile spreading across his face. "Consulting. Corporate security. Risk assessment. You know how people tick, Joe. You know what makes them tick, and more importantly, what makes them break. That's a valuable commodity in a world that's always trying to pull a fast one." He'd then produced a worn business card, its edges softened with age, bearing the embossed letters: 'Frank Harrison – Strategic Security Solutions.' "Got a small operation. Mostly freelance, but it's steady. Could use someone with your… unique skillset."

The offer was a revelation. It wasn't the adrenaline-fueled rush of his past life, nor was it the passive acceptance of retirement. It was a challenge, a chance to apply his hard-won experience in a constructive, even respectable, way. It was a path that required him to use his mind, his intuition, his understanding of human nature, but to do so within the framework of law and order, albeit on its fringes. This was it. This was the clean slate he'd been searching for.

He spent the next few weeks in a whirlwind of activity, the sale of the shop finalized, his belongings packed into a single, sturdy suitcase. He visited Mike one last time, not in the sterile anonymity of a roadside diner, but in a small, nondescript apartment Mike had managed to secure. The air was still thick with the lingering scent of cheap disinfectant and desperation, but there was a quiet dignity about

Mike now, a fragile resolve that Joe hadn't seen before. They didn't rehash the past, didn't delve into the labyrinthine complexities of their shared history. Instead, they talked about the future, about the small, tentative steps Mike was taking towards sobriety and stability. Joe left him with a modest sum, a gesture of support that felt both inadequate and necessary.

"You sure about this, Joe?" Mike had asked, his voice raspy with emotion, as Joe stood at the door.

"It's time, Mike," Joe had replied, a quiet certainty in his voice. "Time for me to build something new."

As he drove west, the city skyline receding in his rearview mirror, a profound sense of release washed over him. The miles unspooled before him, each one a further detachment from the life he'd known. He was no longer Joe, the shop owner, the brother of a fugitive, the reluctant participant in a dangerous game. He was simply Joe, a man with a new direction, a new purpose, and a future that was entirely his own to shape. He was an architect of his own destiny, laying the foundation for a life built not on the ruins of the past, but on the solid ground of his own making. The road ahead was long, and the challenges would undoubtedly be significant, but for the first time in a long time, Joe felt a sense of genuine optimism, a quiet understanding that his resilience, his capacity for reinvention, was his greatest asset. He was leaving behind the suffocating embrace of what was, and stepping into the liberating expanse of what could be. The new horizon wasn't just a geographical destination; it was a state of being, a testament to his unwavering spirit.

## Lessons Learned

The hum of the engine, a steady drone against the vast, indifferent canvas of the prairie, had become a sort of meditative mantra for Joe. Each mile devoured was a further severing of the threads that had bound him to a life he no longer recognized. The city, with its suffocating familiarity and the indelible imprint of his brother's downfall, was now a receding memory, a distant shore he'd intentionally sailed away from. He carried with him not just the physical remnants of his former existence – a worn suitcase, a modest savings account – but a far heavier cargo: the hard-won, deeply ingrained lessons forged in the crucible of his family's implosion. These weren't the abstract platitudes found in self-help books; they were visceral truths, learned through the raw, unflinching gaze of experience, truths that had carved themselves into the very bedrock of his character.

The most profound of these lessons, he understood now, was the devastating, all-consuming nature of addiction. He'd seen it firsthand, not just in the hollowed-out eyes and erratic behavior of his brother, Mike, but in the ripple effect it had on everyone caught in its orbit. It was a parasitic entity, feeding on trust, on love, on hope, leaving behind a desolate landscape of regret and destruction. The dream he'd inherited, the meticulously crafted legacy of his father's business, had been systematically dismantled, piece by agonizing piece, by the insatiable hunger of this sickness. He'd witnessed the slow erosion of a man's soul, the gradual surrender to a craving that eclipsed all else, and the realization had left an indelible mark. It wasn't a moral failing, not entirely; it was a disease, insidious and relentless, that could reduce even the strongest to a shadow of their former selves. This understanding, bleak as it was, offered a strange sort of clarity. It explained the inexplicable, provided a framework for the chaos, and, most importantly, instilled in him a profound respect for the fragile resilience of the human spirit when faced with such an adversary.

Loyalty, too, had been a complex and often brutal teacher. He'd always believed in standing by family, in a steadfast adherence to the bonds that connected them. But the ordeal had revealed the insidious ways in which misguided loyalty could be twisted and exploited. He'd seen how readily people could rationalize their involvement in unsavory activities, cloaking their complicity in the guise of familial obligation. There were lines, he now knew, that even the closest bonds shouldn't compel one to cross. The desire to protect, to shield those he cared about, had often blinded him to the inherent dangers, to the moral compromises he was being nudged towards. He'd learned, through painful experience, that true loyalty wasn't about blind obedience or a refusal to see fault; it was about holding each other accountable, about demanding better, even when it meant confronting uncomfortable truths. It was about recognizing that sometimes, the most loving act was to refuse to be an enabler, to step back and allow consequences to unfold, however harsh. This was a difficult and often lonely lesson, one that required him to recalibrate his understanding of what it meant to be a true brother, a true son.

The darker corners of society, the underbelly he'd always skirted with a certain practiced detachment, had become a far more intimate acquaintance. He'd navigated the intricate webs of debt, deception, and desperation, witnessing the often-desperate measures people took to survive, or simply to subsist. He'd seen the predatory nature of certain individuals and institutions, preying on vulnerability, on weakness, on the very desperation that addiction so often breeds. His skills, honed in a more clandestine environment, had been tested and sharpened by these encounters. He'd learned to read the subtle tells, the unconscious gestures, the veiled threats that spoke volumes in the hushed exchanges of back rooms and dimly lit alleys. But beyond the mechanics of survival, he'd also glimpsed the shared humanity, the common threads of fear and hope that pulsed beneath the surface, even in the most hardened individuals. He understood now that the lines between 'good' and 'bad' were often blurred, painted in shades of grey rather than stark black and white, a realization that fostered a grudging, if wary, empathy.

He'd learned the agonizing fragility of dreams. The business, the tangible manifestation of his father's ambition and his own inherited responsibility, had seemed so solid, so unshakeable. Yet, it had crumbled with a speed that belied its apparent strength, a victim of circumstances and choices that had spun wildly out of control. The meticulous planning, the years of dedication, the very foundation of their family's stability – all had proven surprisingly susceptible to the corrosive forces of addiction and poor judgment. It was a stark reminder that success was not a guarantee, that stability was often an illusion, and that the future, no matter how carefully charted, remained inherently unpredictable. This understanding instilled in him a profound sense of humility, a recognition of the sheer luck and privilege that often underpinned outward success.

However, the most enduring lesson, the one that fueled his westward journey, was the indomitable strength of the human spirit. He had witnessed Mike's flicker of desire for redemption, the tentative steps towards sobriety, the raw courage it took to confront the demons that had held him captive for so long. He had seen the resilience of the human will, the capacity to endure, to adapt, to find glimmers of hope even in the deepest despair. This was the fuel that propelled him forward, the quiet affirmation that while dreams could be fragile, the spirit that dared to dream was anything but. It was the knowledge that even after immense loss and betrayal, the capacity for rebuilding, for reinvention, remained. This was the core truth he carried with him, a silent, unwavering conviction that the human capacity for resilience was, perhaps, our greatest and most enduring strength.

These lessons were not abstract principles to be intellectually dissected. They were etched into his being, the scar tissue of a painful but necessary apprenticeship. They informed his every decision, his every interaction. As he drove, the landscape shifting from urban sprawl to endless horizons, he felt the weight of this knowledge, not as a burden, but as a guiding force. It was a quiet determination, an inner compass that had been recalibrated by fire. He understood that his past, with all its complexities and consequences, was not something to be erased or forgotten, but something to be integrated, to be learned from. He carried the ghosts of his family's struggles, not as specters to be feared, but as silent counselors, reminding him of the precipice he had narrowly avoided and the path he was determined to forge. The road ahead was unwritten, but he approached it with a newfound clarity, armed with the hard-won wisdom that had been purchased at such a steep price. He was not just leaving a place; he was leaving behind a way of being, and embracing a new one, shaped by the crucible of his experiences, ready to confront whatever lay beyond the horizon. He understood that the sale of the shop, the severing of those ties, was merely the first step in a far more profound process of self-creation, a journey back to himself, armed with a clarity born of hardship and a quiet, unshakeable resolve. The lessons, though painful, had illuminated his path, clearing away the fog of inherited expectations and the shadows of past mistakes, revealing a future that was, for the very first time, entirely his own to shape.

## Hope on the Horizon

The drone of the tires on the asphalt was no longer just a sound; it was a rhythm, a counterpoint to the quiet hum of nascent hope that had begun to resonate within him. Joe's gaze, usually fixed with a grim intensity on the immediate stretch of highway, now drifted towards the vast expanse that unfolded before him. The prairie, an endless tapestry of greens and browns under a sky that stretched into an impossible blue, offered a stark contrast to the claustrophobic confines of the city he'd left behind. It was a different kind of space, one that didn't crowd or suffocate, but rather invited an exhale, a deep, cleansing breath that seemed to scrub away the lingering residue of his past. He hadn't sought out this journey with any grand illusions. The path he'd walked had been stained with the bitter realities of addiction's relentless grip, the corrosive effects of misplaced loyalty, and the stark vulnerability of dreams shattered against the rocks of poor choices. He'd witnessed the slow, agonizing unraveling of his family, the systematic dismantling of a legacy built on hard work and aspiration, all brought down by the insatiable maw of a disease that consumed everything in its path. This wasn't the stuff of fairy tales; it was the gritty, unvarnished truth of lives irrevocably altered.

Yet, in the midst of that devastation, something unexpected had taken root. It wasn't the effervescent, unearned optimism that often masqueraded as hope, but a more grounded, resilient kind of belief. It was the quiet acknowledgment that survival itself was a testament, a declaration that even after enduring the crushing weight of loss and betrayal, life possessed an astonishing capacity to persist, to bloom again in the most unlikely of soils. He'd seen it in Mike's own flickering desire for redemption, in the sheer, raw courage it took for his brother to confront the demons that had held him captive for so long. He'd observed the unwavering strength of the human will, its tenacious grip on existence, its remarkable ability to adapt, to find slivers of light even in the deepest, most oppressive darkness. This was the fuel that now propelled him westward, a silent, unwavering affirmation that while dreams might be fragile, the spirit that dared to dream, the spirit that persevered, was anything but.

The decision to sell the shop, the tangible symbol of his father's ambition and his own inherited burden, had been agonizing. It felt like severing a physical limb, a tangible link to a past that was both a source of pride and profound pain. But it was also the necessary amputation, the surgical removal of a diseased growth that was preventing anything new from taking hold. He understood, with a clarity born of harsh experience, that the future wasn't about clinging to the remnants of what was, but about embracing the possibility of what could be. The meticulously charted course of his father's business, the predictable trajectory he'd been expected to follow, had been a mirage. The reality was far messier, far more unpredictable, and ultimately, far more freeing. He carried with him not just the financial proceeds of that sale, but the weight of those lessons, the hard-won wisdom that had been purchased at such a steep price. They were the scar tissue of a painful but essential apprenticeship, etched into the very fabric of his being.

He felt the subtle shift in the landscape, the air growing cleaner, the horizon expanding with each mile. The city, with its cacophony of sounds and its suffocating familiarity, was now a fading imprint on his rearview mirror. He wasn't just leaving a place behind; he was shedding a way of being, a persona that had been shaped and constrained by the circumstances of his past. He was stepping into a new one, one that was still amorphous, still undefined, but undeniably his own. The journey had been devastating, a brutal confrontation with the fragility of life and the insidious nature of addiction. But it had also been a crucible, forging within him a resilience he hadn't known he possessed. The disorientation of his brother's fall, the subsequent unraveling of their family's stability, had stripped him bare, leaving him exposed to the rawest elements of human experience. And in that vulnerability, he'd discovered a core of strength, a quiet determination that had been amplified by the very forces that sought to break him.

The horizon beckoned, a clean, unblemished line where the earth met the sky. It represented not an end, but a beginning, a vast, open space where new possibilities could unfurl. He wasn't naive enough to believe that his troubles were entirely behind him. The scars of the past ran deep, and the memory of the battles fought, both within himself and with the external forces that had sought to derail him, would forever remain. But he faced that horizon with a newfound sense of self-awareness, a sober understanding of his own capabilities and limitations. He'd learned that hope wasn't a passive waiting for good things to happen, but an active engagement with the present, a commitment to moving forward, even when the path was uncertain. It was the quiet understanding that even after experiencing profound loss, the capacity for rebuilding, for reinvention, remained an intrinsic part of the human spirit.

He recalled the hushed conversations in the back rooms, the desperate exchanges in dimly lit alleys, the predatory glances that often accompanied offers of dubious assistance. He'd learned to read the subtle tells, the unconscious gestures that betrayed hidden intentions, the veiled threats that whispered in the silence between words. These experiences, though often unsettling, had honed his instincts, sharpening his ability to navigate the often-treacherous currents of human interaction. He'd learned to discern genuine concern from calculated manipulation, to recognize the desperation that could drive people to extraordinary lengths, and to understand the shared humanity that often pulsed beneath the surface of even the most hardened exteriors. It was a valuable, if grim, education, one that had stripped away any lingering illusions about the inherent goodness of all people. The world, he now knew, was a complex tapestry woven with threads of both light and shadow, and understanding both was crucial for survival.

The journey had also recalibrated his understanding of loyalty. He'd always believed in the sanctity of familial bonds, in an unwavering commitment to those closest to him. But he'd witnessed how easily that loyalty could be twisted, how it could be used as a shield for complicity, a justification for overlooking or even participating in destructive behavior. He'd learned that true loyalty wasn't about blind adherence or a refusal to acknowledge fault. It was about accountability, about demanding better, even when it meant confronting uncomfortable truths. It was about recognizing that sometimes, the most profound act of love was to refuse to enable, to step back and allow consequences to unfold, however painful they might be. This was a difficult lesson, one that had forced him to re-evaluate his own motivations and to acknowledge the fine line between support and enabling.

He thought about the fragility of dreams, how easily they could be crushed by the weight of circumstance or the consequences of poor decisions. The business, the symbol of his father's hard work and his own anticipated future, had seemed so solid, so unshakeable. Yet, it had crumbled with a speed that belied its apparent strength, a victim of forces that had spiraled wildly out of control. This realization instilled a profound sense of humility, a recognition of the sheer luck and privilege that often underpinned outward success. It was a stark reminder that stability was often an illusion, and that the future, no matter how carefully planned, remained inherently unpredictable. This understanding, while somber, also brought a sense of liberation. It freed him from the paralyzing fear of failure, from the need to always maintain an unblemished façade of control.

The landscape continued to unfold, a panorama of wide-open spaces that mirrored the burgeoning sense of possibility within him. He wasn't returning to the city, not yet, and perhaps not ever. The journey westward was more than a geographical displacement; it was a conscious act of self-reclamation. He was moving away from the ghosts of his past, not to forget them, but to outrun their suffocating grip. He carried the lessons learned, the hard-won wisdom that had been purchased at such a steep price, not as a burden, but as a guiding force. They were the compass that had been recalibrated by fire, pointing him towards a future that was, for the first time, entirely his own to shape. The road ahead was unwritten, a blank canvas waiting for his touch, and he approached it with a quiet determination, armed with the knowledge that the human spirit, even when battered and bruised, possessed an indomitable capacity for resilience and renewal.

The hum of the engine was a constant reminder of the miles traveled and the miles yet to go, a soundtrack to his quiet, resolute pursuit of a new horizon. He was not just driving away from something; he was driving towards himself. The journey had been devastating, a brutal confrontation with the deepest sorrows and failures, but it had ultimately led him to a place of hard-earned peace, a profound self-awareness that resonated with the quiet strength of the vast, open sky. The hope he felt wasn't a naive wish, but a deep-seated conviction, forged in the fires of adversity, that life, in all its messy, unpredictable glory, could indeed continue. He was ready to face whatever came next, not with the bravado of someone who had never fallen, but with the quiet wisdom of someone who had risen. The setting sun, painting the clouds in hues of orange and purple, cast long shadows across the prairie, a reminder of the darkness he had navigated, but also a promise of the dawn that would inevitably follow. He finally understood that the most important horizon wasn't the one he saw in the distance, but the one he carried within himself.

# EPILOGUE

These drives offered solace, a moving meditation through life's uncertainties. They allowed for reflection on past experiences.

The hushed conversations spoke of unspoken fears and enduring hopes. Resilience bloomed in unexpected places, a quiet defiance.

This narrative explores that inner fortitude. It delves into the strength discovered when the road ahead seems daunting.

# AUTHOR'S NOTE

This tapestry, woven from the raw threads of a thousand whispered confessions and the salt-stained pages of lives unraveled and rebuilt, burns with a truth that transcends mere ink. It's a descent into the gnawing maw of addiction, where the body screams and the spirit Withers, only to claw its way back, gasping for breath, towards a dawn no one dared imagine. We've lived the phantom itch, the gnawing hunger, the deafening silence where hope once echoed. Through fractured mirrors, we glimpsed not just ourselves, but the defiant spark that ignites, against all odds, in the human heart – a stubborn ember refusing to be extinguished, a primal scream of resilience that reshapes the very air around us. To name the ghosts that bled into these pages would be to dilute their power, to invite the cold logic of citation where the tempest of raw experience must rage.

Drawing upon a profound grasp of human nature, P. Hartwell forges tales saturated with unvarnished truth and profound introspection. With an acute perception of life's encroaching darkness, his writings explore the enduring strength of the soul and the delicate interplay between utter desolation and flickering optimism. His prose stands out for its dedication to genuine character representation and a courageous confrontation of existence's most arduous circumstances.

# Glossary

**The Grip:** Refers to the pervasive and destructive influence of addiction on an individual's life and their relationships.

**The Unraveling:** Denotes the process by which a family's stability and emotional structure deteriorates due to addiction and its associated consequences.

**Scar Tissue:** Metaphorically represents the lasting emotional and psychological impact of trauma, loss, and difficult experiences, signifying resilience and survival.

**Crucible:** An intense experience or period of intense difficulty that serves to forge character and reveal inner strength.

**Reclamation:** The act of regaining control over one's life, identity, and future after significant personal struggle or loss.

# ABOUT THE AUTHOR

P. Hartwell is a fiction mystery author drawn to the places where history falters and secrets endure. Raised along the windswept shores of Lake Erie and shaped by global travels and ancestral lore, he writes stories that stir beneath the surface—where grief haunts, truth hides, and the past refuses to stay buried. With a cinematic eye for atmosphere and a deep reverence for forgotten histories, Hartwell crafts mysteries steeped in emotional tension and elemental unease. His work invites readers into shadowy worlds where every clue carries weight, and every silence speaks volumes.

www.ingramcontent.com/pod-product-compliance
Lightning Source LLC
Chambersburg PA
CBHW021235310726
48971CB00006B/1835